Andersen's Fairy Tales

Hans Christian Andersen's stories of kings and paupers, common folk and legendary characters, have charmed generations of readers—probably because they represent the accumulated unconscious wisdom and creative imagination of mankind.

Who has not laughed at the false pride of royalty, the hypocrisy of courtiers, the honesty of childhood recorded in THE EMPEROR'S NEW CLOTHES? Who has failed to rejoice at the final triumph of THE UGLY DUCKLING or to commiserate with the hard-won knowledge of THE FIR TREE? Who has missed the underlying moral in THE RED SHOES or the sense of love and of the infinite in the solution to THE SNOW QUEEN'S promise?

Though not originally written for children, these stories, nonetheless, are enchanting to the childish imagination, and will serve as a delightful storehouse of pleasure and learning long after the things of childhood have been put aside.

ANDERSEN'S
Fairy Tales

By HANS CHRISTIAN ANDERSEN

TRANSLATED BY E. V. LUCAS
AND MRS. H. B. PAULL

WITH ILLUSTRATIONS BY
LEONARD VOSBURGH

COMPANION LIBRARY

PUBLISHERS *Grosset & Dunlap* NEW YORK

Contents

Contents

Andersen's Fairy Tales

The Garden of Paradise

THERE was once a king's son. Nobody had so many or such beautiful books as he had. He could read about everything which had ever happened in the world, and see it all represented in the most beautiful pictures. He could get information about every nation and every country, but as to where the Garden of Paradise was to be found, not a word could he discover; and this was the very thing he thought most about. When he was quite little and was about to start to school, his grandmother had told him that every flower in the Garden of Paradise was a delicious cake, and that the pistils were full of wine. In one flower, history was written; in another, geography or tables. You had only to eat the cake and you knew the lesson. The more you ate, the more history, geography, and tables you knew. All this he believed then, but as he grew older and wiser and learned more, he easily perceived that the delights of the Garden of Paradise must be far beyond all this.

"Oh, why did Eve take of the tree of knowledge? Why did Adam eat the forbidden fruit? If it had only been I, it would not have happened, and sin would never have entered the world."

That is what he said then, and he still said it when he was seventeen. His thoughts were full of the Garden of Paradise.

One day he went walking into the woods. He went alone, for that was his greatest pleasure. Evening came on, clouds gathered, and it rained as if the whole heaven had become a sluice from which the water poured in sheets. It was as dark as it is in the deepest well. Now he slipped on the wet grass, and then he fell on the bare stones which jutted out of the rocky ground. Everything was dripping, and at last the poor Prince hadn't a dry thread left on him. He had to climb over huge rocks where the water oozed out of the thick moss. He was almost fainting, when he heard a curious murmuring and saw in front of him a big lighted cave. A fire was burning in the middle, big enough to roast a stag, which was in fact being done. A splendid stag with its huge antlers was stuck on a spit, being slowly turned round between the hewn trunks of two fir trees. An oldish woman, tall and strong enough to be a man in disguise, sat by the fire, throwing on logs from time to time.

"Come in by all means," she said. "Sit down by the fire so that your clothes may dry."

"There is a shocking draft here," said the Prince, as he sat down on the ground.

"It will be worse than this when my sons come home!" said the woman. "You are in the cavern of the winds, and my sons are the four winds of the world. Do you understand?"

"Where are your sons?" asked the Prince.

"Well, that's not easy to answer when the question is so stupidly put," said the woman. "My sons do as they like. They are playing ball now with the clouds up there in the great hall." And she pointed up to the sky.

"Oh indeed!" said the Prince. "You seem to speak very harshly, and you are not so gentle as the women I generally see about me."

"Oh, I daresay they have nothing else to do. I have to be harsh if I am to keep my boys under control. But I can do it, although they are a stiff-necked lot. Do you see those four sacks hanging on the wall? They are just as frightened of them as you used to be of the cane behind the looking glass. I can double the boys up, I can tell you, and then they have to go into the bag. We don't stand upon ceremony, and there they stay. They can't get out to play their tricks till it suits me to let them out. But here comes one of them now."

It was the North Wind who came in with an icy blast. Great hailstones peppered about the floor and snowflakes drifted in. He was dressed in bearskin trousers and jacket, and he had a sealskin cap drawn over his ears. Long icicles hung from his beard, and one hailstone after another dropped from the collar of his jacket.

"Don't go straight to the fire," said the Prince. "You might easily get chilblains."

"Chilblains!" said the North Wind with a loud laugh. "Why, they are my greatest delight. What sort of a feeble creature are you? How did you get into the cave of the winds?"

"He is my guest," said the old woman. "And if you are not pleased with that explanation you may go into the bag. Do you understand me?"

This had its effect, and the North Wind now told where he came from and where he had been for the last month.

"I come from the Arctic seas," he said. "I have been on Behring Island with the Russian walrus hunters. I sat at the helm and slept when they sailed from the north cape, and when I woke now and then the stormy petrels were flying about my legs. They are queer birds. They flap their wings briskly and then stretch them out motionless; even then they have speed enough."

"Don't be too long-winded," said the mother of the winds. "So at last you got to Behring Island?"

"It's perfectly splendid! There you have a floor to dance

on, as flat as a pancake; the island is covered with half-thawed snow and moss. Bones of whales and polar bears lie about, which look like the legs and arms of giants covered with green mold. One would think that the sun had never shone on them. I gave a little puff to the fog and discovered a house. It was built of wreckage and covered with whale skins, the flesh side turned outwards. It was all red and green, and a live polar bear sat on the roof growling. I went to the shore to look at the bird nests and saw the featherless young birds screaming and gaping. I blew down thousands of their throats and that taught them to shut their mouths. A little further, the walruses were rolling about like monster maggots, with pigs' heads and teeth a yard long!"

"You're a good storyteller, my boy," said his mother. "It makes my mouth water to hear you!"

"Then there was a hunt. The harpoons were plunged into the walruses' breasts, and the steaming blood spurted out over the ice like fountains. Then I remembered my part of the game. I blew my ships, the mountain-high icebergs, against the boats. Whew! how the crews whistled and screamed, but I whistled louder. They were obliged to throw the dead walruses, chests, and ropes out upon the ice. I shook the snowflakes over them and let them drift south to taste the salt water. They will never come back to Behring Island!"

"Then you've been doing evil!" said the mother of the winds.

"What good I did, the others may tell you," said he. "But here we have my brother from the west. I like him best of all. He smells of the sea and brings a splendid cool breeze with him!"

"Is that the little Zephyr?" asked the Prince.

"Yes, certainly it is Zephyr, but he is not so little as all that. He used to be a fine boy, but that was long ago."

He looked like a wild man of the woods, but he had a broad-brimmed hat on to protect his face. He carried a mahogany club cut in the American mahogany forest. Nothing else would do for him.

"Where do you come from?" asked his mother.

"From the forest wildernesses," he said, "where the thorny creepers make a fence between every tree, where the water snake lies in the wet grass, and where human beings seem to be superfluous!"

"What did you do there?"

"I looked at the mighty river, saw where it dashed over the rocks in dust and flew with the clouds to carry the rainbow. I saw a wild buffalo swimming in the river, but the stream carried him away. He floated with the wild duck, which soared into the sky at the rapids, but the buffalo was carried over with the water. I liked that and blew up a storm so big that it whirled the primeval trees about like shavings."

"And you have done nothing else?" asked the old woman.

"I have been turning somersaults in the savannas, patting the wild horse, and shaking down coconuts. Oh, I have plenty of stories to tell, but one need not tell everything. You know that very well, old woman!" Then he kissed his mother so heartily that she nearly fell backwards. He was indeed a wild boy.

The South Wind appeared now in a turban and a Bedouin's flowing cloak.

"It is fearfully cold in here," he said, throwing wood on the fire. "It is easy to see that the North Wind got here first."

"It is hot enough to roast a polar bear," said the North Wind.

"You are a polar bear yourself," said the South Wind.

"Do you want to go into the bag?" asked the old woman. "Sit down on that stone and tell us where you have been."

"In Africa, mother," he answered. "I have been chasing the lion with the Hottentots in Kaffirland. What grass there is on those plains—as green as an olive. The gnu was dancing about and the ostriches ran races with me, but I am still the fastest. I went to the desert with its yellow sand. It looks like the bottom of the sea. I met a caravan. They were killing their last camel to get water to drink, but it wasn't much they got. The sun was blazing above and the sand burning below. There was no end to the desert. I burrowed into the fine loose sand and whirled it up in great columns —that was a dance! You should have seen how despondently the dromedaries stood, and how the merchant drew his caftan over his head. He threw himself down before me as if I had been Allah, his god. Now they are buried, and there is a pyramid of sand over them all. When I blow it away sometime the sun will bleach their bones, and then travelers will see that people have been there before. Otherwise you would hardly believe it in the desert!"

"Then you have been doing only harm!" said the mother. "Into the bag you go!" And before he knew where he was, she had the South Wind by the waist and in the bag. It rolled about on the ground, but she sat upon it and then it had to be quiet.

"Your sons are lively fellows," said the Prince.

"Yes indeed," she said, "but I can master them. Here comes the fourth."

It was the East Wind, and he was dressed like a Chinaman.

"Oh, have you come from that quarter?" said the mother. "I thought you had been in the Garden of Paradise."

"I am going there tomorrow," said the East Wind. "It will be a hundred years tomorrow since I have been there. I have just come from China, where I danced round the porcelain tower till all the bells jingled. The officials were flogged in the streets. The bamboo canes were broken over their shoulders, and they were all people ranging from the first to the ninth rank. They shrieked 'Many thanks, Father and benefactor,' but they didn't mean what they said. And I went on ringing the bells and singing 'Tsing, tsang, tsu!' "

"You're quite uproarious about it!" said the old woman. "It's a good thing you are going to the Garden of Paradise tomorrow; it always has a good effect on your behavior. Mind you drink deep of the well of wisdom, and bring a little bottleful home for me."

"That I will," said the East Wind. "But why have you put my brother from the south into the bag? Out with him! He must tell me about the phoenix. The Princess always wants to hear about that bird when I call every hundred years. Open the bag! Then you'll be my sweetest mother, and I'll give you two pockets full of tea as green and fresh as when I picked it."

"Well, for the sake of the tea, and because you are my darling, I will open my bag."

She did open it and the South Wind crept out, but he was quite crestfallen because the strange Prince had seen his disgrace.

"Here is a palm leaf for the Princess!" said the South Wind. "The old phoenix, the only one in the world, gave it to me. He has scratched his whole history on it with his bill, for the hundred years of his life, and she can read it for herself. I saw how the phoenix set fire to his nest himself and sat on it while it burnt, like the widow of a Hindu. Oh, how the dry branches crackled, how it smoked, and what a smell there was! At last it all burst into flame and the old bird was burnt to ashes, but his egg lay glowing in the fire. It broke with a loud bang and the young one flew out. Now it rules over all the birds, and it is the only phoenix in the world. He bit a hole in the leaf I gave you. That is his greeting to the Princess."

"Let us have something to eat now," said the mother of the winds, and they all sat down to eat the roast stag. The Prince sat beside the East Wind, and they soon became good friends.

"I say," said the Prince, "just tell me who is this Princess, and where is the Garden of Paradise?"

"Oh, ho!" said the East Wind, "if that is where you want to go, you must fly with me tomorrow. But I may as well tell you that no human being has been there since Adam and Eve. You know all about them, I suppose, from your Bible stories?"

"Of course," said the Prince.

"When they were driven out, the Garden of Eden sank into the ground, but it kept its warm sunshine, its mild air, and all its charms. The queen of the fairies lives there. The Island of Bliss, where death never enters, and where living is a delight, is there. Get on my back tomorrow and I will take you with me. I think I can manage it. But you mustn't talk now! I want to go to sleep."

When the Prince woke up in the early morning, he was not a little surprised to find that he was already high above the clouds. He was sitting on the back of the East Wind, who was holding him carefully. They were so high up that woods and fields, rivers and lakes, looked like a large colored map.

"Good morning," said the East Wind. "You may as well sleep a little longer, for there is not much to be seen in this flat country below, unless you want to count the churches. They look like chalk dots on the green board."

He called the fields and meadows "the green board."

"It was very rude of me to leave without saying good-by to your mother and brothers," said the Prince.

"One is excused when one is asleep," said the East Wind, and they flew on faster than ever. You could mark their flight by the rustling of the trees as they passed over the woods. And whenever they crossed a lake or the sea, the waves rose and the great ships dipped low down in the water like floating swans. Towards evening the large towns were amusing as it grew dark, with all their lights twinkling, now here, now there, just as when one burns a piece of paper and sees all the little sparks like children coming home from school. The Prince clapped his hands, but the East Wind told him he had better hold tight, or he might fall and find himself hanging onto a church steeple.

The eagle in the great forest flew swiftly, but the East Wind flew more swiftly still. The Cossack on his little horse sped fast over the plains, but the Prince sped faster still.

"Now you can see the Himalayas," said the East Wind. "They are the highest mountains in Asia. We shall soon reach the Garden of Paradise."

They took a more southerly direction, and the air became scented with spices and flowers. Figs and pomegranates grew wild, and the wild vines were covered with blue and green grapes. They both descended here and stretched themselves on the soft grass, where the flowers nodded to the wind, as much as to say, "Welcome back."

"Are we in the Garden of Paradise now?" asked the Prince.

"No, certainly not," answered the East Wind. "But we shall soon be there. Do you see that wall of rock and the great cavern where the wild vine hangs like a big curtain? We have to go through there. Wrap yourself up in your cloak. The sun is burning here, but a step further on it is icy cold. The bird which flies past the cavern has one wing out here in the heat of summer, and the other is there in the cold of winter."

"So that is the way to the Garden of Paradise!" said the Prince.

Now they entered the cavern. Oh, how icily cold it was, but it did not last long. The East Wind spread his wings, and they shone like the brightest flame. But what a cave it was! Large blocks of stone, from which the water dripped, hung over them in the most extraordinary shapes. At one moment it was so low and narrow that they had to crawl on hands and knees. The next it was as wide and lofty as if they were in the open air. It looked like a chapel of the dead, with mute organ pipes and banners turned into stone.

"We seem to be journeying along Death's road to the Garden of Paradise," said the Prince, but the East Wind never answered a word. He only pointed before them where a beautiful blue light was shining. The blocks of stone above them grew dimmer and dimmer, and at last they became as transparent as a white cloud in the moonshine. The air was also deliciously soft, as fresh as on the mountaintops and as scented as down among the roses in the valley.

A river ran there as clear as the air itself, and the fish in it were like gold and silver. Purple eels, which gave out blue sparks with every curve, gamboled about in the water, and the broad leaves of the water lilies were tinged with the hues of the rainbow. The flowers themselves were like fiery orange flames, nourished by the water, just as oil keeps a lamp constantly burning. A firm bridge of marble, as delicately and skillfully carved as if it were lace and glass beads, led over the water to the Island of Bliss, where the Garden of Paradise bloomed.

The East Wind took the Prince in his arms and bore him over. The flowers and leaves there sang all the beautiful old songs of his childhood, but sang them more wonderfully than any human voice could sing them.

Were these palm trees or giant water plants growing here? The Prince had never seen such rich and mighty trees. The most wonderful climbing plants hung in wreaths, such as are only to be found in gold and colors on the margins of old books of the Saints or entwined among their initial letters. It was the most extraordinary combination of birds, flowers, and scrolls.

Close by on the grass stood a flock of peacocks with their brilliant tails outspread. Yes indeed, it seemed so, but when the Prince touched them he saw that they were not birds but plants. They were big dock leaves, which shone like peacock tails. Lions and tigers sprang like agile cats among the green hedges, which were scented with the blossom of the olive; and the lions and tigers were tame. A wild dove, glistening like a pearl, beat a lion's mane with his wings, and an antelope, otherwise so shy, stood by nodding, just as if he wanted to join the game.

The Fairy of the Garden now advanced to meet them. Her garments shone like the sun, and her face beamed like that of a happy mother rejoicing over her child. She was young and very beautiful and was surrounded by a band of lovely girls, each with a gleaming star in her hair.

When the East Wind gave her the inscribed leaf from the phoenix, her eyes sparkled with delight. She took the Prince's hand and led him into her palace, where the walls were the color of the brightest tulips in the sunlight. The ceiling was one great shining flower, and the longer one gazed into it the deeper the calyx seemed to be. The Prince went to the window, and looking through one of the panes saw the tree of knowledge, with the serpent, and Adam and Eve standing by.

"Weren't they driven out?" he asked. The Fairy smiled and explained that Time had burned a picture into each pane, but not of the kind one usually sees. They were alive, the leaves moved, and people came and went like the reflections in a mirror.

Then he looked through another pane and he saw Jacob's dream, with the ladder going straight up into heaven, and angels with great wings were fluttering up and down. All that had ever happened in this world lived and moved on these windowpanes. Only Time could imprint such wonderful pictures.

The Fairy smiled and led him into a large, lofty room, the walls of which were like transparent paintings of faces, one more beautiful than the other. There were millions of the Blessed who smiled and sang, and all their songs melted into one perfect melody. The highest ones were so tiny that they seemed smaller than the very smallest rosebud—no bigger than a pin point in a drawing. In the middle of the room stood a large tree, with handsome drooping branches. Golden apples hung like oranges among its green leaves. It was the tree of knowledge, of whose fruit Adam and Eve had eaten. From every leaf hung a shining red drop of dew. It was as if the tree wept tears of blood.

"Now let us get into the boat," said the Fairy. "We shall find refreshment on the swelling waters. The boat rocks, but it does not move from the spot. Yet all the countries of the world will pass before our eyes."

It was a curious sight to see the whole coast move. Here came lofty snow-clad Alps, with their clouds and dark fir trees. The horn echoed sadly among them, and the shepherd yodeled sweetly in the valleys. Banyan trees bent their long drooping branches over the boat. Black swans floated on the water, and the strangest animals and flowers appeared on the shore. This was New Holland, the fifth portion of the world, which glided past them with a view of its blue mountains. They heard the song of priests, and saw the dances of the savages to the sound of drums and pipes of bone. The pyramids of Egypt, reaching to the clouds, and fallen columns, and sphinxes half buried in sand, next sailed past them. Then came the Aurora Borealis blazing over the peaks of the north; they were fireworks which could not be imitated. The Prince was very happy, and he saw a hundred times more than we have described.

"Can I stay here always?" he asked.

"That depends upon you," answered the Fairy. "If you do not, like Adam, allow yourself to be tempted to do what is forbidden, you can stay here always."

"I will not touch the apples on the tree of knowledge," said the Prince. "There are thousands of other fruits here as beautiful."

"Test yourself, and if you are not strong enough, go back with the East Wind who brought you. He is going away now, and will not come back for a hundred years. The time will fly in this place like a hundred hours, but that is a long time for temptation and sin. Every evening when I leave you I must say, 'Come with me,' and I must beckon to you. But stay behind! Do not come with me, for with every step you take your longing will grow stronger. You will reach the hall where grows the tree of knowledge. I sleep beneath its fragrant drooping branches. You will bend over me and I must smile, but if you press a kiss upon my lips, Paradise will sink deep down into the earth, and it will be lost to you. The sharp winds of the winderness will whistle round you. The cold rain will drop from your hair. Sorrow and labor will be your lot."

"I will remain here," said the Prince.

And the East Wind kissed him on the mouth and said, "Be strong then, and we shall meet again in a hundred years. Farewell!" Then the East Wind spread his great wings. They shone like poppies at the harvest time or like the Northern Lights in a cold winter.

"Good-by, good-by!" whispered the flowers. Storks and pelicans flew in a line like waving ribbons, conducting him to the boundaries of the Garden.

"Now we begin our dancing," said the Fairy. "At the end when I dance with you, as the sun goes down, you will see me beckon to you and cry, 'Come with me.' But do not come. I have to repeat it every night for a hundred years.

The East Wind spread his great wings

Every time you resist you will grow stronger, and at last you will not even think of following. Tonight is the first time, so remember my warning."

And the Fairy led him into a large hall of white transparent lilies. The yellow stamens in each formed a little golden harp which echoed the sound of strings and flutes. Lovely girls, slender and graceful, dressed in floating gauze which revealed their exquisite limbs, glided in the dance, and sang of the joy of living—they who would never die—and of the Garden of Paradise that would bloom forever.

The sun went down and the sky was bathed in golden light which made the lilies look like roses. The Prince drank the foaming wine handed to him by the maidens. He felt such joy as he had never known before. He saw the background of the hall opening, where the tree of knowledge stood in a radiance that blinded him. The song coming from it was soft and lovely as his mother's voice, and she seemed to say, "My child! My beloved child!"

Then the Fairy beckoned to him and said so tenderly, "Come with me," that he rushed towards her, forgetting his promise, forgetting everything, on the very first evening that she smiled and beckoned to him.

The fragrance in the scented air grew stronger, the harps sounded sweeter than ever, and it seemed as if the millions of smiling heads in the hall where the tree grew, nodded and sang, "One must know everything. Man is lord of the earth." They were no longer tears of blood which fell from the tree. They seemed to him to be red shining stars.

"Come with me, come with me," spoke those trembling tones, and at every step the Prince's cheeks burnt hotter and hotter and his blood coursed more rapidly.

"I must go," he said. "It is no sin. I must see her asleep. Nothing will be lost if I do not kiss her, and that I will not do. My will is strong."

The Fairy dropped her shimmering garment, drew back

the branches, and a moment after was hidden within their depths.

"I have not sinned yet," said the Prince, "nor shall I!" Then he drew back the branches. There she lay asleep already, beautiful as only the Fairy in the Garden of Paradise can be. She smiled in her dreams, but he bent over her and saw the tears welling up under her eyelashes.

"Do you weep for me?" he whispered. "Weep not, beautiful maiden. I only now understand the full bliss of Paradise. It surges through my blood and through my thoughts. I feel the strength of the angels and of everlasting life in my mortal limbs. Even if everlasting night comes over me, a moment like this is worth it." And he kissed away the tears from her eyes. His mouth touched hers.

Then came a sound like thunder, louder and more awful than any he had ever heard before, and everything around collapsed. The beautiful Fairy, the flowery Paradise sank deeper and deeper. The Prince saw it sink into the darkness of night. It shone far off like a tiny twinkling star. The chill of death crept over his limbs. He closed his eyes and lay long as if dead.

The cold rain fell on his face, and the sharp wind blew around his head, and at last his memory came back.

"What have I done?" he sighed. "I have sinned like Adam—sinned so heavily that Paradise has sunk low beneath the earth."

He opened his eyes, and he could still see the star, the faraway star, which twinkled like Paradise. It was the morning star in the sky. He got up and found himself in the woods near the cave of the winds, and the mother of the winds sat by his side. She looked angry and raised her hand.

"On the very first evening!" she said. "I thought as much. If you were my boy, you should go into the bag!"

"Ah, he shall soon go there!" said Death. He was a strong old man, with a scythe in his hand and great black wings.

"He shall be laid in a coffin, but not now. I only mark him and then leave him for a time to wander about on the earth to expiate his sin and to grow better. I will come sometime. When he least expects me, I shall come back, lay him in a black coffin, put it on my head, and fly to the skies. The Garden of Paradise blooms there too, and if he is good and holy he shall enter into it. But if his thoughts are wicked and his heart still full of sin, he will sink deeper in his coffin than Paradise sank. And I shall go only once in every thousand years to see if he is to sink deeper or to rise to the stars—the bright stars up there!"

Little Tiny

THERE was once a woman who wished very much to have a child, but she could not obtain her wish. At last she went to a fairy and said, "I should so very much like to have a little child. Can you tell me where I can find one?"

"Oh, that can be easily managed," said the fairy. "Here is a grain of barley different from the kind that grows in the fields and that the chickens eat. Plant it in a flowerpot and see what will happen."

"Thank you," said the woman and gave the fairy twelve pennies, which was the price of the barleycorn. Then she went home and planted it. Immediately there grew up a large handsome flower, something like a tulip in appearance, but with leaves tightly closed as if it were still a bud.

"It is a beautiful flower," said the woman, and she kissed the red and golden colored leaves. While she did so the flower opened and she could see that it was a real tulip. Within the flower, upon the green velvet stamens, sat a very delicate and graceful little maiden. She was scarcely half as long as a thumb, and they gave her the name of Little Thumb, or Tiny, because she was so small. A walnut shell, elegantly polished, served her for a cradle. Her bed was formed of blue violet leaves, with a rose leaf for a counterpane. Here she slept at night, but during the day she amused herself on a table, where the woman placed a plate full of water. Round this plate were flowers with their stems in the water, and upon it floated a large tulip petal which served Tiny for a boat. Here the little maiden sat and rowed from side to side, with two oars made of white horsehair. It really was a very pretty sight. Tiny could sing so softly and sweetly that nothing like her singing had ever before been heard.

One night as she lay in her pretty bed, a large, ugly, wet toad crept through a broken pane of glass in the window, and leaped right upon the table where Tiny lay sleeping under her rose leaf quilt. "What a pretty little wife she would make for my son!" said the toad, and she took up the walnut shell in which little Tiny lay asleep, and jumped through the window with it into the garden.

In the swampy margin of a broad stream in the garden lived the toad with her son. He was uglier even than his mother! When he saw the pretty little maiden in her elegant bed, he could only cry, "Croak, croak, croak."

"Don't speak so loud or she will awake," said the old toad. "And then she might run away, for she is as light as swan's down. We will place her on one of the water lily leaves out in the stream. It will be like an island to her— she is so light and small—and then she cannot escape. And while she is away we will make haste and prepare the stateroom under the marsh, in which you are to live when you are married."

Far out in the stream grew a number of water lilies with broad green leaves, which seemed to float on the top of the water. The largest of these leaves appeared farther off than the rest, and the old toad swam out to it with the walnut shell, in which little Tiny lay still asleep. The little creature woke very early in the morning, and began to cry bitterly when she found where she was. She could see nothing but water on every side of the large green leaf and no way of reaching the land. Meanwhile the old toad was very busy under the marsh, decking her room with rushes and wild yellow flowers, to make it look pretty for her new daughter-in-law. Then she swam out with her ugly son to the leaf on which she had placed poor little Tiny. She wanted to fetch the pretty bed, that she might put it in the bridal chamber to be ready for her.

The old toad bowed low to her in the water and said, "Here is my son. He will be your husband and you will live happily together in the marsh by the stream."

"Croak, croak, croak," was all her son could say for himself. So the toads took up the elegant little bed and swam away with it, leaving Tiny all alone on the green leaf, where she sat and wept. She could not bear to think of living with the old toad and having her ugly son for a husband. The little fishes who swam about in the water beneath her had seen the toad and had heard what she said, so they lifted their heads above the water to look at the little maiden. As soon as they caught sight of her they saw she was very pretty, and it made them sorry to think that she must go and live with the ugly toads. "No, that must never be!" So they assembled together in the water around the green stalk which held the leaf on which the little maiden stood, and gnawed it away at the root with their teeth. Then the leaf floated down the stream, carrying Tiny far away, out of reach of land.

Tiny sailed past many towns, and the little birds in the bushes saw her and sang, "What a lovely little creature!" The leaf swam with her farther and farther till it brought her to other lands. A graceful white butterfly constantly fluttered round her, and at last alighted on the leaf. Tiny pleased him, and she was glad of it for now the toad could not possibly reach her, and the country through which she sailed was beautiful, and the sun shone upon the water till it glittered like liquid gold. She took off her sash and tied one end of it round the butterfly and fastened the other end to the leaf, which now glided on much faster than ever, taking little Tiny with it. Presently a large cockchafer flew by. The moment he caught sight of her, he seized her round her delicate waist with his claws and flew with her into a tree. The green leaf floated away on the brook, and the butterfly flew with it, for he was fastened to it and could not get away.

Oh, how frightened little Tiny felt when the cockchafer flew with her to the tree! But especially was she sorry for the beautiful white butterfly which she had fastened to the leaf, for if he could not free himself he would die of hunger. But the cockchafer did not trouble himself at all about the matter. He seated himself by her side on a large green leaf, gave her some honey from the flowers to eat, and told her she was very pretty, though not in the least like a cockchafer. After a time, all the cockchafers who lived in the tree came to visit her. They stared at Tiny, and then the young lady cockchafers turned up their feelers and said, "She has only two legs. How ugly that looks!"

"She has no feelers," said another.

"Her waist is quite slim. She is just like a human being. Oh, she is ugly!" said all the lady cockchafers, although Tiny was very pretty.

The cockchafer who had run away with her believed all the others when they said she was ugly, and would have nothing more to do with her, and told her she might go where she liked. Then he flew down with her from the tree and placed her on a daisy, and she wept at the thought that she was so ugly that even the cockchafers would have nothing to say to her. And all the while she was really the loveliest creature that one could imagine, and as tender and delicate as a beautiful roseleaf.

During the whole summer poor little Tiny lived quite alone in the wide forest. She wove herself a bed with blades of grass, and hung it up under a broad leaf to protect herself from the rain. She sucked the honey from the flowers for food, and drank the dew from their leaves every morning. So passed away the summer and the autumn, and then came the winter—the long, cold winter. All the birds who had sung to her so sweetly had flown away, and the trees and the flowers had withered. The large clover leaf under which she had lived was now rolled together and shriveled up; nothing remained of it but a yellow withered stalk. She felt dreadfully cold, for her clothes were torn and she was herself so frail and delicate that poor little Tiny was nearly frozen to death. It began to snow too, and the snowflakes, as they fell upon her, were like a whole shovelful falling upon one of us, for we are tall while she was only an inch high. Then she wrapped herself up in a dry leaf, but it cracked in the middle and could not keep her warm, and she shivered with cold.

Near the wood in which she had been living lay a large grain field, but the grain had been cut a long time. Nothing remained but the bare dry stubble standing up out of the frozen ground. It was to her like struggling through a large wood. Oh, how she shivered with the cold! She came at last to the door of a field mouse, who had a little den under the stubble. There dwelt the field mouse in warmth and comfort, with a whole roomful of grain, a kitchen, and a beautiful dining room. Poor little Tiny stood before the door just like a little beggar girl, and begged for a handful of barley, for she had been without a morsel to eat for two days.

"You poor little creature," said the field mouse, who was really a good old field mouse. "Come into my warm room and dine with me." She was so pleased with Tiny that she said, "You are quite welcome to stay with me all winter, if you like. But you must keep my rooms clean and neat, and tell me stories, for I like to hear them very much." And Tiny did all the field mouse asked her, and found herself very comfortable.

"We shall have a visitor soon," said the field mouse one day. "My neighbor pays me a visit once a week. He is even better off than I am. He has large rooms, and wears a beautiful black velvet coat. If you could only have him for a husband, you would be well provided for indeed. But he is blind; so you must tell him some of your prettiest stories."

Tiny did not feel at all interested about this neighbor, for he was a mole. However, he came and paid his visit, dressed in his black velvet coat.

"He is very rich and learned, and his house is twenty times larger than mine," said the field mouse.

He was rich and learned, no doubt, but he always spoke slightingly of the sun and the pretty flowers, because he had never seen them. Tiny was obliged to sing to him, "Ladybird, ladybird, fly away home," and many other pretty songs. And the mole fell in love with her because she had such a sweet voice, but he said nothing yet, for he was very cautious. A short time before, the mole had dug a long passage under the earth, which led from the dwelling of the field mouse to his own, and here she had permission to walk with Tiny whenever she liked. But he warned them not to be alarmed at the sight of a dead bird which lay in the passage. It was a perfect bird, with a beak and feathers, and could not have been dead long, and was lying just where the mole had made his passage.

The mole took a piece of phosphorescent wood in his mouth, and it glittered like fire in the dark. Then he went before them to light them through the long, dark passage. When they came to the spot where lay the dead bird, the mole pushed his broad nose through the ceiling, the earth gave way so that there was a large hole, and the daylight shone into the passage. In the middle of the floor lay a dead swallow, his beautiful wings folded close to his sides, his feet and his head drawn up under his feathers. The poor bird had evidently died of the cold. It made little Tiny very sad to see it, for she greatly loved the little birds who had sung and twittered for her so beautifully all the summer.

But the mole pushed it aside with his crooked legs and said, "He will sing no more now. How miserable it must be to be born a little bird. I am thankful that none of my children will ever be birds, who can do nothing but cry, 'Tweet, tweet,' and always die of hunger in the winter."

"Yes, you may well say that, you clever mole," exclaimed the field mouse. "What is the use of his twittering, for when winter comes he must either starve or be frozen to death? Still birds are very highbred, I suppose."

Tiny said nothing, but when the two others had turned their backs on the bird, she stooped down and stroked aside the soft feathers which covered the head, and kissed the closed eyelids. "Perhaps this was the one who sang to me so sweetly in the summer," she said. "And how much pleasure you gave me, you dear pretty bird."

The mole now stopped up the hole through which the daylight shone, and then accompanied the ladies home. But during the night, as Tiny could not sleep, she got out of bed and wove a large beautiful carpet of hay. Then she carried it to the dead bird and spread it over him, with some down from the flowers which she had found in the field mouse's room. It was as soft as wool, and she spread some of it on each side of the bird so that he might lie warmly in the cold earth. "Farewell, you pretty little bird," said she. "Farewell. Thank you for your delightful singing during the summer, when all the trees were green and the warm sun shone upon us." Then she laid her head on the bird's breast, and she was alarmed immediately, for it seemed as if something inside the bird went thump, thump. It was the bird's heart. He was not really dead—only benumbed with the cold—and the warmth had restored him to life.

In autumn, all the swallows fly away into warm countries, but if one happens to linger and the cold seizes it, it becomes frozen and falls down as if dead. It remains where it fell, and the cold snow covers it. Tiny trembled very much: she was quite frightened, for the bird was large, a great deal larger than herself—she was only an inch high. But she took courage, laid the wool more thickly over the poor swallow, and then brought a leaf which she had used for her own counterpane and laid it over the head of the poor bird. The next night she again stole out to see him. He was alive but very weak. He could only open his eyes for a moment to look at Tiny, who stood holding a piece of decayed wood in her hand, for she had no other lantern.

"Thank you, pretty little maiden," said the sick swallow. "I have been so nicely warmed that I shall soon regain my strength and be able to fly about in the warm sunshine."

"Oh," said she, "it is cold out of doors now. It is snowing and freezing. Stay in your warm bed. I will take care of you."

Then she brought the swallow some water in a flower leaf. And after he had drunk, he told her that he had wounded one of his wings in a thornbush and could not fly as fast as the others, who were soon far away on their journey to warm countries. Then at last he had fallen to the earth and could remember no more. He did not know how he came to where she had found him. The whole winter the swallow remained underground, and Tiny nursed him with care and love. Neither the mole nor the field mouse knew anything about it, for they did not like swallows.

Very soon the springtime came and the sun warmed the earth. Then the swallow bade farewell to Tiny, and she opened the hole in the ceiling which the mole had made. The sun shone in upon them so beautifully that the swallow asked her if she would go with him. She could sit on his back, he said, and he would fly away with her into the green woods. But Tiny knew it would make the field mouse feel very sad if she left her in that manner and said, "No, I cannot."

"Farewell, then. Farewell, you good, pretty little maiden," said the swallow and flew out into the sunshine.

Tiny looked after him, and the tears rose in her eyes. She was very fond of the poor swallow.

"Tweet, tweet," sang the bird as he flew out into the green woods, and Tiny felt very sad. She was not allowed to go out into the warm sunshine. The corn which had been sown in the field over the house of the field mouse had grown up high into the air, and formed a thick wood to Tiny, who was only an inch in height.

"You are going to be married, Tiny," said the field mouse. "My neighbor has asked for you. What good fortune for a poor child like you! Now we will prepare your wedding clothes. They must be both woolen and linen. Nothing must be wanting when you are the mole's wife."

Tiny had to turn the spindle, and the field mouse hired four spiders who were to weave day and night. Every evening the mole visited her and was continually speaking of the time when the summer would be over. Then he would keep his wedding day with Tiny, but now the heat of the sun was so great that it burned the earth and made it quite hard, like a stone. As soon as the summer was over, the wedding should take place, but Tiny was not at all pleased, for she did not like the tiresome mole. Every morning when the sun rose, and every evening when it went down, she would creep out at the door. And as the wind blew aside the leaves of the corn so that she could see the blue sky, she thought how beautiful and bright it seemed out there, and wished so much to see her dear swallow again. But he never returned. By this time he had flown far away into the lovely green forest.

When autumn arrived, Tiny had her outfit quite ready, and the field mouse said to her, "In four weeks the wedding must take place." Then Tiny wept, and said she would not marry the disagreeable mole.

"Nonsense," replied the field mouse. "Now don't be obstinate, or I shall bite you with my teeth. He is a very handsome mole. The queen herself does not wear more beautiful velvets and furs. His kitchens and cellars are quite full. You ought to be thankful for such good fortune."

So the wedding day was fixed, on which the mole was to fetch Tiny away to live with him deep under the earth, and never again to see the warm sun, because *he* did not like it. The poor child was very unhappy at the thought of saying farewell to the beautiful sun, and as the field mouse had given her permission to stand at the door, she went to look at it once more.

"Farewell, bright sun," she cried, stretching out her arm towards it. And then she walked a short distance from the house. The corn had been cut, and only the dry stubble remained in the fields. "Farewell, farewell," she repeated, twining her arm round a little red flower that grew just by her side. "Greet the little swallow for me, if you should see him again."

"Tweet, tweet," sounded over her head suddenly. She looked up, and there was the swallow himself flying close by. As soon as he spied Tiny, he was delighted. And then she told him how unwilling she felt to marry the ugly mole, and to live always beneath the earth and never see the bright sun any more. And as she told him she wept.

"Cold winter is coming," said the swallow, "and I am going to fly away into warmer countries. Will you go with me? You can sit on my back and fasten yourself on with your sash. Then we can fly away from the ugly mole and his gloomy rooms—far away over the mountains into warmer countries, where the sun shines more brightly than here; where it is always summer and the flowers bloom in greater beauty. Fly now with me, dear little Tiny. You saved my life when I lay frozen in that dark dreary passage."

"Yes, I will go with you," said Tiny. And she seated herself on the bird's back with her feet on his outstretched wings, and tied her sash to one of his strongest feathers.

Then the swallow rose in the air and flew over forest and over sea, high above the highest mountains, covered with eternal snow. Tiny would have been frozen in the cold air, but she crept under the bird's warm feathers, keeping her little head uncovered so that she might admire the beautiful lands over which they passed. At length they reached the warm countries, where the sun shines brightly and the sky seems much higher above the earth. Here on the hedges and by the wayside grew purple, green, and white grapes. Lemons and oranges hung from trees in the woods, and the air was fragrant with myrtles and orange blossoms. Beautiful children ran along the country lanes, playing with large gay butterflies, and as the swallow flew farther and farther, every place appeared still more lovely.

At last they came to a blue lake, and by the side of it, shaded by trees of the deepest green, stood a palace of dazzling white marble, built in the olden times. Vines clustered round its lofty pillars and at the top were many swallows' nests, and one of these was the home of the swallow who carried Tiny.

"This is my house," said the swallow, "but it would not do for you to live there. You would not be comfortable. You must choose for yourself one of those lovely flowers, and I will put you down upon it. And then you shall have everything that you can wish to make you happy."

"That will be delightful," she said, and clapped her little hands for joy.

A large marble pillar lay on the ground, which in falling had been broken into three pieces. Between these pieces grew the most beautiful large white flowers. So the swallow flew down with Tiny and placed her on one of the broad leaves. How surprised she was to see, in the middle of the flower, a tiny little man, as white and transparent as if he had been made of crystal! He had a gold crown on his head, and delicate wings at his shoulders, and was not much larger than Tiny herself. He was the angel of the flower—for a tiny man or a tiny woman dwells in every flower—and this was the king of them all.

"How beautiful he is!" whispered Tiny to the swallow.

The little prince was at first quite frightened at the bird, who was like a giant compared to such a delicate little creature as himself. But when he saw Tiny, he was delighted and thought her the prettiest little maiden he had ever seen. He took the gold crown from his head, placed it on hers, asked her name, and asked if she would be his wife and the queen over all the flowers.

This certainly was a very different sort of husband from the son of the toad, or the mole with his black velvet and fur. So she said, "Yes," to the handsome prince. Then all the flowers opened and out of each came a little lady or a tiny lord, all so pretty it was quite a pleasure to look at them. Each of them brought Tiny a present, but the best gift was a pair of beautiful wings which had belonged to a large white fly. And they fastened them to Tiny's shoulders so that she might fly from flower to flower. Then there was much rejoicing, and the little swallow, who sat above them in his nest, was asked to sing a wedding song, which he did as well as he could. But in his heart he felt sad, for he was very fond of Tiny and would have liked never to part from her again.

"You must not be called Tiny any more," said the spirit of the flowers to her. "It is an ugly name and you are so very pretty. We will call you Maia."

"Farewell, farewell," said the swallow, with a heavy heart, as he left the warm countries to fly back to Denmark. There he had a nest over the window of a house in which dwelt the writer of fairy tales. The swallow sang, "Tweet, tweet," and from his song came the whole story.

The Fir Tree

FAR down in the forest, where the warm sun and the fresh air made a sweet resting place, grew a pretty little fir tree. And yet it was not so happy—it wished so much to be tall like its companions, the pines and firs which grew around it. The sun shone, the soft air fluttered its leaves, and the little peasant children passed by, prattling merrily, but the fir tree heeded them not. Sometimes the children would bring a large basket of raspberries or strawberries, wreathed on a straw, and seat themselves near the fir tree and say, "Is this not a pretty little tree?" which made it feel more unhappy than before.

And yet all this while the tree grew a notch or joint taller every year—for by the number of joints in the stem of a fir tree we can discover its age. Still, as it grew it complained, "Oh, how I wish I were as tall as the other trees. Then I would spread out my branches on every side, and my top would overlook the wide world. I should have the birds building their nests on my boughs, and when the wind blew, I should bow with stately dignity like my tall companions."

The tree was so discontented that it took no pleasure in the warm sunshine, the birds, or the rosy clouds that floated over it morning and evening. Sometimes in winter, when the snow lay white and glittering on the ground, a hare would come springing along and would jump right over the little tree, and then how mortified it would feel!

Two winters passed; and when the third arrived, the tree

had grown so tall that the hare was obliged to run round it. Yet it remained dissatisfied and would exclaim, "Oh, if I could but keep on growing tall and old! There is nothing else worth caring for in the world."

In the autumn, as usual, the woodcutters came and cut down several of the tallest trees. And the young fir tree, which was not grown to its full height, shuddered as the noble trees fell to the earth with a crash. After the branches were lopped off, the trunks looked so slender and bare that they could scarcely be recognized. Then they were placed upon wagons and drawn by horses out of the forest. "Where were they going? What would become of them?" The young fir tree wished very much to know. So in the spring, when the swallows and the storks came, it asked, "Do you know where those trees were taken? Did you meet them?"

The swallows knew nothing, but the stork, after a little reflection, nodded his head and said, "Yes, I think I do. I met several new ships when I flew from Egypt, and they had masts that smelt like fir. I think these must have been the trees. I assure you they were stately, very stately."

"Oh, how I wish I were tall enough to go on the sea," said the fir tree. "What is this sea, and what is it like?"

"It would take too much time to explain," said the stork, flying quickly away.

"Rejoice in thy youth," said the sunbeam. "Rejoice in thy fresh growth and the young life that is in thee." And the wind kissed the tree and the dew watered it with tears, but the fir tree regarded them not.

Christmas drew near and many young trees were cut down, some even smaller and younger than the fir tree, who enjoyed neither rest nor peace from longing to leave its forest home. These young trees, chosen for their beauty, kept their branches, but they too were laid on wagons and drawn by horses out of the forest.

"Where are they going?" asked the fir tree. "They are no taller than I am. Indeed, one is much shorter. And why are the branches not cut off? Where are they going?"

"We know. We know," sang the sparrows. "We have looked in at the windows of the houses in town, and we know what is done with them. They are dressed up in the most splendid manner. We have seen them standing in the middle of a warm room, and adorned with all sorts of beautiful things—honey cakes, gilded apples, playthings, and many hundreds of wax tapers."

"And then," asked the fir tree, trembling through all its branches, "and then what happens?"

"We did not see any more," said the sparrows. "But that was enough for us."

"I wonder whether anything so brilliant will ever happen to me," thought the fir tree. "It would be much better than crossing the sea. I long for it almost with pain. Oh, when will Christmas be here? I am now as tall and well grown as those which were taken away last year. Oh, that I were now laid on the wagon, or standing in the warm room, with all that brightness and splendor around me! Something better and more beautiful is to come after, or the trees would not be so decked out. Yes, what follows will be grander and more splendid. What can it be? I am weary with longing. I scarcely know how I feel."

"Rejoice with us," said the air and the sunlight. "Enjoy thine own bright life in the fresh air."

But the tree would not rejoice, though it grew taller every day. And winter and summer its dark green foliage might be seen in the forest, while passers-by would say, "What a beautiful tree!"

A short time before Christmas, the discontented fir tree was the first to fall. As the ax cut through the stem and divided the pith, the tree fell with a groan to the earth, conscious of pain and faintness, and forgetting all its anticipations of happiness in sorrow at leaving its home in the forest. It knew that it should never again see its dear old companions, the trees, nor the little bushes and many-colored flowers that had grown by its side; perhaps not even the birds. Neither was the journey at all pleasant. The tree first recovered itself while being unpacked with several other trees in the courtyard of a house, and it heard a man say, "We want only one, and this is the prettiest."

Then came two servants in grand livery and carried the fir tree into a large and beautiful apartment. On the walls hung pictures and near the great stove stood great china vases, with lions on the lids. There were rocking chairs, silken sofas, and large tables covered with pictures, books, and playthings worth a great deal of money. At least, the children said so. Then the fir tree was placed in a large tub full of sand, but green baize hung all around it so that no one could see it was a tub, and it stood on a very handsome carpet. How the fir tree trembled! "What is going to happen to me now?" Some young ladies came and the servants helped them to adorn the tree. On one branch they hung little bags cut out of colored paper, and each bag was filled with sweetmeats. From other branches hung gilded apples and walnuts as if they had grown there. And above and all around were hundreds of red, blue, and white tapers, which were fastened on the branches. Dolls exactly like real babies were placed under the green leaves—the tree had never seen such things before! And at the very top was fastened a glittering star made of tinsel. Oh, it was very beautiful!

"This evening," they all exclaimed, "how bright it will be!" "Oh, that the evening were here!" thought the tree. "And the tapers lighted! Then I shall know what else is going to happen. Will the trees of the forest come to see me? I wonder if the sparrows will peep in at the windows as they fly? Shall I grow faster here, and keep on all these ornaments during summer and winter?" But guessing was of very little use. It made his bark ache, and this pain is as bad for a slender fir tree as a headache is for us. At last the tapers were lighted and then what a glistening blaze of light the tree presented! It trembled so with joy in all its branches that one of the candles fell among the green leaves and burnt some of them. "Help! Help!" exclaimed the young ladies, but there was no danger, for they quickly extinguished the fire. After this the tree tried not to tremble at all, though the fire frightened him. He was so anxious not to hurt any of the beautiful ornaments, even while their brilliancy dazzled him. And now the folding doors were thrown open and a troop of children rushed in as if they intended to upset the tree. They were followed more slowly by their elders. For a moment the little ones stood silent with astonishment, and then they shouted for joy till the room rang, and they danced merrily round the tree, while one present after another was taken from it.

"What are they doing? What will happen next?" thought the fir. At last the candles burnt down to the branches and were put out. Then the children received permission to plunder the tree.

Oh, how they rushed upon it, till the branches cracked, and had it not been fastened with the glistening star to the ceiling, it must have been thrown down. The children then danced about with their pretty toys, and no one noticed the tree except the children's maid, who came and peeped among the branches to see if an apple or a fig had been forgotten. "A story! A story!" cried the children, pulling a little fat man towards the tree.

"Now we shall be in the green shade," said the man, as he seated himself under it, "and the tree will have the pleasure of hearing also, but I shall only relate one story. What shall it be? Ivede-Avede? Or Humpty Dumpty, who fell downstairs but soon got up again, and at last married a princess?"

"Ivede-Avede," cried some. "Humpty Dumpty," cried others, and there was a fine shouting and crying out. The fir tree remained quite still and thought to himself, "Shall I have anything to do with all this?" But he had already amused them as much as they wished. Then the old man told them the story of Humpty Dumpty—how he fell downstairs, and was raised up again, and married a princess. And the children clapped their hands and cried, "Tell another! Tell another!" They wanted to hear the story of Ivede-Avede, but they only had Humpty Dumpty. After this the fir tree became quite silent and thoughtful. Never had the birds in the forest told such tales as Humpty Dumpty, who fell downstairs and yet married a princess.

"Ah, yes, so it happens in the world," thought the fir tree. He believed it all, because it was related by such a nice man. "Ah, well," he thought, "who knows? Perhaps I may fall down too, and marry a princess." And he looked forward joyfully to the next evening, expecting to be again decked out with lights and playthings, gold and fruit. "To-morrow I will not tremble," thought he. "I will enjoy all my splendor, and I shall hear the story of Humpty Dumpty again, and perhaps Ivede-Avede." And the tree remained quiet and thoughtful all night. In the morning the servants and the housemaid came in.

"Now," thought the fir, "all my splendor is going to begin again." But they dragged him out of the room and upstairs to the garret and threw him on the floor, in a dark corner where no daylight shone, and there they left him. "What does this mean?" thought the tree. "What am I to do here? I can hear nothing in a place like this!" And he leaned against the wall and thought and thought.

He had time enough to think, for days and nights passed and no one came near him, and when at last somebody did come, it was only to put away large boxes in a corner. So the tree was completely hidden from sight as if it had never existed. "It is winter now," thought the tree. "The ground is hard and covered with snow, so that people cannot plant me. I shall be sheltered here, I daresay, until spring comes. How thoughtful and kind everybody is to me! Still I wish this place were not so dark as well as lonely, with not even a little hare to look at. How pleasant it was out in the forest when the snow lay on the ground. Then the hare would run by, yes, and jump over me too, although I did not like it then. Oh, it is terribly lonely here!"

"Squeak, squeak," said a little mouse, creeping cautiously towards the tree. Then came another, and they both sniffed at the fir tree and crept between the branches.

"Oh, it is very cold," said the mouse, "or else we should be so comfortable here, shouldn't we, you old fir tree?"

"I am not old," said the fir tree. "There are many who are older than I am."

"Where do you come from and what do you know?" asked the mice, who were full of curiosity. "Have you seen the most beautiful places in the world, and can you tell us all about them? And have you been in the storeroom, where cheeses lie on the shelf and hams hang from the ceiling? One can run about on tallow candles there, and go in thin and come out fat."

"I know nothing of that place," said the fir tree. "But I know the wood where the sun shines and the birds sing." And then the tree told the little mice all about its youth. They had never heard such an account in their lives. After they had listened to it attentively, they said, "What a number of things you have seen! You must have been very happy."

"Happy?" exclaimed the fir tree. And then as he reflected upon what he had been telling them, he said, "Ah, yes. After all, those were happy days." But when he went on and related all about Christmas Eve, and how he had been dressed up with cakes and lights, the mice said, "How happy you must have been, you old fir tree!"

"I am not old at all," replied the tree. "I only came from the forest this winter. I am now checked in my growth."

"What splendid stories you can relate," said the little mice. And the next night four other mice came with them to hear what the tree had to tell. The more he talked, the more he remembered, and then he thought to himself, "Those were happy days, but they may come again. Humpty Dumpty fell downstairs, and yet he married the princess. Perhaps I may marry a princess too." And the fir tree thought of the pretty little birch tree that grew in the forest, which was to him a real beautiful princess.

"Who is Humpty Dumpty?" asked the little mice, and then the tree related the whole story. He could remember every single word, and the little mice were so delighted with it that they were ready to jump to the top of the tree. The next night a great many more mice came, and on Sunday two rats came with them. But the rats said it was not a pretty story at all, and the little mice were very sorry, for it made them also think less of it.

"Do you know only one story?" asked the rats.

"Only one," replied the fir tree. "I heard it on the happiest evening in my life, but I did not know I was so happy at the time."

"We think it is a very miserable story," said the rats. "Don't you know any story about bacon or tallow in the storeroom?"

"No," replied the tree.

"Many thanks to you then," replied the rats, and they marched off.

The little mice also kept away after this, and the tree sighed and said, "It was very pleasant when the merry little mice sat round me and listened while I talked. Now that is all past too. However, I shall consider myself happy when someone comes to take me out of this place." But would this ever happen? Yes, one morning people came to clear out the garret. The boxes were packed away, and the tree was pulled out of the corner and thrown roughly on the garret floor. Then the servant dragged it out upon the staircase where the daylight shone.

"Now life is beginning again," said the tree, rejoicing in the sunshine and fresh air. Then it was carried downstairs and taken into the courtyard so quickly that it forgot to think of itself, and could only look about. There was so much to be seen! The court was close to a garden, where everything looked blooming. Fresh and fragrant roses hung over the little palings. The linden trees were in blossom, while the swallows flew here and there, crying, "Twit, twit, twit, my mate is coming." But it was not the fir tree they meant.

"Now I shall live," cried the tree, joyfully spreading out its branches. But alas, they were all withered and yellow, and it lay in a corner amongst weeds and nettles. The star of gold paper still stuck in the top of the tree and glittered in the sunshine. In the same courtyard were playing two of the merry children who had danced round the tree at Christmas and had been so happy. The youngest saw the gilded star and ran and pulled it off the tree.

"Look what is sticking to the old ugly fir tree," said the child, treading on the branches till they crackled under his boots. And the tree saw all the fresh bright flowers in the garden, and then looked at itself and wished it had remained in the dark corner of the garret. It thought of its fresh youth in the forest, of the merry Christmas evening, and of the little mice who had listened to the story of Humpty Dumpty.

"Past! past!" said the old tree. "Oh, had I but enjoyed myself while I could have done so! Now it is too late."

Then a lad came and chopped the tree into small pieces, till a large bundle lay in a heap on the ground. The pieces were placed in a fire under the kettle, and they quickly blazed up brightly, while the tree sighed so deeply that each sigh was like a little pistol shot. Then the children, who were at play, came and seated themselves in front of the fire, and looked at it and cried, "Pop, pop." But at each "pop," which was a deep sigh, the tree was thinking of a summer day in the forest, or of some winter night there when the stars shone brightly, and of Christmas evening, and of Humpty Dumpty, the only story it had ever heard or knew how to relate—till at last it was consumed.

The boys still played in the garden, and the youngest wore on his breast the golden star with which the tree had been adorned during the happiest evening of its existence. Now all was past: the tree's life was past, and the story also—for all stories must come to an end at last.

The Storks

A STORK had built his nest on the roof of a house at the very edge of a little town. The mother stork was sitting on the nest with her little ones, who stuck out their little black beaks, which had not yet turned red. The father stork stood a little way off on the ridge of the roof, erect and stiff, with one leg drawn up under him, so as at least to be at some trouble while standing sentry. He stood so still that he seemed to be carved out of wood.

"It will look so grand for my wife to have a sentry on guard by the nest," he thought. "People won't know that I am her husband. I daresay they think I have orders to stand there. It looks smart!" And so he remained standing on one leg.

A party of children were playing in the street, and when they saw the stork, one of the boldest boys, followed by the others, sang the old song about the storks. But he sang it just as it came into his head:

"Oh, father stork, father stork, fly to your nest;
Three featherless fledglings await your return.
The first of your chicks shall be stuck through the breast,
The second shall hang, and the third shall burn."

"Listen! What are the boys singing?" asked the little storks. "Did they say we are to be hanged and burnt?"

"Don't bother your heads about them!" said the mother stork. "Don't listen to them and then it won't do you any harm."

But the boys went on singing and pointing their fingers at the storks. Only one boy, whose name was Peter, said that it was a shame to make fun of creatures and he would take no part in it.

The mother bird comforted her little ones saying, "Do not trouble yourselves about it. Look at your father. See how quietly he stands, and on one leg too!"

"But we are so frightened," said the young ones, burying their heads in the nest.

The next day when the children came back to play and saw the storks, they began their old song:

"The first of your chicks shall be stuck through the breast,
The second shall hang, and the third shall burn."

"Are we to be hanged and burnt?" asked the little storks.

"No, certainly not," said the mother. "You are to learn to fly. See if I don't drill you! Then we will go into the fields and visit the frogs. They curtsey in the water to us and sing 'Koax, Koax,' and then we gobble them up. That's a treat if you like one!"

"And what next?" asked the young ones.

"Oh, then all the storks in the country assemble for the autumn maneuvers, and you will have to fly your best, for the one who cannot fly will be run through the body by the general's beak. So you must take good care to learn something when the drills begin."

"After all then we may be staked just as the boys said—and listen, they are singing it again now!"

"Listen to me and not to them," said the mother stork. "After the grand maneuvers we shall fly away to the warm countries, a very long way off, over the woods and mountains. We go to Egypt where they have houses with three-cornered sides, which reach above the clouds. They are called pyramids, and they are older than any stork can remember. Then there is a river which overflows its banks and all the land round turns to mud. You walk about in mud eating frogs!"

"Oh!" said all the young ones.

"Yes, it is splendid, you do nothing but eat all day. And while we are so well off there, there is not a leaf on the trees in this country. It is so cold here that the clouds freeze all to pieces and fall down in little bits."

She meant snow, but did not know how to describe it any better.

"Do the naughty boys freeze to pieces?" asked the young storks.

"No, they don't freeze to pieces, but they come very near to it and have to sit moping in dark rooms. You, on the other hand, fly about in strange countries, in the warm sunshine among flowers."

Some time passed and the little ones were big enough to stand up in the nest and look about them. The father stork flew back and forth every day with nice frogs and little snakes, and every kind of delicacy he could find. It was so funny to see the tricks he did to amuse them. He would turn his head right around onto his tail, and he would clatter with his beak as if it were a rattle. And then he told them all the stories he had heard in the swamps.

"Well, now you must learn to fly," said the mother stork one day, and all the young ones had to stand on the ridge of the roof. Oh, how they wobbled, trying to keep their balance with their wings, and how nearly they fell down.

"Now look at me!" said the mother. "This is how you must hold your heads. And move your legs so: one, two; one, two. This will help you get on in the world."

Then she flew a little way, and the young ones made a clumsy little hop, and down they came with a bump, for their bodies were too heavy.

"I don't want to fly," said one of the young ones, creeping down into the nest again. "I don't care about going to the warm countries."

"Do you want to freeze to death here when the winter comes? Shall the boys come and hang or burn or stake you? I will soon call them!"

"No, no!" said the young one, hopping out upon the roof again just like the others.

By the third day they could all fly fairly well. Then they thought they could hover in the air too, and they tried it. But flop!—they soon found they had to move their wings again.

Then the boys began their song again:

"Oh, father stork, father stork, fly to your nest."

"Shall we fly down and pick their eyes out?" asked the young ones.

"No, leave them alone," said their mother. "Pay attention only to me—that is much more important. One, two, three! Now we fly to the right. One, two, three! Now to the left and round the chimney. That was good! That last stroke of the wings was so pretty and the flap so well done that I will allow you to go to the swamp with me tomorrow. Several nice storks go there with their children, and just let me see that mine are the nicest. Don't forget to carry your heads high. It looks well, and gives you an air of importance."

"But are we not to have our revenge on the naughty boys?" asked the young storks.

"Let them scream as much as they like! You will fly away with the clouds to the land of the pyramids, while they will perhaps be freezing. There won't be a green leaf or a sweet apple here then!"

"But we *will* have our revenge!" they whispered to each other, and then they began their drilling again.

Of all the boys in the street, not one was worse at making

fun of the storks than he who first began the derisive song. He was a tiny little fellow, not more than six years old. It is true that the young storks thought he was at least a hundred, for he was so much bigger than their father and mother, and they had no idea how old children and grown-up people could be. They reserved all their vengeance for the boy who first began to tease them, and who never would leave off. The young storks were frightfully irritated by the teasing, and the older they grew the less they would stand it. At last their mother was obliged to promise that they should have their revenge, but not till the last day before they left.

"We shall first have to see how you behave at the maneuvers. If you come to grief and the general has to run you through the breast with his beak, the boys will be right after all, at least in one way! Now let us see!"

"That you shall!" said the young ones. And what pains they took! They practiced every day, till they could fly as lightly as any feather. It was quite a pleasure to watch them.

Then came the autumn. All the storks began to assemble, before they started on their flight to the warm countries where they spend their winters.

Those were indeed maneuvers! They had to fly over woods and towns to try their wings, because they had such a long journey before them. The young storks did everything so well that they got no end of frogs and snakes as prizes. They had the best characters, and then they could eat the frogs and snakes afterwards, which you may be sure they did.

"Now we shall have our revenge!" they said.

"Yes, certainly," said the mother stork. "My plan is this —and I think it is the right one. I know the pond where all the little human babies lie, till the storks fetch them and give them to their parents. The pretty little creatures lie there asleep, dreaming sweet dreams, sweeter than any they ever dream afterwards. Every parent wishes for such a little baby, and every child wants a baby brother or sister. Now we shall fly to the pond and fetch a little brother or sister for each of those children who did not join in singing that horrid song, or in making fun of the storks. But those who sang it shall not have one."

"But what about that bad wicked boy who first began the song?" shrieked the young storks. "What is to be done to him?"

"In the pond there is a little dead baby—it has dreamed itself to death. We will take it to him, and then he will cry because we have brought him a little dead brother. But you have surely not forgotten the good boy who said, 'It is a shame to make fun of the creatures!' We will take him both a brother and a sister, and, because his name is Peter, you shall all be called Peter too."

It happened just as she said, and all the storks are called Peter to this day.

Little Ida's Flowers

"MY poor flowers are dead," said little Ida. "They were so pretty yesterday evening, and now all the leaves are hanging down quite withered. Why do they do that?" she asked of the student who sat on the sofa. She liked him very much; he could tell the most amusing stories and cut out the prettiest pictures—hearts, and ladies dancing, castles with doors that opened, as well as flowers. He was a delightful student. "Why do the flowers look so faded today?" she asked again, and pointed to her nosegay, which was quite withered.

"Don't you know what is the matter with them?" said the student. "The flowers were at a ball last night, and it is no wonder they hang their heads."

"But flowers cannot dance?" cried little Ida.

"Yes, indeed, they can," replied the student. "When it grows dark, and everybody is asleep, they jump about quite merrily. They have a ball almost every night."

"Can children go to these balls?"

"Yes," said the student, "little daisies and lilies of the valley."

"Where do the flowers dance?" asked little Ida.

"Have you not often seen the large castle outside the gates of the town, where the king lives in summer and where the beautiful garden is full of flowers? And have you not fed the swans with bread when they swam towards you in the lake? Well, the flowers have capital balls there, believe me."

"I was in the garden yesterday with my mother," said

Ida. "But all the leaves were off the trees and there was not a single flower left. Where are they? I used to see so many in the summer."

"They are in the castle," replied the student. "You must know that as soon as the king and all the court are gone into the town, the flowers run out of the garden into the castle, and you should see how merry they are. The two most beautiful roses seat themselves on the throne, and are called the king and queen. Then all the red cockscombs range themselves on each side and bow. These are the lords-in-waiting. After that the pretty flowers come in and there is a grand ball. The blue violets represent little naval cadets, and dance with hyacinths and crocuses, which they call young ladies. The tulips and tiger lilies are the old ladies who sit and watch the dancing, so that everything may be conducted with order and propriety."

"But," said little Ida, "is there no one there to hurt the flowers for dancing in the king's castle?"

"No one knows anything about it," said the student. "The old steward of the castle, who has to watch there at night, sometimes comes in. He carries a great bunch of keys, and as soon as the flowers hear the keys rattle, they run and hide themselves behind the long curtains and stand quite still, just peeping their heads out. Then the steward says, 'I smell flowers here,' but he cannot see them."

"Oh, how capital!" said little Ida, clapping her hands. "Should I be able to see these flowers?"

"Yes," said the student. "Mind you think of it next time you go out. No doubt you will see them if you peep through the window. I did so today, and I saw a long yellow lily lying stretched out on the sofa. She was a court lady."

"Can the flowers from the Botanical Gardens go to these balls?" asked Ida. "It is such a distance!"

"Oh, yes," said the student, "whenever they like, for they can fly. Have you not seen those beautiful red, white, and yellow butterflies that look like flowers? They were flowers once. They have flown off their stalks into the air, and flap their leaves as if they were little wings to make them fly. Then, if they behave well, they obtain permission to fly about during the day, instead of being obliged to sit still on their stems at home. And so in time their leaves become real wings. It may be, however, that the flowers in the Botanical Gardens have never been to the king's palace, and, therefore, they know nothing of the merry doings which take place there at night. I will tell you what to do, and the botanical professor, who lives close by here, will be so surprised. You know him very well, do you not? Well, next time you go into his garden, you must tell one of the flowers that there is going to be a grand ball at the castle. Then that flower will tell all the others and they will fly away to the castle as soon as possible. And when the professor walks into his garden, there will not be a single flower left. How he will wonder what has become of them!"

"But how can one flower tell another? Flowers cannot speak."

"No, certainly not," replied the student, "but they can make signs. Have you not often seen that when the wind blows they nod at one another and rustle all their green leaves?"

"Can the professor understand the signs?" asked Ida.

"Yes, to be sure he can. He went one morning into his garden and saw a stinging nettle making signs with its leaves to a beautiful red carnation. It was saying, 'You are so pretty, I like you very much.' But the professor did not approve of such nonsense, so he clapped his hands on the nettle to stop it. Then the leaves, which are its fingers, stung him so sharply that he has never ventured to touch a nettle since."

"Oh, how funny!" said Ida, and she laughed.

"How can anyone put such notions into a child's head?"

said a tiresome lawyer, who had come to pay a visit. He did not like the student, and would grumble when he saw him cutting out droll or amusing pictures. Sometimes it would be a man hanging on a gibbet and holding a heart in his hand as if he had been stealing hearts. Sometimes it was an old witch riding through the air on a broom and carrying her husband on her nose. But the lawyer did not like such jokes, and he would say as he had just said, "How can anyone put such nonsense into a child's head? What absurd fancies they are!"

But to little Ida, all these stories which the student told her about the flowers seemed very droll, and she thought over them a great deal. The flowers did hang their heads, because they had been dancing all night and were very tired, and most likely they were ill. Then she took them into the room where a number of toys lay on a pretty little table, and the whole of the table drawer besides was full of beautiful things. Her doll Sophy lay in the doll's bed asleep, and little Ida said to her, "You must really get up, Sophy, and be content to lie in the drawer tonight. The poor flowers are ill, and they must lie in your bed. Then perhaps they will get well again." So she took out the doll, who looked quite cross and said not a single word, for she was angry at being turned out of her bed. Ida placed the flowers in the doll's bed and drew the quilt over them. Then she told them to lie quite still and be good while she made some tea for them, so that they might be quite well and able to get up the next morning. And she drew the curtains close round the little bed, so that the sun might not shine in their eyes. During the whole evening she could not help thinking of what the student had told her. And before she went to bed herself, she peeped behind the curtains into the garden where all her mother's beautiful flowers grew— hyacinths and tulips, and many others. Then she whispered to them quite softly, "I know you are going to a ball tonight." But the flowers appeared as if they did not understand, and not a leaf moved; still Ida felt quite sure she knew all about it.

She lay awake a long time after she was in bed, thinking how pretty it must be to see all the beautiful flowers dancing in the king's garden. "I wonder if my flowers have really been there?" she said to herself, and then she fell asleep. In the night she awoke; she had been dreaming of the flowers and of the student, as well as of the tiresome lawyer who found fault with him. It was quite still in Ida's bedroom; the night lamp burned on the table and her father and mother were asleep. "I wonder if my flowers are still lying in Sophy's bed?" she thought to herself. "How much I should like to know!" She raised herself a little and glanced at the door of the room where all her flowers and playthings lay. It was partly open, and as she listened, it seemed as if someone in the room was playing the piano, but softly and more prettily than she had ever before heard it. "Now all the flowers are certainly dancing in there," she thought. "Oh, how much I should like to see them!" But she did not dare to move for fear of disturbing her father and mother. "If they would only come in here," she thought, but they did not come. And the music continued to play so beautifully, and was so pretty, that she could resist no longer. She crept out of her little bed, went softly to the door, and looked into the room.

Oh, what a splendid sight there was to be sure! There was no night lamp burning, but the room appeared quite light, for the moon shone through the window upon the floor, and made it almost like day. All the hyacinths and tulips stood in two long rows down the room. Not a single flower remained in the window, and the flowerpots were all empty. The flowers were dancing gracefully on the floor, making turns and holding each other by their long green leaves as they swung round. At the piano sat a large yellow lily which little Ida was sure she had seen in the summer, for she remembered the student saying she was very much like Miss Lina, one of Ida's friends. They all laughed at him then, but now it seemed to little Ida as if the tall yellow flower was really like the young lady. She had just the same manners while playing, bending her long yellow face from side to side, and nodding in time to the beautiful music.

Then she saw a large purple crocus jump into the middle of the table where the playthings stood, go up to the doll's bedstead and draw back the curtains. There lay the sick flowers, but they got up directly and nodded to the others as a sign tha they wished to dance with them. The old rough doll with the broken mouth stood up and bowed to the pretty flowers. They did not look ill at all now, but jumped about and were very merry. Yet none of them noticed little Ida. Presently it seemed as if something fell from the table. Ida looked that way and saw a slight carnival rod jumping down among the flowers as if it belonged to them. It was, however, very smooth and neat, and a little wax doll with a broad-brimmed hat on her head, like the one worn by the lawyer, sat upon it. The carnival rod hopped about among the flowers on its three red stilted feet, and stamped quite loud when it danced the mazurka. The flowers could not do this dance—they were too light to stamp in that manner.

All at once the wax doll on the carnival rod seemed to grow larger and taller, and it turned around and said to the flowers, "How can you put such things in a child's head? They are all foolish fancies." And then the doll was exactly like the lawyer with the broad-brimmed hat, and looked as yellow and as cross as he did. But the rough doll struck him on his thin legs, and he shrunk up again and became quite a little wax doll. This was very amusing, and Ida could not help laughing. The carnival rod went on dancing, and the lawyer was obliged to dance also. It made no difference whether he made himself great and tall, or remained a little wax doll with a large black hat; still he must dance. At last some of the flowers interceded for him, especially those who had lain in the doll's bed, and the carnival rod gave up his dancing. At that moment a loud knocking was heard in the drawer, where Ida's doll Sophy lay with many other toys. Then the rough doll ran to the end of the table, laid himself flat down upon it, and began to pull the drawer out a little way.

Sophy raised herself and looked round quite astonished. "There must be a ball here tonight," she said. "Why did not somebody tell me?"

"Will you dance with me?" said the rough doll.

"You are the right sort to dance with, certainly," said she, turning her back upon him.

Then she seated herself on the edge of the drawer and thought that perhaps one of the flowers would ask her to dance, but none of them did. Then she coughed, "Hem, hem, a-hem"—but for all that no partner came. The shabby doll now danced quite alone, and not very badly, after all. As none of the flowers seemed to notice Sophy, she let herself down from the drawer to the floor, so as to make a very great noise. All the flowers came round her directly and asked if she had hurt herself, especially those who had lain in her bed. But she was not hurt at all, and Ida's flowers thanked her for the use of the nice bed and were very kind to her. They led her into the middle of the room, where the moon shone, and danced with her, while all the other flowers formed a circle round them. Then Sophy was very happy and said they might keep her bed: she did not mind lying in the drawer at all. But the flowers thanked her very much and said, "We cannot live long. Tomorrow morning we shall be dead, and you must tell little Ida to bury us in the garden, near the grave of the canary. In the summer we shall wake up again and be more beautiful than ever."

"No, you must not die," said Sophy, as she kissed the flowers.

Then the door of the room opened and a number of beautiful flowers danced in. Ida could not imagine where they could have come from, unless they were the flowers from the king's garden. First came two lovely roses with little golden crowns on their heads. These were the king and queen. Beautiful stocks and carnations followed, bowing to everyone present. They also had music with them. Large poppies and peonies had pea shells for instruments, and blew into them till they were quite red in the face. The bunches of blue hyacinths and the little white snowdrops jingled their bell-like flowers, as if they were real bells. Then came many more flowers: blue violets, purple heart's-ease, daisies, and lilies of the valley, and they all danced together, and kissed each other. It was very beautiful to behold.

At last the flowers wished each other good night. Then little Ida crept back into bed again, and dreamt of all she had seen. When she arose the next morning, she went quickly to the little table to see if the flowers were still there. She drew aside the curtains of the little bed. There they all lay, but quite faded; much more so than the day before. Sophy was lying in the drawer where Ida had placed her, but she looked very sleepy.

"Do you remember what the flowers told you to say to me?" asked little Ida. But Sophy looked quite stupid and said not a single word.

"You are not kind at all," said Ida. "And yet they all danced with you."

Then she took a little paper box on which were painted beautiful birds, and laid the dead flowers in it.

"This shall be your pretty coffin," she said. "And by and by, when my cousins come to visit me, they shall help me to bury you out in the garden, so that next summer you may grow up again more beautiful than ever."

Her cousins were two good-tempered boys whose names were James and Adolphus. Their father had given them each a bow and arrow, and they had brought them to show Ida. She told them about the poor flowers which were dead, and as soon as they obtained permission they went with her to bury them. The two boys walked first with their crossbows on their shoulders, and little Ida followed, carrying the pretty box containing the dead flowers. They dug a little grave in the garden. Ida kissed her flowers, and then laid them, with the box, in the earth. James and Adolphus then fired their crossbows over the grave, as they had neither guns nor cannons.

The Red Shoes

THERE was once a little girl. She was a tiny delicate little thing, but she always had to go about barefoot in summer, because she was very poor. In winter she had only a pair of heavy wooden shoes, and her ankles were terribly chafed.

An old mother shoemaker lived in the middle of the village, and she made a pair of little shoes out of some strips of red cloth. They were very clumsy, but they were made with the best intention, for the little girl was to have them. Her name was Karen.

These shoes were given to her, and she wore them for the first time on the day her mother was buried. They were certainly not mourning-shoes, but she had no others, and so she walked barelegged in them behind the poor pine coffin.

Just then a big old carriage drove by, and a big old lady was seated in it. She looked at the little girl and felt very, very sorry for her, and said to the parson, "Give the little girl to me and I will look after her and be kind to her." Karen thought it was all because of the red shoes, but the old lady said they were hideous, and they were burnt. Karen was well and neatly dressed, and had to learn reading and sewing. People said she was pretty, but her mirror said, "You are more than pretty. You are lovely!"

At this time the Queen was taking a journey through the country, and she had her little daughter the Princess with her. The people, and among them Karen, crowded round the palace where they were staying, to see them. The little Princess stood at a window to show herself. She wore neither a train nor a golden crown, but she was dressed all in white with a beautiful pair of red morocco shoes. They were indeed a contrast to those the poor old mother shoemaker had made for Karen. Nothing in the world could be compared to these red shoes.

The time came when Karen was old enough to be confirmed. She had new clothes and she was also to have a pair of new shoes. The rich shoemaker in the town was to take the measure of her little foot. His shop was full of glass cases of the most charming shoes and shiny leather boots. They looked beautiful but the old lady could not see very well, so it gave her no pleasure to look at them. Among all the other shoes there was one pair of red shoes like those worn by the Princess. Oh, how pretty they were! The shoemaker told them that they had been made for an earl's daughter, but they had not fitted. "I suppose they are patent leather," said the old lady. "They are so shiny."

"Yes, they do shine," said Karen, who tried them on. They fitted and were bought, but the old lady had not the least idea that they were red, or she would never have allowed Karen to wear them for her confirmation. This she did however.

Everybody looked at her feet, and when she walked up the church to the chancel she thought that even the old pictures, those portraits of dead and gone priests and their wives, with stiff collars and long black clothes, fixed their eyes upon her shoes. She thought of nothing else when the minister laid his hand upon her head and spoke to her of holy baptism, the covenant of God, and said that henceforth she was to be a responsible Christian person. The solemn notes of the organ resounded, the children sang with their sweet voices, and the old precentor sang, but Karen thought only about her red shoes.

By the afternoon the old lady had been told on all sides that the shoes were red, and she said it was very naughty and most improper. For the future, whenever Karen went to the church she was to wear black shoes, even if they were old. Next Sunday there was holy communion, and Karen was to receive it for the first time. She looked at the black shoes and then at the red ones. Then she looked again at the red—and at last put them on.

It was beautiful sunny weather. Karen and the old lady went by the path through the cornfield, and it was rather dusty. By the church door stood an old soldier with a crutch. He had a curious long beard; it was more red than white—in fact it was almost red. He bent down to the ground and asked the old lady if he might dust her shoes. Karen put out her little foot too. "See what beautiful dancing shoes!" said the soldier. "Mind you stick fast when you dance." And as he spoke he struck the soles with his hand. The old lady gave the soldier a copper and went into the church with Karen. All the people in the church looked at Karen's red shoes, and all the portraits looked too. When Karen knelt at the altar rails and the chalice was put to her lips, she thought only of the red shoes. She seemed to see them floating before her eyes. She forgot to join in the hymn of praise, and she forgot to say the Lord's Prayer.

Now everybody left the church, and the old lady got into her carriage. Karen lifted her foot to get in after her, but just then the old soldier, who was still standing there, said, "See what pretty dancing shoes!" Karen couldn't help it: she took a few dancing steps, and when she began her feet continued to dance. It was just as if the shoes had a power over them. She danced right round the church. She couldn't stop. The coachman had to run after her, take hold of her, and lift her into the carriage; but her feet continued to dance, so that she kicked the poor lady horribly. At last they got the shoes off and her feet had a little rest.

When they got home the shoes were put away in a cupboard, but Karen could not help going to look at them.

Karen's feet continued to dance

The old lady became very ill. They said she could not live. She had to be carefully nursed and tended, and no one was nearer than Karen to do this. But there was to be a grand ball in the town and Karen was invited. She looked at the old lady, who after all could not live. Then she looked at the red shoes—she thought there was no harm in doing so. She put on the red shoes—that much she thought she might do—and then she went to the ball and began to dance. The shoes would not let her do what she liked: when she wanted to go to the right, they danced to the left. When she wanted to dance up the room, the shoes danced down the room, and then down the stairs, through the streets and out of the town gate. Away she danced, and away she had to dance, right away into the dark forest. Something shone up above the trees and she thought it was the moon, for it was a face, but it was the old soldier with the red beard. He nodded and said, "See what pretty dancing shoes!"

This frightened her terribly and she wanted to throw off the red shoes, but they stuck fast. She tore off her stockings, but the shoes had grown fast to her feet. So off she danced, and off she had to dance, over fields and meadows, in rain and sunshine, by day and by night, but at night it was fearful.

She danced into the open churchyard, but the dead did not join her dance; they had something much better to do. She wanted to sit down on a pauper's grave where the bitter wormwood grew, but there was no rest nor repose for her. When she danced towards the open church door, she saw an angel standing there in long white robes and wings which reached from his shoulders to the ground. His face was grave and stern, and in his hand he held a broad and shining sword.

"Dance you shall!" said he. "You shall dance in your red shoes till you are pale and cold. Till your skin shrivels up and you are a skeleton! You shall dance from door to door, and wherever you find proud vain children, you must knock at the door so that they may see you and fear you. Yea, you shall dance—"

"Mercy!" shrieked Karen, but she did not hear the angel's answer, for the shoes bore her through the gate into the fields, and over roadways and paths. Ever and ever she was forced to dance.

One morning she danced past a door she knew well. She heard the sound of a hymn from within, and a coffin covered with flowers was being carried out. Then she knew that the old lady was dead, and it seemed to her that she was forsaken by all the world and cursed by the holy angels of God.

On and ever on she danced. Dance she must, even through the dark nights. The shoes bore her away over briars and stubble till her feet were torn and bleeding. She danced away over the heath till she came to a little lonely house. She knew the executioner lived here, and she tapped with her fingers on the window pane and said, "Come out! Come out! I can't come in for I am dancing!"

The executioner said, "Don't you know who I am? I chop the bad people's heads off, and I see that my ax is quivering."

"Don't chop my head off," said Karen, "for then I can never repent of my sins. But pray, pray chop off my feet with the red shoes!"

Then she confessed all her sins and the executioner chopped off her feet with the red shoes, but the shoes danced right away with the little feet into the depths of the forest.

Then he made her a pair of wooden feet and crutches, and he taught her a psalm, the one penitents always sing. And she kissed the hand which had wielded the ax and went away over the heath.

"I have suffered enough for those red shoes!" said she. "I will go to church now, so that they may see me." And she went as fast as she could to the church door. When she got there, the red shoes danced right up in front of her, and she was frightened and went home again.

She was very sad all the week and shed many bitter tears, but when Sunday came she said, "Now then, I have suffered long enough. I should think I am quite as good as many who sit holding their heads so high in church."

She went along quite boldly, but she did not get further than the gate before she saw the red shoes dancing in front of her. She was more frightened than ever and turned back, this time with real repentance in her heart. Then she went to the parson's house and begged to be taken into service. She would be very industrious and work as hard as she could. She didn't care what wages they gave her, if only she might have a roof over her head and live among kind people. The parson's wife was sorry for her, and took her into her service. She proved to be very industrious and thoughtful. She sat very still and listened most attentively in the evening when the parson read the Bible. All the little ones were very fond of her, but when they chattered about finery and dress and about being as beautiful as a queen, she would shake her head.

Next Sunday they all went to church and they asked her if she would go with them, but she looked sadly, with tears in her eyes, at her crutches. And they went without her to hear the word of God, while she sat in her little room alone. It was only big enough for a bed and a chair. She sat there with her prayer book in her hand, and as she read it with a humble mind she heard the notes of the organ, borne from the church by the wind. She raised her tear-stained face and said, "Oh, God help me!"

Then the sun shone brightly round her, and the angel in the white robes whom she had seen that night at the church door stood before her. He no longer held the sharp sword in his hand, but a beautiful green branch covered with roses. He touched the ceiling with it and it rose to a great height, and wherever he touched it a golden star appeared. Then he touched the walls and they spread themselves out, and she saw and heard the organ. She saw the pictures of the old parsons and their wives. The congregation were all sitting in their seats singing aloud—for the church itself had come home to the poor girl in her narrow little chamber, or else she had been taken to it. She found herself on the bench with the other people from the parsonage. And when the hymn had come to an end, they looked up and nodded to her and said, "It was a good thing you came after all, little Karen!"

"It was through God's mercy!" she said. The organ sounded and the children's voices echoed so sweetly through the choir. The warm sunshine streamed brightly in through the window, right up to the bench where Karen sat. Her heart was so overfilled with the sunshine, with peace, and with joy, that it broke. Her soul flew with the sunshine to heaven, and no one there asked about the red shoes.

The Ugly Duckling

THE country was **very** lovely just then—it was summer. The wheat was golden and the oats still green. The hay was stacked in the rich low meadows, where the stork marched about on his long red legs, chattering in Egyptian, the language his mother had taught him.

Round about field and meadow lay great woods, in the midst of which were deep lakes. Yes, the country certainly was lovely. In the sunniest spot stood an old mansion surrounded by a deep moat, and great dock leaves grew from the walls of the house right down to the water's edge. Some of them were so tall that a small child could stand upright under them. In among the leaves, it was as secluded as in the depths of a forest, and there a duck was sitting on her nest. Her little ducklings were just about to be hatched, but she was quite tired of sitting, for it had lasted such a long time. Moreover, she had very few visitors, as the other ducks liked swimming about in the moat better than waddling up to sit under the dock leaves and gossip with her.

At last one egg after another began to crack. "Cheep, cheep!" they said. All the chicks had come to life and were poking their heads out.

"Quack, quack!" said the duck, and then they all quacked their hardest and looked about them on all sides among the green leaves. Their mother allowed them to look as much as they liked, for green is good for the eyes.

"How big the world is, to be sure!" said all the young ones. They certainly now had ever so much more room to move about than when they were inside their eggshells.

"Do you imagine this is the whole world?" said the mother. "It stretches a long way on the other side of the garden, right into the parson's field, though I have never been as far as that. I suppose you are all here now?" She got up and looked about. "No, I declare I have not got you all yet! The biggest egg is still there. How long is this going to take?" she said, and settled herself on the nest again.

"Well, how are you getting on?" said an old duck who had come to pay her a visit.

"This one egg is taking such a long time!" answered the sitting duck. "The shell will not crack. But now you must look at the others. They are the finest ducklings I have ever seen. They are all exactly like their father, the rascal!—yet he never comes to see me."

"Let me look at the egg which won't crack," said the old duck. "You may be sure that it is a turkey's egg! I was cheated like that once and I had no end of trouble and worry with the creatures, for I may tell you that they are afraid of the water. I simply could not get them into it. I quacked and snapped at them, but it all did no good. Let me see the egg! Yes, it is a turkey's egg. You just leave it alone, and teach the other children to swim."

"I will sit on it a little longer. I have sat so long already that I may as well go on till the Midsummer Fair comes round."

"Please yourself," said the old duck, and away she went.

At last the big egg cracked. "Cheep, cheep!" said the young one and tumbled out. How big and ugly he was! The duck looked at him.

"That is a monstrous big duckling," she said. "None of the others looked like that. Can he be a turkey chick? Well, we shall soon find that out. Into the water he shall go, if I have to kick him in myself."

Next day was gloriously fine, and the sun shone on all the green dock leaves. The mother duck with her whole family went down to the moat.

Splash! into the water she sprang. "Quack, quack," she said, and one duckling plumped in after the other. The water dashed over their heads, but they came up again and floated beautifully. Their legs went of themselves, and they were all there. Even the big ugly gray one swam about with them.

"No, that is no turkey," she said. "See how beautifully he uses his legs and how erect he holds himself. He is my own chick, after all, and not bad looking when you come to look at him properly. Quack, quack! Now come with me and I will take you out into the world and introduce you to the duckyard. But keep close to me all the time so that no one will tread upon you. And beware of the cat!"

Then they went into the duckyard. There was a fearful uproar going on, for two broods were fighting for the head of an eel, and in the end the cat captured it.

"That's how things go in this world," said the mother duck, and she licked her bill, because she had wanted the eel's head herself.

"Now use your legs," said she. "Mind you quack properly, and bend your necks to the old duck over there. She is the grandest of us all. She has Spanish blood in her veins and that accounts for her size. And do you see? She has a red rag round her leg. That is a wonderfully fine thing, and the most extraordinary mark of distinction any duck can have. It shows clearly that she is not to be parted with, and that she is worthy of recognition both by beasts and men! Quack, now! Don't turn your toes in! A well brought up duckling keeps his legs wide apart just like father and mother. That's it. Now bend your necks and say quack!"

They did as they were bid, but the other ducks round about looked at them and said, quite loud, "Just look there! Now we are to have that tribe, just as if there were not enough of us already. And, oh dear, how ugly that duckling is! We won't stand him." And a duck flew at him at once and bit him in the neck.

"Let him be," said the mother. "He is doing no harm."

"Very likely not," said the biter. "But he is so ungainly and queer that he must be whacked."

"Those are handsome children mother has," said the old duck with the rag round her leg. "They are all good looking except this one, but he is not a good specimen. It's a pity you can't make him over again."

"That can't be done, your grace," said the mother duck. "He is not handsome, but he is a thoroughly good creature, and he swims as beautifully as any of the others. I think I might venture even to add that I think he will improve as he goes on, or perhaps in time he may grow smaller. He was too long in the egg, and so he has not come out with a very good figure." And then she patted his neck and stroked him down. "Besides, he is a drake," said she. "So it does not matter so much. I believe he will be very strong, and I don't doubt but he will make his way in the world."

"The other ducklings are very pretty," said the old duck. "Now make yourselves quite at home, and if you find the head of an eel you may bring it to me."

After that they felt quite at home. But the poor duckling who had been the last to come out of the shell, and who was so ugly, was bitten, pushed about, and made fun of both by the ducks and the hens. "He is too big," they all said. And the turkey cock, who was born with his spurs on and therefore thought himself quite an emperor, puffed himself up like a vessel in full sail, made for him, and gobbled and gobbled till he became quite red in the face. The poor duckling was at his wit's end, and did not know which way to turn. He was in despair because he was so ugly and the butt of the whole duckyard.

So the first day passed, and afterwards matters grew worse and worse. The poor duckling was chased and hustled by all of them. Even his brothers and sisters ill-used him. They were always saying, "If only the cat would get hold of you, you hideous object!" Even his mother said, "I wish to goodness you were miles away." The ducks bit him, the hens pecked him, and the girl who fed them kicked him aside.

Then he ran off and flew right over the hedge, where the little birds flew up into the air in a fright.

"That is because I am so ugly," thought the poor duckling, shutting his eyes, but he ran on all the same. Then he came to a great marsh where the wild ducks lived. He was so tired and miserable that he stayed there the whole night. In the morning the wild ducks flew up to inspect their new comrade.

"What sort of a creature are you?" they inquired, as the duckling turned from side to side and greeted them as well as he could. "You are frightfully ugly," said the wild ducks, "but that does not matter to us, so long as you do not marry into our family." Poor fellow! He had not thought of marriage. All he wanted was permission to lie among the rushes and to drink a little of the marsh water.

He stayed there two whole days. Then two wild geese came, or rather two wild ganders. They were not long out of the shell and therefore rather pert.

"I say, comrade," they said, "you are so ugly that we have taken quite a fancy to you! Will you join us and be a bird of passage? There is another marsh close by, and there are some charming wild geese there. All are sweet young ladies who can say quack! You are ugly enough to make your fortune among them." Just at that moment, bang! bang! was heard up above, and both the wild geese fell dead among the reeds, and the water turned blood red. Bang! bang! went the guns, and flocks of wild geese flew from the rushes and the shot peppered among them again.

There was a grand shooting party, and the sportsmen lay hidden round the marsh. Some even sat on the branches of the trees which overhung the water. The blue smoke rose like clouds among the dark trees and swept over the pool.

The retrieving dogs wandered about in the swamp— splash! splash! The rushes and reeds bent beneath their tread on all sides. It was terribly alarming to the poor duckling. He twisted his head around to get it under his wing, and just at that moment a frightful big dog appeared close beside him. His tongue hung right out of his mouth and his eyes glared wickedly. He opened his great chasm of a mouth close to the duckling, showed his sharp teeth, and —splash!—went on without touching him.

"Oh, thank Heaven!" sighed the duckling. "I am so ugly that even the dog won't bite me!"

Then he lay quite still while the shots whistled among the bushes, and bang after bang rent the air. It only became quiet late in the day, but even then the poor duckling did not dare to get up. He waited several hours more before he looked about, and then he hurried away from the marsh as fast as he could. He ran across fields and meadows, and there was such a wind that he had hard work to make his way.

Towards night he reached a poor little cottage. It was such a miserable hovel that it could not make up its mind which way even to fall, and so it remained standing. The wind whistled so fiercely around the duckling that he had to sit on his tail to resist it, and it blew harder and ever harder. Then he saw that the door had fallen off one hinge and hung so crookedly that he could creep into the house through the crack, and so he made his way into the room.

An old woman lived here with her cat and her hen. The cat, whom she called "Sonnie," would arch his back, purr, and give off electric sparks if you stroked his fur the wrong way. The hen had quite tiny short legs, and so she was called "Chickie-low-legs." She laid good eggs, and the old woman was as fond of her as if she had been her own child.

In the morning the strange duckling was discovered immediately, and the cat began to purr and the hen to cluck.

"What on earth is that?" said the old woman, looking round, but her sight was not good and she thought the duckling was a fat duck which had escaped. "This is a wonderful find!" said she. "Now I shall have duck's eggs—if only it is not a drake. We must wait and see about that."

So she took the duckling on trial for three weeks, but no eggs made their appearance. The cat was master of this house and the hen its mistress. They always said, "We and the world," for they thought that they represented the half of the world, and that quite the better half.

The duckling thought there might be two opinions on the subject, but the cat would not hear of it.

"Can you lay eggs?" she asked.

"No."

"Have the goodness to hold your tongue then!"

And the cat said, "Can you arch your back, purr, or give off sparks?"

"No."

"Then you had better keep your opinions to yourself when people of sense are speaking!"

The duckling sat in the corner nursing his ill humor. Then he began to think of the fresh air and the sunshine and an uncontrollable longing seized him to float on the water. At last he could not help telling the hen about it.

"What on earth possesses you?" she asked. "You have

nothing to do. That is why you get these freaks into your head. Lay some eggs or take to purring, and you will get over it."

"But it is so delicious to float on the water," said the duckling. "It is so delicious to feel it rushing over your head when you dive to the bottom."

"That would be a fine amusement!" said the hen. "I think you have gone mad. Ask the cat about it. He is the wisest creature I know. Ask him if he is fond of floating on the water or diving under it. I say nothing about myself. Ask our mistress herself, the old woman. There is no one in the world cleverer than she is. Do you suppose she has any desire to float on the water or to duck underneath it?"

"You do not understand me," said the duckling.

"Well, if we don't understand you, who should? I suppose you don't consider yourself cleverer than the cat or the old woman, not to mention me! Don't make a fool of yourself, child, and thank your stars for all the good we have done you. Have you not lived in this warm room, and in such society that you might have learned something? But you are an idiot, and there is no pleasure in associating with you. You may believe me: I mean you well. I tell you home truths, and there is no surer way than that of knowing who are one's friends. You just set about laying some eggs, or learn to purr, or to emit sparks."

"I think I will go out into the wide world," said the duckling.

"Oh, do so by all means," said the hen.

So away went the duckling. He floated on the water and ducked underneath it, but he was looked at askance and was slighted by every living creature for his ugliness. Now autumn came. The leaves in the woods turned yellow and brown. The wind took hold of them, and they danced about. The sky looked very cold and the clouds hung heavy with snow and hail. A raven stood on the fence and croaked "Caw, caw!" from sheer cold. It made one shiver only to think of it. The poor duckling certainly was in a bad case!

One evening, the sun was just setting in wintry splendor when a flock of beautiful large birds appeared out of the bushes. The duckling had never seen anything so beautiful. They were dazzlingly white with long waving necks. They were swans, and uttering a peculiar cry they spread out their magnificent broad wings and flew away from the cold regions to warmer lands and open seas. They mounted so high, so very high, and the ugly little duckling became strangely uneasy. He circled round and round in the water like a wheel, craning his neck up into the air after them. Then he uttered a shriek so piercing and so strange that he was quite frightened by it himself. Oh, he could not forget those beautiful birds, those happy birds. And as soon as they were out of sight, he ducked right down to the bottom, and when he came up again he was quite beside himself. He did not know what the birds were, or whither they flew, but all the same he was more drawn towards them than he had ever been by any creatures before. He did not envy them in the least. How could it occur to him even to wish to be such a marvel of beauty? He would have been thankful if only the ducks would have tolerated him among them—the poor ugly creature.

The winter was so bitterly cold that the duckling was obliged to swim about in the water to keep it from freezing over, but every night the hole in which he swam got smaller and smaller. Then it froze so hard that the surface ice cracked, and the duckling had to use his legs all the time so that the ice should not freeze around him. At last he was so weary that he could move no more, and he was frozen fast into the ice.

Early in the morning a peasant came along and saw him. He went out onto the ice and hammered a hole in it with his heavy wooden shoe, and carried the duckling home to his wife. There he soon revived. The children wanted to play with him, but the duckling thought they were going to ill-use him, and rushed in his fright into the milk pan, and the milk spurted out all over the room. The woman shrieked and threw up her hands. Then he flew into the butter cask, and down into the meal tub and out again. Just imagine what he looked like by this time! The woman screamed and tried to hit him with the tongs. The children tumbled over one another in trying to catch him, and they screamed with laughter. By good luck the door stood open, and the duckling flew out among the bushes and the newly fallen snow. And he lay there thoroughly exhausted.

But it would be too sad to mention all the privation and misery he had to go through during the hard winter. When the sun began to shine warmly again, the duckling was in the marsh, lying among the rushes. The larks were singing and the beautiful spring had come.

Then all at once he raised his wings and they flapped with much greater strength than before and bore him off vigorously. Before he knew where he was, he found himself in a large garden where the apple trees were in full blossom and the air was scented with lilacs, the long branches of which overhung the indented shores of the lake. Oh, the spring freshness was delicious!

Just in front of him he saw three beautiful white swans advancing towards him from a thicket. With rustling feathers they swam lightly over the water. The duckling recognized the majestic birds, and he was overcome by a strange melancholy.

"I will fly to them, the royal birds, and they will hack me to pieces because I, who am so ugly, venture to approach them. But it won't matter! Better be killed by them than be snapped at by the ducks, pecked by the hens, spurned by the henwife, or suffer so much misery in the winter."

So he flew into the water and swam towards the stately swans. They saw him and darted towards him with ruffled feathers.

"Kill me!" said the poor creature, and he bowed his head towards the water and awaited his death. But what did he see reflected in the transparent water?

He saw below him his own image, but he was no longer a clumsy dark gray bird, ugly and ungainly. He was himself a swan! It does not matter in the least having been born in a duckyard, if only you come out of a swan's egg!

He felt quite glad of all the misery and tribulation he had gone through, for he was the better able to appreciate his good fortune now and all the beauty which greeted him. The big swans swam round and round him and stroked him with their bills.

Some little children came into the garden with corn and pieces of bread which they threw into the water, and the smallest one cried out, "There is a new one!" The other children shouted with joy, "Yes, a new one has come." And they clapped their hands and danced about, running after their father and mother. They threw the bread into the water, and one and all said, "The new one is the prettiest of them all. He is so young and handsome." And the old swans bent their heads and did homage before him.

He felt quite shy, and hid his head under his wing. He did not know what to think. He was very happy, but not at all proud, for a good heart never becomes proud. He thought of how he had been pursued and scorned, and now he heard them all say that he was the most beautiful of all beautiful birds. The lilacs bent their boughs right down into the water before him, and the bright sun was warm and cheering. He rustled his feathers and raised his slender neck aloft, saying with exultation in his heart, "I never dreamt of so much happiness when I was the Ugly Duckling!"

The Girl Who Trod on a Loaf

I DARESAY you have heard of the girl who stepped on a loaf so as not to soil her shoes, and all the misfortunes that befell her in consequence. At any rate the story has been written and printed too.

She was a poor child of a proud and arrogant nature, and her disposition was bad from the beginning. When she was quite tiny, her greatest delight was to catch flies and pull their wings off, to make creeping insects of them. Then she would catch chafers and beetles and stick them on a pin, after which she would push a leaf or a bit of paper close enough for them to seize with their feet, for the pleasure of seeing them writhe and wriggle in their efforts to free themselves from the pins.

"The chafer is reading now," said little Inger. "Look at it turning over the page!"

She got worse rather than better as she grew older. But she was very pretty, and that no doubt was her misfortune, or she might have had many a beating which she never got.

"It will take a heavy blow to bend that head," said her own mother. "As a child you have often trampled on my apron. I fear when you are grown up you will trample on my heart."

This she did with a vengeance.

She was sent into service in the country with some rich

people. They treated her as if she had been their own child and dressed her in the same style. She grew prettier and prettier, but her pride grew too.

When she had been with them a year, her employers said to her, "You ought to go home to see your parents, little Inger."

So she went, but she only went to show herself, so that they might see how grand she was. When she got to the town gates, and saw the young men and maids gossiping round the pond, and her mother sitting among them with a bundle of sticks she had picked up in the woods, Inger turned away. She was ashamed that one so fine as herself should have for her mother such a ragged old woman who picked up sticks. She was not a bit sorry that she had turned back, only angry.

Another half year passed.

"Little Inger, you really ought to go and see your old parents," said her mistress. "Here is a large loaf of wheaten bread that you may take to them. They will be pleased to see you."

Inger put on all her best clothes and her fine new shoes. She held up her skirts and picked her steps carefully so as to keep her shoes nice and clean. Now no one could blame her for this. But when she came to the path through the marsh a great part of it was wet and muddy, and she threw the loaf into the mud for a stepping stone, to get over with dry shoes. As she stood there with one foot on the loaf and was lifting up the other for the next step, the loaf sank deeper and deeper with her till she entirely disappeared. Nothing was to be seen but a black bubbling pool.

Now this is the story.

But what had become of her? She went down to the Marsh Wife who has a brewery down there. The Marsh Wife is own sister to the Elf King, and aunt to the Elf maidens who are well enough known. They have had verses written about them and pictures painted, but all that people know about the Marsh Wife is that when the mist rises over the meadows in the summer, she is at her brewing. It was into this brewery that little Inger fell, and no one can stand being there long. A scavenger's cart is sweet compared to the Marsh Wife's brewery. The smell from the barrels is enough to make people faint, and the barrels are so close together that no one can pass between them, but wherever there is a little chink it is filled up with noisome toads and slimy snakes. Little Inger fell among all this horrid living filth. It was so icy cold that she shuddered from head to foot and her limbs grew quite stiff. The loaf stuck fast to her feet and it drew her down just as an amber button draws a bit of straw.

The Marsh Wife was at home. Old Bogey and his great-grandmother were paying her a visit. The great-grandmother is a very venomous old woman, and she is never idle. She never goes out without her work, and she had it with her to-day too. She was busily making gadabout leather to put into people's shoes so that the wearer might have no rest. She embroidered lies and strung together all the idle words which fell to the ground, to make mischief of them. Oh yes, old great-grandmother can knit and embroider in fine style.

As soon as she saw little Inger, she put up her eyeglass and looked at her through it. "That girl has got something in her," she said. "I should like to have her as a remembrance of my visit. She would make a very good statue in my great-grandson's outer corridor."

So Inger was given to her and this was how she got to Bogeyland. People don't always get there by such a direct route, though it is easy enough to get there in more round-about ways.

What a never-ending corridor that was, to be sure. It made one giddy to look either backwards or forwards. Here

"*She would make a very good statue*"

stood an ignominious crew waiting for the door of mercy to be opened, but long might they wait. Great, fat, sprawling spiders spun webs of a thousand years round and round their feet. And these webs were like footscrews and held them as in a vice, or as though bound with a copper chain. Besides, there was such everlasting unrest in every soul—the unrest of torment. The miser had forgotten the key of his money chest; he knew he had left it sticking in the lock. But it would take far too long to enumerate all the various tortures here. Inger experienced the torture of standing like a statue with a loaf tied to her feet.

"This is what comes of trying to keep one's feet clean," said she to herself. "Look how they stare at me!" They did indeed stare at her. All their evil passions shone out of their eyes and spoke without words from their lips. They were a terrible sight. "It must be a pleasure to look at me!" thought Inger, "for I have a pretty face and nice clothes." She turned her eyes to look at them; her neck was too stiff to turn.

But oh, how dirty she had got in the Marsh Wife's brewery; she had never thought of that. Her clothes were covered with slime. A snake had got among her hair and hung dangling down her back. A toad looked out of every fold of her dress, croaking like an asthmatic pug dog. It was most unpleasant. "But all the others down here look frightful too," was her consolation.

Worse than anything was the terrible hunger she felt, and she could not stoop down to break a bit of bread off the loaf she was standing on. No, her back had stiffened, her arms and hands had stiffened, and her whole body was like a pillar of stone. She could turn her eyes, but she could only turn them entirely around, so as to look backwards—and a horrible sight that was. And then came the flies! They crept upon her eyes, and however much she winked they would not fly away. They could not, for she had pulled off their wings and made creeping insects of them. That was indeed a torment added to her gnawing hunger. She seemed at last to be absolutely empty.

"If this is to go on long, I shan't be able to bear it," said she. But it did go on, and bear it she must.

Then a scalding tear fell upon her forehead. It trickled over her face and bosom right down to the loaf. Then another fell, and another, till there was a perfect shower.

Who was crying for little Inger? Had she not a mother on earth? Tears of sorrow shed by a mother for her child will always reach it, but they do not bring healing. They burn and make the torment fifty times worse. Then this terrible hunger again, and she not able to get at the bread under her feet. She felt at last as if she had been feeding upon herself, and had become a mere hollow reed which conducts every sound. She distinctly heard everything that was said on earth about herself, and she heard nothing but hard words.

Certainly her mother wept bitterly and sorrowfully, but at the same time she said, "Pride goes before a fall. There was your misfortune, Inger. How you have grieved your mother!" Her mother and everyone on earth knew all about her sin: how she had stepped upon the loaf and sunk down under the earth, and so was lost. The cowherd had told them so much. He had seen it himself from the hillock where he was standing.

"How you have grieved your mother, Inger," said the poor woman. "But then I always said you would."

"Oh, that I had never been born!" thought Inger then. "I should have been much better off. My mother's tears are no good now."

She heard the good people her employers, who had been like parents to her, talking about her. "She was a sinful child," they said. "She did not value the gifts of God but trod them under foot. She will find it hard to open the door of mercy."

"They ought to have brought me up better," thought

Inger. "They should have knocked the nonsense out of me if it was there."

She heard that a song had been written about her and sung all over the country: "The arrogant girl who trod on a loaf to keep her shoes clean."

"That I should hear that old story so often and have to suffer so much for it!" thought Inger.

"The others ought to be punished for their sins, too," said Inger. "There would be plenty to punish. Oh how I am being tormented!"

And her heart grew harder than her outer shell.

"Nobody will ever get any better in this company, and I won't be any better. See how they are all staring at me!"

Her heart was full of anger and malice towards everybody.

"Now they have got something to talk about up there! Oh, this torture!"

She heard people telling her story to children, and the little ones always called her "wicked Inger"—"she was so naughty that she had to be tormented." She heard nothing but hard words from the children's mouths.

But one day when anger and hunger were gnawing at her hollow shell, she heard her name mentioned and her story being told to an innocent child, a little girl, and the little creature burst into tears at the story of proud, vain Inger.

"But will she never come up here again?" asked the child. And the answer was, "She will never come up again."

"But if she were to ask pardon and promise never to do it again?"

"She won't ask pardon," they said.

"But I want her to do it," said the little girl, who refused to be comforted. "I will give my doll's house if she may only come up again. It is so dreadful for poor Inger."

These words reached down into Inger's heart and they seemed to do her good. It was the first time that anyone had said, "Poor Inger," without adding anything about her misdeeds. A little innocent child was weeping and praying for her, and it made her feel quite odd. She would have liked to cry herself, but she could not shed a tear, and this was a further torment.

As the years passed above, so they went on below without any change. She less often heard sounds from above, and she was less talked about. But one day she was aware of a sigh. "Inger, Inger, what a grief you have been to me, but I always knew you would." It was her mother who was dying. Occasionally she heard her name mentioned by her old employers, and the gentlest words her mistress used were, "Shall I ever see you again, Inger? One never knows whither one may go."

But Inger knew very well that her good kindly mistress could never come to the place where she was.

Again a long bitter period passed. Then Inger again heard her name pronounced, and saw above her head what seemed to be two bright stars. They were in fact two kind eyes which were closing on earth. So many years had gone by since the little girl had cried so bitterly at the story of "Poor Inger," that the child had grown to be an old woman whom the Lord was now calling to Himself. In the last hour when one's whole life comes back to one, she remembered how as a little child she had wept bitter tears at the story of Inger. The impression was so clear to the old woman in the hour of death that she exclaimed aloud, "O Lord, may I not, like Inger, have trodden on Thy blessed gifts without thinking? And may I not also have nourished pride in my heart? But in Thy mercy Thou didst not let me fall! Forsake me not now in my last hour!"

The old woman's eyes closed and the eyes of her soul were opened to see the hidden things, and as Inger had been so vividly present in her last thoughts, she saw now how deep she had sunk. And at the sight she burst into tears.

Then she stood in the Kingdom of Heaven, as a child, weeping for poor Inger. Her tears and prayers echoed into the hollow, empty shell which surrounded the imprisoned, tortured soul, and it was quite overwhelmed by all this unexpected love from above. An angel of God weeping over her! Why was this vouchsafed to her? The tortured soul recalled every earthly action it had ever performed, and at last it melted into tears, in a way Inger had never done.

She was filled with grief for herself. It seemed as though the gate of mercy could never be opened to her. But as in humble contrition she acknowledged this, a ray of light shone into the gulf of destruction. The strength of the ray was far greater than that of the sunbeam which melts the snowman built up by the boys in the garden. And sooner, much sooner, than a snowflake melts on the warm lips of a child, did Inger's stony form dissolve before it. And a little bird with lightning speed winged its way to the upper world. It was terribly shy and afraid of everything. It was ashamed of itself and afraid to meet the eye of any living being, so it hastily sought shelter in a chink in the wall. There it cowered, shuddering in every limb. It could not utter a sound, for it had no voice. It sat for a long time before it could survey calmly all the wonders around. Yes, they were wonders indeed! The air was so sweet and fresh, the moon shone so brightly, the trees and bushes were so fragrant. And then the comfort of it all; its feathers were so clean and dainty.

How all creation spoke of love and beauty! The bird would gladly have sung aloud all these thoughts stirring in its breast, but it had not the power. Gladly would it have caroled as do the cuckoos and nightingales in summer. The good God, who hears the voiceless hymn of praise even of a worm, was also aware of this psalm of thanksgiving trembling in the breast of the bird, as the psalms of David echoed in his heart before they shaped themselves into words and melody. These thoughts and these voiceless songs grew and swelled for weeks. They must have an outlet, and at the first attempt at a good deed this would be found.

Then came the holy Christmas feast. The peasants raised a pole against a well, and tied a sheaf of oats on to the top so that the little birds might have a good meal on the happy Christmas Day.

The sun rose bright and shone upon the sheaf of oats, and the twittering birds surrounded the pole. Then from the chink in the wall came a feeble tweet-tweet. The swelling thoughts of the bird had found a voice, and this faint twitter was its hymn of praise. The thought of a good deed was awakened, and the bird flew out of its hiding place. In the Kingdom of Heaven this bird was well known.

It was a very hard winter and all the water had thick ice over it. The birds and wild creatures had great difficulty in finding food. The little bird flew along the highways, finding here and there in the tracks of the sledges a grain of corn. At the baiting places it also found a few morsels of bread, of which it would only eat a crumb, and gave the rest to the other starving sparrows which it called up. Then it flew into the town and peeped about. Wherever a loving hand had strewn bread crumbs for the birds, it ate only one crumb and gave the rest away.

In the course of the winter the bird had collected and given away so many crumbs of bread that they equaled in weight the whole loaf which little Inger had stepped upon to keep her shoes clean. When the last crumbs were found and given away, the bird's gray wings became white and spread themselves wide.

"A tern is flying away over the sea," said the children who saw the white bird. Now it dived into the sea, and now it soared up into the bright sunshine. It gleamed so brightly that it was not possible to see what became of it. They said it flew right into the sun.

The Bottle Neck

CLOSE to the corner of a street, among other abodes of poverty stood an exceedingly tall, narrow house, which had been so knocked about by time that it seemed out of joint in every direction. This house was inhabited by poor people, but the deepest poverty was apparent in the garret lodging in the gable. In front of the little window, an old bent bird cage hung in the sunshine, which had not even a proper water glass. Instead there was the broken neck of a bottle turned upside down and with a cork stuck in to make it hold the water with which it was filled. An old maid stood at the window. She had hung chickweed over the cage, and the little linnet in it hopped from perch to perch and sang and twittered merrily.

"Yes, it's all very well for you to sing," said the bottle neck. He did not really speak the words as we do, for the neck of a bottle cannot speak, but he thought them to himself in his own mind, just as people sometimes talk quietly to themselves.

"Yes, you may very well sing. You have all your limbs uninjured. You should feel what it is like to lose your body and have only a neck and a mouth left, with a cork stuck in it as I have. You wouldn't sing then, I know. After all, it is just as well that there are some who can be happy. I have no reason to sing, nor could I sing now if I were ever so happy. But when I was a whole bottle and they rubbed me with a cork, didn't I sing then? I used to be called a complete lark. I remember when I went out to a picnic with the furrier's family, on the day his daughter was betrothed. It seems as if it only happened yesterday. I have gone through a great deal in my time, when I come to recollect. I have been in the fire and in the water. I have been deep in the earth, and I have mounted higher in the air than most people. And now I am swinging here, outside a bird cage, in the air and the sunshine. Oh indeed, it would be worth while to hear my history, but I do not speak it aloud for a very good reason—I cannot."

Then the bottle neck related his history, which was really rather remarkable. He in fact related it to himself, or at least thought it in his own mind. The little bird sang his own song merrily. In the street below there was driving and running to and fro. Everyone thought of his own affairs, or perhaps of nothing at all—but the bottle neck thought deeply.

He thought of the blazing furnace in the factory, where he had been blown into life. He remembered how hot it felt when he was placed in the heated oven, the home from which he sprang, and that he had a strong inclination to leap out again directly; but after a while it became cooler, and he found himself very comfortable. He had been placed in a row with a whole regiment of his brothers and sisters, all brought out of the same furnace. Some of them had certainly been blown into champagne bottles, and others into beer bottles, which made a little difference between them. In the world it often happens that a beer bottle may later contain precious wine, and a champagne bottle be filled with blacking. But even in decay it may always be seen whether a man has been well born. Nobility remains noble, as a champagne bottle remains the same, even with blacking in its interior.

When the bottles were packed, our bottle was packed among them. It little expected then to finish its career as a bottle neck, or to be used as a water glass in a bird cage, which is after all a place of honor, for it is to be of some use in the world. The bottle did not behold the light of day again until it was unpacked with the rest in the wine merchant's cellar, and for the first time rinsed with water, which caused very curious sensations. There it lay empty and without a cork, and it had a peculiar feeling as if it wanted something; it knew not what.

At last it was filled with rich and costly wine, and a cork was placed in it and sealed down. Then it was labeled "first quality," as if it had carried off the first prize at an examination. However, the wine and the bottle were both new, and while we are young is the time for poetry. There were sounds of song within the bottle, of things it could not understand, of green sunny mountains where the vines grow and where the merry vine dressers laugh, sing, and are merry. "Ah, how beautiful is life!" All these tones of joy and song in the bottle were like the working of a young poet's brain, who often knows not the meaning of the tones which are sounding within him.

One morning the bottle found a purchaser in the furrier's apprentice, who was told to bring one of the best bottles of wine. It was placed in the provision basket with ham and cheese and sausages. The sweetest fresh butter and the finest bread were put into the basket by the furrier's daughter, for she packed it. She was young and pretty. Her brown eyes laughed, and a smile lingered round her mouth as sweet as that in her eyes. She had delicate hands, beautifully white, and her neck was whiter still. It could easily be seen that she was a very lovely girl, and as yet she was not engaged. The provision basket lay in the young girl's lap as the family drove out to the forest, and the neck of the bottle peeped out from between the folds of the white napkin. There was red wax on the cork, and the bottle looked straight at the young girl's face and also at the face of the young sailor who sat near her. He was a young friend, the son of a portrait painter.

He had lately passed his examination with honor, as mate, and the next morning he was to sail in his ship to a distant coast. There had been a great deal of talk on this subject while the basket was being packed, and during the conversation the eyes and the mouth of the furrier's daughter did not wear a very joyful expression.

The young people wandered away into the green wood and talked together. What did they talk about? The bottle could not say, for he was in the provision basket. It remained there for a long time, but when at last it was brought forth it appeared as if something pleasant had happened, for everyone was laughing. The furrier's daughter laughed too, but she said very little, and her cheeks were like two roses. Then her father took the bottle and the corkscrew into his hands. What a strange sensation it was to have the cork drawn for the first time! The bottle could never after that forget the performance of that moment. Indeed there was quite a convulsion within him as the cork flew out, and a gurgling sound as the wine was poured forth into the glasses. "Long life to the betrothed!" cried the papa, and every glass was emptied to the dregs, while the young sailor kissed his beautiful bride.

"Happiness and blessing to you both!" said the old people—father and mother; and the young man filled the glasses again.

"Safe return, and a wedding this day next year!" he cried. And when the glasses were empty he took the bottle, raised it on high, and said, "Thou hast been present here on the happiest day of my life. Thou shalt never be used by others!" So saying, he hurled it high in the air.

The furrier's daughter thought she should never see it again, but she was mistaken. It fell among the rushes on the borders of a little woodland lake. The bottle neck remembered well how long it lay there unseen. "I gave them wine, and they gave me muddy water," he had said to himself. "But I suppose it was all well meant."

He could no longer see the betrothed couple nor the cheerful old people, but for a long time he could hear them rejoicing and singing. At length there came by two peasant boys, who peeped in among the reeds and spied the bottle. Then they took it up and carried it home with them, so that once more it was provided for.

At home in their wooden cottage these boys had an elder brother, a sailor, who was about to start on a long voyage. He had been there the day before to say farewell, and his mother was now very busy packing up various things for him to take with him on his voyage. In the evening his father was going to carry the parcel to the town, to see his son once more and take him a farewell greeting from his mother. A small bottle had already been filled with herb tea mixed with brandy, and wrapped in a parcel. But when the boys came in, they brought with them the larger and stronger bottle which they had found. This bottle would hold much more than the little one, and they all said the brandy would be good for stomach complaints, especially as it was mixed with medicinal herbs. The liquid which they now poured into the bottle was not like the red wine with which it had once been filled. These were bitter drops, but they are of great use sometimes—for the stomach. The new large bottle was to go, not the little one. So the bottle once more started on its travels.

It was taken on board (for Peter Jensen was one of the crew) the very same ship in which the young mate was to sail. But the mate did not see the bottle. Indeed if he had, he would not have known it nor supposed it was the one out of which they had drunk to the felicity of the betrothed and to the prospect of a marriage on his own happy return. Certainly the bottle no longer poured forth wine, but it contained something quite as good. And so it happened that whenever Peter Jensen brought it out, his messmates gave it the name of "the apothecary," for it contained the best medicine to cure his stomach, and he gave it out quite willingly as long as a drop remained. Those were happy days, and the bottle would sing when rubbed with a cork, and it was called a "great lark," "Peter Jensen's lark."

Long days and months rolled by during which the bottle stood empty in a corner, when a storm arose—whether on the passage out or home it could not tell, for it had never been ashore. It was a terrible storm. Great waves arose, darkly heaving and tossing the vessel to and fro. The mainmast was split asunder, the ship sprang a leak, and the pumps became useless, while all around was black as night. At the last moment, when the ship was sinking, the young mate wrote on a piece of paper, "We are going down. God's will be done." Then he wrote the name of his betrothed, his own name, and that of the ship. Then he put the leaf in an empty bottle that happened to be at hand, corked it down tightly, and threw it into the foaming sea. He knew not that it was the very same bottle from which the goblet of joy and hope had once been filled for him. And now it was tossing on the waves with his last greeting, and a message from the dead.

The ship sank, and the crew sank with her. But the bottle flew on like a bird, for it bore within it a loving letter from a loving heart. And as the sun rose and set, the bottle felt as at the time of its first existence, when in the heated glowing stove it had a longing to fly away. It outlived the storms and the calm. It struck against no rocks, and was not devoured by sharks. But it drifted on for more than a year, sometimes towards the north, sometimes towards the south, just as the current carried it. It was in all other ways its own master, but even of that one may get tired. The written leaf, the last farewell of the bridegroom to his bride, would only bring sorrow when once it reached her hands. But where were those hands so soft and delicate, which had once spread the tablecloth on the fresh grass in the green wood, on the day of her betrothal? Ah yes, where was the furrier's daughter? And where was the land which might lie nearest to her home?

The bottle knew not. It traveled onward and onward, and at last all this wandering about became wearisome. At all events it was not its usual occupation. But it had to travel, till at length it reached land—a foreign country. Not a word spoken in this country could the bottle understand. It was a language it had never before heard, and it is a great loss not to be able to understand a language. The bottle was fished out of the water and examined on all sides. The little letter contained within it was discovered, taken out, and turned and twisted in every direction, but the people could not understand what was written upon it. They could be quite sure that the bottle had been thrown overboard from a vessel, and that something about it was written on this paper. But what was written? That was the question. So the paper was put back into the bottle, and then both were put away in a large cupboard of one of the great houses of the town.

Whenever any strangers arrived, the paper was taken out and turned over and over, so that the address, which was only written in pencil, became almost illegible. At last no one could distinguish any letters on it at all. For a whole year the bottle remained standing in the cupboard, and then it was taken up to the loft, where it soon became covered with dust and cobwebs. Ah, how often then it thought of those better days—of the times when in the fresh green wood it had poured forth rich wine; or while rocked by the swelling waves it had carried in its bosom a secret, a letter, a last parting sigh.

For twenty years it stood in the loft, and it might have

stayed longer but that the house was going to be rebuilt. The bottle was discovered when the roof was taken off. They talked about it, but the bottle did not understand what they said. A language is not to be learned by living in a loft, even for twenty years. "If I had been downstairs in the room," thought the bottle, "I might have learned it."

It was now washed and rinsed, which process was really quite necessary, and afterwards it looked clean and transparent and felt young again in its old age. But the paper which it had carried so faithfully was destroyed in the washing. They filled the bottle with seeds, though it scarcely knew what had been placed in it. Then they corked it down tightly and carefully wrapped it up. There not even the light of a torch or lantern could reach it, much less the brightness of the sun or moon. "Men go on a journey that they may see as much as possible," thought the bottle. "And yet I can see nothing." However, it did something quite as important. It traveled to the place of its destination and was unpacked.

"What trouble they have taken with the bottle over yonder," said one. "And very likely it is broken after all." But the bottle was not broken, and better still, it understood every word that was said. This language it had heard at the furnaces and at the wine merchant's, in the forest and on the ship—it was the only good old language it could understand. It had returned home, and the language was as a welcome greeting. For very joy it felt ready to jump out of people's hands, and scarcely noticed that its cork had been drawn and its contents emptied out, till it found itself carried to a cellar, to be left there and forgotten. "There's no place like home, even if it's a cellar." It never occurred to him to think that he might lie there for years—he felt so comfortable. For many long years he remained in the cellar, till at last some people came to carry away the bottles, and he was among the number.

Out in a garden there was a great festival. Brilliant lamps hung in festoons from tree to tree, and paper lanterns through which the light shone till they looked like transparent tulips. It was a beautiful evening, and the weather mild and clear. The stars twinkled. And on the new moon, which was in the form of a crescent, lay the shadowy disc of the whole moon, that looked like a gray globe with a golden rim. It was a beautiful sight for those who had good eyes. The illumination extended even to the most retired of the garden walks, though none were so retired that anyone need lose himself there. In the borders were placed bottles, each containing a light, and among them the bottle with which we are acquainted, and whose fate it was one day to be only a bottle neck, and to serve as a water glass in a bird cage.

Everything here appeared lovely to our bottle, for it was again in the green wood amid joy and feasting. Again it heard music and song, and the noise and murmur of a crowd, especially in that part of the garden where the lamps blazed and the paper lanterns displayed their brilliant colors. It stood in a distant walk certainly, but a place pleasant for contemplation; and it carried a light and was at once useful and ornamental. In such an hour it is easy to forget that one has spent twenty years in a loft, and it is a good thing to be able to do so.

Close before the bottle passed a single pair, like the bridal pair—the mate and the furrier's daughter—who had so long ago wandered in the wood. It seemed to the bottle as if he were living that time over again. Not only the guests were walking in the garden, but the other people who were allowed to witness the splendor and the festivities. Among the latter came an old maid who seemed to be quite alone in the world. She was thinking, like the bottle, of the green wood and of a young betrothed pair who were closely connected with herself. She was thinking of that hour, the happiest of her life, in which she had taken part, when she had herself been one of that betrothed pair. Such hours are never to be forgotten, let a maiden be as old as she may. But she did not recognize the bottle. Neither did the bottle notice the old maid. And so we often pass each other in the world when we meet without recognizing each other, as did these two, even while together in the same town.

The bottle was taken from the garden and again sent to a wine merchant. It was once more filled with wine, and was sold to an aeronaut who was to make an ascent in his balloon on the following Sunday. A great crowd assembled to witness the sight. Military music had been engaged and many other preparations made. The bottle saw it all from the basket in which he lay close to a live rabbit. The rabbit was quite excited because he knew that he was to be taken up and let down again in a parachute. The bottle, however, knew nothing of the "up," or of the "down." He saw only that the balloon was swelling larger and larger till it could swell no more, and began to rise and be restless. Then the ropes which held it were cut through, and the aerial ship rose in the air with the aeronaut and the basket containing the bottle and the rabbit, while the music sounded and all the people shouted "Hurrah!"

"This is a wonderful journey up into the air," thought the bottle. "It is a new way of sailing, and here at least there is no fear of striking against anything."

Thousands of people gazed at the balloon, and the old maid who was in the garden saw it also. She stood at the open window of the garret, by which hung the cage containing the linnet, who then had no water glass but was obliged to be contented with an old cup. On the window sill stood a myrtle in a pot, and this had been pushed a little to one side that it might not fall out. For the old maid was leaning out of the window that she might see. And she did see distinctly the aeronaut in the balloon, and how he let down the rabbit in the parachute, and then drank to the health of all the spectators in the wine from the bottle. After doing this, he hurled it high into the air. How little she thought that this was the very same bottle which her friend had thrown aloft in her honor, on that happy day of rejoicing in the green wood, in her youthful days! The bottle had no time to think, when raised so suddenly, and before it was aware, it reached the highest point it had ever attained in its life. Steeples and roofs lay far, far beneath it, and the people looked as tiny as possible.

Then it began to descend much more rapidly than the rabbit had done. It made somersaults in the air, and felt itself quite young and unfettered, although it was half full of wine. But this did not last long. What a journey it was! All the people could see the bottle, for the sun shone upon it. The balloon was already far away and very soon the bottle was far away also, for it fell on a roof and broke in pieces. But the pieces had got such an impetus that they could not stop. They went jumping and rolling about till at last they fell into the courtyard and were broken into still smaller pieces. Only the neck of the bottle managed to keep whole, and it was broken off as clean as if it had been cut with a diamond.

"That would make a capital bird's glass," said one of the cellar men. But none of them had either a bird or a cage, and it was not to be expected they would acquire one just because they had found a bottle neck that could be used as a glass. But the old maid who lived in the garret had a bird, and it really might be useful to her. So the bottle neck was provided with a cork and taken up to her. And as it often happens in life, the part that had been uppermost was now turned downwards, and it was filled with fresh water. Then they hung it in the cage of the little bird, who sang and twittered more merrily than ever.

"Ah, you have good reason to sing," said the bottle neck,

which was looked upon as something very remarkable because it had been in a balloon. Nothing further was known of its history. As it hung there in the bird cage, it could hear the noise of the people in the street below, as well as the conversation of the old maid in the room. A friend had just come to visit her and they talked, not about the bottle neck, but of the myrtle in the window.

"No, you must not spend a dollar for your daughter's bridal bouquet," said the old maid. "You shall have a beautiful little bunch for a nosegay, full of blossoms. Do you see how splendidly the tree has grown? It has been raised from only a little sprig of myrtle that you gave me on the day after my betrothal, and from which I was to make my own bridal bouquet when a year had passed. But that day never came! The eyes were closed which were to have been my light and joy through life. In the depths of the sea my beloved sleeps sweetly. The myrtle is an old tree, and I am a still older woman. Before the sprig you gave me faded, I took a spray and planted it. It has become a large tree. Its blossoms shall at last appear at a wedding festival, in your daughter's bouquet."

There were tears in the eyes of the old maid, as she spoke of the beloved of her youth and of their betrothal in the wood. Many thoughts came into her mind. But the thought never came that quite close to her, in that very window, was a remembrance of those olden times—the neck of the bottle which had, as it were, shouted for joy when the cork flew out with a bang on the betrothal day. But the bottle neck did not recognize the old maid. He had not been listening to what she had related, perhaps because he was thinking so much about her.

The Snow Queen

A TALE IN SEVEN STORIES

FIRST STORY

Deals with a Mirror and Its Fragments

NOW we are about to begin and you must attend! And when we get to the end of the story, you will know more than you do now about a very wicked hobgoblin. He was one of the worst kind; in fact he was a real demon.

One day this demon was in a high state of delight because he had invented a mirror with this peculiarity: that every good and pretty thing reflected in it shrank away to almost nothing. On the other hand, every bad and good-for-nothing thing stood out and looked its worst. The most beautiful landscapes reflected in it looked like boiled spinach, and the best people became hideous, or else they were upside down and had no bodies. Their faces were distorted beyond recognition, and if they had even one freckle it appeared to spread all over the nose and mouth. The demon thought this immensely amusing. If a good thought passed through anyone's mind, it turned to a grin in the mirror, and this caused real delight to the demon.

All the pupils in the demon's school—for he kept a school —reported that a miracle had taken place: now for the first time, they said, it was possible to see what the world and mankind were really like. They ran about everywhere with the mirror, till at last there was not a country or a person which had not been seen in this distorting mirror.

They even wanted to fly up to heaven with it to mock the angels. But the higher they flew the more it grinned, so much so that they could hardly hold it. And at last it slipped out of their hands and fell to the earth, shivered into hundreds of millions and billions of bits. Even then it did more harm than ever. Some of these bits were not as big as a grain of sand, and these flew about all over the world, getting into people's eyes. Once in, they stuck there and distorted everything they looked at, or made them see everything that was amiss. Each tiniest grain of glass kept the same power as that possessed by the whole mirror. Some people even got a bit of the glass into their hearts, and that was terrible for the heart became like a lump of ice. Some of the fragments were so big that they were used for window panes, but it was not advisable to look at one's friends through these panes. Other bits were made into spectacles, and it was a bad business when people meaning to be just put on these spectacles.

The bad demon laughed till he split his sides! It tickled him to see the mischief he had done. But some of these fragments were still left floating about the world, and you shall hear what happened to them.

SECOND STORY

About A Little Boy and A Little Girl

IN a big town crowded with houses and people, where there is no room for gardens, people have to be content with flowers in pots instead. In one of these towns lived two children who managed to have something bigger than a flowerpot for a garden. They were not brother and sister, but they were just as fond of each other as if they had been. Their parents lived opposite each other in two attic rooms. The roof of one house just touched the roof of the next one, with only a rain-water gutter between them. They each had a little dormer window, and one had only to step over the gutter to get from one house to the other.

Each of the parents had a large window box in which they grew pot herbs and a little rose tree. There was one in each box and they both grew splendidly. Then it occurred to the parents to put the boxes across the gutter, from house to house, and they looked just like two banks of flowers. The pea vines hung down over the edges of the boxes, and the roses threw out long creepers which twined round the windows. It was almost like a green triumphal arch. The boxes were high and the children knew they must not climb up onto them, but they were often allowed to have their little stools out under the rose trees; and there they had delightful games.

Of course in the winter there was an end to these amusements. The windows were often covered with hoar frost. Then they would warm coppers on the stove and stick them on the frozen panes, where they made lovely peepholes as round as possible. Then bright eyes would peep through these holes, one from each window. The little boy's name was Kay and the little girl's Gerda.

In the summer they could reach each other with one bound, but in the winter they had to go down all the stairs in one house and up all the stairs in the other, and outside there were snowdrifts.

"Look! The white bees are swarming," said the old grandmother.

"Have they a queen bee too?" asked the little boy, for he knew that there was a queen among the real bees.

"Yes, indeed they have," said the grandmother. "She flies where the swarm is thickest. She is the biggest of them all and she never remains on the ground. She always flies up again to the sky. Many a winter's night she flies through the streets and peeps in at the windows, and then the ice freezes on the panes into wonderful patterns like flowers."

"Oh yes, we have seen that," said both children, and then they knew it was true.

"Can the Snow Queen come in here?" asked the little girl.

"Just let her come," said the boy, "and I will put her on the stove, where she will melt."

But the grandmother smoothed his hair and told him more stories.

In the evening when little Kay was at home and half undressed, he crept up onto the chair by the window and peeped out of the little hole. A few snowflakes were falling, and one of these, the biggest, remained on the edge of the window box. It grew bigger and bigger, till it became the figure of a woman dressed in the finest white gauze, which appeared to be made of millions of starry flakes. She was delicately lovely, but all ice—glittering, dazzling ice. Still she was alive. Her eyes shone like two bright stars, but there was no rest or peace in them. She nodded to the window and waved her hand. The little boy was frightened and jumped down off the chair, and then he fancied that a big bird flew past the window.

The next day was bright and frosty, and then came the thaw—and after that the spring. The sun shone, green buds began to appear, the swallows built their nests, and people began to open their windows. The little children began to play in their garden on the roof again. The roses were in splendid bloom that summer. The little girl had learned a hymn, and there was something in it about roses, and that made her think of her own. She sang it to the little boy, and then he sang it with her:

> "Where roses deck the flowery vale,
> There, Infant Jesus, we thee hail!"

The children took each other by the hands, kissed the roses and rejoiced in God's bright sunshine, and spoke to it as if the Child Jesus were there. What lovely summer days they were, and how delightful it was to sit under the fresh rose trees which seemed never to tire of blooming.

Kay and Gerda were looking at a picture book of birds and animals one day—it had just struck five by the church clock—when Kay said, "Oh! Something struck my heart and I have got something in my eye."

The little girl put her arms round his neck. He blinked his eye, but there was nothing to be seen.

"I believe it is gone," he said, but it was not gone. It was one of those very grains of glass from the mirror, the magic mirror. You remember that horrid mirror in which all good and great things reflected in it became small and mean, while the bad things were magnified and every flaw became very apparent.

Poor Kay! A grain of it had gone straight to his heart and would soon turn it to a lump of ice. He did not feel it any more but it was still there.

"Why do you cry?" he asked. "It makes you look ugly. There's nothing the matter with me. How horrid!" he suddenly cried. "There's a worm in that rose, and that one is quite crooked. After all, they are nasty roses and so are the boxes they are growing in!" He kicked the box and broke off two of the roses.

"What are you doing, Kay?" cried the little girl. When he saw her alarm, he broke off another rose, and then ran in by his own window and left dear little Gerda alone.

When she next got out the picture book he said it was only fit for babies in long clothes. When his grandmother told them stories he always had a *but*—. And if he could manage it, he liked to get behind her chair, put on her spectacles, and imitate her. He did it very well and people laughed at him. He was soon able to imitate everyone in the street. He could make fun of all their peculiarities and failings. "He will turn out a clever fellow," said people. But it was all that bit of glass in his heart, that bit of glass in his eye, and it made him tease little Gerda who was so devoted to him. He played quite different games now; he seemed to have grown older. One winter's day when the snow was falling fast, he brought in a big magnifying glass. He held out the tail of his blue coat and let the snowflakes fall upon it.

"Now look through the glass, Gerda!" he said. Every snowflake was magnified and looked like a lovely flower or a sharply pointed star.

"Do you see how cleverly they are made?" **said** Kay. "Much more interesting than looking at real flowers and there is not a single flaw in them. They are perfect. If only they would not melt!"

Shortly afterwards he appeared in his thick gloves, with his sled on his back. He shouted right into Gerda's ear, "I have got leave to drive in the big square where the other boys play." And away he went.

In the big square the bolder boys used to tie their little sleds to the farm carts and go a long way in this fashion. They had no end of fun over it. Just in the middle of their games, a big sled came along. It was painted white and the occupant wore a white fur coat and cap. The sled drove twice round the square, and Kay quickly tied his sled on behind. Then off they went, faster and faster, into the next street. The driver turned round and nodded to Kay in the most friendly way, just as if they knew each other. Every time Kay wanted to loose his sled, the person nodded again and Kay stayed where he was, and they drove right out through the town gates. Then the snow began to fall so heavily that the little boy could not see a hand before him as they rushed along. He undid the cords and tried to get away from the big sled, but it was no use. His little sled stuck fast. And on they rushed, faster than the wind. He shouted aloud but nobody heard him, and the sled tore on through the snowdrifts. Every now and then it gave a bound, as if they were jumping over hedges and ditches. He was very frightened and he wanted to say his prayers, but he could only remember the multiplication tables.

The snowflakes grew bigger and bigger till at last they looked like big white chickens. All at once they sprang on one side, the big sled stopped, and the person who drove got up, coat and cap smothered in snow. It was a tall and upright lady all shining white, the Snow Queen herself.

"We have come along at a good pace," she said, "but it's cold enough to kill one. Creep inside my bearskin coat."

She took him into the sled by her, wrapped him in her furs, and he felt as if he were sinking into a snowdrift.

"Are you still cold?" she asked and kissed him on the forehead. Ugh! It was colder than ice. It went to his very heart, which was already more than half ice. He felt as if he were dying, but only for a moment, and then it seemed to have done him good. He no longer felt the cold.

"My sled! Don't forget my sled!" He only now remembered it. It was tied to one of the white chickens which flew along behind them. The Snow Queen kissed Kay again and then he forgot all about little Gerda, Grandmother, and all the others at home.

"Now I mustn't kiss you any more," she said, "or I should kiss you to death!"

Kay looked at her and she was so pretty! A more beautiful face could hardly be imagined. She did not seem to be made of ice now, as she was when she waved her hand to him outside the window. In his eyes she was quite perfect, and he was not a bit afraid of her. He told her that he could do mental arithmetic as far as fractions, and that he knew the number of square miles and the number of inhabitants of the country. She always smiled at him, and he then thought that he surely did not know enough; and he looked up into the wide expanse of heaven, into which they rose higher and higher as she flew with him on a dark cloud, while the storm surged around them, the wind ringing in their ears like well-known old songs.

They flew over woods and lakes, over oceans and islands. The cold wind whistled down below them, the wolves howled, the black crows flew screaming over the sparkling snow. But up above, the moon shone bright and clear—and Kay looked at it all the long, long winter nights. In the day he slept at the Snow Queen's feet.

THIRD STORY

The Garden of the Woman Learned in Magic

BUT how was little Gerda getting on all this long time since Kay left her? Where could he be? Nobody knew. Nobody could say anything about him. All that the other boys knew was that they had seen him tie his little sled to a splendid big one which drove away down the street and out of the town gates. Nobody knew where he was, and many tears were shed. Little Gerda cried long and bitterly. At last, people said he was dead. He must have fallen into the river which ran close by the town. Oh, what long, dark, winter days those were!

At last the spring came and the sunshine.

"Kay is dead and gone," said little Gerda.

"I don't believe it," said the sunshine.

"He is dead and gone," she said to the swallows.

"We don't believe it," said the swallows, and at last little Gerda did not believe it either.

"I will put on my new red shoes," she said one morning. "Kay never saw them. And then I will go down to the river and ask it about him."

It was very early in the morning. She kissed the old grandmother, who was still asleep, put on the red shoes, and went quite alone out by the gate to the river.

"Is it true that you have taken my little playfellow? I will give you my red shoes if you will bring him back to me again."

She thought the little ripples nodded in such a curious way that she took off her red shoes, her most cherished possessions, and threw both into the river. They fell close by the shore and were carried straight back to her by the little wavelets. It seemed as if the river would not accept her offering, as it had not taken little Kay.

She only thought she had not thrown them far enough, so she climbed into a boat which lay among the rushes. Then she went right out to the further end of it and threw the shoes into the water again. But the boat was loose and her movements started it off, and it floated away from the shore. She felt it moving and tried to get out, but before she reached the other end the boat was more than a yard from the shore and was floating away quite quickly.

Little Gerda was terribly frightened and began to cry, but nobody heard her except the sparrows. They could not carry her ashore, but they flew alongside twittering as if to cheer her, "We are here! We are here!"

The boat floated rapidly away with the current. Little Gerda sat quite still with only her stockings on. Her little red shoes floated behind but they could not catch up with the boat, which drifted away faster and faster.

The banks on both sides were very pretty with beautiful flowers, fine old trees, and slopes dotted with sheep and cattle, but not a single person.

"Perhaps the river is taking me to little Kay," thought Gerda, and that cheered her. She sat up and looked at the beautiful green banks for hours.

Then they came to a big cherry garden. There was a little house in it with curious blue and red windows. It had a thatched roof, and two wooden soldiers stood outside, who presented arms as she sailed past. Gerda called out to them.

She thought they were alive, but of course they did not answer. She was quite close to them, for the current drove the
boat close to the bank. Gerda called out again louder than
before, and then an old, old woman came out of the house.
She was leaning upon a big hooked stick, and she wore a big
sun hat which was covered with beautiful painted flowers.

"You poor little child," said the old woman. "However
were you driven out on this big strong river into the wide,
wide world alone?" Then she walked right into the water
and caught hold of the boat with her hooked stick. She drew
it ashore and lifted little Gerda out.

Gerda was delighted to be on dry land again, but she was
a little bit frightened by the strange old woman.

"Tell me who you are and how you got here," said she.

When Gerda had told her the whole story and asked her if
she had seen Kay, the woman said she had not seen him
but that she expected him. Gerda must not be sad; she was
to come and taste her cherries and see her flowers, which
were more beautiful than any picture book. Each one had a
story to tell. Then she took Gerda by the hand, they went
into the little house, and the old woman locked the door.

The windows were very high up, and they were red, blue,
and yellow. They threw a very curious light into the room.
On the table were quantities of the most delicious cherries,
of which Gerda had leave to eat as many as ever she liked.
While she was eating, the old woman combed her hair with
a golden comb, so that her hair curled and shone like gold
round the pretty little face, which was as sweet as a rose.

"I have long wanted a little girl like you," said the old
woman. "You will see how well we shall get on together."
While she combed her hair Gerda had forgotten all about
Kay, for the old woman was learned in the magic art. But
she was not a bad witch. She only cast spells over people for
a little amusement, and she wanted to keep Gerda. She
therefore went into the garden and waved her hooked stick

over all the rosebushes, and however beautifully they were flowering, all sank down into the rich black earth without leaving a trace behind them. The old woman was afraid if Gerda saw the roses she would be reminded of Kay and would want to run away. Then she took Gerda into the flower garden. What a delicious scent there was! Every imaginable flower for every season was in that lovely garden. No picture book could be brighter or more beautiful. Gerda jumped for joy and played till the sun went down behind the tall cherry trees. Then she was put into a lovely bed with rose-colored silken coverings stuffed with violets. She slept and dreamt as lovely dreams as any queen on her wedding day.

The next day she played with the flowers in the garden again—and many days passed in the same way. Gerda knew every flower, but however many there were she always thought there was one missing, but which it was she did not know.

One day she was sitting looking at the old woman's sun hat with its painted flowers, and the very prettiest one of them all was a rose. The old woman had forgotten her hat when she charmed the others away. This is the consequence of being absent-minded.

"What!" said Gerda, "are there no roses here?" And she sprang in among the flower beds and sought, but in vain. Her hot tears fell on the very places where the roses used to be. When the warm drops moistened the earth, the rose trees shot up again just as full of bloom as when they sank. Gerda embraced the roses and kissed them, and then she thought of the lovely roses at home, and this brought the thought of little Kay.

"Oh, how I have been delayed," said the little girl. "I ought to have been looking for Kay. Don't you know where he is?" she asked the roses. "Do you think he is dead and gone?"

"He is not dead," said the roses. "We have been down underground, you know, and all the dead people are there, but Kay is not among them."

"Oh, thank you!" said little Gerda. And then she went to the other flowers and looked into their cups and said, "Do you know where Kay is?"

But each flower stood in the sun and dreamt its own dreams. Little Gerda heard many of these but never anything about Kay.

And what said the tiger lilies?

"Do you hear the drum? Rub-a-dub. It has only two notes: rub-a-dub. Always the same. The wailing of women and the cry of the preacher. The Hindu woman in her long red garment stands on the pile, while the flames surround her and her dead husband. But the woman is only thinking of the living man in the circle round, whose eyes burn with a fiercer fire than that of the flames which consume the body. Do the flames of the heart die in the fire?"

"I understand nothing about that," said little Gerda.

"That is my story," said the tiger lily.

"What does the convolvulus say?"

"An old castle is perched high over a narrow mountain path. It is closely covered with ivy, almost hiding the old red walls and creeping up leaf upon leaf right round the balcony where stands a beautiful maiden. She bends over the balustrade and looks eagerly up the road. No rose on its stem is fresher than she. No apple blossom wafted by the wind moves more lightly. Her silken robes rustle softly as she bends over and says, 'Will he never come?' "

"Is it Kay you mean?" asked Gerda.

"I am only talking about my own story—my dream," answered the convolvulus.

What said the little snowdrop?

"Between two trees a rope with a board is hanging. It is a swing. Two pretty little girls in snowy frocks and green ribbons fluttering on their hats are seated on it. Their brother, who is bigger than they are, stands up behind them. He has his arms round the ropes for supports, and holds in one hand a little bowl and in the other a clay pipe. He is blowing soap bubbles. As the swing moves the bubbles fly upwards in all their changing colors. The last one still hangs from the pipe swayed by the wind, and the swing goes on. A little black dog runs up. He is almost as light as the bubbles. He stands up on his hind legs and wants to be taken into the swing, but it does not stop. The little dog falls with an angry bark. They jeer at it. The bubble bursts. A swinging plank, a fluttering foam picture—that is my story!"

"I daresay what you tell me is very pretty, but you speak so sadly and you never mention little Kay."

What said the hyacinth?

"There were three beautiful sisters, all most delicate and quite transparent. One wore a crimson robe, the other a blue, and the third was pure white. These three danced hand in hand by the edge of the lake in the moonlight. They were human beings, not fairies of the wood. The fragrant air attracted them and they vanished into the wood. Here the fragrance was stronger still. Three coffins glide out of the wood towards the lake, and in them lie the maidens. The fireflies flutter lightly round them with their little flickering torches. Do these dancing maidens sleep, or are they dead? The scent of the flower says that they are corpses. The evening bell tolls their knell."

"You make me quite sad," said little Gerda. "Your perfume is so strong it makes me think of those dead maidens. Oh, is little Kay really dead? The roses have been down underground, and they say no."

"Ding, dong," tolled the hyacinth bells. "We are not tolling for little Kay. We know nothing about him. We sing our song, the only one we know."

And Gerda went on to the buttercups, shining among their dark green leaves.

"You are a bright little sun," said Gerda. "Tell me if you know where I shall find my playfellow."

The buttercup shone brightly and returned Gerda's glance. What song could the buttercup sing? It would not be about Kay.

"God's bright sun shone into a little court on the first day of spring. The sunbeams stole down the neighboring white wall, close to which bloomed the first yellow flower of the season. It shone like burnished gold in the sun. An old woman had brought her armchair out into the sun. Her granddaughter, a poor and pretty little maidservant, had come to pay her a short visit, and she kissed her. There was gold, heart's gold, in the kiss. Gold on the lips, gold on the ground, and gold above, in the early morning beams! Now that is my little story," said the buttercup.

"Oh, my poor old grandmother!" sighed Gerda. "She will be longing to see me and grieving about me, as she did about Kay. But I shall soon go home again and take Kay with me. It is useless for me to ask the flowers about him. They know only their own stories and have no information to give me."

Then she tucked up her little dress so that she might run the faster, but the narcissus blossoms struck her on the legs as she jumped over them. So she stopped and said, "Perhaps you can tell me something."

She stooped down close to the flower and listened. What did it say?

"I can see myself. I can see myself," said the narcissus. "Oh, how sweet is my scent. Up there in an attic window stands a little dancing girl half dressed. First she stands on one leg, then on the other, and looks as if she would tread the whole world under her feet. She is only a delusion. She pours some water out of a teapot onto a bit of stuff that she is holding. It is her bodice. 'Cleanliness is a good thing,' she says. Her white dress hangs on a peg. It has been washed in the teapot, too, and dried on the roof. She puts it on and wraps a saffron colored scarf round her neck, which makes the dress look whiter. See how high she carries her head, and all upon one stem. I see myself. I see myself."

"I don't care a bit about all that," said Gerda. "It's no use telling me such stuff."

And then she ran to the end of the garden. The door was fastened, but she pressed the rusty latch and it gave way. The door sprang open and little Gerda ran out with bare feet into the wide world. She looked back three times, but nobody came after her. At last she could run no farther and she sat down on a big stone. When she looked around she saw that the summer was over. It was quite late autumn. She would never have known it inside the beautiful garden, where the sun always shone and the flowers of every season were always in bloom.

"Oh, how I have wasted my time," said little Gerda. "It is autumn. I must not rest any longer." And she got up to go on.

Oh, how weary and sore were her little feet, and everything round looked so cold and dreary. The long willow leaves were quite yellow. The damp mist fell off the trees like rain. One leaf dropped after another from the trees, and only the sloe thorn still bore its fruit, but the sloes were sour and set one's teeth on edge. Oh, how gray and sad it looked, out in the wide world!

FOURTH STORY

The Prince and the Princess

GERDA was soon obliged to rest again. A big crow hopped onto the snow, just in front of her. He had been sitting looking at her for a long time and wagging his head. Now he said

"Caw! caw! Good day, good day," as well as he could. He meant to be kind to the little girl, and asked her where she was going alone in the wide world.

Gerda understood the word "alone" and knew how much there was in it, and she told the crow the whole story of her life and adventures and asked if he had seen Kay.

The crow nodded his head gravely and said, "Maybe I have. Maybe I have."

"What, do you really think you have?" cried the little girl, nearly smothering him with her kisses.

"Gently, gently!" said the crow. "I believe it may have been Kay, but he has forgotten you by this time, I expect, for the Princess."

"Does he live with a Princess?" asked Gerda.

"Yes, listen," said the crow. "But it is so difficult to speak your language. If you understand crow's language, I can tell you about it much better."

"No, I have never learned it," said Gerda. "But grandmother did and used to speak it. If only I had learned it!"

"It doesn't matter," said the crow. "I will tell you as well as I can, although I may do it rather badly."

Then he told her what he had heard.

"In this kingdom where we are now," said he, "there lives a Princess who is very clever. She has read all the newspapers in the world and forgotten them again, so clever is she. One day she was sitting on her throne, which is not such an amusing thing to do either, they say. And she began humming a tune, which happen to be:

'Why should I not be married, oh why?'

'Why not, indeed?' said she. And she made up her mind to marry, if she could find a husband who had an answer ready when a question was put to him. She called all the court ladies together, and when they heard what she wanted they were delighted.

" 'I like that now,' they said. 'I was thinking the same thing myself the other day.' "

"Every word I say is true," said the crow, "for I have a tame sweetheart who goes about the palace whenever she likes. She told me the story."

Of course his sweetheart was a crow, for "birds of a feather flock together," and one crow always chooses another. "The newspapers all came out immediately with borders of hearts and the Princess' initials. They gave notice that any young man who was handsome enough might go up to the palace to speak to the Princess. The one who spoke as if he were quite at home, and spoke well, would be chosen by the Princess as her husband. Yes, yes, you may believe me. It's as true as I sit here," said the crow. "The people came crowding in. There was such running and crushing, but no one was fortunate enough to be chosen, either on the first day or on the second. They could all of them talk well enough in the street, but when they entered the castle gates and saw the guard in silver uniforms, and when they went up the stairs through rows of lackeys in gold embroidered liveries, their courage forsook them. When they reached the brilliantly lighted reception rooms and stood in front of the throne where the Princess was seated, they could think of nothing to say. They only echoed her last words, and of course that was not what she wanted.

"It was just as if they had all taken some kind of sleeping powder which made them lethargic. They did not recover themselves until they got out into the street again, and then they had plenty to say. There was quite a long line of them, reaching from the town gates up to the palace.

"I went to see them myself," said the crow. "They were hungry and thirsty but they got nothing at the palace, not even as much as a glass of tepid water. Some of the wise ones had taken sandwiches with them, but they did not share them with their neighbors. They thought if the others went in to the Princess looking hungry, there would be more chance for themselves."

"But Kay, little Kay!" asked Gerda, "when did he come? Was he amongst the crowd?"

"Give me time! Give me time! We are just coming to him. It was on the third day that a little person came marching cheerfully along, without either carriage or horse. His eyes sparkled like yours and he had beautiful long hair, but his clothes were very shabby."

"Oh, that was Kay!" said Gerda gleefully. "Then I have found him!" And she clapped her hands.

"He had a little knapsack on his back," said the crow.

"No, it must have been his sled. He had it with him when he went away," said Gerda.

"Maybe so," said the crow. "I did not look very particularly. But I know from my sweetheart that when he entered the palace gates and saw the lifeguards in the silver uniforms, and the lackeys on the stairs in their gold-laced liveries, he was not the least bit abashed. He just nodded to them and said, 'It must be very tiresome to stand upon the stairs. I am going inside.' The rooms were blazing with lights. Privy councilors and excellencies without number were walking about barefoot, carrying golden vessels. It was enough to make you solemn! His boots creaked fearfully too, but he wasn't a bit upset."

"Oh, I am sure that was Kay!" said Gerda. "I know he had a pair of new boots. I heard them creaking in grandmother's room."

"Yes, indeed they did creak!" said the crow. "But nothing daunted, he went straight up to the Princess, who was sitting on a pearl as big as a spinning wheel. Poor, simple boy! All the court ladies and their attendants, and the courtiers and their gentlemen, each attended by a page, were standing round. The nearer the door they stood, the greater was their haughtiness. The footman's boy, who always wore slippers and stood in the doorway, was almost too proud even to be looked at."

"It must be awful!" said little Gerda, "and yet Kay has won the Princess!"

"If I had not been a crow, I should have taken her myself, notwithstanding that I am engaged. They say he spoke as well as I could have done myself when I speak crow language, at least so my sweetheart says. He was a picture of good looks and gallantry, and then he had not come with any idea of wooing the Princess, but simply to hear her wisdom. He admired her just as much as she admired him."

"Indeed it was Kay then," said Gerda. "He was so clever he could do mental arithmetic up to fractions. Oh, won't you take me to the palace?"

"It's easy enough to talk," said the crow, "but how are we to manage it? I will talk to my tame sweetheart about it; she will have some advice to give us, I daresay, but I am bound to tell you that a little girl like you will never be admitted."

"Oh, indeed I shall," said Gerda. "When Kay hears that I am here, he will come out at once to fetch me."

"Wait here for me by the stile," said the crow. Then he wagged his head and flew off.

The evening had darkened in before he came back. "Caw, caw," he said. "She sends you greeting, and here is a little roll for you. She got it out of the kitchen, where there is bread enough, and I daresay you are hungry. It is not possible for you to get into the palace. You have bare feet and the guards in silver and the lackeys in gold would never allow you to pass. But don't cry. We shall get you in somehow. My sweetheart knows a little back staircase which leads up to the bedroom, and she knows where the key is kept."

Then they went quietly into the garden, into the great

avenue where the trees were. And when the palace lights went out one after the other, the crow led little Gerda to the back door, which was ajar.

Oh, how Gerda's heart beat with fear and longing! It was just as if she were about to do something wrong, and yet she only wanted to know if this really was little Kay. Oh, it must be he, she thought, picturing to herself his clever eyes and his long hair. She could see his very smile when they used to sit under the rose trees at home. She thought he would be very glad to see her and to hear what a long way she had come to find him, and to hear how sad they had all been at home when he did not come back. Oh, it was joy mingled with fear.

They had now reached the stairs, where a little lamp was burning on a shelf. There stood the tame sweetheart, twisting and turning her head to look at Gerda, who made a curtsey, as grandmother had taught her.

"My betrothed has spoken so charmingly to me about you, my little miss," she said. "Your life, 'Vita,' as it is called, is most touching! If you will take the lamp, I will go on in front. We shall take the straight road here and we shall meet no one."

"It seems to me that someone is coming up behind us," said Gerda, as she fancied something rushed past her throwing a shadow on the walls: horses with flowing manes and slender legs; huntsmen, ladies and gentlemen, on horseback.

"Oh, those are only the dreams!" said the crow. "They come to take the thoughts of the noble ladies and gentlemen out hunting. That's a good thing, for you will be able to see them all the better in bed. But don't forget, when you are taken into favor, that you show a grateful spirit."

"Now, there's no need to talk about that," said the crow from the woods.

They now came into the first apartment; it was hung with

rose-colored satin embroidered with flowers. Here again the dreams overtook them, but they flitted by so quickly that Gerda could not distinguish them. The apartments became one more beautiful than the other. There were enough to bewilder anybody. They now reached the bedroom. The ceiling was like a great palm with crystal leaves, and in the middle of the room were two beds, each like a lily hung from a golden stem. One was white, and in it lay the Princess. The other was red, and there lay he whom Gerda had come to seek—little Kay! She bent aside one of the crimson leaves, and she saw a little brown neck. It was Kay! She called his name aloud and held the lamp close to him. Again the dreams rushed through the room on horseback. He awoke, turned his head—and it was not little Kay.

It was only the Prince's neck which was like his, but he was young and handsome. The Princess peeped out of her lily-white bed and asked what was the matter. Then little Gerda cried and told them all her story, and what the crows had done to help her.

"You poor little thing!" said the Prince and Princess. And they praised the crows and said that they were not at all angry with them, but they must not do it again. Then they gave them a reward.

"Would you like your liberty?" said the Princess. "Or would you prefer permanent posts about the court as court crows with perquisites from the kitchen?"

Both crows curtsied and begged for the permanent posts. They thought of their old age and said it would be good to have something for "the old man," as they called it.

The Prince got up and allowed Gerda to sleep in his bed, and he could not have done more. She folded her little hands and thought, "How good the people and the animals are!" Then she shut her eyes and fell fast asleep. All the dreams came flying back again. This time they looked like angels, and they were dragging a little sled with Kay sitting on it, and he nodded. But it was only a dream, so it all vanished when she woke.

Next day she was dressed in silk and velvet from head to foot. They asked her to stay at the palace and have a good time, but she only begged them to give her a little carriage and horse and a little pair of boots, so that she might drive out into the wide world to look for Kay.

They gave her a pair of boots and a muff. She was beautifully dressed, and when she was ready to start, there before the door stood a new chariot of pure gold. The Prince's and Princess' coat of arms were emblazoned on it and shone like a star. Coachman, footman, and outrider, for there was even an outrider, all wore golden crowns. The Prince and Princess themselves helped her into the carriage and wished her joy. The wood crow, who was now married, accompanied her for the first three miles. He sat beside Gerda, for he could not ride with his back to the horses. The other crow stood at the door and flapped her wings. She did not go with them, for she suffered from headache since she had been a kitchen pensioner—the consequence of eating too much. The chariot was stored with sugar biscuits, and there were fruit and ginger nuts under the seat.

"Good-by! good-by!" cried the Prince and Princess. Little Gerda wept and the crow wept too. At the end of the first few miles the crow said good-by, and this was the hardest parting of all. He flew up into a tree and flapped his big black wings as long as he could see the chariot, which shone like the brightest sunshine.

FIFTH STORY

The Little Robber Girl

THEY drove on through a dark wood, where the chariot lighted the way and blinded some robbers by its glare. It was more than they could bear.

"It is gold! It is gold!" they cried, and darting forward they seized the horses and killed the postilions, the coachman, and footman. Then they dragged little Gerda out of the carriage.

"She is fat and she is pretty! She has been fattened on nuts," said the old robber woman, who had a long beard, and eyebrows that hung down over her eyes. "She is as good as a fat lamb, and how nice she will taste!" She drew out her sharp knife as she said this. It glittered horribly. "Oh!" screamed the old woman at the same moment, for her little daughter had come up behind her and was biting her ear. She hung on her back, as wild and as savage a little animal as you could wish to find. "You bad, wicked child!" said the mother, but she was prevented from killing Gerda on this occasion.

"She shall play with me," said the little robber girl. "She shall give me her muff and her pretty dress, and she shall sleep in my bed." Then she bit her mother again and made her dance. All the robbers laughed and said, "Look at her dancing with her cub!"

"I want to get into the carriage," said the little robber girl, and she always had her own way because she was so spoilt and stubborn. She and Gerda got into the carriage, and then they drove over stubble and stones farther and farther into the wood. The little robber girl was as big as Gerda, but much stronger. She had broad shoulders and a darker skin. Her eyes were quite black, with almost a melancholy expression. She put her arm round Gerda's waist and said, "They shan't kill you as long as I don't get angry with you. You must surely be a Princess!"

"No," said little Gerda, and then she told her all her adventures and how fond she was of Kay.

The robber girl looked earnestly at her, gave a little nod, and said, "They shan't kill you even if I am angry with you. I will do it myself." Then she dried Gerda's eyes and stuck her own hands into the pretty muff, which was so soft and warm.

At last the chariot stopped. They were in the courtyard of a robber's castle, the walls of which were cracked from top to bottom. Ravens and crows flew in and out of every hole, and big bulldogs, each of whom looked ready to devour somebody, jumped as high as they could. But they did not bark, for it was not allowed. A big fire was burning in the middle of the stone floor of the smoky old hall. The smoke all went up to the ceiling where it had to find a way out for itself. Soup was boiling in a big caldron over the fire, and hares and rabbits were roasting on the spits.

"You shall sleep with me and all my little pets tonight," said the robber girl.

When they had had something to eat and drink they went along to one corner which was spread with straw and rugs. There were nearly a hundred pigeons roosting overhead on the rafters and beams. They seemed to be asleep, but they fluttered about a little when the children came in.

"They are all mine," said the little robber girl, seizing one of the nearest. She held it by the legs and shook it until it flapped its wings. "Kiss it," she cried, dashing it at Gerda's face. "Those are the wood pigeons," she added, pointing to some laths fixed across a big hole high up on the walls. "They are a regular rabble. They would fly away directly if they were not locked in. And here is my old sweetheart, Be!" Here she dragged forward a reindeer by the horn. He was tied up, and he had a bright copper ring round his neck. "We have to keep him close too, or he would run off. Every single night I tickle his neck with my bright knife. He is so frightened of it!" The little girl produced a long knife out of a hole in the wall and drew it across the reindeer's neck. The poor animal laughed and kicked, and the robber girl laughed and pulled Gerda down into the bed with her.

"Do you have that knife by you while you are alseep?" asked Gerda, looking rather frightened.

"I always sleep with a knife," said the little robber girl. "You never know what will happen. But now tell me again what you told me before about little Kay, and why you went out into the world."

So Gerda told her all about it again, and the wood pigeons cooed up in their cage above them. The other pigeons were asleep. The little robber girl put her arm round Gerda's neck and went to sleep with the knife in her other hand, and she was soon snoring. But Gerda would not close her eyes. She did not know whether she was to live or to die. The robbers sat round the fire, eating and drinking, and the old woman was turning somersaults. This sight terrified the poor little girl.

Then the wood pigeons said, "Coo, coo! We have seen little Kay. His sled was drawn by a white chicken, and he was sitting in the Snow Queen's sled. It was floating low over the trees, while we were in our nests. She blew upon us young ones, and they all died except us two. Coo, coo."

"What are you saying up there?" asked Gerda. "Where was the Snow Queen going? Do you know anything about it?"

"She was most likely going to Lapland, because there is always snow and ice there. Ask the reindeer who is tied up below."

"There is ice and snow, and it's a splendid place," said the reindeer. "You can run and jump about where you like on those big glittering plains. The Snow Queen has her summer tent there, but her permanent castle is up at the North Pole, on the island which is called Spitzbergen."

"Oh Kay, little Kay!" sighed Gerda.

"Lie still, or I shall stick the knife into you," said the robber girl.

In the morning Gerda told her all that the wood pigeons had said, and the little robber girl looked quite solemn, but she nodded her head and said, "No matter! No matter! Do you know where Lapland is?" she asked the reindeer.

"Who should know better than I," said the animal, his eyes dancing. "I was born and brought up there, and I used to leap about on the snowfields."

"Listen," said the robber girl. "You see that all our men folks are away, but mother is still here and she will stay. But later on in the morning she will take a drink out of the big bottle there, and after that she will have a nap. Then I will do something for you." Then she jumped out of bed, ran along to her mother and pulled her beard, and said, "Good morning, my own dear nanny goat!" And her mother filliped her nose till it was red and blue, but it was all affection.

As soon as her mother had had her draught from the bottle and had dropped asleep, the little robber girl went along to the reindeer and said, "I should have the greatest pleasure in the world in keeping you here, to tickle you with my knife, because you are such fun then. However, it does not matter. I will untie your halter and help you outside so that you may run away to Lapland, but you must put your best foot foremost and take this little girl for me to the Snow Queen's palace, where her playfellow is. I suppose you heard what she was telling me, for she spoke loudly enough and you are generally eavesdropping."

The reindeer jumped up into the air for joy. The robber girl lifted little Gerda up, and had the forethought to tie her on, nay, even to give her a little cushion to sit upon. "Here, after all, I will give you your fur boots back, for it will be very cold, but I will keep your muff. It is too pretty to part with. Still you shan't be cold. Here are my mother's big mittens for you. They will reach up to your elbows. Here,

The reindeer darted off for Lapland

stick your hands in! Now your hands look just like my nasty mother's."

Gerda shed tears of joy.

"I don't like you to whimper!" said the little robber girl. "You ought to be looking delighted. And here are two loaves and a ham for you so that you will not starve."

These things were tied onto the back of the reindeer. The little robber girl opened the door and called in all the big dogs, and then she cut the halter with her knife and said to the reindeer, "Now run, but take care of my little girl!"

Gerda stretched out her hands in the big mittens to the robber girl and said good-by. And then the reindeer darted off over briars and bushes, through the big wood, over swamps and plains, as fast as he could go. The wolves howled and the ravens screamed, while the red lights quivered up in the sky.

"There are my old northern lights," said the reindeer. "See how they flash!" And on he rushed faster than ever, day and night. The loaves were eaten, and the ham too, and then they were in Lapland.

SIXTH STORY

The Lapp Woman and the Finn Woman

THEY stopped by a little hut, a very poverty-stricken one. The roof sloped right down to the ground, and the door was so low that the people had to creep on hands and knees when they wanted to go in or out. There was nobody at home here but an old Lapp woman who was frying fish over a whale-oil lamp. The reindeer told her all Gerda's story, but he told his own first, for he thought his much the most important. Gerda was so overcome by the cold that she could not speak at all.

"Oh, you poor creatures!" said the Lapp woman. "You've got a long way to go yet. You will have to go hundreds of miles into the Finmark, for the Snow Queen is paying a country visit there, and she burns blue lights every night. I will write a few words on a dried codfish, for I have no paper. I will give it to you to take to the Finn woman up there. She will be better able to direct you than I can."

So when Gerda was warmed and had eaten and drunk something, the Lapp woman wrote a few words on a dried codfish and gave it to her, bidding her take good care of it. Then she tied her onto the reindeer again and off they flew. Flicker, flicker, went the beautiful blue northern lights up in the sky all night long. At last they came to the Finmark, and knocked on the Finn woman's chimney, for she had no door at all.

There was such a heat inside that the Finn woman went about almost naked. She was little and very grubby. She at once loosened Gerda's things and took off the mittens and the boots, or she would have been too hot. Then she put a piece of ice on the reindeer's head, and after that she read what was written on the codfish. She read it three times, and then she knew it by heart, and put the fish into the pot for dinner. There was no reason why it should not be eaten, and she never wasted anything.

Again the reindeer told his own story first and then little Gerda's. The Finn woman blinked with her wise eyes but she said nothing.

"You are so clever," said the reindeer. "I know you can bind all the winds of the world with a bit of sewing cotton. When a skipper unties one knot, he gets a good wind. When he unties two, it blows hard. And if he undoes the third and the fourth, he brings a storm about his head wild enough to blow down the forest trees. Won't you give the little girl a drink, so that she may have the strength of twelve men to overcome the Snow Queen?"

"The strength of twelve men?" said the Finn woman. "Yes, that will be about enough."

She went along to a shelf and took down a big folded skin, which she unrolled. There were curious characters written on it, and the Finn woman read till the perspiration poured down her forehead.

But the reindeer implored her to give Gerda something, and Gerda looked at her with such beseeching eyes, full of tears, that the Finn woman began blinking again and drew the reindeer into a corner, where she whispered to him, at the same time putting fresh ice on his head.

"Little Kay is certainly with the Snow Queen, and he is delighted with everything there. He thinks it is the best place in the world, but that is because he has got a splinter of glass in his heart and a grain of glass in his eye. They will have to come out first, or he will never be human again, and the Snow Queen will keep him in her power."

"But can't you give little Gerda something to take which will give her power to conquer it all?"

"I can't give her greater power than she already has. Don't you see how great it is? Don't you see how both man and beast have to serve her? How she has got on as well as she has on her bare feet? We must not tell her what power she has. It is in her heart, because she is such a sweet innocent child. If she can't reach the Snow Queen herself, then we can't help her. The Snow Queen's gardens begin just two miles from here. You can carry the little girl as far as that. Put her down by the big bush standing there in the snow covered with red berries. Don't stand gossiping, but hurry back to me!" Then the Finn woman lifted Gerda onto the reindeer's back, and he rushed off as hard as he could.

"Oh, I have not got my boots, and I have not got my mittens!" cried little Gerda.

She soon felt the want of them in that cutting wind, but the reindeer did not dare to stop. He ran on till he came to the bush with the red berries. There he put Gerda down and kissed her on the mouth, while big shining tears trickled down his face. Then he ran back again as fast as ever he could. There stood poor little Gerda without shoes or gloves, in the middle of the freezing icebound Finmark.

She ran forward as quickly as she could. A whole regiment of snowflakes came towards her. They did not fall from the sky, for it was quite clear, with the northern lights shining brightly. No. These snowflakes ran along the ground, and the nearer they came the bigger they grew. Gerda remembered well how big and strange they looked under the magnifying glass. But the size of these was monstrous! They were alive. They were the Snow Queen's advance guard, and they took the most curious shapes. Some looked like big, horrid porcupines; some like bundles of knotted snakes with their heads sticking out. Others again like fat little bears with bristling hair, but all were dazzling white and living snowflakes.

Then little Gerda said the Lord's Prayer, and the cold was so great that her breath froze as it came out of her mouth, and she could see it like a cloud of smoke in front of her. It grew thicker and thicker till it formed itself into bright little angels who grew bigger and bigger when they touched the ground. They all wore helmets and carried shields and spears in their hands. More and more of them appeared, and when Gerda had finished her prayer she was surrounded by a whole legion. They pierced the snowflakes with their spears and shivered them into a hundred pieces, and little Gerda walked fearlessly and undauntedly through them. The angels touched her hands and her feet, and then she hardly felt how cold it was but walked quickly on towards the Palace of the Snow Queen.

Now we must see what Kay was about. He was not thinking about Gerda at all—least of all that she was just outside the Palace.

SEVENTH STORY

What Happened in the Snow Queen's Palace and Afterwards

THE palace walls were made of drifted snow, and the windows and doors of the biting winds. There were over a hundred rooms in it, shaped just as the snow had drifted. The biggest one stretched for many miles. They were all lighted by the strongest northern lights, and were immensely big and empty, and glittering in their iciness. There was never any gaiety in them, not even so much as a ball for the little bears, when the storms might have tuned up as the orchestra, and the polar bears might have walked about on their hind legs and shown off their grand manners. There was never even a little game-playing party for such games as "touch last" or "the biter bit"—no, not even a little gossip over the coffee cups for the white fox misses.

Immense, vast, and cold were the Snow Queen's halls. The northern lights came and went with such regularity that you could count the seconds between their coming and going. In the midst of these never-ending snow halls was a frozen lake. It was broken up on the surface into a thousand bits, but each piece was so exactly like the others that the whole formed a perfect work of art. The Snow Queen sat in the very middle of it when she sat at home. She then said that she was sitting on "The Mirror of Reason," and that it was the best and only one in the world.

Little Kay was blue with cold—nay, almost black—but he did not know it, for the Snow Queen had kissed away the icy shiverings, and his heart was little better than a lump of ice. He went about dragging some sharp flat pieces of ice which he placed in all sorts of patterns, trying to make something out of them, just as when we at home have little tablets of wood, with which we make patterns and call them a "Chinese puzzle."

Kay's patterns were most ingenious, because they were the "Ice Puzzles of Reason." In his eyes they were excellent and of the greatest importance: this was because of the grain of glass still in his eye. He made many patterns forming words, but he never could find the right way to place them for one particular word, a word he was most anxious to make. It was "Eternity." The Snow Queen had said to him that if he could find out this word he should be his own master, and she would give him the whole world and a new pair of skates. But he could not discover it.

"Now I am going to fly away to the warm countries," said the Snow Queen. "I want to go and peep into the black caldrons." She meant the volcanoes Etna and Vesuvius. "I must whiten them a little. It does them good, and the lemons and the grapes too!" And away she flew.

Kay sat quite alone in all those many miles of empty ice halls. He looked at his bits of ice and thought and thought, till something gave way within him. He sat so stiff and immovable that one might have thought he was frozen to death.

Then it was that little Gerda walked into the palace, through the great gates in a biting wind. She said her evening prayer, and the wind dropped as if lulled to sleep, and she walked on into the big empty hall. She saw Kay and knew him at once. She flung her arms round his neck, held him fast, and cried, "Kay, little Kay, have I found you at last?"

But he sat still, rigid and cold.

Then little Gerda shed hot tears. They fell upon his breast and penetrated to his heart. Here they thawed the lump of ice and melted the little bit of the mirror which was in it. He looked at her, and she sang:

"Where roses deck the flowery vale,
There, Infant Jesus, thee we hail!"

Then Kay burst into tears. He cried so much that the grain of glass was washed out of his eye. He knew her and shouted with joy, "Gerda! Dear little Gerda! Where have you been for such a long time? And where have I been?" He looked round and said, "How cold it is here! How empty and vast!"

He kept tight hold of Gerda, who laughed and cried for joy. Their happiness was so heavenly that even the bits of ice danced for joy around them. And when they settled down, there they lay in just the very position the Snow Queen had told Kay he must find out, if he was to become his own master and have the whole world and a new pair of skates.

Gerda kissed his cheeks and they grew rosy. She kissed his eyes and they shone like hers. She kissed his hands and his feet and he became well and strong. The Snow Queen might come home whenever she liked; his order of release was written there in shining letters of ice.

They took hold of each other's hands and wandered out of the big palace. They talked about grandmother and about the roses upon the roof. Wherever they went, the winds lay still and the sun broke through the clouds. When they reached the bush with the red berries, they found the reindeer waiting for them, and he had brought another young reindeer with him whose udders were full. The children drank her warm milk and kissed her on the mouth. Then they carried Kay and Gerda, first to the Finn woman, in whose heated hut they warmed themselves and received directions about the homeward journey. Then they went to the Lapp woman. She had made new clothes for them and prepared her sled. Both the reindeer ran by their side to the boundaries of the country. Here the first green buds appeared, and they said "Good-by" to the reindeer and the Lapp woman. They heard the first little birds twittering and saw the buds in the forest. Out of it came riding a young girl on a beautiful horse which Gerda knew, for it had drawn the golden chariot. She had a scarlet cap on her head and pistols in her belt. It was the little robber girl, who had tired of staying at home. She was riding northwards to see how she liked it before she tried some other part of the world. She knew them again, and Gerda recognized her with delight.

"You are a nice fellow to go tramping off!" she said to little Kay. "I should like to know if you deserve to have somebody running to the end of the world for your sake."

But Gerda patted her cheek and asked about the Prince and Princess.

"They are traveling in foreign countries," said the robber girl.

"But the crow?" asked Gerda.

"Oh, the crow is dead," she answered. "The tame sweetheart is a widow and goes about with a bit of black wool tied round her leg. She pities herself bitterly, but it's all nonsense! But tell me how you got on yourself, and where you found him."

Gerda and Kay both told her all about it.

"Snip, snap, snur-r! It's all right at last then!" she said. And she took hold of their hands and promised that if she ever passed through their town she would pay them a visit. Then she rode off into the wide world. But Kay and Gerda walked on, hand in hand, and wherever they went they found the most delightful spring and blooming flowers. Soon they recognized the big town where they lived, with its tall towers in which the bells still rang their merry peals. They went straight on to grandmother's door, up the stairs, and into her room.

Everything was just as they had left it. The old clock

ticked in the corner, and the hands pointed to the time. As they went through the door into the room, they perceived that they were grown up. The roses clustered round the open window, and there stood their two little chairs. Kay and Gerda sat down upon them, still holding each other by the hand. All the cold empty grandeur of the Snow Queen's palace had passed from their memory like a bad dream. Grandmother sat in God's warm sunshine reading from her Bible.

"Without ye become as little children ye cannot enter into the Kingdom of Heaven."

Kay and Gerda looked into each other's eyes, and then all at once the meaning of the old hymn came to them:

> *"Where roses deck the flowery vale,*
> *There, Infant Jesus, thee we hail!"*

And there they both sat, grown up and yet children, children at heart. And it was summer—warm, beautiful summer.

The Marsh King's Daughter

THE storks have a great many stories which they tell their little ones, all about the bogs and the marshes. They suit them to their ages and capacities. The youngest ones are quite satisfied with "Kribble krabble," or some such nonsense, but the older ones want something with more meaning in it, or at any rate something about the family. We all know one of the two oldest and longest tales which have been kept up among the storks: the one about Moses, who was placed by his mother on the waters of the Nile and found there by the King's daughter. How she reared him and how he became a great man whose burial place nobody to this day knows. This is all common knowledge.

The other story is not known yet because the storks have kept it among themselves. It has been handed on from one mother stork to another for more than a thousand years, and each succeeding mother has told it better and better. And now we shall tell it best of all.

The first pair of storks who told it—and they actually lived it—had their summer quarters on the roof of the Viking's timbered house up by the Wild Bog in Wendsyssel. It is in the county of Hjorring, high up towards the Skaw in the north of Jutland, if we are to describe it according to the authorities. There is still a great bog there which we may read about in the county chronicles. This district used to be under the sea at one time, but the ground has risen and it stretches for miles. It is surrounded on every side by marshy meadows, quagmires, and peat bogs, on which grow cloud berries and stunted bushes. There is nearly always a damp mist hanging over it, and seventy years ago it was still overrun with wolves. It may well be called the Wild Bog, and one can imagine how desolate and dreary it was among these swamps and pools a thousand years ago.

In detail everything is much the same now as it was then. The reeds grow to the same height and have the same kind of long purple-brown leaves with feathery tips as now. The birch still grows there with its white bark and its delicate, loosely hanging leaves. As for living creatures, the flies still wear their gauzy draperies of the same cut, and the storks, now as then, still dress in black and white, with long red stockings.

The people then certainly wore a very different cut of clothes from those worn nowadays, but if any of them, serf or huntsman or anybody at all, stepped on the quagmires, the same fate befell him a thousand years ago as would overtake him now. In he would go and down he would sink to the Marsh King, as they call him. He rules down below over the whole kingdom of bogs and swamps. He might also be called King of the Quagmires, but we prefer to call him the Marsh King, as the storks did. We know very little about his rule, but that is perhaps just as well.

Near the bogs, close to the arm of the Cattegat called the Limfiord, lay the timbered hall of the Vikings, with its stone cellar, its tower, and its three stories. The storks had built their nest on the top of the roof, and the mother stork was sitting on the eggs which she was quite sure would soon be successfully hatched.

One evening father stork stayed out rather late, and when he came back he looked somewhat ruffled.

"I have something terrible to tell you," he said to the mother stork.

"Don't tell it to me then," she answered. "Remember that I am sitting! It might upset me and that would be bad for the eggs."

"You will have to know it," said he. "She has come here —the daughter of our host in Egypt. She has ventured to take the journey, and now she has disappeared."

"She who is related to the fairies? Tell me all about it. You know I can't bear to be kept waiting now I am sitting."

"Look here, mother! She must have believed what the doctor said, as you told me. She believed that the marsh flowers up here would do something for her father, and she flew over here in feather plumage with the other two Princesses, who have to come north every year to take the baths to make themselves young. She came, and she has vanished."

"You go into too many particulars," said the mother stork. "The eggs might get a chill, and I can't stand being kept in suspense."

"I have been on the outlook," said father stork, "and tonight when I was among the reeds where the quagmire will hardly bear me, I saw three swans flying along, and there was something about their flight which said to me, 'Watch them! They are not real swans. They are only in swan's plumage.' You know, mother, as well as I do, that one feels intuitively whether or not things are what they seem to be."

"Yes, indeed!" she said, "But tell me about the Princess. I am quite tired of hearing about swan's plumage."

"You know that in the middle of the bog there is a kind of lake," said father stork. "You can see a bit of it from here if you raise your head. Well, there was a big alder stump between the bushes and the quagmire, and on this the three swans settled, flapping their wings and looking about them. Then one of them threw off the swan's plumage and I at once recognized her as our Princess from Egypt. There she sat with no covering but her long black hair. I heard her beg the two others to take good care of the swan's plumage while she dived under the water to pick up the marsh flower which she thought she could see. They nodded and raised their heads, and lifted up the loose plumage. 'What shall they do with it?' thought I, and she no doubt asked the same thing. And the answer came: she had ocular demonstration of it. They flew up into the air with the feather garment! 'Just you duck down,' they cried. 'Never again will you fly about in the guise of a swan. Never more will you see the land of Egypt. You may sit in your swamp!' Then they tore the feather garment into a hundred bits, scattering the feathers all over the place like a snowstorm. Then away flew those two good-for-nothing Princesses."

"What a terrible thing!" said mother stork. "But I must have the end of it."

"The Princess moaned and wept. Her tears trickled down upon the alder stump and then it began to move, for it was the Marsh King himself who lives in the bog. I saw the stump turn round and saw that it was no longer a stump. It stretched out long miry branches like arms. The poor child was terrified, and she sprang away onto the shaking quagmire where it would not even bear my weight, far less hers. She sank at once and the alder stump after her. It was dragging her down. Great black bubbles rose in the slime, and then there was nothing more to be seen. Now she is buried in the Wild Bog, and never will she take back to Egypt the flowers she came for. You could not have endured the sight, mother."

"You shouldn't even tell me anything of the sort just now. It might have a bad effect upon the eggs. The Princess must look after herself! She will get help somehow. If it had been you or I now, or one of our sort, all would have been over with us."

"I mean to keep a watch though, every day," said the stork, and he kept his word.

A long time passed, and then one day he saw that a green stem shot up from the fathomless depth. When it reached the surface of the water a leaf appeared at the top, which grew broader and broader. Next a bud appeared close by it, and one morning at dawn, just as the stork was passing, the bud opened out in the warm rays of the sun. And in the middle of it lay a lovely baby, a little girl, looking just as fresh as if she had just come out of a bath. She was so exactly like the Princess from Egypt that at first the stork thought it was she who had grown small. But when he put two and two together, he came to the conclusion that it was her child and the Marsh King's. This explained why she appeared in a water lily.

"She can't stay there very long," thought the stork. "There are too many of us in my nest as it is, but an idea has just come into my head! The Viking's wife has no child, and she has often wished for one. As I am always said to bring the babies, this time I will do so in earnest. I will fly away to the Viking's wife with the baby, and that will indeed be a joy for her."

So the stork took up the little girl and flew away with her to the timbered house, where he picked a hole in the bladder skin which covered the window and laid the baby in the arms of the Viking's wife. This done, he flew home and told the mother stork all about it, and the young ones heard what he said. They were old enough now to understand.

"So you see, the Princess is not dead. She must have sent the baby up here, and I have found a home for her."

"I said so from the very first," said mother stork. "Now just give a little attention to your own children! It is almost time to start on our own journey. I feel a tingling in my wings every now and then. The cuckoo and the nightingale are already gone, and I hear from the quails that we shall soon have a good wind. Our young ones will do themselves credit at the maneuvers if I know them aright!"

How delighted the Viking's wife was when she woke in the morning and found the little baby on her bosom. She kissed and caressed it, but it screamed and kicked terribly and seemed anything but happy. At last it cried itself to sleep, and as it lay there a prettier little thing could not have been seen. The Viking's wife was delighted. Her body and soul were filled with joy. She was sure that now her husband and all his men would soon come back as unexpectedly as the baby had come. So she and her household busied themselves in putting the house in order against their return. The long, colored tapestries which she and her handmaids had woven with pictures of their gods—Odin, Thor, and Freya as they were called—were hung up. The serfs had to scour and polish the old shields which hung round the walls. Cushions were laid on the benches, and logs upon the great hearth in the middle of the hall, so that the fire might be lighted at once. The Viking's wife helped with all this work herself, so that when evening came she was very tired and slept soundly.

When she woke towards morning, she was much alarmed at finding that the little baby had disappeared. She sprang up and lighted a pine chip and looked about. There was no baby, but at the foot of the bed sat a hideous toad. She was horrified at the sight and seized a heavy stick to kill it, but it looked at her with such curious sad eyes that she had not the heart to strike it. Once more she looked round, and the toad gave a faint pitiful croak which made her start. She jumped out of bed and threw open the window shutter. The sun was just rising and its beams fell upon the bed and the great toad. All at once the monster's wide mouth seemed to contract and to become small and rosy, the limbs stretched and again took their lovely shapes, and it was her own dear little baby which lay there, and not a hideous frog.

"Whatever is this?" she cried. "I had a bad dream. This is my own darling elfin child." She kissed it and pressed it to her heart, but it struggled and bit like a wild kitten.

Neither that day nor the next did the Viking lord come home, although he was on his way. But the winds were against him—they were blowing southward to help the storks. "It is an ill wind that blows nobody good."

In the course of a few days and nights it became clear to the Viking's wife how matters stood with her little baby. Some magic power had a terrible hold over her. In the daytime it was as beautiful as any fairy, though it had a bad wicked temper. At night on the other hand, she became a hideous toad, quiet and pathetic, with sad mournful eyes. There were two natures in her, both in soul and body, continually shifting. The reason was that the little girl brought by the stork had by day her mother's form and her father's evil nature, but at night her kinship with him appeared in her outward form, and her mother's sweet nature and gentle spirit beamed out of the misshapen monster.

Who could release her from the power of this witchcraft? It caused the Viking's wife much grief and trouble, and yet her heart yearned over the unfortunate being. She knew that she would never dare tell her husband the true state of affairs, because he would without doubt, according to custom, have the poor child exposed on the highway for anyone who chose to look after it. The good woman had not the heart to do this, and so she determined that he should see the child only by broad daylight.

One morning there was a sound of storks' wings swishing over the roof. During the night more than a hundred pairs of storks had made it their resting place after the great maneuvers, and they were now trying their wings before starting on their long southward flight.

"Every man ready!" they cried. "All the wives and children too!"

"How light we feel," cried the young storks. "Our legs tingle as if we were full of live frogs. How splendid it is to be traveling to foreign lands!"

"Keep in line," said the father and mother. "And don't let your beaks clatter so fast! It isn't good for the chest." Then away they flew.

At the very same moment a horn sounded over the heath. The Viking had landed with all his men. They were bringing home no end of rich booty from the Gallic coast, where the people cried in terror as did the people of Britain, "Deliver us from the wild Northmen!"

What life and noise came to the Viking's home by the Wild Bog now! The mead cask was brought into the hall, the great fire was lighted, and horses were slaughtered for the feast, which was to be uproarious. The priest sprinkled the thralls with the warm blood of the horses as a consecration. The fire crackled and roared, driving the smoke up under the roof, and the soot dripped down from the beams, but they were used to all that. Guests were invited and they received handsome presents. All feuds and double dealing were forgotten. They drank deeply, and threw the bones in each other's faces when they had gnawed them, but that was a mark of good feeling. The skald—the minstrel of the times, but he was also a warrior, for he went with them on their expeditions and he knew what he was singing about —gave them one of his ballads recounting all their warlike deeds and their prowess. After every verse came the same refrain: "Fortunes vanish, friends die, one dies oneself, but a glorious name never dies!" Then they banged on the shields and hammered with knives or the knucklebones on the table before them till the hall rang.

The Viking's wife sat on the cross-bench in the banqueting hall. She was dressed in silk with gold bracelets and large amber beads. The skald brought her name into the song too. He spoke of the golden treasure she had brought to her wealthy husband, and of his delight at the beautiful child which he had seen only under its charming daylight guise. He rather admired her passionate nature, and said she would grow into a doughty shield maiden or Valkyrie, able to hold her own in battle. She would be of the kind who would not blink if a practised hand cut off her eyebrows in jest with a sharp sword.

The barrel of mead came to an end, and a new one was rolled up in its place. This one too was soon drained to the dregs, but they were a hard-headed people who could stand a great deal. They had a proverb then: "The beast knows when it is time to go home from grass, but the fool never knows when he has had enough." They knew it very well, but people often know one thing and yet do another. They also knew that "The dearest friend becomes a bore if he sits too long in one's house!" but yet they sat on. Meat and drink are such good things! They were a jovial company. At night the thralls slept among the warm ashes, and they dipped their fingers in the sooty grease and licked them. Those were rare times indeed.

The Viking went out once more that year on a raid, although the autumn winds were beginning. He sailed with his men to the coast of Britain. "It is just over the water," he said. His wife remained at home with the little girl, and certain it was that the foster mother soon grew fonder of the poor toad with the pathetic eyes and plaintive sighs than she was of the little beauty who tore and bit.

The raw, wet autumn fog, the "Gnaw-worm," which gnaws the leaves off the trees lay over wood and heath. And "Bird loose-feather," as they call the snow, followed closely upon the fog. Winter was on its way. The sparrows took the storks' nest under their protection and discussed the absent owners in their own fashion. The stork couple and their young—where were they now?

The storks were in the land of Egypt under such a sun as

we have on a warm summer's day. They were surrounded by flowering tamarinds and acacias. Mahomet's crescent glittered from every cupola on the mosques, and many a pair of storks stood on the slender towers, resting after their long journey. Whole flocks of them had their nests side by side on the mighty pillars, or on the ruined arches of the deserted temples. The date palm lifted high its screen of branches as if to form a sunshade. The grayish-white pyramids stood like shadowy sketches against the clear atmosphere of the desert where the ostrich knew it would find space for its stride. The lion crouched gazing with its great wise eyes at the marble sphinx half buried in the sand. The Nile waters had receded, and the land teemed with frogs. To the storks this was the most splendid sight in all the land. The eyes of the young ones were quite dazzled with the sight.

"See what it is to be here, and we always have the same in our warm country," said the mother stork, and the stomachs of the little ones tingled.

"Is there anything more to see?" they asked. "Shall we go any further inland?"

"There is not much more to see," said the mother stork. "On the fertile side there are only secluded woods where the trees are interlaced by creeping plants. The elephant with its strong clumsy legs is the only creature which can force a way through. The snakes there are too big for us, and the lizards are too nimble. If you go out into the desert, you will get sand in your eyes if the weather is good; and if bad, you may be buried in a sandstorm. No, we are best here. There are plenty of frogs and grasshoppers. Here I stay and you too!" And so she stayed.

The old ones stayed in their nests on the slender minarets, resting themselves but at the same time busily smoothing their feathers and rubbing their beaks upon their red stockings. Or they would lift up their long necks and gravely bow their heads, their brown eyes beaming wisely. The young stork misses walked about gravely among the juicy reeds, casting glances at the young bachelor storks or making acquaintance with them. They would swallow a frog at every third step, or walk about with a small snake dangling from their beak. It had such a good effect, they thought, and then it tasted so good.

The young he-storks engaged in many a petty quarrel, in which they flapped their wings furiously and stabbed each other with their beaks till the blood came. Then they took mates and built nests for themselves. That was what they lived for. New quarrels soon arose, for in these warm countries people are terribly passionate. All the same it was very pleasant to the old ones; nothing that their young ones did could be wrong. There was sunshine every day, and plenty to eat. Nothing to think of but pleasure!

But in the great palace of their Egyptian host, as they called him, matters were not so pleasant. The rich and mighty lord lay stretched upon his couch, as stiff in every limb as if he had been a mummy. The great painted hall was as gorgeous as if he had been lying within a tulip. Relatives and friends stood around him. He was not dead—yet he could hardly be called living. The healing marsh flower from the northern lands, which was to be found and plucked by the one who loved him best, would never be brought. His young and lovely daughter, who in the plumage of a swan had flown over sea and land to the far north, would never return. The two other swan Princesses had come back, and this is the tale they told:

"We were all flying high up in the air when a huntsman saw us and shot his arrow. It pierced our sister to the heart and she slowly sank. As she sank she sang her farewell song and fell into the midst of a forest pool. There by the shore under a drooping birch we buried her. But we had our revenge: we bound fire under the wings of a swallow which had its nest under the eaves of his cottage. The roof took fire and the cottage blazed up, and he was burnt in it. The flames shone on the pool where she lay, earth of the earth, under a birch tree. Never more will she come back to the land of Egypt."

Then they both wept, and the father stork who heard it clattered with his beak and said, "Pack of lies! I should like to drive my beak right into their breasts."

"Where it would break off, and a nice sight you would be then," said the mother stork. "Think of yourself first, and then of your family! Everything else comes second to that."

"I will perch upon the open cupola tomorrow when all the wise and learned folk assemble to talk about the sick man. Perhaps they will get a little nearer to the truth."

The sages met together and talked long and learnedly, but the stork could make neither head nor tail of it. Nothing came of it, however, either for the sick man or for his daughter who was buried in the Wild Bog, but we may just as well hear what they said. We may perhaps understand the story better—or at least as well as the stork did.

"Love is the food of life. The highest love nourishes the highest life. Only through love can this life be won back." This had been said and well said declared the sages.

"It is a beautiful idea," said the father stork at once.

"I don't rightly understand it," said the mother stork. "However, that is not my fault, but the fault of the idea. It really does not matter to me, though. I have other things to think about!"

The sages then talked a great deal about love: the difference between the love of lovers and that of parent and child; the love of vegetation for the light; and how sunbeams kiss the mire and forthwith young shoots spring into being. The whole discourse was so learned that the father stork could not take it in, far less repeat it. He became quite pensive, however, and stood on one leg for a whole day with his eyes half shut. Learning was a heavy burden to him.

Yet one thing the stork had thoroughly comprehended. He had heard from high and low alike what a misfortune it was to thousands of people and to the whole country that this man should be lying sick without hope of recovery. It would indeed be a blessed day which should see his health restored.

"But where blossoms the flower of healing for him?" they had asked of one another. They had also consulted all their learned writings, the twinkling stars, the winds, and the waves. But the only answer that the sages had been able to give was, "Love is the food of life!" How to apply the saying they knew not.

At last all had agreed that succor must come through the Princess, who loved her father with her heart and soul. And they had at last decided what she was to do. It was more than a year and a day since they had sent her at night, when there was a new moon, out into the desert of the sphinx. Here at the base of it she had to push away the sand from the door, and walk through the long passage which led right into the middle of the pyramid, where one of the mightiest of their ancient kings lay swathed in his mummy's bands in the midst of his wealth and glory. Here she had to bend her head to the corpse, and it was revealed to her where she would find healing and salvation for her father.

All this she had done, and the exact spot had been shown her in dreams where in the depths of the morass she would find the lotus flower that would touch her bosom beneath the water. And this she was to bring home. So she flew away in her swan's plumage to the Wild Bog in the far north.

Now all this the father and mother stork had known from the beginning, and we understand the matter better than we did. We know that the Marsh King dragged her down to himself and that to those at home she was dead and gone. The wisest of them said like the mother stork, "She will look out for herself!" So they awaited her return, not knowing in fact what else to do.

"I think I will snatch away the swans' plumage from the two deceitful Princesses," said the father stork. "Then they can not go to the Wild Bog to do any more mischief. I will keep the plumages up there till we find a use for them."

"Up where will you keep them?" asked the mother stork.

"In our nest at the Wild Bog," said he. "The young ones and I can carry them betwen us. If they are too cumbersome, there are places enough on the way where we can hide them till our next flight. One plumage would be enough for her, but two are better. It is a good plan to have plenty of wraps in a northern country."

"You will get no thanks for it," said the mother stork, "but you are the master. I have nothing to say except when I am sitting."

In the meantime the little child in the Viking's hall by the Wild Bog, whither the storks flew in the spring, had been given a name. It was Helga, but such a name was far too gentle for such a wild spirit as dwelt within her. Month by month it showed itself more. And year by year, while the storks took the same journey, in autumn towards the Nile and in spring towards the Wild Bog, the little child grew to be a big girl. Before anyone knew how, she was the loveliest maiden possible of sixteen. The husk was lovely, but the kernel was hard and rough—wilder than most, even in those hard, wild times.

Her greatest pleasure was to dabble her white hands in the blood of the horses slaughtered for sacrifice. In her wild freaks she would bite the heads off the black cocks which the priest was about to slay, and she said in full earnest to her foster father, "If thy foe were to come and throw a rope round the beams of thy house and pull it about thine ears, I would not wake thee if I could. I should not hear him for the tingling of the blood in the ear thou once boxed years ago. I do not forget!"

But the Viking did not believe what she said. Like everybody else he was infatuated by her beauty, nor did he know how body and soul changed places in his little Helga in the dark hours of the night. She rode a horse barebacked as if she were a part of it, nor did she jump off while her steed bit and fought with the other wild horses. She would often throw herself from the cliff into the sea in all her clothes, and swim out to meet the Viking when his boat neared the shore; and she cut off the longest strand of her beautiful long hair to string her bow. "Self-made is well made," said she.

The Viking's wife, though strong-willed and strong-minded after the fashion of the times, became towards her daughter like any other weak, anxious mother, because she knew that a spell rested over the terrible child. Often when her mother stepped out onto the balcony, Helga, from pure love of teasing, it seemed, would sit down upon the edge of the well, throw up her hands and feet, and go backwards plump into the dark narrow hole. Here with her frog's nature she would rise again and clamber out like a cat dripping with water, carrying a perfect stream into the banqueting hall, washing aside the green twigs strewn on the floor.

One bond, however, always held little Helga in check, and that was twilight. When it drew near she became quiet and pensive, allowing herself to be called and directed. An inner perception, as it were, drew her towards her mother, and when the sun sank and the transformation took place, she sat sad and quiet, shriveled up into the form of a toad. Her body was now much bigger than those creatures ever are, but for that reason all the more unsightly. She looked like a wretched dwarf with the head of a frog and webbed fingers. There was something so piteous in her eyes, and voice she had none—only a hollow croak like the smothered sobs of a dreaming child.

Then the Viking's wife would take it on her knee, and looking into its eyes would forget the misshapen form and would often say, "I could almost wish that thou would always remain my dumb frog child. Thou art more terrible to look at when thou art clothed in beauty." Then she would write runes against sickness and sorcery and throw them over the miserable girl, but they did no good at all.

"One would never think that she had been small enough to lie in a water lily," said the father stork. "Now that she is grown up, she is the very image of her Egyptian mother, whom we never saw again. She did not manage to take such good care of herself as you and the sages said she would. I have been flying across the marsh, year in and year out, and never have I seen a trace of her. Yes, I may as well tell you that all these years, when I have flown on ahead of you to look after the nest and set it to rights, I have spent many a night flying about like an owl or a bat, scanning the open water, but all to no purpose. Nor have we had any use for the two swan plumages which the young ones and I dragged up here with so much difficulty. It took us three journeys to get them here. They have lain for years now in the bottom of the nest and if ever a disaster happens, such as a fire in the timbered house, they will be entirely lost."

"And our good nest would be lost too," said the mother stork. "But you think less of that than you do of your feather dresses and your marsh Princess. You had better go down to her one day and stay in the mire for good. You are a bad father to your own chicks, and I have always said so since the first time I hatched a brood. If only we or the young ones don't get an arrow through our wings from that mad Viking girl! She doesn't know what she is about. We are rather more at home here than she is, and she ought to remember that. We never forget our obligations. Every year we pay our toll of a feather, an egg, and a young one, as it is only right we should. Do you think that while she is about I care to go down there as I used to do, and as I do in Egypt where I am 'hail fellow well met' with everybody, and where I peep into their pots and kettles if I like? No, indeed. I sit up here vexing myself about her, the vixen, and you too. You should have left her in the water lily, and there would have been an end of her."

"You are much more estimable than your words," said the father stork. "I know you better than you know yourself, my dear." Then he gave a hop and flapped his wings thrice, proudly stretched out his neck, and soared away without moving his outspread wings. When he had gone some distance he made some more powerful strokes, his head and neck bending proudly forward, while his plumage gleamed in the sunshine. What strength and speed there were in his flight!

"He is still the handsomest of them all," said the mother stork, "but I don't tell him so."

The Viking came home early that autumn with his booty and prisoners. Among these was a young Christian priest, one of those men who persecuted the heathen gods of the north. There had often been discussions of late, both in the hall and in the women's bower, about the new faith which was spreading in all the countries to the south. Through Saint Ansgarius it had spread as far as Hedeby on the Schlei. Even little Helga had heard of the belief in the "White Christ," who for love of mankind had given His life for their salvation. As far as Helga was concerned, it had all gone in at one ear and out at the other, as one says. The very meaning of the word "love" seemed to dawn upon her only when she was shriveled up into the form of a frog in her secret chamber. But the Viking's wife had listened to the story and had felt herself strangely moved by these tales about the Son of the only true God.

The men on their return from their raids told them all about the temples of costly polished stone which were raised to Him whose message was love. Once a couple of heavy golden vessels of cunning workmanship were brought home and about them hung a peculiar spicy odor. They were censers used by the Christian priests to swing before the altars on which blood never flowed, but where the bread and wine were changed to the body and blood of Him who gave Himself for the yet unborn generations.

The young priest was imprisoned in the deep stone cellars of the timber house, and his feet and hands were bound with strips of bark. He was "as beautiful as Baldur," said the Viking's wife, and she felt pity for him, but young Helga proposed that he should be hamstrung and be tied to the tails of wild oxen.

"Then would I loose the dogs on him. Hie and away over marshes and pools! That would be a merry sight, and merrier still would it be to follow in his course."

However, this was not the death the Viking wished him to die. Instead, he intended to offer him up in the morning upon the bloodstone in the groves, as a denier and a persecutor of the great gods. It would be the first man to be sacrificed there. Young Helga begged that she might sprinkle his blood over the images of the gods and over the people. She polished her sharp knife, and when one of the great ferocious dogs, of which there were so many about the place, sprang towards her, she dug her knife into its side, "just to test it," she said.

The Viking's wife looked sadly at this wild, badly disposed girl, and when night came and the girl's beauty of body and soul changed places, she spoke tender words of grief from her sorrowful heart. The ugly toad stood fixing its sad brown eyes upon her, listening and seeming to understand with the mind of a human being.

"Never once has a word of my double grief through you

passed my lips to my husband," said the Viking's wife. "My heart is full of grief for you. Great is a mother's love! But love never entered your heart; it is like a lump of cold clay. From whence did you come into my house?"

Then the ungainly creature trembled as if the words touched some invisible chord between body and soul, and great tears came into its eyes.

"A bitter time will come to you," said the Viking's wife. "And it will be a terrible one to me too! Better would it have been if as a child you had been exposed on the highway, and lulled by the cold to the sleep of death!" And the Viking's wife shed bitter tears and went away in anger and sorrow, passing under the curtain of skins which hung from the beams and divided the hall.

The shriveled-up toad crouched in the corner, and a dead silence reigned. At intervals a half stifled sigh rose within her. It was as if in anguish something came to life in her heart. She took a step forward and listened. Then she stepped forward again and grasped the heavy bar of the door with her clumsy hands. Softly she drew it back and silently lifted the latch. Then she took up the lamp which stood in the anteroom. It seemed as if a strong power gave her strength. She drew out the iron bolt from the barred cellar door and slipped in to the prisoner. He was asleep. She touched him with her cold clammy hand, and when he awoke and saw the hideous creature, he shuddered as if he beheld an evil apparition. She drew out her knife and cut his bonds asunder, and then beckoned him to follow her. He named the Holy Name and made the sign of the cross, and as the form remained unchanged, he repeated the words of the psalmist: "Blessed is the man who hath pity on the poor and needy. The Lord will deliver him in time of trouble." Then he asked, "Who art thou, whose outward appearance is that of an animal, while thou willingly perform deeds of mercy?"

The toad beckoned him and led him behind the sheltering curtains and down a long passage to the stable. She pointed to a horse, onto which he sprang and she after him. She sat in front of him, clutching the mane of the animal. The prisoner understood her and they rode at a quick pace along a path he never would have found to the heath. He forgot her hideous form, knowing that the mercy of God worked through the spirits of darkness. He prayed and sang holy songs, which made her tremble. Was it the power of prayer and his singing working upon her? Or was it the chill air of the advancing dawn? What were her feelings? She raised herself and wanted to stop and jump off the horse, but the Christian priest held her tightly with all his strength, and sang aloud a psalm as if this could lift the spell which held her.

The horse bounded on more wildly than before, the sky grew red, and the first sunbeams pierced the clouds. As the stream of light touched her the transformation took place. She was once more a lovely maiden, but her demoniac spirit was the same. The priest held a blooming maiden in his arms and he was terrified at the sight. He stopped the horse and sprang down, thinking he had met with a new device of the evil one. But young Helga sprang to the ground too. The short child's frock only reached to her knee. She tore the sharp knife from her belt and rushed upon the startled man. "Let me get at thee!" she cried. "Let me reach thee, and my knife shall pierce thee! Thou art ashen pale, beardless slave!"

She closed upon him and they wrestled together, but an invisible power seemed to give strength to the Christian. He held her tight, and the old oak under which they stood seemed to help him, for the loosened roots above the ground tripped her up. Close by rose a bubbling spring, and he sprinkled her with water and commanded the unclean spirit to leave her, making the sign of the cross over her according to Christian usage. But the baptismal water has no power if the spring of faith flows not from within.

Yet even here something more than man's strength opposed itself through him against the evil which struggled within her. Her arms fell and she looked with astonishment and paling cheeks at this man who seemed to be a mighty magician skilled in secret arts. These were dark runes he was repeating, and cabalistic signs he was tracing in the air. She would not have blanched had he flourished a shining sword or a sharp ax before her face, but she trembled now as he traced the sign of the cross upon her forehead and bosom, and she sat before him with drooping head like a wild bird tamed.

He spoke gently to her about the deed of love she had performed for him this night, when she came in the hideous shape of a toad, cut his bands asunder, and led him out to light and life. She herself was bound, he said, and with stronger bonds than his. But she also, through him, should reach to light and life everlasting. He would take her to Hedeby to the holy Ansgarius, and there in that Christian city the spell would be removed. But she must no longer sit in front of him on the horse, even if she went of her own free will. He dared not carry her thus.

"Thou must sit behind me, not before. Thy magic beauty has a power given by the Evil One which I dread. Yet shall I have the victory through Christ!"

He knelt down and prayed humbly and earnestly. It seemed as if the quiet wood became a holy church consecrated by his worship. The birds began to sing as if they too were also of this new congregation, and the fragrance of the wild flowers was as the ambrosial perfume of incense, while the young priest recited the words of Holy Writ: "The Dayspring from on high hath visited us, to give light to them that sit in darkness and in the shadow of death; to guide their feet into the way of peace."

He spoke of the yearning of all nature for redemption, and while he spoke the horse which had carried them stood quietly by, only rustling among the bramble bushes, making the ripe juicy fruit fall into little Helga's hands, as if inviting her to refresh herself. Patiently she allowed herself to be lifted onto the horse's back, and she sat there like one in a trance, who neither watches nor wanders. The Christian man bound together two branches in the shape of a cross, which he held aloft in his hand as he rode through the wood.

The brushwood grew thicker and thicker till at last it became a trackless wilderness. Bushes of the wild sloe blocked the way and they had to ride round them. The bubbling springs turned to standing pools and these they also had to ride round. Still they found strength and refreshment in the pure breezes of the forest, and no less a power in the tender words of faith and love spoken by the young priest in his fervent desire to lead this poor straying one into the way of light and love.

It is said that raindrops can wear a hollow in the hardest stone, and that the waves of the sea can smooth and round the jagged rocks. So did the dew of mercy, falling upon little Helga, soften all that was hard and smooth, all that was rough in her. Not that these effects were yet to be seen. She did not even know that they had taken place, any more than the buried seed lying in the earth knows that the refreshing showers and the warm sunbeams will cause it to flourish and bloom.

As the mother's song unconsciously falls upon the child's heart, it stammers the words after her without understanding them, but later they crystallize into thoughts and in time become clear. In this way the Word also worked here in the heart of Helga.

They rode out of the wood, over a heath, and again

through trackless forests. Towards evening they met a band of robbers. "Where hast thou stolen this beautiful child?" they cried, stopping the horse and pulling down the two riders, for they were a numerous party.

The priest had no weapon but the knife which he had taken from little Helga, and with this he struck out right and left. One of the robbers raised his ax to strike him, but the Christian succeeded in springing to one side, or he would certainly have been hit. But the blade flew into the horse's neck so that the blood gushed forth and it fell to the ground dead. Then little Helga, as if roused from a long deep trance, rushed forward and threw herself onto the gasping horse. The priest placed himself in front of her as a shield and defense, but one of the robbers swung his iron club with such force at his head that the blood and the brains were scattered about, and he fell dead upon the ground.

The robbers seized little Helga by her white arms, but the sun was just going down and as the last rays vanished she was changed into the form of a frog. A greenish white mouth stretched half over her face. Her arms became thin and slimy. And broad hands with webbed fingers spread themselves out like fans. The robbers in terror let her go and she stood among them a hideous monster. Then according to frog nature, she bounded away with great leaps as high as herself and disappeared in the thicket. Then the robbers perceived that this must be Loki's evil spirit or some withcraft, and they hurried away affrighted.

The full moon had risen and was shining in all its splendor when poor little Helga, in the form of a frog, crept out of the thicket. She stopped by the body of the Christian priest and the dead horse. She looked at them with eyes which seemed to weep. A sob came from the toad like that of a child bursting into tears. She threw herself down, first upon one and then on the other, and brought water in her hand, which from being large and webbed formed a cup. This she sprinkled them with, but they were dead, and dead they must remain! This she understood. Soon wild animals would come and devour them—but no, that should never be. So she dug into the ground as deep as she could. She wished to dig a grave for them.

She had nothing but the branch of a tree and her two hands, and she tore the web between her fingers till the blood ran from them. She soon saw that the task would be beyond her, so she fetched fresh water and washed the face of the dead man, and strewed fresh green leaves over it. She also brought large boughs to cover him and scattered dried leaves between the branches. Then she brought the heaviest stones she could carry and laid them over the dead body, filling up the spaces with moss. Now she thought the mound was strong and secure enough, but the difficult task had employed the whole night. The sun was just rising and there stood little Helga in all her beauty, with bleeding hands and maidenly tears for the first time on her blushing cheeks.

It was in this transformation as if two natures were struggling in her. She trembled and glanced round as if she were just awakening from a troubled dream. She leaned for support against a slender beech, and at last climbed to the topmost branches like a cat and seated herself firmly upon them. She sat there for the whole livelong day, like a frightened squirrel in the solitude of the wood where all is still and dead, as they say!

Dead—well, there flew a couple of butterflies whirling round and round each other, and close by were some ant hills, each with its hundreds of busy little creatures swarming to and fro. In the air danced countless midges and swarm upon swarm of flies, ladybirds, dragonflies with golden wings, and other little winged creatures. The earthworm crept forth from the moist ground, and the moles—but excepting these, all was still and dead around. When people say this they don't quite understand what they mean. None noticed little Helga but a flock of jackdaws which flew chattering round the tree where she sat. They hopped along the branch towards her, boldly inquisitive, but a glance from her eyes was enough to drive them away. They could not make her out though, any more than she could understand herself.

When the evening drew near and the sun began to sink, the approaching transformation roused her to fresh exertion. She slipped down gently from the tree, and when the last sunbeam was extinguished she sat there once more, the shriveled-up frog with her torn webbed hands. But her eyes now shone with a new beauty which they had hardly possessed in all the pride of her loveliness. These were the gentlest and tenderest maiden's eyes which now shone out of the face of the frog. They bore witness to the existence of deep feeling and a human heart, and the beauteous eyes overflowed with tears, weeping precious drops that lightened the heart.

The cross made of branches, the last work of him who now was dead and cold, still lay by the grave. Little Helga took it up—the thought came unconsciously—and she placed it between the stones which covered man and horse. At the sad recollection her tears burst forth again, and in this mood she traced the same sign in the earth round the grave. And as she formed with both hands the sign of the cross, the webbed skin fell away from her fingers like a torn glove. She washed her hands at the spring, and gazed in astonishment at their delicate whiteness. Again she made the holy sign in the air, between herself and the dead man. Her lips trembled, her tongue moved, and the name which she had so often heard in her ride through the forest rose to her lips, and she uttered the words "Jesus Christ."

The frog's skin fell away from her. She was the beautiful young maiden, but her head bent wearily and her limbs required rest. She slept, but her sleep was short. She was awakened at midnight, and before her stood the dead horse, prancing and full of life, which shone forth from his eyes and his wounded neck. Close by his side appeared the murdered Christian priest, "more beautiful than Baldur," the Viking's wife might indeed have said, and yet he was surrounded by flames of fire.

There was such earnestness in his large mild eyes, and such righteous judgment in his penetrating glance which pierced into the remotest corner of her heart. Little Helga trembled, and every memory within her was awakened as if it had been the Day of Judgment. Every kindness which had ever been shown her, every loving word which had been said to her, came vividly before her. She now understood that it was love which had sustained her in those days of trial, through which all creatures formed of dust and clay, soul and spirit, must wrestle and struggle. She acknowledged that she had but followed whither she was called, had done nothing for herself. All had been given her. She bent now in lowly humility and full of shame, before Him who could read every impulse of her heart. And in that moment she felt the purifying flame of the Holy Spirit thrill through her soul.

"Thou daughter of earth," said the Christian martyr, "out of the earth art thou come and from the earth shalt thou rise again! The sunlight within thee shall consciously return to its origin—not the beams of the actual sun, but those from God! No soul will be lost. Things temporal are full of weariness, but eternity is life-giving. I come from the land of the dead. Thou also must one day journey through the deep valleys to reach the radiant mountain summits where dwell grace and all perfections. I cannot lead thee to Hedeby for Christian baptism. First must thou break the watery shield that covers the deep morass, and bring forth from its depths the living author of thy being and thy life. Thou must first carry out thy vocation before thy consecration may take place!"

Then he lifted her up onto the horse and gave her a golden censer like those she had seen in the Viking's hall. A fragrant perfume arose from it, and the open wound on the martyr's forehead gleamed like a radiant diadem. He took the cross from the grave, holding it high above him, while they rode rapidly through the air—across the murmuring woods and over the heights where the mighty warriors of old lay buried, each seated on his dead war horse. These strong men of war arose and rode out to the summits of the mounds. The broad golden circlets round their foreheads gleamed in the moonlight and their cloaks fluttered in the wind. The great dragon hoarding his treasure raised his head to look at them, and whole hosts of dwarfs peeped forth from their hillocks, swarming with red, green, and blue lights, like sparks from the ashes of burnt paper.

Away they flew over wood and heath, rivers and pools, up north towards the Wild Bog. Arrived here, they hovered round in great circles. The martyr raised high the cross which shone like gold, and his lips chanted the holy mass. Little Helga sang with him as a child joins in its mother's song. She swung the censer, and from it issued a fragrance of the altar so strong and so wonder-working that the reeds and rushes burst into blossom, and numberless flower stems shot up from the bottomless depths. Everything that had life within it lifted itself up and blossomed. The water lilies spread themselves over the surface of the pool like a carpet of wrought flowers, and on this carpet lay a sleeping woman. She was young and beautiful. Little Helga fancied she saw herself, her picture, mirrored in the quiet pool. It was her mother she saw, the wife of the Marsh King, the princess from the river Nile.

The martyred priest commanded the sleeping woman to be lifted up onto the horse, but the animal sank beneath the burden as though it had no more substance than a winding sheet floating on the wind. But the sign of the cross gave strength to the phantom and all three rode on through the air to dry ground. Just then the cock crew from the Viking's hall and the vision melted away in the mist which was driven along by the wind, but mother and daughter stood side by side.

"Is it myself I see reflected in the deep water?" said the mother.

"Do I see myself mirrored in a bright shield?" said the daughter. But as they approached and clasped each other heart to heart, the mother's heart beat the fastest and she understood.

"My child! My own heart's blossom! My lotus out of the deep waters!"—and she wept over her daughter. Her tears were a new baptism of love and life for little Helga.

"I came hither in a swan's plumage, and here I threw it off," said the mother. "I sank down into the bog, which closed around me. Some power always dragged me down, deeper and deeper. I felt the hand of sleep pressing upon my eyelids. I fell asleep, and I dreamt. I seemed to be again in the vast Egyptian pyramid, but still before me stood the moving alder stump which had frightened me on the surface of the bog. I gazed at the fissures of the bark and they shone out in bright colors and turned to hieroglyphs. It was the mummy's wrappings I was looking at. The coverings burst asunder and out of them walked the mummy king of a thousand years ago, black as pitch, black as the shining wood snail or the slimy mud of the swamp. Whether it were the mummy king or the Marsh King I knew not. He threw his arms around me and I felt that I must die. When life came back to me, I felt something warm upon my bosom. It was a little bird fluttering its wing and twittering.

It flew from my bosom high up towards the heavy dark canopy, but a long green ribbon still bound it to me. I heard and understood its notes of longing: 'Freedom! Sunshine! To the Father!' Then I remembered my own father in the sunlit land of my home, my life, and my love. And I loosened the ribbon and let it flutter away—home to my father. Since that hour I have dreamt no more. I must have slept a long and heavy sleep till this hour, when sweet music and fragrant odors awoke me and set me free."

Where did now the green ribbon flutter which bound the mother's heart to the wings of the bird? Only the stork had seen it. The ribbon was the green stem, the bow was the gleaming flower which cradled the little baby, now grown up to her full beauty and once more resting on her mother's breast. While they stood there pressed heart to heart, the stork was wheeling above their heads in great circles. At length he flew away to his nest and brought back the swan plumages so long cherished there. He threw one over each of them. The feathers closed over them, and mother and daughter rose into the air as two white swans.

"Now let us talk," said the father stork. "Now we can understand each other's language, even if one sort of bird has a different shaped beak from another. It is the most fortunate thing in the world that you appeared this evening. Tomorrow we should have been off, mother and I and the young ones. We are going to fly southwards. Yes, you may look at me. I am an old friend from the Nile, and so is mother, too. Her heart is not so sharp as her beak! She always said that the Princess would take care of herself. I and the young ones carried the swans' plumage up here. How delighted I am and how lucky it is that I am still here! As soon as the day dawns we will set off, a great company of storks. We will fly in front. You had better follow us, and then you won't lose your way. We will keep an eye upon you."

"And the lotus flower which I was to take with me," said the Egyptian Princess, "flies by my side in a swan's plumage. I take the flower of my heart with me, and so the riddle is solved. Now for home! home!"

But Helga said she could not leave the Danish land without seeing her loving foster mother once more, the Viking's wife. For in Helga's memory now rose up every happy recollection, every tender word, and every tear her foster mother had shed over her, and it almost seemed as if she loved this mother best.

"Yes, we must go to the Viking's hall," said the father stork. "Mother and the young ones are waiting for us there. How they will open their eyes and flap their wings! Mother doesn't say much. She is somewhat short and abrupt, but she means very well. Now I will make a great clattering to let them know we are coming."

So he clattered with his beak, and he and the swans flew off to the Viking's hall.

They all lay in a deep sleep within. The Viking's wife had gone late to rest for she was in great anxiety about little Helga, who had not been seen for three days. She had disappeared with the Christian priest, and she must have helped him away. It was her horse which was missing from the stable. By what power had this been brought to pass? The Viking's wife thought over all the many miracles which were said to have been performed by the White Christ and by those who believed in Him and followed Him.

All these thoughts took form in her dreams, and it seemed to her that she was still awake, sitting thoughtfully upon her bed while darkness reigned without. A storm arose. She heard the rolling of the waves east and west of her from the North Sea and from the waters of the Cattegat. The monstrous serpent which, according to her faith, encompassed the earth in the depths of the ocean, was trembling in convulsions from the dread of Ragnarok, the night of the gods. He personified the Day of Judgment, when everything should pass away, even the great gods themselves. The war horn sounded, and away over the rainbow rode the gods, clad in steel, to fight their last battle. Before them flew the shield maidens, the Valkyries, and the ranks were closed by the phantoms of the dead warriors. The whole atmosphere shone in the radiance of the northern lights, but darkness conquered in the end.

It was a terrible hour, and in her dream little Helga sat close beside the frightened woman, crouching on the floor in the form of the hideous frog. She trembled and crept closer to her foster mother, who took her on her knee and in her love pressed her to her bosom, notwithstanding the hideous frog's skin. The air resounded with the clashing of sword and club and the whistling of arrows, as though a fierce hailstorm were passing over them. The hour had come when heaven and earth were to pass away, the stars to fall, and everything to succumb to Surtur's fire. And yet a new earth and a new heaven would arise, and fields of corn would wave where the seas now rolled over the golden sands. The God whom none might name would reign, and to Him would ascend Baldur the mild, the loving, redeemed from the kingdom of the dead. He was coming! The Viking's wife saw him plainly. She saw his face. It was that of the Christian priest, their prisoner.

"White Christ," she cried aloud, and as she spoke the name she pressed a kiss upon the forehead of the loathsome toad. The frog's skin fell away, and before her stood little Helga in all the radiance of her beauty, gentle as she had never been before, and with beaming eyes. She kissed her foster mother's hands and blessed her for all the care and love she had shown in the days of her trial and misery. She thanked her for the thoughts she had instilled into her, and for naming the name which she now repeated, "White Christ!" Little Helga rose up as a great white swan and spread her wings, with the rushing sound of a flock of birds of passage on the wing.

The Viking's wife was awakened by the rushing sound of wings outside. She knew it was the time when the storks took their flight, and it was these she heard. She wanted to see them all once more and to bid them farewell, so she got up and went out onto the balcony. She saw stork upon stork sitting on the roofs of the outbuildings round the courtyard, and flocks of them were flying round and round in great circles.

Just in front of her, on the edge of the well where little Helga so often had frightened her with her wildness, sat two white swans who gazed at her with their wise eyes. Then she remembered her dream, which still seemed quite real to her. She thought of little Helga in the form of a swan. She thought of the Christian priest, and suddenly a great joy arose in her heart. The swans flapped their wings and bent their heads as if to greet her, and the Viking's wife stretched out her arms towards them as if she understood all about it, and she smiled at them with tears in her eyes.

"We are not going to wait for the swans," said the mother stork. "If they want to travel with us they must come. We can't dawdle here till the plovers start! It is very nice to travel as we do, the whole family together, not like the chaffinches and the ruffs, whose males and females fly separately. It's hardly decent! And why are those swans flapping their wings like that?"

"Well, everyone flies in his own way," said the father stork. "The swans fly in an oblique line, the cranes in the form of a triangle, and the plovers in a curved line like a snake."

"Don't talk about snakes while we are flying up here,"

said the mother stork. "It puts desires into the young ones' heads which they can't gratify."

"Are those the high mountains I used to hear about?" asked Helga in the swan's plumage.

"Those are thunder clouds driving along beneath us," said her mother.

"What are those white clouds that rise so high?" again enquired Helga.

"Those are mountains covered with perpetual snows that you see yonder," said her mother, as they flew across the Alps down towards the blue Mediterranean.

"Africa's land! Egypt's strand!" said the daughter of the Nile in her joy, as from far above in her swan's plumage her eye fell upon the narrow waving yellow line, her birthplace. The other birds saw it too and hastened their flight.

"I smell the Nile mud and the frogs!" said the mother stork. "I am tingling all over. Now you will have something nice to taste, and something to see too. There are the marabouts, the ibises, and the cranes. They all belong to our family, but they are not nearly so handsome as we are. They are very stuck up too, especially the ibises, who have been so spoilt by the Egyptians. They make mummies of them and stuff them with spices. I would rather be stuffed with living frogs. And so would you, and so you shall be! Better have something in your crops while you are alive than have a great fuss made over you after you are dead. That is my opinion and I am always right."

"The storks have come back," was said in the great house on the Nile, where its lord lay in the great hall on his downy cushions covered with a leopard skin. He was scarcely alive and yet not dead either, waiting and hoping for the lotus flower from the deep morass in the north.

Relatives and servants stood round his couch, when two great white swans who had come with the storks flew into the hall. They threw off their dazzling plumage, and there stood two beautiful women as like each other as twin drops of dew. They bent over the pale withered old man, throwing back their long hair.

As little Helga bent over her grandfather, the color came back to his cheeks and new life returned to his limbs. The old man rose with health and energy renewed. His daughter and granddaughter clasped him in their arms, as if with a joyous morning greeting after a long troubled night.

Joy reigned through the house and in the storks' nest too; but there the rejoicing was chiefly over the abundance of food, especially the swarms of frogs. And while the sages hastily sketched the story of the two Princesses and the flower of healing, which brought such joy and blessing to the land, the parent storks told the same story in their own way to their family—but not until they had all satisfied their appetites, or they would have had something better to do than to listen to stories.

"Surely you will be made something at last," whispered the mother stork. "It wouldn't be reasonable otherwise."

"Oh, what should I be made?" said the father stork. "And what have I done? Nothing at all!"

"You have done more than all the others. Without you and the young ones the two Princesses would never have seen Egypt again, nor would the old man have recovered his health. You will become something. They will at least give you a doctor's degree, and our young ones will be born with the title, and their young ones after them. Why, you look like an Egyptian doctor already, at least in my eyes!"

And now the learned men and the sages set to work to propound the inner principle, as they called it, that lay at the root of the matter. "Love is the food of life," was their text. Then came the explanations. "The Princess was the warm sunbeam. She went down to the Marsh King and from their meeting sprang forth the blossom."

"I can't exactly repeat the words," said the father stork.

He had been listening on the roof and now wanted to tell those in the nest all about it. "What they said was so involved and so clever that they not only received rank, but presents too. Even the head cook had a mark of distinction —most likely for the soup."

"And what did you get?" asked the mother stork. "They ought not to forget the most important person, and that is what you are. The sages have only cackled about it all. But your turn will come, no doubt."

Late at night when the whole happy household were wrapped in peaceful slumbers, there was still one watcher. It was not father stork, although he stood up in the nest on one leg like a sentry asleep at his post. No, it was little Helga. She was watching, bending out over the balcony in the clear air, gazing at the shining stars. They were bigger and purer in their radiance than she had ever seen them in the north, and yet they were the same. She thought of the Viking's wife by the Wild Bog. She thought of her foster mother's gentle eyes and the tears she had shed over the poor frog child, who now stood in the bright starlight and delicious spring air by the waters of the Nile. She thought of the love in the heathen woman's breast, the love she had lavished on a miserable creature who in human guise was a wild animal, and when in the form of an animal was hateful to the sight and to the touch. She looked at the shining stars and remembered the dazzling light on the forehead of the martyred priest as he flew over moorland and forest. The tones of his voice came back to her, and the words that he had said while she sat overwhelmed and crushed—words concerning the sublime source of love, the highest love embracing all mankind.

What had not been won and achieved by this love? Day and night little Helga was absorbed in the thought of her happiness. She entirely lost herself in the contemplation of it, like a child who turns hurriedly from the giver to examine the beautiful gifts. Happy she was indeed, and her happiness seemed ever growing. Yet more might come, would come. In these thoughts she indulged until she thought no more of the Giver. It was in the wantonness of youth that she thus sinned. Her eyes sparkled with pride, but suddenly she was roused from her vain dream. She heard a great clatter in the courtyard below and, looking out, saw two great ostriches rushing hurriedly round in circles. Never before had she seen this great, heavy, clumsy bird which looked as if its wings had been clipped, and the birds themselves had the appearance of having been roughly used. She asked what had happened to them, and for the first time heard the legend the Egyptians tell concerning the ostrich.

Once, they say, the ostriches were a beautiful and glorious race of birds, with large strong wings. One evening the great birds of the forest said to it, "Brother, shall we tomorrow, God willing, go down to the river to drink?" And the ostrich answered, "I will."

At the break of day then they flew off, first rising high in the air towards the sun, the eye of God. Still higher and higher the ostrich flew, far in front of the other birds, in its pride flying close up to the light. He trusted in his own strength, and not on that of the Giver. He would not say "God willing!" But the avenging angel drew back the veil from the flaming ocean of sunlight, and in a moment the wings of the proud bird were burnt and he sank miserably to the earth. Since that time the ostrich and his race have never been able to rise in the air. He can only fly terror-stricken along the ground, or around and around in narrow circles. It is a warning to mankind, reminding us in every thought and action to say, "God willing!"

Helga thoughtfully and seriously bent her head and looked at the hunted ostrich. She noticed its fear and its miserable pride at the sight of its own great shadow on the white moonlit wall. Her thoughts grew graver and more earnest. A life so rich in joy had already been given her. What more was to come? The best of all perhaps—"God willing!"

Early in the spring, when the storks were again about to take flight to the north, little Helga took off her gold bracelet, scratched her name on it, beckoned to father stork, and put it round his neck. She told him to take it to the Viking's wife, who would see by it that her foster daughter still lived, was happy, and had not forgotten her.

"It is a heavy thing to carry," thought father stork, as it slipped onto his neck. "But neither gold nor honor are to be thrown upon the highway. The stork brings good luck, they say up there."

"You lay gold, and I lay eggs," said mother stork. "But you lay only once and I lay every year. Yet no one appreciates us. I call it very mortifying!"

"One always has the consciousness of one's own worth, mother," said father stork.

"But you can't hang it outside," said mother stork. "It gives neither a fair wind nor a full meal!" And they took their departure.

The little nightingale singing in the tamarind bushes was also going north soon. Helga had often heard it singing by the Wild Bog, so she determined to send a message by it too. She knew the bird language from having worn a swan's plumage, and she had kept it up by speaking to the storks and the swallows. The nightingale understood her quite well, so she begged it to fly to the beechwood in Jutland, where she had made the grave of stones and branches. She bade it tell all the other little birds to guard the grave and to sing over it. The nightingale flew away—and time flew away too.

In the autumn an eagle perched on one of the pyramids saw a gorgeous train of heavily laden camels, and men clad in armor riding fiery Arab steeds as white as silver, with quivering red nostrils and flowing manes reaching to the ground. A royal prince from Arabia, as handsome as a prince should be, was arriving at the stately mansion where now the storks' nest stood empty. Its inhabitants were still in their northern home, but they would soon return. Indeed they came on the very day when the rejoicings were at their height.

There were bridal festivities, and little Helga was the bride, clad in rich silk and many jewels. The bridegroom was the young prince from Arabia, and they sat together at the upper end of the table between her mother and her grandfather. But Helga was not looking at the bridegroom's handsome face round which his black beard curled, nor did she look into his fiery dark eyes which were fixed upon hers. She was gazing up at a brilliant twinkling star which was beaming in the heavens.

Just then there was a rustle of great wings in the air outside. The storks had come back. And the old couple, tired as they were and needing rest, flew straight down to the railing of the veranda. They knew nothing about the festivities. They had heard on the frontiers of the country that little Helga had had them painted on the wall, for they belonged to the story of her life.

"It was prettily done of her," said father stork.

"It is little enough," said mother stork. "She could hardly do less."

When Helga saw them she rose from the table and went out on to the veranda to stroke their wings. The old storks bowed their heads and the very youngest ones looked on and felt honored. And Helga looked up at the shining star, which seemed to grow brighter and purer. Between herself and the star floated a form purer even than the air, and therefore visible to her. It floated quite close to her and she saw that it was the martyred priest. He also had come to her great festival—come even from the heavenly kingdom.

"The glory and bliss yonder far outshine these earthly splendors," he said.

Little Helga prayed, more earnestly and meekly than she had ever done before, that for one single moment she might gaze into the kingdom of Heaven. Then she felt herself lifted up above the earth in a stream of sweet sounds and thoughts. The unearthly music was not only around her—it was within her. No words can express it.

"Now we must return," said the martyr, "or you will be missed."

"Only one glance more," she pleaded. "Only one short moment more."

"We must return to earth. The guests are departing."

"Only one look—the last!"

Little Helga stood once again on the veranda, but all the torches outside were extinguished and the lights in the banqueting hall were out too. The storks were gone. No guests were to be seen, and no bridegroom. All had vanished in those three short minutes.

A great fear seized upon Helga. She walked through the great empty hall into the next chamber where strange warriors were sleeping. She opened a side door which led into her own room, but she found herself in a garden which had never been there before. Red gleams were in the sky, for dawn was approaching. Only three minutes in Heaven, and a whole night on earth had passed away.

Then she saw the storks. She called to them in her own language. Father stork turned his head, listened, and came up to her. "You speak our language," he said. "What do you want? Why do you come here, you strange woman?"

"It is I! It is Helga. Don't you know me? We were talking to each other in the veranda three minutes ago."

"That is a mistake," said the stork. "You must have dreamt it."

"No, no!" she said and reminded him of the Viking's stronghold, of the Wild Bog, and of their journey together.

Father stork blinked his eyes and said, "Why, that is a very old story. I believe it happened in the time of my great-great-grandmother. Yes, there certainly was a princess in Egypt who came from the Danish land, but she disappeared on her wedding night many hundreds of years ago. You may read all about it here, on the monument in the garden. There are both storks and swans carved on it, and you are at the top yourself, all in white marble."

And so it was. Helga understood all about it now and sank upon her knees.

The sun burst forth, and, as in former times, the frog's skin fell away before his beams and revealed the beautiful girl, who now, in the baptism of light, a vision of beauty brighter and purer than the air itself, rose to the Father. The earthly body dropped away in dust. Only a withered lotus flower lay where she had stood.

"Well, that is a new ending to the story," said father stork. "I hadn't expected that, but I like it very well."

"What will the young ones say about it?" asked mother stork.

"Ah, that is a very important matter," said father stork.

The Wild Swans

FAR away, where the swallows take refuge in winter, lived a King who had eleven sons and one daughter, Elise. The eleven brothers—they were all princes—used to go to school with stars on their breasts and swords at their sides. They wrote upon golden slates with diamond pencils, and could read just as well without a book as with one, so there was no mistake about their being real princes. Their sister Elise sat upon a little footstool of looking glass, and she had a picture book which had cost the half of a kingdom. Oh, these children were very happy, but it was not to last thus forever.

Their father, who was King over all the land, married a wicked Queen who was not at all kind to the poor children. They found that out on the first day. All was festive at the castle, but when the children wanted to play at having company, instead of letting them have all the cakes and baked apples they wanted, she would only let them have some sand in a teacup, and said they must make-believe.

In the following week she sent little Elise into the country to board with some peasants, and it did not take her long to make the King believe so many bad things about the boys that he cared no more about them.

"Fly out into the world and look after yourselves," said the wicked Queen. "You shall fly about like birds without voices."

But she could not make things as bad for them as she would have liked: they turned into eleven beautiful wild swans. They flew out of the palace window with a weird scream, right across the park and the woods.

It was very early in the morning when they came to the place where their sister Elise was sleeping in the peasant's house. They hovered over the roof of the house, turning and twisting their long necks and flapping their wings, but no one either heard or saw them. They had to fly away again, and they soared up towards the clouds, far out into the wide world, and they settled in a big dark wood which stretched down to the shore.

Poor little Elise stood in the peasant's room playing with a green leaf, for she had no other toys. She made a little hole in it which she looked through at the sun, and it seemed to her as if she saw her brothers' bright eyes. Every time the warm sunbeams shone upon her cheek it reminded her of their kisses.

One day passed just like another. When the wind whistled through the rose hedges outside the house, it whispered to the roses, "Who can be prettier than you are?" But the roses shook their heads and answered, "Elise." And when the old woman sat in the doorway reading her psalms, the wind turned over the leaves and said to the book, "Who can be more pious than you?" "Elise," answered the book. Both the roses and the book of psalms spoke only the truth.

She was to go home when she was fifteen, but when the Queen saw how pretty she was, she got very angry and her heart was filled with hatred. She would willingly have turned her into a wild swan like her brothers, but she did not dare to do it at once, because the King wanted to see his daughter.

The Queen always went to the bath in the early morning. It was built of marble and adorned with soft cushions and beautiful carpets.

She took three toads, kissed them, and said to the first,

"Sit upon Elise's head when she comes to the bath, so that she may become sluggish like yourself. Sit upon her forehead," she said to the second, "that she may become ugly like you, and then her father won't know her. Rest upon her heart," she whispered to the third. "Let an evil spirit come over her which may be a burden to her."

Then she put the toads into the clean water and a green tinge immediately came over it. She called Elise, undressed her, and made her go into the bath. When she ducked under the water, one of the toads got among her hair, the other got onto her forehead, and the third onto her bosom. But when she stood up, three scarlet poppies floated on the water! Had the creatures not been poisonous, and been kissed by the sorceress, they would have been changed into crimson roses. Yet they became flowers from merely having rested a moment on her head and her heart. She was far too good and innocent for the sorcery to have any power over her.

When the wicked Queen saw this, she rubbed her over with walnut juice and smeared her face with some evil-smelling salve. She also matted up her beautiful hair. It would have been impossible to recognize pretty Elise. When her father saw her, he was quite horrified and said that she could not be his daughter. Nobody would have anything to say to her, except the yard dog and the swallows, but they were poor dumb animals whose opinion went for nothing.

Poor Elise wept and thought of her eleven brothers who were all lost. She crept sadly out of the palace and wandered about all day, over meadows and marshes and into a big forest. She did not know in the least where she wanted to go, but she felt very sad and longed for her brothers, who, no doubt, like herself had been driven out of the palace.

She made up her mind to go and look for them, but she had only been in the wood for a short time when night fell. She had quite lost her way, so she lay down upon the soft moss, said her evening prayer, and rested her head on a little hillock. It was very still and the air was mild. Hundreds of glowworms shone around her on the grass and in the marsh like green fire. When she gently moved one of the branches over her head, the little shining insects fell over her like a shower of stars.

She dreamt about her brothers all night long. Again they were children playing together. They wrote upon the golden slates with their diamond pencils, and she looked at the picture book which had cost half a kingdom. But they no longer wrote strokes and noughts upon their slates as they used to do. No, they wrote down all their boldest exploits and everything that they had seen and experienced. Everything in the picture book was alive. The birds sang, and the people walked out of the book and spoke to Elise and her brothers. When she turned over a page they skipped back into their places again, so that there should be no confusion among the pictures.

When she woke the sun was already high. It is true she could not see it very well through the thick branches of the lofty forest trees, but the sunbeams cast a golden shimmer around beyond the forest. There was a fresh delicious scent of grass and herbs in the air, and the birds were almost ready to perch upon her shoulders. She could hear the splashing of water, for there were many springs around, which all flowed into a pond with a lovely sandy bottom. It was surrounded with thick bushes but there was one place which the stags had trampled down, and Elise passed through the opening to the waterside. It was so transparent that, had not the branches been moved by the breeze, she must have thought that they were painted on the bottom—so plainly was every leaf reflected, both those on which the sun played and those which were in shade.

When she saw her own face, she was quite frightened to see it so brown and ugly. But when she wet her little hand

and rubbed her eyes and forehead, her white skin shone through again. Then she took off all her clothes and went into the fresh water. A more beautiful royal child than she could not be found in all the world.

When she had put on her clothes again and plaited her long hair, she went to a sparkling spring and drank some of the water out of the hollow of her hand. Then she wandered farther into the wood, though she had not the least idea where she was going. She thought of her brothers, and she thought of a merciful God who would not forsake her. He lets the wild crab apples grow to feed the hungry, and He showed her a tree the branches of which were bending beneath their weight of fruit. Here she made her midday meal. Then, having put props under the branches, she walked on into the thickest part of the forest. It was so quiet that she heard her own footsteps. She heard every little withered leaf which bent under her feet. Not a bird was to be seen. Not a ray of sunlight pierced the leafy branches, and the tall trunks were so close together that when she looked before her it seemed as if a thick fence of heavy beams hemmed her in on every side. The solitude was such as she had never known before.

It was a very dark night. Not a single glowworm sparkled in the marsh. Sadly she lay down to sleep, and it seemed to her as if the branches above her parted asunder, and that the Saviour looked down upon her with His loving eyes and that little angels' heads peeped out above His head and under His arms.

When she woke in the morning, she was not sure if she had dreamt this or whether it was really true.

She walked a little farther when she met an old woman with a basket full of berries, of which she gave her some. Elise asked if she had seen eleven princes ride through the wood.

"No," said the old woman. "But yesterday I saw eleven

swans with golden crowns upon their heads, swimming in the stream close by there."

She led Elise a little farther to a slope, at the foot of which the stream meandered. The trees on either bank stretched out their rich leafy branches towards each other. And where their natural growth did not let them reach each other, they had torn their roots out of the ground and leaned over the water in order to interlace their branches.

Elise said good-by to the old woman and walked along by the river till it flowed out into the great open sea.

The beautiful open sea lay before the maiden, but not a sail was to be seen on it, nor a single boat. How was she ever to get any farther? She looked at the numberless little pebbles on the beach. They were all worn quite round by the water. Glass, iron, stone—whatever was washed up— had taken their shapes from the water, which yet was much softer than her little hand.

"With all its rolling, it is untiring, and everything hard is smoothed down," she said. "I will be just as untiring. Thank you for your lessons, you clear rolling waves! Sometime, so my heart tells me, you will bear me to my beloved brothers."

Eleven white swans' feathers were lying on the seaweed. She picked them up and made a bunch of them. There were still drops of water on them, but whether these were dew or tears no one could tell. It was very lonely there by the shore, but she did not feel it, for the sea was everchanging. There were more changes on it in the course of a few hours than could be seen on an inland fresh-water lake in a year. If a big black cloud arose, it was just as if the sea wanted to say, "I can look black too." And then the wind blew up and the waves showed their white crests. But if the clouds were red and the wind dropped, the sea looked like a rose leaf, now white, now green. But however still it was, there was always a little gentle motion just by the shore. The water rose and fell softly like the bosom of a sleeping child.

When the sun was about to go down, Elise saw eleven wild swans with golden crowns upon their heads flying towards the shore. They flew in a swaying line one behind the other, like a white ribbon streamer. Elise climbed up onto the bank and hid behind a bush. The swans settled close by her and flapped their great white wings.

As soon as the sun had sunk beneath the water the swans shed their feathers and became eleven handsome princes. They were Elise's brothers. Although they had altered a good deal, she knew them at once. She felt that they must be her brothers and she sprang into their arms, calling them by name. They were delighted when they recognized their little sister who had grown so big and beautiful. They laughed and cried and told each other how wickedly their stepmother had treated them all.

"We brothers," said the eldest, "have to fly about in the guise of swans as long as the sun is above the horizon. When it goes down we regain our human shapes. So we always have to look out for a resting place near sunset, for should we happen to be flying up among the clouds when the sun goes down, we should be hurled to the depths below. We do not live here. There is another land just as beautiful as this, beyond the sea, but the way to it is very long and we have to cross the mighty ocean to get to it. There is not a single island on the way where we can spend the night. Only one solitary little rock rises just above the water midway. It is only just big enough for us to stand upon close together, and if there is a heavy sea the water splashes over us. Yet we thank our God for it. We stay there overnight in our human forms, and without it we could never revisit our beloved fatherland, for our flight takes two of the longest days in the year. We are permitted to visit the home of our fathers only once a year, and we dare stay for only eleven days. We hover over this big forest from whence we catch a glimpse of the palace where we were born, and where our father lives. Beyond it we can see the high church towers where our mother is buried. We fancy that the trees and bushes here are related to us, and the wild horses gallop over the moors as we used to see them in our childhood. The charcoal burners still sing the old songs we used to dance to when we were children. This is our fatherland. We are drawn towards it and here we have found you again, dear little sister. We may stay here two days longer, and then we must fly away again across the ocean, to a lovely country indeed, but it is not our own dear fatherland. How shall we ever take you with us? We have neither ship nor boat."

"How can I deliver you?" said their sister, and they went on talking to each other nearly all night. They only dozed for a few hours.

Elise was awakened in the morning by the rustling of the swans' wings above her. Her brothers were again transformed and were wheeling round in great circles, till she lost sight of them in the distance. One of them, the youngest, stayed behind. He laid his head against her bosom and she caressed it with her fingers. They remained together all day. Towards evening the others came back, and as soon as the sun went down they took their natural forms.

"Tomorrow we must fly away and we dare not come back for a whole year, but we can't leave you like this. Have you courage to go with us? My wings are strong enough to carry you over the forest, so our united strength ought to be sufficient to bear you across the ocean."

"Oh yes! Take me with you," said Elise.

They spent the whole night in weaving a kind of net of the elastic bark of the willow, bound together with tough rushes. They made it both large and strong. Elise lay down upon it, and when the sun rose and the brothers became swans again, they took up the net in their bills and flew high up among the clouds with their precious sister, who was fast asleep. As the sunbeams fell straight onto her face, one of the swans flew over her head so that his broad wings should shade her.

They were far from land when Elise woke. She thought she must still be dreaming—it seemed so strange to be carried through the air so high up above the sea. By her side lay a branch of beautiful ripe berries and a bundle of savory roots, which her youngest brother had collected for her and for which she gave him a grateful smile. She knew it was he who flew above her head, shading her from the sun. They were so high up that the first ship they saw looked like a gull floating on the water. A great cloud came up behind them like a mountain, and Elise saw the shadow of herself on it, and those of the eleven swans looking like giants. It was a more beautiful picture than any she had ever seen before, but as the sun rose higher, the cloud fell behind and the shadow picture disappeared.

They flew on and on all day like arrows whizzing through the air, but they went slower than usual for now they had their sister to carry. A storm came up, and night was drawing on. With terror in her heart Elise saw the sun sinking, for the solitary rock was nowhere to be seen. The swans seemed to be taking stronger strokes than ever. Alas, she was the cause of their not being able to get on faster. As soon as the sun went down they would become men, and they would be hurled into the sea and drowned. She prayed to God from the bottom of her heart, but still no rock was to be seen. Black clouds gathered and strong gusts of wind announced a storm. The clouds looked like a great threatening leaden wave, and the flashes of lightning followed each other rapidly.

The sun was now at the edge of the sea. Elise's heart quaked, when suddenly the swans shot downwards so suddenly that she thought they were falling. Then they hovered again. Half of the sun was below the horizon, and there for the first time she saw the little rock below, which did not look bigger than the head of a seal above the water. The sun sank very quickly. It was no bigger than a star, but her foot touched solid earth. The sun went out like the last sparks of a bit of burning paper. Her brothers stood arm in arm around her, but there was only just room enough for them. The waves beat upon the rock and washed over them like drenching rain. The heaven shone with continuous fire and the thunder rolled, peal upon peal. But the sister and brothers held each other's hands and sang a psalm which gave them comfort and courage.

The air was pure and still at dawn. As soon as the sun rose, the swans flew off with Elise away from the islet. The sea still ran high. It looked from where they were as if the white foam on the dark green water were millions of swans floating on the waves.

When the sun rose higher, Elise saw before her, half floating in the air, great masses of ice with shining glaciers on the heights. Midway was perched a palace, a mile in length, with one bold colonnade built above another. Below swayed palm trees and gorgeous blossoms as big as mill wheels. She asked if this was the land to which she was going, but the swans shook their heads because what she saw was a mirage. It was the beautiful and ever-changing palace of Fata Morgana. No mortal dared enter it. Elise gazed at it, but as she gazed the palace, gardens, and mountains melted away. And in their place stood twenty proud churches with their high towers and pointed windows. She seemed to hear the notes of the organ, but it was the sea she heard. When she got close to the seeming churches, they changed to a great navy sailing beneath her, but it was only a sea mist floating over the waters.

Yes, she saw constant changes passing before her eyes, but now she saw the real land she was bound to. Beautiful blue mountains rose before her with their cedar woods and palaces. Long before the sun went down, she sat among the hills in front of a big cave covered with delicate green creepers. It looked like a piece of embroidery.

"Now we shall see what you will dream here tonight," said the youngest brother, as he showed her where she was to sleep.

"If only I might dream how I could deliver you!" she said, and this thought filled her mind entirely. She prayed earnestly to God for His help, and even in her sleep she continued her prayer. It seemed to her that she was flying up to Fata Morgana in her castle in the air. The fairy came towards her. She was charming and brilliant, and yet she was very like the old woman who gave her the berries in the wood and told her about the swans with the golden crowns.

"Your brothers can be delivered," she said. "But have you courage and endurance enough for it? The sea is indeed softer than your hands, and it molds the hardest stones, but it does not feel the pain your fingers will feel. It has no heart and does not suffer the pain and anguish you must feel. Do you see the stinging nettle I hold in my hand? Many of this kind grow round the cave where you sleep. Only these and the ones which grow in the churchyards may be used. Mark that! Those you may pluck, although they will burn and blister your hands. Crush the nettles with your feet and you will have flax, and of this you must weave eleven coats of mail with long sleeves. Throw these over the eleven wild swans and the charm is broken. But remember, from the moment you begin this work till it is finished, even if it takes years, you must not utter a word.

The first word you say will fall like a murderer's dagger into the hearts of your brothers. Their lives hang on your tongue. Mark this well."

She touched her hand at the same moment. The touch was like burning fire and it woke Elise. It was bright daylight, and close to where she slept lay a nettle like those in her dream. She fell upon her knees with thanks to God and left the cave to begin her work.

She seized the horrid nettles with her delicate hands, and they burnt like fire. Great blisters rose on her hands and arms, but she suffered it willingly if only it would deliver her beloved brothers. She crushed every nettle with her bare feet and twisted it into green flax.

When the sun went down and the brothers came back, they were alarmed at finding her mute. They thought it was some new witchcraft exercised by their wicked stepmother. But when they saw her hands, they understood that it was for their sakes. The youngest brother wept, and wherever his tears fell she felt no more pain and the blisters disappeared.

She spent the whole night at her work, for she could not rest till she had delivered her dear brothers. All the following day, while her brothers were away, she sat solitary, but never had the time flown so fast. One coat of mail was finished and she began the next. Then a hunting horn sounded among the mountains. She was frightened. The sound came nearer and she heard dogs barking. In terror she rushed into the cave and tied the nettles she had collected and woven into a bundle upon which she sat.

At this moment a big dog bounded forward from the thicket, and another and another. They barked loudly and ran backwards and forwards. In a few minutes all the huntsmen were standing outside the cave. The handsomest of them was the King of the country, and he stepped up to Elise. Never had he seen so lovely a girl.

"How came you here, beautiful child?" he said.

Elise shook her head. She dared not speak. The salvation and the lives of her brothers depended upon her silence. She hid her hands under her apron so that the King should not see what she suffered.

"Come with me," he said. "You cannot stay here. If you are as good as you are beautiful, I will dress you in silks and velvets, put a golden crown upon your head, and you shall live with me and have your home in my richest palace." Then he lifted her upon his horse. She wept and wrung her hands, but the King said, "I think only of your happiness. You will thank me one day for what I am doing." Then he darted off across the mountains, holding her before him on his horse, and the huntsmen followed.

When the sun went down, the royal city with churches and cupolas lay before them, and the King led her into the palace. Here great fountains played in the marble halls and the walls and ceilings were adorned with paintings, but she had no eyes for them. She only wept and sorrowed. Passively she allowed the women to dress her in royal robes, to twist pearls into her hair, and to draw gloves onto her blistered hands.

She was dazzlingly lovely as she stood there in all her magnificence. The courtiers bent low before her and the King wooed her as his bride, although the archbishop shook his head and whispered that he feared the beautiful wood maiden was a witch, who had dazzled their eyes and infatuated the King.

The King refused to listen to him. He ordered the music to play, the richest food to be brought, and the loveliest girls to dance before her. She was led through scented gardens into gorgeous apartments, but nothing brought a smile to her lips or into her eyes. Sorrow sat there like a heritage and a possession for all time. Last of all, the King opened the door of a little chamber close by the room where she was to sleep. It was adorned with costly green carpets and made exactly to resemble the cave where he found her. On the floor lay the bundle of flax she had spun from the nettles, and from the ceiling hung the shirt of mail which was already finished. One of the huntsmen had brought all these things away as curiosities.

"Here you may dream that you are back in your former home," said the King. "Here is the work upon which you were engaged. In the midst of your splendor it may amuse you to think of those times."

When Elise saw all these things so dear to her heart, a smile for the first time played upon her lips and the blood rushed back to her cheeks. She thought of the deliverance of her brothers and she kissed the King's hand. He pressed her to his heart and ordered all the church bells to ring marriage peals. The lovely dumb girl from the woods was to be Queen of the country.

The archbishop whispered evil words into the ear of the King, but they did not reach his heart. The wedding was to take place and the archbishop himself had to put the crown upon her head. In his anger he pressed the golden circlet so tightly upon her head that it gave her pain. But a heavier circlet pressed upon her heart, her grief for her brothers, so she thought nothing of the bodily pain. Her lips were sealed. A single word from her mouth would cost her brothers their lives, but her eyes were full of love for the good and handsome King, who did everything he could to please her.

Every day she grew more and more attached to him. She longed to confide in him and tell him her sufferings, but dumb she must remain and in silence must bring her labor to completion. Therefore at night she stole away from his side into her secret chamber, which was decorated like a cave, and here she knitted one shirt after another. When she came to the seventh, all her flax was worked up. She knew that these nettles which she was to use grew in the churchyard, but she had to pluck them herself. How was she to get there?

"Oh, what is the pain of my fingers compared with the anguish of my heart?" she thought. "I must venture out. The good God will not desert me."

With as much terror in her heart as if she were doing some evil deed, she stole down one night into the moonlit garden and through the long alleys out into the silent streets to the churchyard. It was very dark and lonely, but she picked the stinging nettles and hurried back to the palace with them. Only one person saw her but that was the archbishop, who watched while others slept. Surely now all his bad opinions of the Queen were justified. All was not as it should be with her. She must be a witch, and therefore she had bewitched the King and all the people.

He told the King in the confessional what he had seen and what he feared. When those bad words passed his lips, the pictures of the saints shook their heads as if to say, "It is not so. Elise is innocent." The archbishop, however, took it differently. He thought they were bearing witness against her and shaking their heads at her sin.

Two big tears rolled down the King's cheeks, and he went home with doubt in his heart. He pretended to sleep at night, but no quiet sleep came to his eyes. He perceived how Elise got up and went to her private closet. Day by day his face grew darker. Elise saw it but could not imagine what was the cause of it. It alarmed her, and what was she not already suffering in her heart because of her brothers? Her salt tears ran down upon the royal purple velvet and lay there like sparkling diamonds, and all who saw their splendor wished to be Queen.

She had, however, almost reached the end of her labors. Only one shirt of mail was wanting, but again she had no more flax and not a single nettle was left. Once more, for the last time, she must go to the churchyard to pluck a few handfuls. She thought with dread of the solitary walk and the darkness, but her will was as strong as her trust in God.

Elise went, but the King and the archbishop followed her. They saw her disappear within the grated gateway of the churchyard. The King was very sorrowful, because he thought she must surely be a witch.

"The people must judge her," he groaned. And the people judged: "Let her be consumed in the glowing flames."

She was led from her beautiful royal apartments to a dark damp dungeon, where the wind whistled through the grated window. Instead of velvet and silk they gave her the bundle of nettles she had gathered to lay her head upon. The hard burning shirts of mail were to be her covering, but they could have given her nothing more precious.

She set to work again with many prayers to God. Outside her prison the street boys sang derisive songs about her, and not a soul comforted her with a kind word.

Towards evening she heard the rustle of swans' wings close to her window. It was her youngest brother, who at last had found her. He sobbed aloud with joy although he knew that the coming night might be her last. But then her work was almost done and her brothers were there.

The archbishop came to stay with her during her last hours, as he had promised the King. She shook her head at him and by looks and gestures begged him to leave her. She had only this night in which to finish her work, or else all would be wasted—all her pain, her tears and her sleepless nights. The archbishop went away with bitter words against her, but poor Elise knew that she was innocent, and she went on with her work.

The little mice ran about the floor, bringing nettles to her feet so as to give what help they could, and a thrush sat on the grating of the window, where he sang all night as merrily as he could to keep up her courage.

It was still only dawn and the sun would not rise for an hour, when the eleven brothers stood at the gate of the palace, begging to be taken to the King. This could not be done, they were told, for it was still night. The King was asleep and no one dared wake him. All their entreaties and threats were useless. The watch turned out and even the King himself came to see what was the matter. But just then the sun rose, and no more brothers were to be seen— only eleven wild swans hovering over the palace.

The whole populace streamed out of the town gates. They were all anxious to see the witch burnt. A miserable horse drew the cart in which Elise was seated. They had put upon her a smock of green sacking, and all her beautiful long hair hung loose from the lovely head. Her cheeks were deathly pale and her lips moved softly, while her fingers unceasingly twisted the green yarn. Even on the way to her death she could not abandon her unfinished work. Ten shirts lay completed at her feet. She labored away at the eleventh amid the scoffing insults of the populace.

"Look at the witch! How she mutters! She has no book of psalms in her hands. There she sits with her loathsome sorcery. Tear it away from her and into a thousand bits!"

The crowd pressed around her to destroy her work, but just then eleven wild swans flew down and perched upon the cart, flapping their wings. The crowd gave way before them in terror.

"It is a sign from Heaven! She is innocent," they whispered. But they dared not say it aloud.

The executioner seized her by the hand but she hastily threw the eleven shirts over the swans, who were immediately transformed to eleven handsome princes. But the youngest had a swan's wing in place of an arm, for one sleeve was wanting to his shirt of mail. She had not been able to finish it.

"Now I may speak! I am innocent."

The populace who saw what had happened bowed down before her as if she had been a saint, but she sank lifeless in her brother's arms. So great had been the strain, the terror, and the suffering she had endured.

"Yes, innocent she is indeed," said the eldest brother, and he told them all that had happened.

Whilst he spoke a wonderful fragrance spread around, as of millions of roses. Every faggot in the pile had taken root and shot out branches, and a great high hedge of red roses had arisen. At the very top was one pure white blossom. It shone like a star, and the King broke it off and laid it on Elise's bosom, and she woke with joy and peace in her heart.

All the church bells began to ring of their own accord, and the singing birds flocked around them. Surely such a bridal procession went back to the palace as no king had ever seen before!

Great Claus and Little Claus

IN a village there once lived two men of the selfsame name. They were both called Claus, but one of them had four horses and the other had only one. So to distinguish them, people called the owner of the four horses "Great Claus," and he who had only one horse was called "Little Claus." Now I shall tell you what happened to them, for this is a true story.

Throughout the week Little Claus was obliged to plow for Great Claus and to lend him his one horse, but once a week—on Sunday—Great Claus lent him all his four horses. How proudly each Sunday Little Claus would smack his whip over all five, for they were as good as his own on that one day.

The sun shone brightly and the church bells rang merrily as the people passed by, dressed in their best and with their prayer books under their arms. They were going to hear the parson preach. They looked at Little Claus plowing with his five horses, and he was so proud that he smacked his whip and said, "Gee-up, my five horses."

"You mustn't say that," said Great Claus, "for only one of them is yours."

But Little Claus soon forgot what he ought not to say, and when anyone passed he would call out, "Gee-up, my five horses."

"I must really beg you not to say that again," said Great Claus. "If you do, I shall hit your horse on the head so that he will drop down dead on the spot. And that will be the end of him."

"I promise you I will not say it again," said the other. But as soon as anybody came by nodding to him and wishing him "Good day," he was so pleased and thought how grand it was to have five horses plowing in his field that he cried out again, "Gee-up, all my horses!"

"I'll gee-up your horses for you," said Great Claus. And seizing the tethering mallet he struck Little Claus's one horse on the head, and it fell down dead.

"Oh, now I have no horse at all," said Little Claus, weeping. But after a while he flayed the dead horse and hung the skin in the wind to dry.

Then he put the dried skin into a bag, hung it over his shoulder, and went off to the next town to sell it. But he had a long way to go and had to pass through a dark and gloomy forest.

Presently a storm arose and he lost his way. And before he discovered the right path, evening was drawing on, and it was still a long way to the town and too far to return home before nightfall.

Near the road stood a large farmhouse. The shutters outside the windows were closed, but lights shone through the crevices and at the top. "They might let me stay here for the night," thought Little Claus, so he went up to the door and knocked.

The farmer's wife opened the door, but when she heard what he wanted she told him to go away. Her husband was not at home and she could not let any strangers in.

"Then I shall have to lie out here," said Little Claus to himself, as the farmer's wife shut the door in his face.

Close to the farmhouse stood a large haystack, and between it and the house there was a small shed with a thatched roof. "I can lie up there," said Little Claus, as he saw the roof. "It will make a famous bed, but I hope the stork won't fly down and bite my legs." A live stork who had his nest on the roof was standing up there.

So Little Claus climbed on to the roof of the shed. And as he turned about to make himself comfortable, he discovered that the wooden shutters did not reach to the top of the windows. He could see into the room, in which a large table was laid out with wine, roast meat, and a splendid fish. The farmer's wife and the sexton were sitting at table together. Nobody else was there. She was filling his glass and helping him plentifully to fish, which appeared to be his favorite dish.

"If only I could have some too," thought Little Claus. Then he stretched out his neck towards the window and spied a beautiful large cake. Indeed, they had a glorious feast before them.

At that moment he heard someone riding down the road towards the farm. It was the farmer coming home.

He was a good man but he had one very strange prejudice—he could not bear the sight of a sexton. If he happened to see one, he would get into a terrible rage. Because of this dislike, the sexton had gone to visit the farmer's wife during her husband's absence from home, and the good woman had put before him the best of everything she had in the house to eat.

When they heard the farmer they were dreadfully frightened, and the woman made the sexton creep into a large chest which stood in a corner. He went at once, for he was well aware of the poor man's aversion to the sight of a sexton. The woman then quickly hid all the nice things and the wine in the oven, because if her husband had seen it he would have asked why it was provided.

"Oh dear," sighed Little Claus, on the roof, when he saw the food disappearing.

"Is there anyone up there?" asked the farmer, peering up at Little Claus. "What are you doing up there? You had better come into the house."

Then Little Claus told him how he had lost his way, and asked if he might have shelter for the night.

"Certainly," said the farmer. "But the first thing is to have something to eat."

The woman received them both very kindly, laid the table, and gave them a large bowl of porridge. The farmer was hungry and ate it with a good appetite, but Little Claus could not help thinking of the good roast meat, the fish, and the cake, which he knew were hidden in the oven. He had put his sack with the hide in it under the table by his feet, for as we remember he was on his way to the town to sell it. He did not fancy the porridge, so he trod on the sack and made the dried hide squeak quite loudly.

"Hush!" said Little Claus to his sack, at the same time treading on it again so that it squeaked louder than ever.

"What on earth have you got in your sack?" asked the farmer.

"Oh, it's a goblin," said Little Claus. "He says we needn't eat the porridge, for he has charmed the oven full of roast meat and fish and cake."

"What do you say?" said the farmer, opening the oven door with all speed and seeing the nice things the woman had hidden, but which her husband thought the goblin had produced for their special benefit.

The woman dared not say anything but put the food before them, and then they both made a hearty meal of the fish, the meat, and the cake. Then Little Claus trod on the skin and made it squeak again.

"What does he say now?" asked the farmer.

"He says," answered Little Claus, "that he has also charmed three bottles of wine into the oven for us."

So the woman had to bring out the wine too, and the

farmer drank it and became very merry. Wouldn't he like to have a goblin for himself, like the one in Little Claus's sack!

"Can he charm out the devil?" asked the farmer. "I shouldn't mind seeing him, now that I am in such a merry mood."

"Oh yes!" said Little Claus. "My goblin can do everything that we ask him. Can't you?" he asked, trampling on the sack till it squeaked louder than ever. "Did you hear him say yes? But the devil is so ugly, you'd better not see him."

"Oh I'm not a bit frightened. Whatever does he look like?"

"Well, he will show himself in the image of a sexton."

"Oh dear!" said the farmer. "That's bad! I must tell you that I can't bear to see a sexton. However, it doesn't matter. I shall know it's only the devil and then I shan't mind so much. Now my courage is up! But he mustn't come too close."

"I'll ask my goblin about it," said Little Claus, treading on the bag and putting his ear close to it.

"What does he say?"

"He says you can go along and open the chest in the corner, and there you'll see the devil moping in the dark. But hold the lid tight so that he doesn't get out."

"Will you help me to hold it?" asked the farmer, going along to the chest where the woman had hidden the real sexton, who was shivering with fright. The farmer lifted up the lid a wee little bit and peeped in.

"Ha!" he shrieked, and sprang back. "Yes, I saw him and he looked just exactly like our sexton. It was a horrible sight!" They had to have a drink after this, and there they sat drinking till far into the night.

"You must sell me that goblin," said the farmer. "You may ask what you like for him! I'll give you a bushel of money for him."

"No, I can't do that," said Little Claus. "You must remember how useful my goblin is to me."

"Oh, but I should so like to have him," said the farmer and he went on begging for him.

"Well," said Little Claus at last, "as you have been so kind to me I shall have to give him up. You shall have him for a bushel of money, but I must have it full to the brim."

"You shall have it," said the farmer. "But you must take that chest away with you! I won't have it in the house for another hour. I'd never know whether he's there or not."

So Little Claus gave his sack with the dried hide in it to the farmer and received in return a bushel of money, and the measure was full to the brim. The farmer also gave him a large wheelbarrow to take the money and the chest away in.

"Good-by," said Little Claus, and off he went with his money and the big chest with the sexton in it.

There was a wide and deep river on the other side of the wood. The current was so strong that it was almost impossible to swim against it. A large new bridge had been built across it, and when they got into the very middle of it, Little Claus said quite loud, so that the sexton could hear him, "What am I to do with this stupid old chest? It might be full of paving stones—it's so heavy. I am quite tired of wheeling it along, so I'll just throw it into the river. If it floats down the river to my house, well and good; and if it doesn't, I shan't care."

Then he took hold of the chest and raised it up a bit, as if he were about to throw it into the river.

"No, no! Let it be!" shouted the sexton. "Let me get out!"

"Hullo!" said Little Claus, pretending to be frightened. "Why, he's still inside it! Then I must heave it into the river to drown him."

"Oh no! Oh no!" shouted the sexton. "I'll give you a bushel full of money if you'll let me out!"

"Oh, that's another matter," said Little Claus, opening the chest. The sexton crept out at once and pushed the empty chest into the water, and then went home and gave Little Claus a whole bushel full of money. He had already had one from the farmer, you know, so now his wheelbarrow was quite full of money.

"I got a pretty fair price for that horse, I must admit," said he to himself when he got home to his own room and turned the money out of the wheelbarrow into a heap on the floor. "What a rage Great Claus will be in when he discovers how rich I have become through my one horse. But I won't tell him the truth about it." So he sent a boy to Great Claus to borrow a bushel measure.

"What does he want that for?" thought Great Claus. And he rubbed some tallow on the bottom of the measure, so that a little of whatever was to be measured might stick to it. So it did, for when the measure came back three new silver threepenny bits were sticking to it.

"What's this?" said Great Claus, and he ran straight along to Little Claus. "Where on earth did you get all that money?"

"Oh, that was for my horse's hide which I sold last night."

"That was well paid, indeed!" said Great Claus. And he ran home, took an ax, and hit all his four horses on the head. He then flayed them and went off to the town with the hides.

"Skins! Skins! Who will buy skins?" he shouted up and down the streets.

All the shoemakers and tanners in the town came running up and asked him how much he wanted for them.

"A bushel of money for each," said Great Claus.

"Are you mad?" they all said. "Do you imagine we have money by the bushel?"

"Skins! Skins! Who will buy skins?" he shouted again.

The shoemakers took up their measures and the tanners their leather aprons, and beat Great Claus through the town. "Skins! Skins!" they mocked him. "Yes, we'll give you a raw hide. Out of the town with him!" they shouted, and Great Claus had to hurry off as fast as ever he could go. He had never had such a beating in his life.

"Little Claus shall pay for this," he said when he got home. "I'll kill him for it."

Little Claus's old grandmother had just died in his house. She certainly had been very cross and unkind to him, but now that she was dead he felt quite sorry about it. He took the dead woman and put her into his warm bed to see if he could bring her to life again. He meant her to stay there all night, and he would sit on a chair in the corner. He had slept like that before.

As he sat there in the night, the door opened and in came Great Claus with his ax. He knew where Little Claus's bed stood, and he went straight up to it and hit the dead grandmother a blow on the forehead, thinking that it was Little Claus.

"Just see if you'll cheat me again after that," he said. Then he went home again.

"What a bad, wicked man he is," said Little Claus. "He was going to kill me there. What a good thing that poor old granny was dead already, or else he would have killed her."

He now dressed his old grandmother in her best Sunday clothes, borrowed a horse from his neighbor, harnessed it to a cart, and set his grandmother on the back seat so that she could not fall out when the cart moved. Then he started off through the wood. When the sun rose he was just outside a big inn, and Little Claus drew up his horse and went in to get something to eat. The landlord was a very, very rich man and a very good man, but he was fiery-tempered, as if he were made of pepper and tobacco.

"Good morning," said he to Little Claus. "You've got your best clothes on very early this morning!"

"Yes," said Little Claus. "I'm going to town with my old grandmother. She's sitting out there in the cart. I can't get her to come in. Won't you take her out a glass of mead? You'll have to shout at her, for she's very hard of hearing."

"Yes, she shall have it," said the innkeeper, and he poured out a large glass of mead which he took out to the dead grandmother in the cart.

"Here is a glass of mead your son has sent," said the innkeeper, but the dead woman sat quite still and never said a word. "Don't you hear?" shouted the innkeeper as loud as he could. "Here is a glass of mead from your son!"

Again he shouted and then again as loud as ever, but as she did not stir he got angry and threw the glass of mead in her face. The mead ran all over her and she fell backwards out of the cart, for she was only stuck up and not tied in.

"Now," shouted Little Claus, as he rushed out of the inn and seized the landlord by the neck. "You have killed my grandmother! Just look! There's a great hole in her forehead."

"Oh, what a misfortune!" exclaimed the innkeeper, clasping his hands. "That's the consequence of my fiery temper. Good Little Claus, I will give you a bushel of money and bury your grandmother as if she had been my own, if you will only say nothing about it. Otherwise they will chop my head off, and that is so nasty."

So Little Claus had a whole bushel of money, and the innkeeper buried the old grandmother just as if she had been his own.

When Little Claus got home again with all his money, he

immediately sent his boy over to Great Claus to borrow his measure.

"What?" said Great Claus, "Is he not dead? I shall have to go and see about it myself." So he took the measure over to Little Claus himself.

"I say, wherever did you get all that money?" asked he, his eyes round with amazement at what he saw.

"It was my grandmother you killed instead of me," said Little Claus. "I have sold her and got a bushel of money for her."

"That was good pay indeed!" said Great Claus, so he hurried home, took an ax, and killed his old grandmother.

He then put her in a cart and drove off to town with her where the apothecary lived, and asked if he would buy a dead body.

"Who is it, and where did the body come from?" asked the apothecary.

"It is my grandmother, and I have killed her for a bushel of money," said Great Claus.

"Heaven preserve us!" said the apothecary. "You are talking like a madman. Pray don't say such things! You might lose your head." And he pointed out to him what a horribly wicked thing he had done and what a bad man he was, and that he deserved to be punished. Great Claus was so frightened that he rushed straight out of the shop, jumped into the cart, whipped up his horse, and galloped home. The apothecary and everyone else thought he was mad, and so they let him drive off.

"You shall be paid for this!" said Great Claus, when he got out on the highroad. "You shall pay for this, Little Claus!"

As soon as he got home, he took the biggest sack he could find, went over to Little Claus and said, "You have deceived me again. First I killed my horses, and then my old grandmother. It's all your fault, but you shan't have the chance of cheating me again!" Then he took Little Claus by the waist and put him into the sack, put it on his back, and shouted to him, "I'm going to drown you now!"

It was a long way to go before he came to the river, and Little Claus was not so light to carry. The road passed close by a church in which the organ was playing, and the people were singing beautifully. Great Claus put down the sack with Little Claus in it close by the church door. He thought he would like to go and hear a psalm before he went any further. As Little Claus could not get out of the bag, and all the people were in the church, Great Claus went in too.

"Oh dear, oh dear!" sighed Little Claus in the sack. He turned and twisted, but it was impossible to undo the cord. Just then an old cattle drover with white hair and a tall stick in his hand came along. He had a whole drove of cows and bulls before him. They ran against the sack Little Claus was in and upset it.

"Oh dear," sighed Little Claus. "I am so young to be going to the Kingdom of Heaven!"

"And I," said the cattle drover, "am so old and cannot get there yet!"

"Open the sack!" shouted Little Claus. "Get in in place of me, and you will get to Heaven directly."

"That will just suit me," said the cattle drover, undoing the sack for Little Claus, who immediately sprang out. "You must look after the cattle now," said the old man as he crept into the sack. Little Claus tied it up and walked off driving the cattle before him.

A little while afterwards Great Claus came out of the church. He took the sack again on his back and he certainly thought it had grown lighter, for the old cattle drover was not more than half the weight of Little Claus.

"How light he seems to have got! That must be because I have been to church and said my prayers." Then he went on to the river, which was both wide and deep, and threw the sack with the old cattle drover in it into the water.

"Now, you won't cheat me again!" he shouted, for he thought it was Little Claus.

Then he went homewards, but when he reached the crossroads he met Little Claus with his herd of cattle.

"What's the meaning of this?" exclaimed Great Claus. "Didn't I drown you?"

"Yes," said Little Claus. "It's just about half an hour since you threw me into the river."

"But where did you get all those splendid beasts?" asked Great Claus.

"They are sea cattle," said Little Claus. "I will tell you the whole story, and indeed I thank you heartily for drowning me. I'm at the top of the tree now and a very rich man, I can tell you. I was so frightened when I was in the sack! The wind whistled in my ears when you threw me over the bridge into the cold water. I immediately sank to the bottom but I was not hurt, for the grass is beautifully soft down there. The sack was opened at once by a beautiful maiden in snow-white clothes with a green wreath on her wet hair. She took my hand and said, 'Are you there, Little Claus? Here are some cattle for you, and a mile farther up the road you will come upon another herd which I will give you too!' Then I saw that the river was a great highway for the sea folk. Down at the bottom of it they walked and drove about, from the sea right up to the end of the river. The flowers were lovely and the grass was so fresh! The fishes which swam about glided close to me just like birds in the air. How nice the people were, and what a lot of cattle strolled about in the ditches!"

"But why did you come straight up here again then?" asked Great Claus. "I shouldn't have done that if it was so fine down there."

Little Claus walked off driving the cattle

"Oh," said Little Claus, "that's just my cunning. You remember I told you the mermaid said that a mile farther up the road—and by the road she means the river, for she can't go anywhere else—I should find another herd of cattle waiting for me. Well, I know how many bends there are in the river and what a roundabout way it would be. It's ever so much shorter if you can come up on dry land and take the short cuts. You save a couple of miles by it and can get the cattle much sooner."

"Oh, you *are* a fortunate man," said Great Claus. "Do you think I should get some sea cattle if I were to go down to the bottom of the river?"

"I'm sure you would," said Little Claus. "But I can't carry you in the sack to the river. You're too heavy for me. If you'd like to walk there and then get into the sack, I'll throw you into the river with the greatest pleasure in the world."

"Thank you," said Great Claus. "But if I don't get any sea cattle when I get down there, see if I don't give you a sound thrashing."

"Oh, don't be so hard on me!" said Little Claus.

Then they walked off to the river. As soon as the cattle saw the water they rushed down to drink, for they were very thirsty. "See what a hurry they're in," said Little Claus. "They want to get down to the bottom again."

"Now, help me first," said Great Claus, "or else I'll thrash you." He then crept into a big sack which had been lying across the back of one of the cows. "Put a big stone in, or I'm afraid I shan't sink," said Great Claus.

"Oh, have no fear of that," said Little Claus, and he put a big stone into the sack and gave it a push. Plump went the sack and Great Claus was in the river, where he sank to the bottom at once.

"I'm afraid he won't find any cattle," said Little Claus, as he drove his herd home.

The Shepherdess and the Sweep

HAVE you ever seen an old wooden cupboard quite black with age, and ornamented with carved foliage and curious figures? Well, just such a cupboard stood in the parlor, and had been left to the family as a legacy by the great-grandmother. It was covered from top to bottom with carved roses and tulips. The most curious scrolls were drawn upon it, and out of them peeped little stags' heads with antlers.

In the middle of the cupboard door was the carved figure of a most ridiculous man. He grinned at you, for no one could call it laughing. He had goat's legs, little horns on his head, and a long beard. The children in the room always called him "Major-general-field-sergeant-commander Billy-goat's-legs." It was certainly a very difficult name to pronounce and there are very few who ever receive such a title, but then it seemed wonderful how he came to be carved at all. Yet there he was, always looking at the table under the looking glass, where stood a very pretty little shepherdess made of china. Her shoes were gilt, and her dress had a red rose for an ornament. She wore a hat and carried a crook. Both were gilded and looked very bright and pretty.

Close by her side stood a little chimney sweeper, as black as a coal, and also made of china. He was, however, quite as clean and neat as any other china figure. He only represented a black chimney sweeper, and the china workers might just as well have made him a prince, had they felt inclined to do so. He stood holding his ladder quite handily, and his face was as fair and rosy as a girl's. Indeed that was rather a mistake—it should have had some black marks on it. He and the shepherdess had been placed side by side close together, and being so placed they became engaged to each other. They were very well suited, since both were made of the same sort of china and both were equally fragile.

Close to them stood another figure, three times as large as they were and also made of china. He was an old Chinaman, who could nod his head and who used to pretend that he was the grandfather of the shepherdess, although he could not prove it. He, however, assumed authority over her. Therefore, when "Major-general-field-sergeant-commander Billy-goat's-legs" asked for the little shepherdess to be his wife, he nodded his head to show that he consented.

"You will have a husband," said the old Chinaman to her, "who I really believe is made of mahogany. He will make you the lady of Major-general-field-sergeant-commander Billy-goat's-legs. He has the whole cupboard full of silver plate, which he keeps locked up in secret drawers."

"I won't go into the dark cupboard," said the little shepherdess. "I have heard that he has eleven china wives there already."

"Then you shall be the twelfth," said the old Chinaman. "Tonight as soon as you hear a rattling in the old cupboard, you shall be married, as true as I am a Chinaman." And then he bobbed his head and fell asleep.

Then the little shepherdess cried and looked at her sweetheart, the china chimney sweeper. "I must entreat you," said she, "to go out with me into the wide world, for we cannot stay here."

"I will do whatever you wish," said the little chimney

sweeper. "Let us go immediately. I think I shall be able to maintain you with my profession."

"If we only were safely down from the table!" said she. "I shall not be happy till we are really out in the world."

Then he comforted her and showed her how to place her little foot on the carved edge and gilt-leaf ornaments of the table. He brought his little ladder to help her, and so they contrived to reach the floor. But when they looked at the old cupboard, they saw it was all in an uproar. The carved stags pushed out their heads, raised their antlers, and twisted their necks.

The major-general sprang up into the air and cried out to the old Chinaman, "They are running away! They are running away!"

The two were rather frightened at this, so they jumped into the drawer of the window seat. Here were three or four packs of cards not quite complete, and a doll's theater which had been built up very neatly. A comedy was being performed in it and all the queens of diamonds, clubs, and hearts, and spades sat in the first row fanning themselves with tulips. And behind them stood all the knaves, showing that they had heads above and below as playing cards generally have. The play was about two lovers who were not allowed to marry, and the shepherdess wept because it was so like her own story.

"I cannot bear it," said she. "I must get out of the drawer." But when they reached the floor and cast their eyes on the table, there was the old Chinaman awake and shaking his whole body, till all at once down he came on the floor—plump!

"The old Chinaman is coming," cried the little shepherdess in a fright, and down she fell on one knee.

"I have thought of something," said the chimney sweeper. "Let us get into the great potpourri jar which stands in the corner. There we can lie on rose leaves and lavender, and throw salt in his eyes if he comes near us."

"No, that will never do," said she, "because I know that the Chinaman and the potpourri jar were lovers once, and there always remains behind a feeling of goodwill between those who have been so intimate as that. No, there is nothing left for us but to go out into the wide world."

"Have you really courage enough to go out into the wide world with me?" said the chimney sweeper. "Have you thought how large it is, and that we can never come back here again?"

"Yes, I have," she replied.

When the chimney sweeper saw that she was quite firm, he said, "My way is through the stove and up the chimney. Have you courage to creep with me through the firebox and the iron pipe? When we get to the chimney I shall know how to manage very well. We shall soon climb too high for anyone to reach us, and we shall go through a hole in the top out into the wide world." So he led her to the door of the stove.

"It looks very dark," said she. Still she went in with him through the stove and through the pipe, where it was as dark as pitch.

"Now we are in the chimney," said he. "And look! There is a beautiful star shining above it." It was a real star shining down upon them as if it would show them the way. So they clambered and crept on, and a frightfully steep place it was. But the chimney sweeper helped her and supported her, till they got higher and higher. He showed her the best places on which to set her little china feet. So at last they reached the top of the chimney and sat themselves down, for they were very tired, as may be supposed. The sky with all its stars was over their heads, and below were the roofs of the town. They could see for a very long distance out

They reached the top of the chimney

into the wide world, and the poor little shepherdess leaned her head on her chimney sweeper's shoulder and wept till she washed the gilt off her sash. The world was so different from what she expected.

"This is too much," she said. "I cannot bear it. The world is too large. Oh, I wish I were safe back on the table again, under the looking glass. I shall never be happy till I am safe back again. Now I have followed you out into the wide world, you will take me back if you love me."

Then the chimney sweeper tried to reason with her, and spoke of the old Chinaman and of the Major-general-field-sergeant-commander Billy-goat's-legs. But she sobbed so bitterly and kissed her little chimney sweeper, till he was obliged to do all she asked, foolish as it was. And so with a great deal of trouble they climbed down the chimney, and then crept through the pipe and stove, which were certainly not very pleasant places. Then they stood in the dark firebox and listened behind the door, to hear what was going on in the room. As it was all quiet, they peeped out. Alas, there lay the old Chinaman on the floor. He had fallen down from the table as he attempted to run after them, and was broken into three pieces. His back had separated entirely and his head had rolled into a corner of the room. The major-general stood in his old place and appeared lost in thought.

"This is terrible," said the little shepherdess. "My poor old grandfather is broken to pieces and it is our fault. I shall never live after this." And she wrung her little hands.

"He can be riveted," said the chimney sweeper. "He can be riveted. Do not be so hasty. If they cement his back and put a good rivet in it he will be as good as new, and he will be able to say as many disagreeable things to us as ever."

"Do you think so?" said she. And then they climbed up to the table and stood in their old places.

"As we have done no good," said the chimney sweeper, "we might as well have remained here, instead of taking so much trouble."

"I wish grandfather were riveted," said the shepherdess. "Will it cost much, I wonder?" And she had her wish. The family had the Chinaman's back mended and a strong rivet put through his neck. He looked as good as new but he could no longer nod his head.

"You have become very proud since your fall broke you to pieces," said Major-general-field-sergeant-commander Billy-goat's-legs. "You have no reason to give yourself such airs. Am I to have her or not?"

The chimney sweeper and the little shepherdess looked piteously at the old Chinaman, for they were afraid he might nod, but he was not able. Besides, it was so tiresome to be always telling strangers he had a rivet in the back of his neck.

And so the little china people remained together, and they were glad of the grandfather's rivet, and they continued to love each other till they were broken to pieces.

The Bell

IN the evening at sunset, when glimpses of golden clouds could just be seen among the chimney pots, a curious sound would be heard, first by one person, then by another. It was like a church bell, but it only lasted a moment because of the rumble of vehicles and street cries.

"There is the evening bell," people would say. "The sun is setting."

Those who went outside the town where the houses were more scattered, each with its garden or little meadow, saw the evening star and heard the tones of the bell much better. It seemed as if the sound came from a church buried in the silent, fragrant woods, and people looked in that direction, feeling quite solemn.

Time passed and still people said one to the other, "Can there be a church in the woods? That bell has such a wonderfully sweet sound! Shall we go and look at it closer?" The rich people drove and the poor ones walked, but it was a very long way. When they reached a group of willows which grew on the outskirts of the wood, they sat down and looked up among the long branches, thinking that they were really in the heart of the forest. A confectioner from the town came out and pitched a tent there, and then another confectioner, and he hung a bell up over his tent. This bell was tarred so as to stand the rain, and the clapper was wanting. When people went home again they said it had been so romantic, and that meant something beyond mere tea. Three persons protested that they had penetrated right through the forest to the other side. They said that they heard the same curious bell all the time, but that then it sounded as if it came from the town.

One of them wrote a poem about it and said that it sounded like a mother's voice to a beloved child. No melody could be sweeter than the chimes of this bell.

The Emperor's attention was also drawn to it and he promised that anyone who really discovered where the sound came from should receive the title of "World's Bell Ringer," even if there were no bell at all.

A great many people went into the woods for the sake of earning an honest penny, but only one of them brought home any kind of explanation. No one had been far enough, not even he himself, but he said that the sound of the bell came from a very big owl in a hollow tree. It was a wise owl which perpetually beat its head against a tree, but whether the sound came from its head or from the hollow tree he could not say with any certainty. All the same he was appointed "World's Bell Ringer," and every year he wrote a little treatise on the owl, but nobody was much the wiser for it.

Now on a certain confirmation day the priest had preached a very moving sermon, and all the young people about to be confirmed had been much touched by it. It was a very important day for them. They were leaving childhood behind and becoming grown-up persons. The child's soul was, as it were, to be transformed into that of a responsible being. It was a beautiful sunny day and after the confirmation the young people walked out of the town, and they heard the sound of the unknown bell more than usually loud coming from the wood. On hearing it they all felt anxious to go and see it—all except three.

The first of these had to go home to try on her ball dress. It was this very dress and this very ball which were the reason of her having been confirmed this time; otherwise it would have been put off. The second was a poor boy who had borrowed his tailcoat and boots of the landlord's son and had to return them at the appointed time. The third said that he had never been anywhere without his parents, that he had always been a good child and he meant to continue so, although he was confirmed. Nobody ought to have made fun of this resolve, but he did not escape being laughed at.

So these three did not go. The others trudged off. The sun shone and the birds sang, and the newly confirmed young people took each other by the hand and sang with them. They had not yet received any position in life. They were all equal in the eyes of the Lord on the day of their confirmation. Soon two of the smallest ones got tired and returned to town. Two little girls sat down and made wreaths, so they did not go either. When the others reached the willows where the confectioners had their tents, they said, "Now then, here we are. The bell doesn't exist. It is only something people imagine."

Just then the bell with its deep rich notes was heard in the woods and four or five of them decided after all to penetrate farther into the wood. The underwood was so thick and close that it was quite difficult to advance. The woodruff grew almost too high. Convolvulus and brambles hung in long garlands from tree to tree, where the nightingales sang and the sunbeams played. It was deliciously peaceful but there was no path for the girls; their clothes would have been torn to shreds. There were great boulders overgrown with many-colored mosses, and fresh springs trickled among them with a curious little gurgling sound.

"Surely that cannot be the bell," said one of the young people, as he lay down to listen. "This must be thoroughly looked into." So he stayed behind and let the others go on.

They came to a little hut made of bark and branches overhung by a crab apple, as if it wanted to shake all its bloom over the roof, which was covered with roses. The long sprays clustered round the gable, and on it hung a little bell. Could this be the one they sought? Yes, they were all agreed that it must be, except one. He said it was far too small and delicate to be heard so far away as they had heard it, and that the tones which moved all hearts were quite different from these. He who spoke was a king's son and so the others said, "That kind of fellow must always be wiser than anyone else."

So they let him go on alone, and as he went he was more and more overcome by the solitude of the wood, but he still heard the little bell with which the others were so pleased. And now and then when the wind came from the direction of the confectioners, he could hear demands for tea. But the deep-toned bell sounded above them all, and it seemed as if there were an organ playing with it; and the sounds came from the left where the heart is placed.

There was a rustling among the bushes, and a little boy stood before the King's son. He had on wooden shoes and such a small jacket that the sleeves did not cover his wrists. They knew each other, for he was the boy who had had to go back to return the coat and the boots to the landlord's son. He had done this, changed back into his shabby clothes and wooden shoes, and then, drawn by the deep notes of the bell, had returned to the wood again.

"Then we can go together," said the King's son.

But the poor boy in the wooden shoes was too bashful. He pulled down his short sleeves and said he was afraid he could not walk quickly enough and besides he thought the bell ought to be looked for on the right, because that side looked the most beautiful.

"Then we shan't meet at all," said the King's son, nodding to the poor boy, who went into the thickest and darkest part of the wood, where the thorns tore his shabby clothes and scratched his face, hands, and feet till they bled.

The King's son got some good scratches too, but he at least had the sun shining upon his path. We are going to follow him, for he is a bright fellow.

"I must and will find the bell," said he, "if I have to go to the end of the world."

Some horrid monkeys sat up in the trees grinning and showing their teeth. "Shall we pelt him?" said they. "Shall we thrash him? He is a King's son."

But he went confidently on, farther and farther into the wood, where the most extraordinary flowers grew. There were white starlike lilies with blood-red stamens, pale blue tulips which glistened in the sun, and appletrees on which the apples looked like great shining soap bubbles. You may fancy how these trees glittered in the sun. Round about were beautiful green meadows where stags and hinds gamboled under the spreading oaks and beeches. Mosses and creepers grew in the fissures where the bark of the trees was broken away. There were also great glades with quiet lakes, where white swans swam about flapping their wings. The King's son often stopped and listened, for he sometimes fancied that the bell sounded from one of these lakes. Then again he felt sure that it was not there, but farther in the wood.

Now the sun began to go down, and the clouds were fiery red. A great stillness came over the wood and he sank upon his knees, sang his evening psalm, and said, "Never shall I find what I seek, now the sun is going down. The night is coming on—the dark night. Perhaps I could catch one more glimpse of the round, red sun before it sinks beneath the earth. I will climb up onto those rocks. They are as high as the trees."

He seized the roots and creepers and climbed up the slippery stones where the water snakes wriggled and the toads seemed to croak at him, but he reached the top before the sun disappeared. Seen from this height, oh, what splendor lay before him! The ocean, the wide beautiful ocean, with its long waves rolling towards the shore! The sun still stood like a great shining altar, out there where sea and sky met. Everything melted away into glowing colors. The wood sang, the ocean sang, and his heart sang with them. All nature was like a vast holy temple, where trees and floating clouds were as pillars, flowers and grass a woven tapestry, and the heaven itself a great dome. The red colors vanished as the sun went down, but millions of stars peeped out. They were like countless diamond lamps and he spread out his arms towards heaven, sea, and forest. At that moment, from the right-hand path came the poor boy with the short sleeves and wooden shoes. He had reached the same goal just as soon by his own road. They ran towards each other and clasped each other's hands in that great temple of nature and poetry, and above them sounded the invisible holy bell. Happy spirits floated round it to the strains of a joyous hallelujah.

The Angel

"WHENEVER a good child dies, an angel of God comes down from heaven, takes the dead child in his arms, spreads out his great white wings, and flies with him over all the places which the child has loved during his life. Then he gathers a large handful of flowers which he carries up to the Almighty, that they may bloom more brightly in heaven than they do on earth. And the Almighty presses the flowers to His heart, but He kisses the flower that pleases Him best, and it receives a voice and is able to join the song of the chorus of bliss."

These words were spoken by an angel of God as he carried a dead child up to heaven, and the child listened as if in a dream. Then they passed over well-known spots where the little one had often played, and through beautiful gardens full of lovely flowers.

"Which of these shall we take with us to heaven to be transplanted there?" asked the angel.

Close by grew a slender, beautiful rosebush, but some wicked hand had broken the stem, and the half-opened rosebuds hung all faded and withered on the trailing branches.

"Poor rosebush!" said the child. "Let us take it with us to heaven, that it may bloom above in God's garden."

The angel took up the rosebush. Then he kissed the child and the little one half-opened his eyes. The angel gathered also some beautiful flowers, as well as a few humble buttercups and heartsease.

"Now we have flowers enough," said the child, but the angel only nodded. He did not fly upward to heaven.

It was night and quite still in the great town. Here they remained, and the angel hovered over a small narrow street in which lay a large heap of straw, ashes, and sweepings from houses of people who had moved away. There lay fragments of plates, pieces of plaster, rags, old hats, and other rubbish. Amidst all of this confusion, the angel pointed to the pieces of a broken flowerpot, and to a lump of earth which had fallen out of it. The earth had been kept from falling to pieces by the roots of a withered field flower which had been thrown amongst the rubbish.

"We will take this with us," said the angel. "I will tell you why as we fly along."

And as they flew the angel related the history.

"Down in that narrow lane, in a low cellar, lived a poor sick boy. He had been afflicted from his childhood, and even in his best days he could just manage to walk up and down the room on crutches once or twice, but no more. During some days in summer the sunbeams would lie on the floor of the cellar for about half an hour. In this spot the poor sick boy would sit warming himself in the sunshine and watching the red blood through his delicate fingers as he held them before his face. Then he would say he had been out, though he knew nothing of the green forest in its spring verdure till a neighbor's son brought him a green bough from a beech tree. This he would place over his head, and fancy that he was in the beechwood while the sun shone and the birds caroled gaily. One spring day the neighbor's boy brought him some field flowers, and among them was one to which the roots still adhered. This he carefully planted in a flowerpot, and placed in a window seat near his bed. And the flower had been planted by a fortunate hand, for it grew, put forth fresh shoots, and blossomed every year. It became a splendid flower garden to the sick boy, and his little treasure upon earth. He watered it and cherished it, and took care it should have the benefit of every sunbeam that found its way into the cellar, from the earliest morning ray to the evening sunset. The flower entwined itself even in his dreams. For him it bloomed; for him it spread its perfume. And it gladdened his eyes, and to the flower he turned, even in death, when the Lord called him. He has been one year with God. During that time the flower has stood in the window, withered and forgotten, till cast out among the sweepings into the street, on the day the lodgers moved. And this poor flower, withered and faded as it is, we have added to our nosegay, because it gave more real joy than the most beautiful flower in the garden of a queen."

"But how do you know all this?" asked the child whom the angel was carrying to heaven.

"I know it," said the angel, "because I myself was the poor sick boy who walked upon crutches, and I know my own flower well."

Then the child opened his eyes and looked into the glorious happy face of the angel, and at the same moment they found themselves in that heavenly home where all is happiness and joy. And God pressed the dead child to His heart, and wings were given him so that he could fly with the angel, hand in hand. Then the Almighty pressed all the flowers to His heart. But He kissed the withered field flower and it received a voice. Then it joined in the song of the angels, who surrounded the throne, some near, and others in a distant circle, but all equally happy. They all joined in the chorus of praise, both great and small—the good, happy child and the poor field flower, that once lay withered and cast away on a heap of rubbish in a narrow dark street.

The Nightingale

IN China, as you know, the Emperor is a Chinaman, and all the people around him are Chinamen too. It is many years since the story I am going to tell you happened, but that is all the more reason for telling it, lest it should be forgotten.

The Emperor's palace was the most beautiful thing in the world. It was made entirely of finest porcelain, which was very costly, and so fragile that it could be touched only with the very greatest of care. The most extraordinary flowers were to be seen in the garden. The most beautiful ones had little silver bells tied to them which tinkled perpetually, so that no one could pass the flowers without looking at them. Every little detail in the garden had been most carefully thought out, and it was so big that even the gardener himself did not know where it ended.

If one went on walking, one came to beautiful woods with lofty trees and deep lakes. The wood extended to the sea, which was deep and blue, deep enough for large ships to sail up right under the branches of the trees. Among these trees lived a nightingale, which sang so deliciously that even the poor fisherman, who had plenty of other things to do, lay still to listen to it when he was out at night drawing in his nets.

"Heavens, how beautiful it is," he said, but then he had to attend to his business and forgot it. The next night when he heard it again he would again exclaim, "Heavens, how beautiful it is."

Travelers came to the Emperor's capital from every country in the world. They admired everything very much, especially the palace and the gardens, but when they heard the nightingale they all said, "This is better than anything."

When they got home they described it, and learned men wrote many books about the town, the palace, and the garden. But nobody forgot the nightingale—it was always put above everything else. Those among them who were poets wrote the most beautiful poems, all about the nightingale in the woods by the deep blue sea. These books went all over the world, and in course of time some of them reached the Emperor. He sat in his golden chair reading and reading, and nodding his head, well pleased to hear such beautiful descriptions of the town, the palace, and the garden. "But the nightingale is the best of all," he read.

"What is this?" said the Emperor. "The nightingale? Why, I know nothing about it. Is there such a bird in my kingdom, and in my own garden, and I have never heard of it? Imagine my having to discover this from a book."

Then he called his gentleman-in-waiting, who was so grand that when anyone of a lower rank dared to speak to him or to ask him a question, he would only answer, "P," which means nothing at all.

"There is said to be a very wonderful bird called a nightingale here," said the Emperor. "They say that it is better than anything else in all my great kingdom. Why have I never been told anything about it?"

"I have never heard it mentioned," said the gentleman-in-waiting. "It has never been presented at court."

"I wish it to appear here this evening to sing to me," said the Emperor. "The whole world knows what I am possessed of, and I know nothing about it!"

"I have never heard it mentioned before," said the gentleman-in-waiting. "I will seek it, and I will find it." But where was it to be found? The gentleman-in-waiting ran upstairs and downstairs and in and out of all the rooms and corridors. No one of all those he met had ever heard anything about the nightingale. So the gentleman-in-waiting ran back to the Emperor and said that it must be a myth, invented by the writers of the books. "Your Imperial Majesty must not believe everything that is written! Books are often mere inventions, even if they do not belong to what we call the black art."

"But the book in which I read it was sent to me by the powerful Emperor of Japan. Therefore it can't be untrue. I will hear this nightingale. I insist upon its being here tonight. I extend my most gracious protection to it, and if it is not forthcoming, I will have the whole court trampled upon after supper."

"Tsing-pe!" said the gentleman-in-waiting, and away he ran again, up and down all the stairs, in and out of all the rooms and corridors. Half the court ran with him, for none of them wished to be trampled on. There was much questioning about this nightingale, which was known to all the outside world but to no one at court.

At last they found a poor little maid in the kitchen, who said, "Oh heavens! The nightingale? I know it very well. Yes indeed, it can sing. Every evening I am allowed to take broken meat to my poor sick mother who lives down by the shore. On my way back, when I am tired I rest awhile in the wood, and then I hear the nightingale. Its song brings the tears into my eyes. I feel as if my mother were kissing me."

"Little kitchen maid," said the gentleman-in-waiting, "I will procure you a permanent position in the kitchen and permission to see the Emperor dining, if you will take us to the nightingale. It is commanded to appear at court tonight."

Then they all went out into the wood where the nightingale usually sang. Half the court was there. As they were going along at their best pace, a cow began to bellow.

"Oh," said a young courtier, "there we have it. What wonderful power for such a little creature. I have certainly heard it before."

"No, those are the cows bellowing. We are a long way from the place." Then frogs began to croak in the marsh.

"How beautiful!" said the Chinese chaplain. "It is just like the tinkling of church bells."

"No, those are the frogs," said the little kitchen maid. "But I think we shall soon hear it now."

Then the nightingale began to sing.

"Listen, listen! There it sits," said the little girl. And she pointed to a little gray bird up among the branches.

"Is it possible?" said the gentleman-in-waiting. "I should never have thought it was like that. How common it looks. Seeing so many grand people must have frightened all its colors away."

"Little nightingale," called the kitchen maid quite loud, "Our Gracious Emperor wishes you to sing to him."

"With the greatest pleasure," said the nightingale, warbling away in the most delightful fashion.

"It is just like crystal bells," said the gentleman-in-waiting. "Look at its little throat, how active it is. It is extraordinary that we have never heard it before. I am sure it will be a great success at court."

"Shall I sing again to the Emperor?" said the nightingale, who thought he was present.

"My precious little nightingale," said the gentleman-in-waiting, "I have the honor to command your attendance at a court festival tonight, where you will charm His Gracious Majesty the Emperor with your fascinating singing."

"It sounds best among the trees," said the nightingale, but it went with them willingly when it heard that the Emperor wished it.

The palace had been brightened up for the occasion. The

walls and the floors, which were all of china, shone by the light of many thousand golden lamps. The most beautiful flowers, all of the tinkling kind, were arranged in the corridors. There was hurrying to and fro, and a great draught, but this was just what made the bells ring. One's ears were full of the tinkling. In the middle of the large reception room where the Emperor sat, a golden rod had been fixed, on which the nightingale was to perch. The whole court was assembled, and the little kitchen maid had been permitted to stand behind the door, as she now had the actual title of Cook. They were all dressed in their best. Everybody's eyes were turned towards the little gray bird at which the Emperor was nodding.

The nightingale sang delightfully, and the tears came into the Emperor's eyes and rolled down his cheeks. And when the nightingale sang more beautifully than ever, its notes melted all hearts. The Emperor was so charmed that he said the nightingale should have his gold slipper to wear round its neck. But the nightingale declined with thanks— it had already been sufficiently rewarded.

"I have seen tears in the eyes of the Emperor," he said. "That is my richest reward. The tears of an Emperor have a wonderful power. God knows I am sufficiently recompensed." And it again burst into its sweet heavenly song.

"That is the most delightful coquetting I have ever seen!" said the ladies. And they took some water into their mouths to try and make the same gurgling, when anyone spoke to them, thinking so to equal the nightingale. Even the lackeys and the chambermaids announced that they were satisfied, and that is saying a great deal. They are always the most difficult people to please. Yes indeed, the nightingale had made a sensation. It was to stay at court now, and have its own cage, as well as liberty to walk out twice a day and once in the night. It always had twelve footmen, with each one holding a ribbon which was tied round its leg. There was not much pleasure in an outing of that sort.

The whole town talked about the marvelous bird. If two people met, one said to the other "Night," and the other answered "Gale." And then they sighed, perfectly understanding each other. Eleven cheesemongers' children were named after it, but not one among them could sing anything.

One day a large parcel came for the Emperor. Outside was written the word "Nightingale."

"Here we have another new book about this celebrated bird," said the Emperor. But it was not a book. It was a little work of art in a box, an artificial nightingale exactly like the living one, except that it was studded all over with diamonds, rubies, and sapphires.

When the artificial bird was wound up, it could sing one of the songs the real one sang, and it wagged its tail, which glittered with silver and gold. A ribbon was tied round its neck on which was written, "The Emperor of Japan's nightingale is very poor compared to the Emperor of China's."

Everybody said, "Oh, how beautiful!" And the person who brought the artificial bird immediately received the title of Imperial Nightingale-Carrier-in-Chief.

"Now, they must sing together. What a duet that will be!"

Then they had to sing together, but they did not get on very well, for the real nightingale sang in its own way and the artificial one could only sing waltzes.

"There is no fault in that," said the music master. "It is perfectly in time and correct in every way."

Then the artificial bird had to sing alone. It was just as great a success as the real one, and it was much prettier to look at, because it glittered like bracelets and breastpins.

It sang the same tune three and thirty times over, and yet

it was not tired. People would willingly have heard it from the beginning again, but the Emperor said that the real one must have a turn now. But where was it? No one had noticed that it had flown out of the open window, back to its own green woods.

"What is the meaning of this?" said the Emperor.

All the courtiers railed at it and said it was a most ungrateful bird.

"We have got the best bird though," said they, and then the artificial bird had to sing again. This was the thirty-fourth time that they had heard the same tune, but they did not know it thoroughly even yet because it was so difficult.

The music master praised the bird tremendously and insisted that it was better than the real nightingale, not only on the outside with all its diamonds, but inside too.

"You see, my ladies and gentlemen, and the Emperor before all, in the real nightingale you never know what you will hear, but in the artificial one everything is decided beforehand. So it is, and so it must remain. It can't be otherwise. You can account for things: you can open it and show the human ingenuity in arranging how the waltzes go, and how one note follows upon another."

"Those are exactly my opinions," they all said, and the music master got leave to show the bird to the public next Sunday. They were also to hear it sing, said the Emperor. So they heard it, and all became as enthusiastic over it as if they had drunk themselves merry on tea, because that is a thoroughly Chinese habit.

Then they all said, "Oh!" and stuck their forefingers in the air and nodded their heads. But the poor fisherman who had heard the real nightingale said, "It sounds very nice, and it is very nearly like the real one, but there is something wanting. I don't know what." The real nightingale was banished from the kingdom.

The artificial bird had its place on a silken cushion, close

The artificial bird glittered

to the Emperor's bed. All the presents it had received of gold and precious jewels were scattered round it. Its title had risen to be Chief Imperial Singer-of-the-Bed-Chamber. In rank it stood number one on the left side, for the Emperor reckoned that side where the heart was seated was the important one. And even an Emperor's heart is on the left side.

The music master wrote five and twenty volumes about the artificial bird. The treatise was very long, and was written in all the most difficult Chinese characters. Everybody said they had read and understood it, for otherwise they would have been reckoned stupid, and then their bodies would have been trampled upon.

Things went on in this way for a whole year. The Emperor, the court, and all the other Chinamen knew every little gurgle in the song of the artificial bird by heart. But they liked it all the better for this, and they could all join in the song themselves. Even the street boys sang "Zizizi! cluck, cluck, cluck!" And the Emperor sang it too.

But one evening, when the bird was singing its best and the Emperor was lying in bed listening to it, something gave way inside the bird with a "whizz." "Whirr!" went all the wheels, and the music stopped.

The Emperor jumped out of bed and sent for his private physicians, but what good could they do? Then they sent for the watchmaker, who after a good deal of talk and examination got the works to go again somehow. But he said the bird would have to be spared as much as possible, because it was so worn out, and that he could not renew the works so as to be sure of the tune. This was a great blow! They now dared to let the artificial bird sing only once a year, and hardly that. But then the music master made a little speech using all the most difficult Chinese words. He said it was just as good as ever, and his saying it made it so.

Five years passed, and then a great grief came upon the

nation. They were all very fond of their Emperor, and now he was ill and could not live, it was said. A new Emperor was already chosen, and people stood about in the street and asked the gentleman-in-waiting how the Emperor was getting on.

"P," answered he, shaking his head.

The Emperor lay pale and cold in his gorgeous bed. The courtiers thought he was dead, and they all went off to pay their respects to their new Emperor. The lackeys ran off to talk matters over, and the chambermaids gave a great coffee party. Cloth had been laid down in all the rooms and corridors so as to deaden the sounds of footsteps, so it was very, very quiet. But the Emperor was not dead yet. He lay stiff and pale in the gorgeous bed with velvet hangings and heavy golden tassels. There was an open window high above him, and the moon streamed in upon the Emperor and the artificial bird beside him.

The poor Emperor could hardly breathe. He seemed to have a weight on his chest. He opened his eyes and then he saw that it was Death sitting upon his chest, wearing his golden crown. In one hand he held the Emperor's golden sword, and in the other his Imperial banner. From among the folds of the velvet hangings peered many curious faces. Some were hideous, others gentle and pleasant. They were all the Emperor's good and bad deeds, which now looked him in the face when Death was weighing him down.

"Do you remember that?" whispered one after the other. "Do you remember this?" And they told him so many things that the perspiration poured down his face.

"I never knew that," said the Emperor. "Music, music! Sound the great Chinese drums," he cried, "that I may not hear what they are saying." But they went on and on, and Death sat nodding his head like a Chinaman at everything that was said. "Music, music!" shrieked the Emperor. "You precious little golden bird, sing, sing! I have loaded you with precious stones, and even hung my own golden slipper round your neck. Sing, I tell you, sing!"

But the bird stood silent. There was nobody to wind it up, so of course it could not go. Death continued to fix the great empty sockets of its eyes upon him, and all was silent, terribly silent.

Suddenly, close to the window there was a burst of lovely song. It was the living nightingale, perched on a branch outside. It had heard of the Emperor's need and had come to bring comfort and hope to him. As it sang, the faces round became fainter and fainter, and the blood coursed with fresh vigor in the Emperor's veins and through his feeble limbs. Even Death himself listened to the song and said, "Go on, little nightingale, go on!"

"Yes, if you give me the gorgeous golden sword. Yes, if you give me the Imperial banner. Yes, if you give me the Emperor's crown."

And Death gave back each of these treasures for a song, and the nightingale went on singing. It sang about the quiet churchyard where the roses bloom, where the elder flowers scent the air, and where the fresh grass is ever moistened anew by the tears of the mourners. This song brought to Death a longing for his own garden, and like a cold gray mist he passed out of the window.

"Thanks, thanks!" said the Emperor. "You heavenly little bird, I know you. I banished you from my kingdom, and yet you have charmed the evil visions away from my bed by your song, and even Death away from my heart. How can I ever repay you?"

"You have rewarded me," said the nightingale. "I brought tears to your eyes the very first time I ever sang to you, and I shall never forget it. Those are the jewels which gladden the heart of a singer. But sleep now, and wake up fresh and strong. I will sing to you."

Then it sang again, and the Emperor fell into a sweet refreshing sleep. The sun shone in at his window, and he awoke refreshed and well. None of his attendants had yet come back to him, for they thought he was dead, but the nightingale still sat there singing.

"You must always stay with me," said the Emperor. "You shall sing only when you like, and I will break the artificial bird into a thousand pieces."

"Don't do that," said the nightingale. "It did all the good it could. Keep it as you have always done. I can't build my nest and live in this palace, but let me come whenever I like. Then I will sit on the branch in the evening and sing to you. I will sing to cheer you and to make you thoughtful too. I will sing to you of the happy ones and of those that suffer. I will sing about the good and the evil, which are kept hidden from you. The little singing bird flies far and wide, to the poor fisherman and to the peasant's home, to numbers who are far from you and your court. I love your heart more than your crown, and yet there is an odor of sanctity round the crown too! I will come, and I will sing to you. But you must promise me one thing."

"Everything!" said the Emperor, who stood there in his imperial robes which he had just put on, and he held the sword heavy with gold upon his heart.

"Only one thing I ask you. Tell no one that you have a little bird who tells you everything. It will be better so."

Then the nightingale flew away. The attendants came in to look after their dead Emperor—and there he stood, bidding them "Good morning!"

Holger the Dane

THERE is an old castle in Denmark which is called Kronborg. It juts out into the Sound, and great ships sail past it every day by hundreds. There are Russian and English and Prussian ships and ships of many other nationalities. They all fire a salute when they pass the old castle. Boom! they say, and the castle answers, boom! That is the way cannons say, "How do you do!" and "Thank you." No ships sail in the winter, for then the water is frozen over, right up to the Swedish coast, and it becomes a great highroad. Swedish and Danish flags fly, and the Danes and the Swedes say, "How do you do!" and "Thank you!" to each other, not with cannons but with a friendly shake of the hand. They buy fancy bread and cakes of each other, for strange food tastes best.

But old Kronborg is always the chief feature, and down inside it in the deep dark cellar lives Holger the Dane. He is clad in steel and iron and rests his head upon his strong arms, and his long beard hangs over the marble table to which it has grown fast. He sleeps and dreams, but in his dreams he sees all that is happening up there in Denmark. Every Christmas Eve a holy angel comes and tells him that he has dreamt aright, and that he may go to sleep again because Denmark is not yet in any real danger. But should danger come, then old Holger the Dane will rise up, and the table will burst asunder when he wrenches his beard away from it. Then he will come forward and strike a blow that will resound in all parts of the world.

An old grandfather was sitting telling his little grandson all this about Holger the Dane, and the little boy knew that all that his grandfather said was true. While the old man was talking, he sat carving a big wooden figure which was to represent Holger the Dane as the figurehead of a ship. The old grandfather was a carver, the sort of man who carves a figurehead for each ship, according to its name. Here he had carved Holger the Dane, who stood erect and proud, with his long beard. He held in his hand a great broadsword and rested his other hand upon a shield with the Danish Arms. The old grandfather had so much to tell about remarkable Danish men and women that the little boy at last thought he must know as much as Holger the Dane, who after all only dreamt about these things. When the little fellow went to bed, he thought so much about the things he had heard and pressed his chin so hard into the quilt that he thought it was a long beard grown fast to it.

The old grandfather remained sitting at his work, carving away at the last bit of it, which was the arms on the shield. At last it was finished. He looked at it complete, and thought of all the things he had heard and read, and what he had been telling the little boy in the evening. He nodded and wiped his spectacles, and put them on again and said, "Well, I don't suppose Holger the Dane will come in my time, but perhaps the boy in bed there may see him, and will have his share of the fighting when the time comes." Then the old grandfather nodded again, and the more he looked at his Holger the Dane the more plain it became to him that the figure he had made was a good one. He even fancied that the color came into it and that the armor shone like polished steel. The hearts in the Danish Arms [1] got redder and the crowns on the springing lions became golden.

---

[1] The Danish Arms consist of three lions between nine hearts.

"It's the finest coat of arms in the world!" said the old man. "The lions are strength, and the hearts are love and tenderness." He looked at the uppermost lion and thought about King Knut who bound the mighty England to Denmark's throne. He looked at the second lion and thought of Waldemar, who united Denmark and subdued the Vandals. He looked at the third lion and thought of Margaret, who united Denmark, Sweden, and Norway. When he looked at the red hearts, they shone more brightly than ever. They became waving flames of fire, and in his thoughts he followed each of them.

The first led him into a narrow, dark prison. He saw a prisoner—a beautiful woman—Eleonora Ulfeld, daughter of Christian the Fourth. The flame placed itself like a rose on her bosom, and bloomed in harmony with her heart. She was the noblest and best of Denmark's women. "That is one heart in the Arms of Denmark," said the old grandfather. Then his thoughts followed the next heart, which led him out to sea among the thunder of cannon and ships enveloped in smoke. And the flame attached itself like an order to Hvitfield's breast as he, to save the fleet, blew up his ship and himself with it.

The third heart led him to the miserable huts of Greenland, where Hans Egede, the priest, labored with loving words and deeds. The flame was a star upon his breast, one heart more for the Danish Arms.

The old grandfather's heart went in advance of the waving flames, for he knew whither the flames were leading him.

Frederick the Sixth stood in the peasant woman's poor little room and wrote his name with chalk on the beams. The flame trembled on his breast—trembled in his heart. In the peasant's room his heart became a heart in Denmark's Arms. And the old grandfather wiped his eyes, for he had known King Frederick and lived for him—King Frederick with silvery hair and honest blue eyes. Then he folded his hands and sat, looking pensively before him. His daughter-in-law came and told him that it was late and he must rest; the supper was ready.

"What a grand figure you have made, grandfather," she said. "Holger the Dane and all our beautiful coat of arms. I think I have seen that face before."

"No, that you haven't," said the old man. "But I have seen it and have often before tried to carve it in wood, just as I remember it. It was when the English lay in the roads on the second day of April, and we knew we were true old Danes. Where I stood on the *Denmark* in Steen Billé's squadron, I had a man by my side. It seemed as if the balls were afraid of him. There he stood singing old ballads, fighting and struggling as if he were more than a man. I remember his face still, but whence he came or whither he went I haven't an idea, nor has anyone else either. I have often thought it must have been old Holger the Dane himself, who had swum down from Kronborg to help us in the hour of danger. Now that's my idea, and there stands his portrait."

The figure threw its shadow right up the wall as high as the ceiling. It looked as if it were the real Holger the Dane himself standing in the light. The shadow seemed to move, but perhaps that was because the candle was not burning very steadily. The old man's daughter-in-law kissed him and led him to the big armchair by the table, and she and her husband, who was the old man's son and the father of the little boy in bed, sat eating their supper and chatting.

The old grandfather's head was full of Danish lions and Danish hearts and strength and gentleness. He could talk of nothing else. He explained to them that there is another strength besides the strength of the sword, and he pointed to the shelf where his old books lay—all of Holberg's plays, which were so much read because they were so amusing. All the characters from olden times were quite familiar to him.

"You see he knew how to fight too," said the old man. "He spent all his life in showing up in his plays the follies and peculiarities of those around him."

Then the grandfather nodded to a place above the looking glass where an almanac hung with a picture of the Round Tower on it, and he said, "There was Tycho Brahe. He was another who used the sword—not to hack at legs and arms, but to cut out a plainer path among the stars of heaven! And then *he* whose father belonged to my calling, Thorwaldsen the old woodcarver's son. We have seen him ourselves with the silvery locks falling on his broad shoulders, and his name is known to all the world. Ah, he is a sculptor, and I am only a woodcarver. Yes, Holger the Dane comes in many guises, that the strength of Denmark may be known all over the world. Shall we drink to the health of Bertel Thorwaldsen?"

The little boy in bed distinctly saw the castle of Kronborg and the real Holger the Dane, who lived down below it, with his beard grown fast to the marble table, and dreaming about all that happens up above. Holger the Dane also dreamt about the poor little room where the woodcarver lived. He heard everything that was said, and nodded in his dreams, murmuring, "Yes, remember me, ye Danish people! Keep me in mind. I shall come in time of need."

Outside Kronborg it was bright daylight and the wind bore the notes of the huntsman's horn from the opposite shore. The ships sailed past with their greeting—boom, boom! And the answer came from Kronborg—boom, boom! Holger the Dane did not wake, however loud they thundered, because it was only "How do you do!" and "Many thanks!" It will have to be a different kind of firing to rouse him, but he will wake, never fear. There is grit in Holger the Dane.

The Emperor's New Clothes

MANY years ago there was an Emperor who was so excessively fond of new clothes that he spent all his money on them. He cared nothing about his soldiers, nor for the theater, nor for driving in the woods except for the sake of showing off his new clothes. He had a costume for every hour in the day. Instead of saying as one does about any other king or emperor, "He is in his council chamber," the people here always said, "The Emperor is in his dressing room."

Life was very gay in the great town where he lived. Hosts of strangers came to visit it every day, and among them one day were two swindlers. They gave themselves out as weavers and said that they knew how to weave the most beautiful fabrics imaginable. Not only were the colors and patterns unusually fine, but the clothes that were made of this cloth had the peculiar quality of becoming invisible to every person who was not fit for the office he held, or who was impossibly dull.

"Those must be splendid clothes," thought the Emperor. "By wearing them I should be able to discover which men in my kingdom are unfitted for their posts. I shall distinguish the wise men from the fools. Yes, I certainly must order some of that stuff to be woven for me."

The Emperor paid the two swindlers a lot of money in advance, so that they might begin their work at once.

They did put up two looms and pretended to weave, but they had nothing whatever upon their shuttles. At the outset they asked for a quantity of the finest silk and the purest gold thread, all of which they put into their own bags while they worked away at the empty looms far into the night.

"I should like to know how those weavers are getting on with their cloth," thought the Emperor, but he felt a little queer when he reflected that anyone who was stupid or unfit for his post would not be able to see it. He certainly thought that he need have no fears for himself, but still he thought he would send somebody else first to see how it was getting on. Everybody in the town knew what wonderful power the stuff possessed, and everyone was anxious to see how stupid his neighbor was.

"I will send my faithful old minister to the weavers," thought the Emperor. "He will be best able to see how the stuff looks, for he is a clever man and no one fulfills his duties better than he does."

So the good old minister went into the room where the two swindlers sat working at the empty loom.

"Heaven help us," thought the old minister, opening his eyes very wide. "Why, I can't see a thing!" But he took care not to say so.

Both the swindlers begged him to be good enough to step a little nearer, and asked if he did not think it a good pattern and beautiful coloring. They pointed to the empty loom. The poor old minister stared as hard as he could, but he could not see anything, for of course there was nothing to see.

"Good heavens," thought he. "Is it possible that I am a fool? I have never thought so, and nobody must know it. Am I not fit for my post? It will never do to say that I cannot see the stuff."

"Well, sir, you don't say anything about the stuff," said the one who was pretending to weave.

"Oh, it is beautiful—quite charming," said the minister, looking through his spectacles. "Such a pattern and such colors! I will certainly tell the Emperor that the stuff pleases me very much."

"We are delighted to hear you say so," said the swindlers, and then they named all the colors and described the peculiar pattern. The old minister paid great attention to what they said, so as to be able to repeat it when he got home to the Emperor.

Then the swindlers went on to demand more money, more silk, and more gold, to be able to proceed with the weaving. But they put it all into their own pockets. Not a single strand was ever put into the loom, but they went on as before, weaving at the empty loom.

The Emperor soon sent another faithful official to see how the stuff was getting on and if it would soon be ready. The same thing happened to him as to the minister. He looked and looked, but as there was only the empty loom, he could see nothing at all.

"Is not this a beautiful piece of stuff?" said both the swindlers, showing and explaining the beautiful pattern and colors which were not there to be seen.

"I know I am no fool," thought the man, "so it must be that I am unfit for my good post. It is very strange, though. However, one must not let it appear." So he praised the stuff he did not see, and assured them of his delight in the beautiful colors and the originality of the design.

"It is absolutely charming," he said to the Emperor. Everybody in the town was talking about this splendid stuff.

Now the Emperor thought he would like to see it while it was still on the loom. So, accompanied by a number of selected courtiers, among whom were the two faithful officials who had already seen the imaginary stuff, he went to visit the crafty impostors, who were working away as hard as ever they could at the empty loom.

"It is magnificent," said both the honest officials. "Only see, Your Majesty, what a design! What colors!" And they pointed to the empty loom, for they each thought no doubt the others could see the stuff.

"What?" thought the Emperor. "I see nothing at all. This is terrible! Am I a fool? Am I not fit to be Emperor? Why, nothing worse could happen to me!"

"Oh, it is beautiful," said the Emperor. "It has my highest approval." And he nodded his satisfaction as he gazed at the empty loom. Nothing would induce him to say that he could not see anything.

The whole suite gazed and gazed, but saw nothing more than all the others. However, they all exclaimed with His Majesty, "It is very beautiful." And they advised him to wear a suit made of this wonderful cloth on the occasion of a great procession which was just about to take place. "Magnificent! Gorgeous! Excellent!" went from mouth to mouth. They were all equally delighted with it. The Emperor gave each of the rogues an order of knighthood to be worn in their buttonholes and the title of "Gentleman Weaver."

The swindlers sat up the whole night before the day on which the procession was to take place, burning sixteen candles, so that people might see how anxious they were to get the Emperor's new clothes ready. They pretended to take the stuff off the loom. They cut it out in the air with a huge pair of scissors, and they stitched away with needles without any thread in them.

At last they said, "Now the Emperor's new clothes are ready."

The Emperor with his grandest courtiers went to them himself, and both swindlers raised one arm in the air, as if they were holding something. They said, "See, these are the trousers. This is the coat. Here is the mantle," and so on. "It is as light as a spider's web. One might think one had nothing on, but that is the very beauty of it."

"Yes," said all the courtiers, but they could not see anything, for there was nothing to see.

"Will Your Imperial Majesty be graciously pleased to take off your clothes?" said the impostors. "Then we may put on the new ones, along here before the great mirror."

The Emperor took off all his clothes, and the impostors pretended to give him one article of dress after the other of the new ones which they had pretended to make. They pretended to fasten something around his waist and to tie on something. This was the train, and the Emperor turned round and round in front of the mirror.

"How well His Majesty looks in the new clothes! How becoming they are!" cried all the people round. "What a design, and what colors! They are most gorgeous robes."

"The canopy is waiting outside which is to be carried over Your Majesty in the procession," said the master of the ceremonies.

"Well, I am quite ready," said the Emperor. "Don't the clothes fit well?" Then he turned round again in front of the mirror, so that he should seem to be looking at his grand things.

The chamberlains who were to carry the train stooped and pretended to lift it from the ground with both hands, and they walked along with their hands in the air. They dared not let it appear that they could not see anything.

Then the Emperor walked along in the procession under the gorgeous canopy, and everybody in the streets and at the windows exclaimed, "How beautiful the Emperor's new clothes are! What a splendid train! And they fit to perfection!" Nobody would let it appear that he could see nothing, for then he would not be fit for his post, or else he was a fool.

None of the Emperor's clothes had been so successful before.

"But he has got nothing on," said a little child.

"Oh, listen to the innocent," said its father. And one person whispered to the other what the child had said. "He has nothing on—a child says he has nothing on!"

"But he has nothing on!" at last cried all the people.

The Emperor writhed, for he knew it was true. But he thought "The procession must go on now." So he held himself stiffer than ever, and the chamberlains held up the invisible train.

The Steadfast Tin Soldier

THERE were once five and twenty tin soldiers, all brothers, for they were the offspring of the same old tin spoon. Each man shouldered his gun, kept his eyes well to the front, and wore the smartest red and blue uniform imaginable. The first thing they heard in their new world, when the lid was taken off the box, was a little boy clapping his hands and crying, "Soldiers, soldiers!"

It was his birthday and they had just been given to him, so he lost no time in setting them up on the table. All the soldiers were exactly alike with one exception, and he differed from the rest in having only one leg. For he was made last, and there was not quite enough tin left to finish him. However, he stood just as well on his one leg as the others did on two. In fact he was the one who became famous.

On the table where they were being set up were many other toys, but the chief thing which caught the eye was a delightful paper castle. You could see through the tiny windows right into the rooms. Outside there were some little trees surrounding a small mirror, representing a lake, whose surface reflected the waxen swans which were swimming about on it. It was altogether charming, but the prettiest thing of all was a little maiden standing at the open door of the castle.

She too was cut out of paper, but she wore a dress of the lightest gauze, with a dainty little blue ribbon over her shoulders, by way of a scarf, set off by a brilliant spangle as big as her whole face. The little maid was stretching out both arms, for she was a dancer. And in the dance one of her legs was raised so high into the air that the tin soldier could see absolutely nothing of it, and supposed that she like himself had but one leg.

"That would be the very wife for me!" he thought, "but she is much too grand. She lives in a palace, while I only have a box, and then there are five and twenty of us to share it. No, that would be no place for her. But I must try to make her acquaintance!" Then he lay down full length behind a snuffbox which stood on the table. From that point he could have a good look at the lady, who continued to stand on one leg without losing her balance.

Late in the evening the other soldiers were put into their box, and the people of the house went to bed. Now was the time for the toys to play. They amused themselves with paying visits, fighting battles, and giving balls. The tin soldiers rustled about in their box for they wanted to join the games, but they could not get the lid off. The nutcrackers turned somersaults and the pencil scribbled nonsense on the slate. There was such a noise that the canary woke up and joined in, but his remarks were in verse. The only two who did not move were the tin soldier and the little dancer. She stood as stiff as ever on tiptoe, with her arms spread out. He was equally firm on his one leg, and he did not take his eyes off her for a moment.

Then the clock struck twelve, when pop! up flew the lid of the snuffbox, but there was no snuff in it. No! There was a little black goblin, a sort of jack-in-the-box.

"Tin soldier," said the goblin, "have the goodness to keep your eyes to yourself." But the tin soldier feigned not to hear. "Ah! you just wait till tomorrow," said the goblin.

In the morning when the children got up, they put the tin soldier on the window frame, and whether it was caused by the goblin or by a puff of wind, I do not know, but all at once the window burst open and the soldier fell head foremost from the third story.

It was a terrific descent, and he landed at last with his leg in the air and resting on his cap, with his bayonet fixed between two paving stones. The maidservant and the little boy ran down at once to look for him, but although they almost trod on him they could not see him. Had the soldier called out, "Here I am!" they would have found him. But he did not think it proper to shout when he was in uniform.

Presently it began to rain, and the drops fell faster and faster till there was a regular torrent. When it was over, two street boys came along. "Look out!" said one. "There is a tin soldier. He shall go for a sail."

So they made a boat out of a newspaper and put the soldier into the middle of it, and he sailed away down the gutter. Both boys ran alongside clapping their hands. Good heavens! what waves there were in the gutter, and what a current, but then it certainly had rained cats and dogs. The paper boat danced up and down, and now and then whirled round and round. A shudder ran through the tin soldier, but he remained undaunted and did not move a muscle. He only looked straight before him with his gun shouldered. All at once the boat drifted under a long wooden tunnel, and it became as dark as it was in his box.

"Where on earth am I going now?" thought he. "Well, well, it is all the fault of that goblin! Oh, if only the little maiden were with me in the boat, it might be twice as dark for all I should care."

At this moment a big water rat, who lived in the tunnel, came up.

"Have you a pass?" asked the rat. "Hand up your pass."

The tin soldier did not speak, but clung still tighter to his gun. The boat rushed on, the rat close behind. Phew, how he gnashed his teeth and shouted to the bits of stick and straw, "Stop him! Stop him! He hasn't paid his toll. He hasn't shown his pass."

But the current grew stronger and stronger. The tin soldier could already see daylight before him at the end of the tunnel, but he also heard a roaring sound, fit to strike terror to the bravest heart. Just imagine: where the tunnel ended, the stream rushed straight into the big canal. That would be just as dangerous for him as it would be for us to shoot a great rapid.

He was so near the end now that it was impossible to stop. The boat dashed out. The poor tin soldier held himself as stiff as he could. No one should say of him that he even winced!

The boat swirled round three or four times and filled with water to the edge; it must sink. The tin soldier stood up to his neck in water, and the boat sank deeper and deeper. The paper became limper and limper, and at last the water went over his head. Then he thought of the pretty little dancer whom he was never to see again, and this refrain rang in his ears:

> "Onward! Onward! Soldier!
> For death thou canst not shun."

At last the paper gave way entirely and the soldier fell through, but at the same moment he was swallowed by a big fish. Oh, how dark it was inside the fish! It was worse even than being in the tunnel. And then it was so narrow! But the tin soldier was as dauntless as ever and lay full length, shouldering his gun.

The fish rushed about and made the most frantic movements. At last it became quite quiet, and after a time a flash like lightning pierced it. The soldier was once more in the broad daylight, and someone called out loudly, "A tin soldier!" The fish had been caught, taken to market, sold, and brought into the kitchen, where the cook cut it open with a large knife. She took the soldier up by the waist with two fingers and carried him into the parlor, where everyone wanted to see the wonderful man who had traveled about in the stomach of a fish. But the tin soldier was not at all proud. They set him up on the table, and—wonder of wonders! he found himself in the very same room that he had been in before. He saw the very same children, and the toys were still standing on the table, as well as the beautiful castle with the pretty little dancer.

She still stood on one leg and held the other up in the air. You see, she also was unbending. The soldier was so much moved that he was ready to shed tears of tin, but that would not have been fitting. He looked at her and she looked at him, but they said never a word. At this moment one of the little boys took up the tin soldier, and without rhyme or reason threw him into the fire. No doubt the little goblin in the snuffbox was to blame for that. The tin soldier stood there, lighted up by the flame and in the most horrible heat, but whether it was the heat of the real fire, or the warmth of his feelings, he did not know. He had lost all his gay color. It might have been from his perilous journey, or it might have been from grief. Who can tell?

He looked at the little maiden and she looked at him, and he felt that he was melting away, but he still managed to keep himself erect, shouldering his gun bravely.

A door was suddenly opened. The draught caught the little dancer and she fluttered like a sylph, straight into the fire, to the soldier, blazed up and was gone!

By this time the soldier was reduced to a mere lump, and when the maid took away the ashes next morning she found him in the shape of a small tin heart. All that was left of the dancer was her spangle, and that was burned as black as a coal.

The Little Match Girl

IT was late on a bitterly cold New Year's Eve. The snow was falling. A poor little girl was wandering in the dark cold streets; she was bareheaded and barefoot. She had of course had slippers on when she left home, but they were not much good, for they were so huge. They had last been worn by her mother, and they fell off the poor little girl's feet when she was running across the street to avoid two carriages that were rolling rapidly by. One of the shoes could not be found at all, and the other was picked up by a boy who ran off with it, saying that it would do for a cradle when he had children of his own.

So the poor little girl had to walk on with her little bare feet, which were red and blue with the cold. She carried a quantity of matches in her old apron, and held a packet of them in her hand. Nobody had bought any of her during all the long day, and nobody had even given her a copper. The poor little creature was hungry and perishing with cold, and she looked the picture of misery.

The snowflakes fell on her long yellow hair, which curled so prettily round her face, but she paid no attention to that. Lights were shining from every window, and there was a most delicious odor of roast goose in the streets, for it was New Year's Eve. She could not forget that! She found a corner where one house projected a little beyond the next

The poor little girl held a packet of matches

one, and here she crouched, drawing up her feet under her, but she was colder than ever. She did not dare to go home, for she had not sold any matches and had not earned a single penny. Her father would beat her, and besides it was almost as cold at home as it was here. They had only the roof over them, and the wind whistled through it although they stuffed up the biggest cracks with rags and straw.

Her little hands were almost stiff with cold. Oh, one little match would do some good! If she only dared, she would pull one out of the packet and strike it on the wall to warm her fingers. She pulled out one. *R-r-sh-sh!* How it sputtered and blazed! It burnt with a bright clear flame, just like a little candle, when she held her hand round it. Now the light seemed very strange to her! The little girl fancied that she was sitting in front of a big stove with polished brass feet and handles. There was a splendid fire blazing in it and warming her so beautifully, but—what happened? Just as she was stretching out her feet to warm them, the flame went out, the stove vanished—and she was left sitting with the end of the burnt match in her hand.

She struck a new one. It burnt, it blazed up, and where the light fell upon the wall, it became transparent like gauze, and she could see right through it into the room. The table was spread with a snowy cloth and pretty china. A roast goose stuffed with apples and prunes was steaming on it. And what was even better, the goose hopped from the dish with the carving knife sticking in his back and waddled across the floor. It came right up to the poor child, and then—the match went out, and there was nothing to be seen but the thick black wall.

She lit another match. This time she was sitting under a lovely Christmas tree. It was much bigger and more beautifully decorated than the one she had seen when she peeped through the glass doors at the rich merchant's house this very Christmas. Thousands of lighted candles gleamed under its branches. And many colored pictures, such as she had seen in the shop windows, looked down at her. The little girl stretched out both her hands towards them—then out went the match. All the Christmas candles rose higher and higher, till she saw that they were only the twinkling stars. One of them fell and made a bright streak of light across the sky.

"Someone is dying," thought the little girl, for her old grandmother, the only person who had ever been kind to her, used to say, "When a star falls, a soul is going up to God."

Now she struck another match against the wall, and this time it was her grandmother who appeared in the circle of flame. She saw her quite clearly and distinctly, looking so gentle and happy.

"Grandmother!" cried the little creature. "Oh, do take me with you. I know you will vanish when the match goes out. You will vanish like the warm stove, the delicious goose, and the beautiful Christmas tree!"

She hastily struck a whole bundle of matches, because she did so long to keep her grandmother with her. The light of the matches made it as bright as day. Grandmother had never before looked so big or so beautiful. She lifted the little girl up in her arms, and they soared in a halo of light and joy, far, far above the earth, where there was no more cold, no hunger, and no pain—for they were with God.

In the cold morning light the poor little girl sat there, in the corner between the houses, with rosy cheeks and a smile on her face—dead. Frozen to death on the last night of the old year. New Year's Day broke on the little body still sitting with the ends of the burnt-out matches in her hand.

"She must have tried to warm herself," they said. Nobody knew what beautiful visions she had seen, nor in what a halo she had entered with her grandmother upon the glories of the New Year.

The Swineherd

THERE was once a poor prince who had only a tiny king-dom, but it was big enough to allow him to marry, and he was bent upon marrying.

Now it certainly was rather bold of him to say to the Emperor's daughter, "Will you have me?" He did, however, venture to say so, for his name was known far and wide. And there were hundreds of princesses who would have said "Yes," and "Thank you, kindly," but see if *she* would!

Let us hear about it.

A rose tree grew on the grave of the Prince's father. It was such a beautiful rose tree. But it bloomed only every fifth year, and then bore only one blossom. What a rose that was! By merely smelling it one forgot all of one's cares and sorrows.

Then he had a nightingale which sang as if every lovely melody in the world dwelt in her little throat. This rose and this nightingale were to be given to the Princess, so they were put into great silver caskets and sent to her.

The Emperor had them carried before him into the great hall where the Princess was playing at "visiting" with her ladies-in-waiting—they had nothing else to do. When she saw the caskets with the gifts, she clapped her hands with delight.

"If it were only a little pussy cat!" said she. But there was the lovely rose.

"Oh, how exquisitely it is made!" said all the ladies-in-waiting.

"It is more than beautiful," said the Emperor. "It is neatly made." But the Princess touched it, and then she was ready to cry.

"Fie, papa!" she said. "It is not made. It is a real one."

"Fie," said all the ladies-in-waiting. "It is a real one."

"Well, let us see what there is in the other casket, before we get angry," said the Emperor, and out came the nightingale. It sang so beautifully that at first no one could find anything to say against it.

"*Superbe! charmant!*" said the ladies-in-waiting, for they all had a smattering of French; one spoke it worse than the other.

"How that bird reminds me of our lamented Empress' musical box," said an old courtier. "Ah yes, they are the same tunes and the same beautiful execution."

"So they are," said the Emperor, crying like a little child.

"I should hardly think it could be a real one," said the Princess.

"Yes, it is a real one," said those who had brought it.

"Oh, let that bird fly away then," said the Princess, and she would not hear of allowing the Prince to come. But he was not to be crushed. He stained his face brown and black and, pressing his cap over his eyes, he knocked at the door.

"Good morning, Emperor," said he. "Can I be taken into service in the palace?"

"Well, there are so many wishing to do that," said the Emperor. "But let me see. Yes, I need somebody to look after the pigs. We have so many of them."

So the Prince was made imperial swineherd. A horrid little room was given him near the pigsties, and here he had to live. He sat busily at work all day, and by the evening he had made a beautiful little cooking pot. It had bells all round it, and when the pot boiled, they tinkled delightfully and played the old tune:

"Ach du lieber Augustin,
Alles ist weg, weg, weg!" [1]

But the greatest of all its charms was that by holding one's finger in the steam, one could immediately smell all the dinners that were being cooked at every stove in the town. Now this was a very different matter from a rose.

The Princess came walking along with all her ladies-in-waiting, and when she heard the tune she stopped and looked pleased, for she could play "Ach du lieber Augustin" herself. It was her only tune, and she could only play it with one finger.

"Why, that is my tune," she said. "This must be a cultivated swineherd. Ask him what the instrument costs."

So one of the ladies-in-waiting had to go into his room, but before she entered she put on wooden clog-shoes.

"How much do you want for the pot," she asked.

"I must have ten kisses from the Princess," said the swineherd.

"Heaven preserve us!" said the lady.

"I won't take less," said the swineherd.

"Well, what does he say?" asked the Princess.

"I really cannot tell you," said the lady-in-waiting. "It is so shocking."

"Then you must whisper it." And she whispered it.

"He is a wretch!" said the Princess and went away at once. But she had only gone a little way when she heard the bells tinkling beautifully:

"Ach du lieber Augustin."

"Go and ask him if he will take ten kisses from the ladies-in-waiting."

[1] Alas, dear Augustin,
All is lost, lost, lost!

"No, thank you," said the swineherd. "Ten kisses from the Princess, or I keep my pot."

"How tiresome it is," said the Princess. "Then you will have to stand round me, so that no one may see."

So the ladies-in-waiting stood round her and spread out their skirts while the swineherd took his ten kisses, and then the pot was hers.

What a delight it was to them! The pot was kept on the boil day and night. They knew what was cooking on every stove in the town, from the chamberlain's to the shoemaker's. The ladies-in-waiting danced about and clapped their hands.

"We know who has sweet soup and pancakes for dinner, and who has cutlets. How amusing it is."

"Highly interesting," said the mistress of the robes.

"Yes, but hold your tongues, for I am the Emperor's daughter."

"Heaven preserve us!" they all said.

The swineherd—that is to say, the Prince, only nobody knew that he was not a real swineherd—did not let the day pass in idleness, and he now constructed a rattle. When it was swung round it played all the waltzes, galops and jig tunes ever heard since the creation of the world.

"But this is *superbe!*" said the Princess, as she walked by. "I have never heard finer compositions. Go and ask him what the instrument costs, but let us have no more kissing."

"He wants a hundred kisses from the Princess," said the lady-in-waiting.

"I think he is mad!" said the Princess, and she went away, but she had not gone far when she stopped.

"One must encourage art," she said. "I am the Emperor's daughter. Tell him he can have ten kisses, the same as yesterday, and he can take the others from the ladies-in-waiting."

"But we don't like that at all," said the ladies.

"Oh, nonsense! If I can kiss him you can do the same. Remember that I pay you wages as well as give you board and lodging." So the lady-in-waiting had to go again.

"A hundred kisses from the Princess, or let each keep his own."

"Stand in front of me," said she, and all the ladies stood round while he kissed her.

"Whatever is the meaning of that crowd round the pigsties?" said the Emperor as he stepped out on to the veranda. He rubbed his eyes and put on his spectacles. "Why, it is the ladies-in-waiting. What game are they up to? I must go and see!" So he pulled up the heels of his slippers for they were shoes which he had trodden down.

Bless us, what a hurry he was in! When he got into the yard he walked very softly, and the ladies were so busy counting the kisses, so that there should be fair play, and neither too few nor too many kisses, that they never heard the Emperor. He stood on tiptoe.

"What is all this?" he said when he saw what was going on, and he hit them on the head with his slipper just as the swineherd was taking his eighty-sixth kiss.

"Out you go!" said the Emperor. He was very furious, and he put both the Princess and the Prince out of his realm.

There she stood crying, and the swineherd scolded, and the rain poured down in torrents.

"Oh, miserable creature that I am!" said the Princess. "If only I had accepted the handsome Prince. Oh, how unhappy I am!"

The swineherd went behind a tree, wiped the black and brown stain from his face, and threw away his ugly clothes. When he stepped out dressed as a prince, he was so handsome that the Princess could not help curtseying to him.

"I am come to despise thee," he said. "Thou wouldst not have an honorable prince. Thou couldst not prize the rose or the nightingale. But thou wouldst kiss the swineherd for a trumpery musical box! As thou hast made thy bed, so must thou lie upon it."

Then he went back into his own little kingdom and shut and locked the door. So she had to stand outside and sing in earnest:

> "Ach du lieber Augustin,
> Alles ist weg, weg, weg!"

Elder-Tree Mother

THERE was once a little boy who had taken cold by going out and getting his feet wet. No one could think how he managed to do so, for the weather was quite dry. His mother undressed him and put him to bed. Then she brought in the teapot to make him a good cup of elder tea, which is so warming. At the same time, the friendly old man who lived all alone at the top of the house came in at the door. He had neither wife nor child, but he was very fond of children, and he knew so many fairy tales and stories that it was a pleasure to hear him talk.

"Now, if you drink your tea," said the mother, "very likely you will have a story in the meantime."

"Yes, if I can only think of a new one to tell," said the old man. "But how did the little fellow get his feet wet?" asked he.

"Ah," said the mother, "that we cannot find out."

"Will you tell me a story?" asked the little boy.

"Yes, if you can tell me exactly how deep the gutter is in the little street through which you go to school."

"Just halfway up to my knee," said the boy. "That is, if I stand in the deepest part."

"It is easy to see how we got our feet wet," said the old man. "Well, now I suppose I ought to tell a story, but I don't know any more."

"You can make up one, I know," said the boy. "Mother says that you can turn everything you look at into a story, and everything even that you touch."

"Ah, but that kind of tale and story is worth nothing. The real ones come of themselves. They knock at my forehead and say, 'Here we are!' "

"Won't there be a knock soon?" said the boy. And his mother laughed, while she put elder flowers in the teapot and poured boiling water over them. "Oh, do tell me a story!"

"Yes, if a story comes of itself. But tales and stories are very grand—they come only when it pleases them. Stop!" he cried all at once. "Here we have it. Look! There is a story in the teapot now."

The little boy looked at the teapot and saw the lid raise itself gradually. Long branches sprouted out, even from the spout, in all directions, till they became larger and larger, and there appeared a large elder tree, covered with flowers white and fresh. It spread itself even to the bed and pushed the curtains aside. And oh, how fragrant the blossoms smelled!

In the midst of the tree sat a pleasant-looking old woman, in a very strange dress. The dress was green like the leaves of the elder tree, and was decorated with large white elder blossoms. It was not easy to tell whether the border was made of some kind of cloth or of real flowers.

"What is that woman's name?" asked the boy.

"The Romans and Greeks called her a dryad," said the old man, "but we do not understand that name. In the quarter of the town where the sailors live, they call her Elder-Tree Mother, and you must pay attention to her now and listen while you look at the beautiful tree.

"Just such a large blooming tree as this stands in the corner of a poor little yard. And under this tree, one bright sunny afternoon, sat two old people—a sailor and his wife. They had great-grandchildren and would soon celebrate their golden wedding, which is the fiftieth anniversary of the wedding day, as I suppose you know, and the Elder-Tree

Mother sat in the tree and looked as pleased as she does now.

" 'I know when the golden wedding is to be,' said she, but they did not hear her. They were talking of olden times.

" 'Do you remember,' said the old sailor, 'when we were quite little and used to run about and play in the very same yard where we are now sitting, and how we planted little twigs in one corner and made a garden?'

" 'Yes,' said the old woman. 'I remember it quite well; and how we watered the twigs, and one of them was a sprig of elder that took root and put forth green shoots, until it became in time the great tree under which we old people are now seated.'

" 'To be sure,' he replied. 'And in that corner yonder stands the water butt in which I used to sail my boat that I had cut out all myself. And it sailed well, too! But since then I have learned a very different kind of sailing.'

" 'Yes, but before that we went to school,' said she. 'And then we were prepared for confirmation. How we both cried on that day! But in the afternoon we went hand in hand up to the round tower, and saw the view over Copenhagen and across the water. Then we went to Fredericksburg, where the king and queen were sailing in their beautiful boat on the river.'

" 'But I had to sail on a very different voyage elsewhere and be away from home for years on long voyages,' said the old sailor.

" 'Ah yes, and I used to cry about you,' said she, 'for I thought you must be dead, and lying drowned at the bottom of the sea with the waves sweeping over you. And many a time have I got up in the night to see if the weathercock had turned. It turned often enough, but you came not. How well I remember one day. The rain was pouring down from the skies and the man came to the house where I was in service, to fetch away the dust. I went down to him with the dust-box and stood for a moment at the door. What shocking weather it was! And while I stood there, the postman came up and brought me a letter from you. How that letter had traveled about! I tore it open and read it. I laughed and wept at the same time—I was so happy. It said that you were in warm countries where the coffee berries grew, and told what a beautiful country it was and described many other wonderful things. So I stood reading by the dustbin, with the rain pouring down, when all at once somebody came and clasped me round the waist.'

" 'Yes, and you gave me such a box on the ears that they tingled,' said the old man.

" 'I did not know that it was you,' she replied, 'but you had arrived as quickly as your letter, and you looked so handsome, and indeed so you are still. You had a large yellow silk handkerchief in your pocket and a shiny hat on your head. You looked quite fine. And all the time what weather it was and how dismal the street looked!'

" 'And then do you remember,' said he, 'when we were married, and our first boy came, and then Marie, and Niels, and Peter, and Hans Christian?'

" 'Indeed, I do,' she replied. 'And they are all grown up respectable men and women whom everyone likes.'

" 'And now their children have little ones,' said the old sailor. 'There are great-grandchildren for us, strong and healthy too.'

" 'Was it not about this time of the year that we were married?'

" 'Yes. And today is the golden wedding day,' said Elder-Tree Mother, popping her head out just between the two old people, and they thought it was a neighbor nodding to them.

Then they looked at each other and clasped their hands together. Presently came their children and grandchildren, who knew very well that it was the golden wedding day.

They had already wished them joy on that very morning, but the old people had forgotten it, although they remembered so well all that had happened many years before. And the elder tree smelled sweetly, and the setting sun shone upon the faces of the old people till they looked quite ruddy. And the youngest of their grandchildren danced round them joyfully and said they were going to have a feast in the evening, and there were to be hot potatoes.

"Then the Elder-Tree Mother nodded in the tree and cried, 'Hurrah,' with all the rest."

"But that is not a story," said the little boy, who had been listening.

"Not till you understand it," said the old man. "But let us ask the Elder-Tree Mother to explain it."

"It was not exactly a story," said the Elder-Tree Mother, "but the story is coming now, and it is a true one. For out of truth grow the most wonderful stories, just as my beautiful elder bush has sprung out of the teapot."

And then she took the little boy out of bed and laid him on her bosom. And the blooming branches of elder closed over them so that they sat, as it were, in a leafy bower. And the bower flew with them through the air in the most delightful manner.

At once the Elder-Tree Mother changed to a beautiful young maiden. Her dress was still of the same green stuff, ornamented with a border of white elder blossoms, such as the Elder-Tree Mother had worn. In her bosom she wore an elder flower. A wreath of the same was entwined in her golden ringlets. Her large blue eyes were very beautiful to look at. She was the same age as the boy, and they kissed each other and felt very happy. They left the arbor together hand in hand and found themselves in a beautiful flower garden which belonged to their home. On the green lawn their father's stick was tied up. There was life in this stick for the little ones, for no sooner did they place themselves upon it than the white knob changed into a pretty neighing head with a black flowing mane, and four long slim legs sprang forth. The creature was strong and spirited, and galloped with them round the grass plot.

"Hurrah! Now we will ride many miles away," said the boy. "We'll ride to the nobleman's estate where we went last year."

Then they rode round the grass plot again, and the little maiden, who, we know, was Elder-Tree Mother, kept crying out, "Now we are in the country. Do you see the farmhouse with a great baking oven which sticks out from the wall by the roadside like a gigantic egg? There is an elder spreading its branches over it, and a cock is marching about and scratching for the chickens. See how he struts! Now we are near the church. There it stands on the hill, shaded by the great oak trees, one of which is half dead. See, here we are at the blacksmith's forge. How the fire burns! And the half-clad men are striking the hot iron with the hammer, so that the sparks fly about. Now then, away to the nobleman's beautiful estate!"

And the boy saw all that the little girl spoke of as she sat behind him on the stick, for it passed before him, although they were only galloping round the grass plot.

Then they played together on a sidewalk, and raked up the earth to make a little garden. She took elder flowers out of her hair and planted them, and they grew just like those which he had heard the old people talking about, and which they had planted in their young days. They walked about hand in hand too, just as the old people had done when they were children, but they did not go up the round tower nor to Fredericksburg garden. No. But the little girl seized the boy round the waist and they rode all over the whole country. Sometimes it was spring, then summer, then autumn, and then winter followed, while thousands of images were presented to the boy's eyes and heart. And the little girl constantly sang to him, "You must never forget all this."

And through their whole flight the elder tree sent forth the sweetest fragrance. They passed roses and fresh beech trees, but the perfume of the elder tree was stronger than all, for its flowers hung round the little maiden's heart, against which the boy so often leaned his head during their flight.

"It is beautiful here in the spring," said the maiden, as they stood in a grove of beech trees covered with fresh green leaves. At their feet the sweet-scented thyme and blushing anemone lay spread amid the green grass in delicate bloom. "Oh, that it were always spring in the fragrant beech groves!"

"Here it is delightful in summer," said the maiden, as they passed old knights' castles, telling of days gone by, and saw the high walls and pointed gables mirrored in the rivers beneath, where swans were sailing about and peeping into the cool green avenues. In the fields the corn waved to and fro like the sea. Red and yellow flowers grew among the ruins, and the hedges were covered with wild hops and blooming convolvulus. In the evening the moon rose round and full, and the haystacks in the meadows filled the air with their sweet scent. These were scenes never to be forgotten.

"It is lovely here also in autumn," said the little maiden, and then the scene changed.

The sky appeared higher and more beautifully blue, while the forest glowed with colors of red, green, and gold. The hounds were off to the chase. Large flocks of wild birds flew screaming over the Huns' graves, where the blackberry bushes twined around the old ruins. The dark blue sea was dotted with white sails, and in the barns sat old women, maidens, and children, picking hops into a large tub. The young ones sang songs and the old ones told fairy tales of wizards and witches. There could be nothing more pleasant than all this.

"Again," said the maiden, "it is beautiful here in winter." Then in a moment all the trees were covered with hoarfrost and they looked like white coral. The snow crackled beneath the feet as if everyone had on new boots, and one shooting star after another fell from the sky. In warm rooms there could be seen the Christmas trees decked out with presents and lighted up amid festivities and joy. In the country farmhouses could be heard the sound of the violin, and there were games for apples, so that even the poorest child could say, "It is beautiful in winter."

Beautiful indeed were all the scenes which the maiden showed to the little boy. And always around them floated the fragrance of the elder blossom, and ever above them waved the red flag with the white cross under which the old seaman had sailed. The boy, who had become a youth and had gone as a sailor out into the wide world and sailed to warm countries where the coffee grew, and to whom the little girl had given an elder blossom from her bosom for a keepsake when she took leave of him, placed the flower in his hymn book. And when he opened it in foreign lands, he always turned to the spot where this flower of remembrance lay. The more he looked at it, the fresher it appeared. He could, as it were, breathe the homelike fragrance of the woods and see the little girl looking at him with her clear blue eyes from between the petals of the flower, and hear her whispering, "It is beautiful here at home in spring and summer, in autumn and winter," while hundreds of these home scenes passed through his memory.

Many years passed, and he was now an old man seated with his old wife under an elder tree in full blossom. They were holding each other's hands just as the great-grandfather and grandmother had done, and spoke, as they did, of olden times and of the golden wedding.

The little maiden with the blue eyes and the elder blossoms in her hair sat in the tree and nodded to them and said, "Today is the golden wedding." And then she took two flowers out of her wreath and kissed them, and they shone first like silver and then like gold. And as she placed them on the heads of the old people, each flower became a golden crown. And there they sat like a king and queen under the sweetly scented tree, which still looked like an elder bush. Then he related to his old wife the story of the Elder-Tree Mother, just as he had heard it told when he was a little boy. And they both fancied it very much like their own story, especially in some parts which they liked the best.

"Well, and so it is," said the little maiden. "Some call me Elder-Tree Mother, others call me a dryad, but my real name is 'Memory.' It is I who sit in the tree as it grows and grows, and I can think of the past and relate many things. Let me see if you have still preserved the flower."

Then the old man opened his hymn book, and there lay the elder flower as fresh as if it had only just been placed there. And "Memory" nodded, and the two old people with the golden crowns on their heads sat in the red glow of the evening sunlight, and closed their eyes, and—and—the story was ended.

The little boy lay in his bed and did not quite know whether he had been dreaming or listening to a story. The teapot stood on the table, but no elder bush grew out of it, and the old man who had really told the tale was on the threshold and just going out at the door.

"How beautiful it was!" said the little boy. "Mother, I have been to warm countries."

"I can quite believe it," said his mother. "When anyone drinks two full cups of elder flower tea, he may well get into warm countries!" And then she covered him up that he should not take cold. "You have slept well while I have been disputing with the old man as to whether it was a real story or a fairy legend."

"And where is the Elder-Tree Mother?" asked the boy.

"She is in the teapot," said the mother. "And there she may stay."

Hans Clodhopper

THERE was once an old mansion in the country in which lived an old squire with his two sons, and these two sons were too clever by half. They had made up their minds to propose to the King's daughter. And they ventured to do so because she had made it known that she would take any man for a husband who had most to say for himself.

These two took a week over their preparations. It was all the time they had for it, but it was quite enough with all their accomplishments, which were most useful. One of them knew the Latin dictionary by heart, as well as the town newspapers for three years, either forwards or backwards. The second one had made himself acquainted with all the statutes of the Corporations and what every alderman had to know, so he thought he was competent to talk about affairs of state. And he also knew how to embroider harness, for he was clever with his fingers.

"I shall win the King's daughter," they both said, and their father gave each of them a beautiful horse. The one who could repeat the dictionary and the newspapers had a coal-black horse, while the one who was learned in guilds and embroideries had a milk-white one. Then they smeared the corners of their mouths with oil to make them more flexible. All the servants were assembled in the courtyards to see them mount, but just then the third brother came up —for there were three. Only nobody made any account of this one, Hans Clodhopper, as he had no accomplishments like his brothers.

"Where are you going in your fine clothes?" he asked.

"To court, to talk ourselves into favor with the Princess. Haven't you heard the news which is being drummed all over the country?" And then they told him the news.

"Preserve us! Then I must go too," said Hans Clodhopper. But his brothers laughed and rode away.

"Father, give me a horse. I want to get married too. If she takes me she takes me, and if she doesn't take me, I shall take her all the same."

"Stuff and nonsense!" said his father. "I will give no horse to you. Why, you have got nothing to say for yourself, but your brothers are fine fellows."

"If I mayn't have a horse," said Hans Clodhopper, "I'll take the billy goat. He is my own and he can carry me very well!" And he seated himself astride the billy goat, dug his heels into its sides, and galloped off down the highroad. Whew! what a pace they went at.

"Here I come," shouted Hans Clodhopper, and he sang till the air rang.

The brothers rode on in silence. They did not say a word to each other, for they had to store up every good idea which they wanted to produce later on, and their speeches had to be very carefully thought out.

"Hallo!" shouted Hans Clodhopper. "Here I come. See what I've found on the road!" And he showed them a dead crow.

"What on earth will you do with that, Clodhopper?" said they.

"I will give it to the King's daughter."

"Yes, I would do that," said they, and they rode on laughing.

"Hallo, here I come! See what I have found! One doesn't find such a thing as this every day on the road." The brothers turned round to see what it was.

"Clodhopper," said they, "it's nothing but an old wooden shoe with the upper part broken off. Is the Princess to have that too?"

"Yes indeed she is," said Hans, and the brothers again rode on laughing.

"Hallo, hallo, here I am!" shouted Hans Clodhopper. "Now this is something wonderful!"

"What have you found this time?" asked the brothers. "Won't the Princess be delighted!"

"Why," said the brothers, "it's only sand picked up out of the ditch!"

"Yes, that it is," said Hans Clodhopper, "and the finest kind of sand, too. You can hardly hold it." And he filled his pockets with it. His brothers rode on as fast as they could, and arrived at the town gates a whole hour before him. At the gate the suitors received tickets in the order of their arrival, and they were arranged in rows, six in each file and so close together that they could not move their arms. This was a very good thing, or they would have torn each other's garments off, merely because one stood in front of the other. All the other inhabitants of the town stood round the castle, peeping in at the windows to see the King's daughter receive the suitors. And as each one of them came into the room he lost the power of speech.

"No good," said the Princess. "Away with him!"

Now came the brother who could repeat the dictionary, but he had entirely forgotten it while standing in the ranks. The floor creaked and the ceiling was made of looking glass, so that he saw himself standing on his head. And at every window sat three clerks and an alderman, who wrote down all that was said, so that it might be sent to the papers at once and sold for a halfpenny at the street corners. It was terrible, and the stoves had been heated to such a degree that they got red-hot at the top.

"It is terribly hot in here," said the suitor.

"That is because my father is roasting cockerels today," said the Princess.

Bah! There he stood like a fool. He had not expected a conversation of this kind, and he could not think of a word to say, just when he wanted to be specially witty.

"No good," said the King's daughter. "Away with him!" And he had to go.

Then came the second brother. "There's a fearful heat here," said he.

"Yes, we are roasting cockerels today," said the King's daughter.

"What did—what?" said he. And all the reporters duly wrote, "What did—what."

"No good," said the King's daughter. "Away with him!"

Then came Hans Clodhopper. He rode the billy goat right into the room.

"What a burning heat you have here," said he.

"That is because I am roasting cockerels," said the King's daughter.

"That is very convenient," said Hans Clodhopper. "Then I suppose I can get a crow roasted too."

"Yes, very well," said the King's daughter. "But have you anything to roast it in? I have neither pot nor pan."

"But I have," said Hans Clodhopper. "Here is a cooking pot." And he brought out the wooden shoe and put the crow into it.

"Why you have enough for a whole meal," said the King's daughter. "But where shall we get any dripping to baste it with?"

"Oh, I have some in my pocket," said Hans Clodhopper. "I have enough and to spare." And he poured a little of the sand out of his pocket.

"Now I like that," said the Princess. "You have an answer for everything, and you have something to say for yourself. I will have you for a husband. But do you know that every word we have said will be in the paper tomorrow? For at every window sit three clerks and an alderman, and the alderman is the worst, for he doesn't understand." She said this to frighten him. All the clerks sniggered and made blots of ink on the floor.

"Oh, those are the gentry!" said Hans Clodhopper. "Then I must give the alderman the best thing I have." And he turned out his pockets and threw the sand in his face.

"That was cleverly done," said the Princess. "I couldn't have done it, but I will try to learn."

So Hans Clodhopper became King, gained a wife and a crown, and sat upon the throne. We have this straight out of the alderman's newspaper, but it is not to be depended upon.

The Princess and the Pea

THERE was once a prince, and he wanted a princess, but she must be a *real* princess. He traveled all over the world to find one, but there was always something wrong. There were plenty of princesses, but as to whether they were real princesses he had great difficulty in discovering. There was always something which was not quite right about them. So at last he had to come home again, and he was very sad because he wanted a real princess so badly.

One evening there was a terrible storm. It thundered and lightened and the rain poured down in torrents. Indeed it was a fearful night.

In the middle of the storm somebody knocked at the town gate, and the old King himself went to open it.

It was a princess who stood outside, but she was in a terrible state from the rain and the storm. The water streamed out of her hair and her clothes. It ran in at the top of her shoes and out at the heel, but she said that she was a real princess.

"Well we shall soon see if that is true," thought the old Queen, but she said nothing. She went into the bedroom, took all the bedclothes off and laid a single pea on the bedstead. Then she took twenty mattresses and piled them on the top of the pea, and then piled twenty feather beds on the top of the mattresses. Up on top of all these was where the princess was to sleep that night.

In the morning they asked her, "Did you sleep well?"

"Oh, terribly badly!" said the princess. "I hardly closed my eyes the whole night. Heaven knows what was in the bed. I seemed to be lying on something very hard, and my whole body is black and blue this morning. It was terrible!"

They saw at once that she must be a real princess when she felt the pea through twenty mattresses and twenty feather beds. Nobody but a real princess could have such a delicate skin.

So the prince took her to be his wife, for now he was sure that he had found a real princess. And the pea was put into a museum, where it may still be seen if no one has stolen it.

Now this is a true story.

What the Good Man Does Is Always Right

I WILL tell you a story which was told to me when I was a little boy. Every time I thought of the story, it seemed to me to become more and more charming, for it is with stories as it is with many people—they become better as they grow older.

I take it for granted that you have been in the country and seen a very old farmhouse with a thatched roof, with mosses and small plants growing wild upon the thatch. There is a stork's nest on the summit of the gable; for we can't do without the stork. The walls of the house are sloping and the windows are low, and only one of the latter is made so that it will open. The baking oven sticks out of the wall like a little fat body. The elder tree hangs over the paling, and beneath its branches, at the foot of the paling, is a pool of water in which a few ducks are disporting themselves. There is a yard dog too, who barks at all comers.

Just such a farmhouse stood out in the country, and in this house dwelt an old couple—a peasant and his wife. Small as was their property, there was one article among it that they could do without—a horse, which made a living out of the grass it found by the side of the highroad. The old peasant rode into the town on this horse, and often his neighbors borrowed it of him and rendered the old couple some service in return for the loan of it. But they thought it would be best if they sold the horse or exchanged it for something that might be more useful to them. But what might this *something* be?

"You'll know that best, old man," said the wife. "It is a fair day today, so ride into town and get rid of the horse for money, or make a good exchange. Whichever you do will be right to me. Ride off to the fair."

And she fastened his neckerchief for him, for she could do that better than he could. And she tied it in a double bow, for she could do that very prettily. Then she brushed his hat round and round with the palm of her hand, and gave him a kiss. So he rode away upon the horse that was to be sold or to be bartered for something else. Yes, the old man knew what he was about.

The sun shone hotly down and not a cloud was to be seen in the sky. The road was very dusty, for many people, who were all bound for the fair, were driving or riding or walking upon it. There was no shelter anywhere.

Among the rest, a man was trudging along and driving a cow to the fair. The cow was as beautiful a creature as any cow can be.

"She gives good milk, I'm sure," said the peasant. "That would be a very good exchange—the cow for the horse."

"Hallo, you there with the cow!" he said. "I tell you what: I fancy a horse costs more than a cow, but I don't care for that. A cow would be more useful to me. If you like, we'll exchange."

"To be sure I will," said the man, and they exchanged accordingly.

So that was settled and the peasant might have turned back, for he had done the business he came to do. But as he had once made up his mind to go to the fair, he determined to go on, merely to have a look at it. And so he went on to the town with his cow.

Leading the animal, he strode sturdily on, and after a short time he overtook a man who was driving a sheep. It was a good fat sheep with a fine fleece on its back.

"I should like to have that fellow," said our peasant. "He would find plenty of grass by our palings, and in the winter we could keep him in the room with us. Perhaps it would be more practical to have a sheep instead of a cow. Shall we exchange?"

The man with the sheep was quite ready and the bargain was struck. So our peasant went on in the highroad with his sheep. Soon he overtook another man, who came into the road from a field, carrying a great goose under his arm.

"That's a heavy thing you have there. It has plenty of feathers and plenty of fat, and would look well tied to a string and paddling in the water at our place. That would be something for my old woman. She could make all kinds of profit out of it. How often she has said, 'If we only had a goose!' Now perhaps she can have one, and if possible it shall be hers. Shall we exchange? I'll give you my sheep for your goose and thank you into the bargain."

The other man had not the least objection. And accordingly they exchanged, and our peasant became the proprietor of the goose.

By this time he was very near the town. The crowd on the highroad became greater and greater. There was quite a crush of men and cattle. They walked in the road, close by the palings, and at the barrier they even walked into the tollman's potato field, where his own fowl was strutting about with a string to its leg, lest it should take fright at the crowd and stray away, and so be lost. This fowl had short tail feathers, and winked with both its eyes, and looked very cunning. "Cluck, cluck!" said the fowl.

What it thought when it said this I cannot tell you, but directly our good man saw it, he thought, "That's the finest fowl I've ever seen in my life! Why, it's finer than our parson's brood hen. On my word, I should like to have that fowl. A fowl can always find a grain or two, and can almost keep itself. I think it would be a good exchange if I could get that for my goose."

"Shall we exchange?" he asked the toll taker.

"Exchange?" repeated the man. "Well, that would not be a bad thing."

And so they exchanged. The toll taker at the barrier kept the goose and the peasant carried away the fowl.

Now he had done a good deal of business on his way to the fair, and he was hot and tired. He wanted something to eat and a glass of brandy to drink, and soon he was in front of the inn. He was just about to step in when the hostler came out, so they met at the door. The hostler was carrying a sack.

"What have you in that sack?" asked the peasant.

"Rotten apples," answered the hostler. "A whole sackful of them—enough to feed the pigs with."

"Why, that's a terrible waste! I should like to take them to my old woman at home. Last year the old tree by the turf-hole bore only a single apple, and we kept it in the cupboard till it was quite rotten and spoiled. 'It was always property,' my old woman said. But here she could see a quantity of property—a whole sackful. Yes, I shall be glad to show them to her."

"What will you give me for the sackful?" asked the hostler.

"What will I give? I will give my fowl in exchange."

And he gave the fowl accordingly and received the apples, which he carried into the guest room. He leaned the sack carefully by the stove, and then went to the table. But the stove was hot: he had not thought of that. Many guests were present—horse dealers, oxherds, and two Englishmen. And the two Englishmen were so rich that their pockets bulged out with gold coins and almost burst. And they could bet too, as you shall hear.

Hiss-s-s! hiss-s-s! What was that by the stove? The apples were beginning to roast!

"What is that?"

"Why, do you know—" said our peasant.

And he told the whole story of the horse he had changed for a cow, and all the rest of it, down to the apples.

"Well, your old woman will give it to you well when you get home!" said one of the two Englishmen. "There will be a disturbance."

"What? Give me what?" said the peasant. "She will kiss me and say, 'What the old man does is always right.' "

"Shall we wager?" said the Englishman. "We'll wager coined gold by the ton—a hundred pounds to the hundred-weight!"

"A bushel will be enough," replied the peasant. "I can only set the bushel of apples against it, and I'll throw myself and my old woman into the bargain. And I fancy that's piling up the measure."

"Done! Taken!"

And the bet was made. The host's carriage came up, and the Englishmen got in and the peasant got in. Away they went, and soon they stopped before the peasant's farm.

"Good evening, old woman."

"Good evening, old man."

"I've made the exchange."

"Yes, you understand what you're about," said the woman. And she embraced him, and paid no attention to the strange guests, nor did she notice the sack.

"I got a cow in exchange for the horse," said he.

"Heaven be thanked!" said she. "What glorious milk we

shall now have, and butter and cheese on the table. That was a most capital exchange!"

"Yes, but I changed the cow for a sheep."

"Ah, that's better still!" cried the wife. "You always think of everything. We have just pasture enough for a sheep. Ewe's milk and cheese, and woolen jackets and stockings! The cow can not give those, and her hairs will only come off. How you think of everything!"

"But I changed away the sheep for a goose."

"Then this year we shall really have roast goose to eat, my dear old man. You are always thinking of something to give me pleasure. How charming that is! We can let the goose walk about with a string to her leg, and she'll grow fatter still before we roast her."

"But I gave away the goose for a fowl," said the man.

"A fowl? That *was* a good exchange!" replied the woman. "The fowl will lay eggs and hatch them, and we shall have chickens. We shall have a whole poultry yard! Oh, that's just what I was wishing for."

"Yes, but I exchanged the fowl for a sack of shriveled apples."

"What! I must positively kiss you for that!" exclaimed the wife. "My dear good husband! Now I'll tell you something. Do you know, you had hardly left me this morning before I began thinking how I could give you something very nice this evening. I thought it should be pancakes with savory herbs. I had eggs, and bacon too. But I lacked herbs. So I went over to the schoolmaster's, as they have herbs there, I know. But the schoolmistress is a mean woman, though she looks so sweet. I begged her to lend me a handful of herbs. 'Lend!' she answered me, 'nothing at all grows in our garden, not even a shriveled apple. I could not even lend you a shriveled apple, my dear woman.' But now I can lend *her* ten, or a whole sackful. That I'm very glad of.

That makes me laugh." And with that she gave him a resounding kiss.

"I like that!" exclaimed both the Englishmen together. "Always going downhill, and always merry! That's worth the money."

So they paid a hundredweight of gold to the peasant, who was not scolded, but kissed.

Yes, it always pays, when the wife sees and always asserts that her husband knows best and that whatever he does is right.

You see, that is my story. I heard it when I was a child. And now you have heard it too, and know that "What the good man does is always right."

The Roses and the Sparrows

IT really appeared as if something very important was going on by the duck farm, but this was not the case. A few minutes before, all the ducks had been resting on the water or standing on their heads, for they can do so, and then they all swam in a bustle to the shore. The traces of their feet could be seen on the wet earth, and far and wide could be heard their quacking. The water, so lately clear and bright as a mirror, became disturbed.

A moment before, every tree and bush near the old farmhouse, and the house itself, with the holes in the roof and the swallows' nests, and above all the beautiful rosebush covered with roses, had been clearly reflected in the water. The rosebush on the wall hung over the water, which resembled a picture, only everything appeared upside down. But when the water was set in motion, it all vanished and the picture disappeared. Two feathers dropped by the fluttering ducks floated to and fro on the water. All at once they took a start, as if the wind were coming, but it did not come and they were obliged to lie still, as the water again became quiet and at rest. The roses could once more behold their own reflections. They were very beautiful but they knew it not, for no one had told them. The sun shone between the delicate leaves. Everywhere the sweet fragrance spread itself, creating a feeling of deep happiness.

"How beautiful is our existence!" said one of the roses. "I feel as if I should like to kiss the sun. It is so bright and warm! I should like to kiss the roses, too, our images in the water, and the pretty birds there in their nests. There are some birds, too, in a nest above us. They stretch out their heads and cry 'Tweet, tweet,' very faintly. They have no feathers yet, as their father and mother have. They are good neighbors both above us and below us. How beautiful is our life!"

The young birds above and the young ones below were the same ones. They were sparrows, and their nest was reflected in the water. Their parents were sparrows also, and they had taken possession of an empty swallow's nest of the year before, and occupied it now as if it were their own.

"Are those ducks' children that are swimming about?" asked the young sparrows, as they spied the feathers on the water.

"If you must ask questions, pray ask sensible ones," said the mother. "Can you not see that these are feathers, the living stuff for clothes, which I wear and which you will wear soon? But ours are much finer. I should like, however, to have them up here in the nest. They would make it so warm. I am rather curious to know why the ducks were so alarmed just now. It could not be from fear of us, certainly, though I did say 'tweet' rather loudly. The thickheaded roses really ought to know, but they are very ignorant. They only look at one another and smell. I am heartily tired of such neighbors."

"Listen to the sweet little birds above us," said the roses. "They are trying to sing. They cannot manage it yet, but it will be done in time. What a pleasure it will be to have such lively neighbors."

Suddenly two horses came prancing along to drink at the water. A peasant boy rode one of them. He had a broad-brimmed black hat on, but had taken off most of his other clothes that he might ride into the deepest part of the pond. He whistled like a bird, and while passing the rosebush he plucked a rose and placed it in his hat and then rode on, thinking himself very fine. The other roses looked at their sister and asked each other where she could be going, but they did not know.

"I should like for once to go out into the world," said one, "although it is very lovely here in our home of green leaves. The sun shines warmly by day, and in the night we can see that heaven is more beautiful still, as it sparkles through the holes in the sky."

She meant the stars, for she knew no better.

"We make the house very lively," said the mother sparrow. "Since people say that a swallow's nest brings luck, they are pleased to see us. But as to our neighbors, a rosebush on the wall produces damp. It will most likely be removed, and perhaps grain will grow here instead of it. Roses are good for nothing but to be looked at and smelled, or perhaps one may chance to be stuck in a hat. I have heard from my mother that they fall off every year. The farmer's wife preserves them by laying them in salt, and then they receive a French name, which I neither can nor will pronounce. Then they are sprinkled on the fire to produce a pleasant smell. Such, you see, is their life. They are formed only to please the eye and the nose. Now you know all about them."

As evening approached, the gnats played about in the warm air beneath the rosy clouds, and the nightingale came and sang to the roses. She sang that *the beautiful* was like sunshine to the world, and that *the beautiful* lives forever. The roses thought that the nightingale was singing of herself, which anyone, indeed, could easily suppose. They never imagined that her song could refer to them. But it was a joy to them, and they wondered to themselves whether all the little sparrows in the nest would become nightingales.

"We understood that bird's song very well," said the young sparrows, "but one word was not clear. What is *the beautiful?*"

"Oh, nothing of any consequence," replied the mother sparrow. "It is something relating to appearances over yonder at the nobleman's house. The pigeons have a house of their own, and every day they have corn and peas spread for them. I have dined there with them sometimes, and so shall you by and by, for I believe the old maxim 'Tell me what company you keep, and I will tell you what you are.' Well, over at the noble house there are two birds with green throats and crests on their heads. They can spread out their tails like large wheels, and they reflect so many beautiful colors that it dazzles the eyes to look at them. These birds are called peacocks, and they belong to the beautiful, but if even a few of their feathers were plucked off, they would not appear better than we do. I would myself have plucked some out had they not been so large."

"I will pluck them," squeaked the youngest sparrow, who had no feathers of his own yet.

In the cottage dwelt two young married people, who loved each other very much, and who were so industrious and active that everything looked neat and pretty around them. Early on Sunday mornings the young wife came out, gathered a handful of the most beautiful roses, and put them in a glass of water, which she placed on a side table.

"I see now that it is Sunday," said the husband as he kissed his little wife. Then they sat down and read their hymn books, holding each other's hands, while the sun shone down upon the young couple and upon the fresh roses in the glass.

"This sight is really too wearisome," said the mother sparrow, who from her nest could look into the room. Then she flew away.

The same thing occurred the next Sunday, and indeed

every Sunday fresh roses were gathered and placed in a glass, but the rose tree continued to bloom in all its beauty. After a while the young sparrows were fledged and wanted to fly, but the mother would not allow it. So they were obliged to remain in the nest for the present, while she flew away alone. It so happened that some boys had fastened a snare made of horsehair to the branch of a tree, and before she was aware, her leg became entangled in the horsehair so tightly as almost to cut it through. What pain and terror she felt! The boys ran up quickly and seized her, not in a very gentle manner.

"It is only a sparrow," they said. However, they did not let her fly away but took her home with them, and every time she squeaked they knocked her on the beak.

In the farmyard they met an old man who knew how to make soap for shaving and washing, in cakes or in balls. When he saw the sparrow which the boys had brought home and which they said they did not know what to do with, he said "Shall we make it beautiful?"

A cold shudder passed over the sparrow when she heard this. The old man then took a shell containing a quantity of glittering gold leaf, from a box full of beautiful colors, and told the youngsters to fetch the white of an egg. With this he besmeared the sparrow all over, and then laid the gold leaf upon it, so that the mother sparrow was now gilded from head to tail. Though she thought not of her appearance, she trembled in every limb. Then the soapmaker tore a little piece out of the red lining of his jacket, cut notches in it so that it looked like a cock's comb, and stuck it on the bird's head.

"Now you will see Gold-jacket fly," said the old man. And he released the sparrow, which flew away in deadly terror with the sunlight shining upon her.

How she did glitter! All the sparrows, and even a crow, who is a knowing old boy, were scared at the sight. Yet still they followed it to discover what foreign bird it could be. Driven by anguish and terror she flew homewards, almost ready to sink to the earth for want of strength. The flock of birds that were following increased, and some even tried to peck her.

"Look at him! Look at him!" they all cried. "Look at him! Look at him!" cried the young ones as their mother approached the nest, but they did not know her. "That must be a young peacock, for he glitters in all colors. It quite hurts one's eyes to look at him. As mother told us: 'Tweet, this is *the beautiful*.'"

Then they pecked the bird with their little beaks, so that she was quite unable to get into the nest. She was too much exhausted even to say "Tweet," much less to say "I am your mother." So the other birds fell upon the sparrow and pulled out feather after feather, till she sunk bleeding into the rosebush.

"You poor creature," said the roses. "Be at rest. We will hide you. Lean your little head against us."

The sparrow spread out her wings once more and drew them in close to her, and then lay dead amongst the roses, her fresh and lovely neighbors.

"Tweet," sounded from the nest. "Where can our mother be staying? It is quite unaccountable. Can this be a trick of hers to show us that we are now to take care of ourselves? She has left us the house as an inheritance, but as it cannot belong to us all when we have families, who is to have it?"

"It won't do for you all to stay with me when I increase my household with a wife and children," remarked the youngest.

"I shall have more wives and children than you," said the second.

"But I am the eldest," cried a third.

Then they all became angry. They beat each other with

their wings and pecked with their beaks, till one after another bounded out of the nest. There they lay in a rage, holding their heads on one side and twinkling the eye that looked upwards. This was their way of looking sulky. They could all fly a little, and by practice they soon learned to do so much better. At length they agreed upon a sign by which they might be able to recognize each other, in case they should meet in the world after they had separated. This sign was to be the cry of "Tweet," and a scratching on the ground three times with the left foot.

The youngest, who was left behind in the nest, spread himself out as broad as ever he could, for he was the householder now. But his glory did not last long. During that night red flames of fire burst through the windows of the cottage. They seized the thatched roof and blazed up frightfully. The whole house was burned down and the sparrow perished with it, while the young couple fortunately escaped with their lives. When the sun rose again, and all nature looked refreshed as after a quiet sleep, nothing remained of the cottage but a few blackened charred beams, leaning against the chimney that now was the only master of the place. Thick smoke still rose from the ruins, but outside on the wall the rosebush still remained unhurt, blooming and fresh as ever, while each flower and each spray was mirrored in the clear water beneath.

"How beautifully the roses are blooming on the walls of that ruined cottage," said a passer-by. "A more lovely picture could scarcely be imagined. I must draw it."

The speaker took out of his pocket a little book full of white leaves of paper, for he was an artist, and with a pencil he sketched the smoking ruins, the blackened rafters, and the chimney that overhung them, and which seemed more and more to totter. Quite in the foreground stood the large, blooming rosebush, which added beauty to the picture. Indeed, it was for the sake of the roses that the sketch had been made. Later in the day two of the sparrows who had been born there came by.

"Where is the house?" they asked. "Where is the nest? Tweet, tweet. All is burnt down, and our strong brother with it. That is all he got by keeping the nest. The roses have escaped—they look as well as ever, with their rosy cheeks. They do not trouble themselves about their neighbor's misfortunes! I won't speak to them. Really, in my opinion, the place looks very ugly!" So they flew away.

On a fine, bright sunny day in autumn, so bright that anyone might have supposed it was still the middle of summer, a number of pigeons were hopping about in the nicely kept courtyard of the nobleman's house, in front of the great steps. Some were black, others white, still others of various colors, and their plumage glittered in the sunshine. An old mother pigeon said to her young ones, "Place yourselves in groups! Place yourselves in groups! That makes a much better appearance."

"What are those little gray creatures that are running about behind us?" asked an old pigeon, with red and green round her eyes. "Little gray ones, little gray ones," she cried.

"They are sparrows—good enough little creatures. We have always had the character of being very good-natured, so we allow them to pick up some grain with us. They do not interrupt our conversation, and they draw back their left foot so prettily."

Sure enough so they did, three times each, and with the left foot too. And they said "Tweet," by which we recognize them as the sparrows that were brought up in the nest on the house that was burnt down.

"The food here is very good indeed," said the sparrows. The pigeons strutted round each other, puffed out their throats, and formed their own opinions on everything they observed.

"Do you see the pouter pigeon?" said one of another. "Do you see how he swallows the peas? He takes too much, and always chooses the best of everything. Coo-oo, coo-oo. How the ugly, spiteful creature lifts his crest." And all their eyes sparkled with malice. "Place yourselves in groups, place yourselves in groups. Little gray coats; little gray coats. Coo-oo, coo-oo."

So they went on, and it will be the same a thousand years hence. The sparrows feasted bravely, and listened attentively. They even stood in ranks like the pigeons, but it did not suit them. So having satisfied their hunger, they left the pigeons passing their own opinions upon them to each other, and slipped through the garden railings. The door of a room in the house leading into the garden stood open, and one of them who felt brave after his good dinner, hopped upon the threshold, crying, "Tweet! I can venture so far."

"Tweet," said another. "I can venture that and a great deal more." And into the room he hopped.

The first followed and, seeing no one there, the third became courageous and flew right across the room, saying, "Venture everything, or do not venture at all. This is a wonderful place, a man's nest I suppose. And look! What can this be?"

Just in front of the sparrows stood the ruins of the burnt cottage. Roses were blooming over it, and their reflection appeared in the water beneath. The black charred beams rested against the tottering chimney. How could it be? How came the cottage and the roses in a room in the nobleman's house? Then the sparrows tried to fly over the roses and the chimney, but they only struck themselves against a flat wall. It was a picture—a large beautiful picture, which the artist had painted from his little sketch.

"Tweet," said the sparrows. "It is really nothing after all. It only looks like reality. Tweet, I suppose that is *the beautiful*. Can you understand it? I can not." Then some persons entered the room, and the sparrows flew away.

Years and days passed. The pigeons had often "coo-oo-d," we must not say quarreled, though perhaps they did, naughty things. The sparrows had suffered from cold in the winter and had lived gloriously in summer. They were all betrothed, or married, or whatever you like to call it. They had little ones, and of course each considered his own brood the wisest and the prettiest. One flew in this direction, and another in that, and when they met, they recognized each other by saying "Tweet," and by three times drawing back the left foot. The eldest remained single. She had no nest nor young ones. Her great wish was to see a large town, so she flew to Copenhagen.

Near to the castle that stood by the channel could be seen a large house, richly decorated with various colors. Down the channel sailed many ships, laden with apples and earthenware. The windows were broader below than at the top, and when the sparrows peeped through, they saw a room that looked to them like a tulip, with beautiful colors of every shade. Within the tulip were white figures of human beings, made of marble. Some few were made of plaster, but this is the same thing to a sparrow. Upon the roof stood a metal chariot and horses, and the goddess of victory, also of metal, was seated in the chariot driving the horses. It was Thorwaldsen's Museum. "How it shines and glitters!" said the maiden sparrow. "This must be *the beautiful*—tweet— only this is larger than a peacock." She remembered what her mother had told them in her childhood: that the peacock was one of the greatest examples of *the beautiful*. She flew down into the courtyard, where everything also was very grand. The walls were painted to represent palm branches, and in the midst of the court stood a large, blooming rose tree, spreading its young, sweet, rose-covered branches over a grave. Thither the maiden sparrow flew, for she saw many others of her own kind.

"Tweet," said she, drawing back her foot three times. During the years that had passed, she had often made the usual greeting to the sparrows she met, but without receiving any acknowledgment, for friends who are once separated do not meet every day. This manner of greeting had become a habit to her, and today two old sparrows and a young one returned the greeting.

"Tweet," they replied, and drew back the left foot three times. They were two old sparrows out of the nest, and a young one belonging to the family. "Ah, good day. How do you do? To think of our meeting here! This is a very grand place, but there is not much to eat. This is *the beautiful*. Tweet."

A great many people now came out of the side rooms in which the marble statues stood, and approached the grave where slept the remains of the great master who had carved these marble statues. Each face had a reflected glory as they stood round Thorwaldsen's grave, and some few gathered up the fallen rose leaves to preserve them. They had all come from afar: one from mighty England, others from Germany and France. One very handsome lady plucked a rose and concealed it in her bosom.

Then the sparrows thought that the roses ruled in this place and that the whole house had been built for them, which seemed really too much honor. But as all the people showed their love for the roses, the sparrows thought they would not remain behindhand in paying their respects.

"Tweet," they said and swept the ground with their tails, and they glanced with one eye at the roses. They had not looked at them very long, however, before they felt convinced that they were old acquaintances, and so they actually were. The artist who had sketched the rosebush and the ruins of the cottage had since then received permission to transplant it, and had given it to the architect, for more beautiful roses had never been seen. The architect had planted it on the grave of Thorwaldsen, where it continued to bloom, the image of *the beautiful,* scattering its fragrant rosy leaves to be gathered and carried away into distant lands in memory of the spot on which they fell.

"Have you obtained a situation in town?" asked the sparrows of the roses.

The roses nodded. They recognized their little gray neighbors, and were rejoiced to see them again.

"It is very delightful," said the roses, "to live here and to blossom, to meet old friends, and to see cheerful faces every day. It is as if each day were a holiday."

"Tweet," said the sparrows to each other. "Yes, these really are our old neighbors. We remember their origin near the pond. Tweet. How they have risen, to be sure. Some people seem to get on while they are asleep. Ah, there's a withered leaf. I can see it quite plainly."

And they pecked at the leaf till it fell. But the rosebush continued fresher and greener than ever. The roses bloomed in the sunshine on Thorwaldsen's grave, and thus became linked with his immortal name.

The Old Street Lamp

DID you ever hear the story of the old street lamp? If not, you may as well listen to it. It was a most respectable old lamp which had seen many, many years of service and now was to retire with a pension. It was this evening at its post for the last time, giving light to the street. Its feelings were something like those of an old dancer at the theater, who is dancing for the last time and knows that tomorrow she will be in her garret, alone and forgotten.

The lamp had very great anxiety about the next day, for he knew that he had to appear for the first time at the town hall, to be inspected by the mayor and the council, who were to decide if he were fit for further service or not: whether the lamp was good enough to be used to light the inhabitants of one of the suburbs, or in the country at some factory. If not, it would be sent at once to an iron foundry to be melted down. In this latter case it might be turned into anything, and he wondered very much whether he would then be able to remember that he had once been a street lamp, and this troubled him exceedingly.

Whatever might happen, one thing seemed certain: that he would be separated from the watchman and his wife, whose family he looked upon as his own. The lamp had been first hung up on the very evening that the watchman, then a robust young man, had entered upon the duties of his office. Ah well, it was a very long time since one became a lamp and the other a watchman. The watchman's wife had pride in those days; she seldom condescended to glance at the lamp, excepting when she passed by in the evening, never in the daytime. But in later years, when all these— the watchman, the wife, and the lamp—had grown old, she had attended to it, cleaned it, and supplied it with oil. The old people were thoroughly honest; they had never cheated the lamp of a single drop of the oil provided for it.

This was the lamp's last night in the street, and tomorrow he must go to the town hall—two very dark things to think of. No wonder he did not burn brightly. Many other thoughts also passed through his mind: how many persons he had lighted on their way, and how much he had seen; as much, very likely, as the mayor and corporation themselves. None of these thoughts were uttered aloud, however. He was a good, honorable old lamp, who would not willingly do harm to anyone, especially to those in authority. As many things were recalled to his mind, the light would flash up with sudden brightness. At such moments, he had a conviction that he would be remembered.

"There was a handsome young man once," thought he. "It is certainly a long time ago, but I remember he had a little note, written on pink paper with a gold edge. The writing was elegant, evidently a lady's hand. Twice he read it through and kissed it, and then looked up at me with eyes that said quite plainly, 'I am the happiest of men!' Only he and I know what was written on this his first letter from his ladylove. Ah yes, and there was another pair of eyes that I remember. It is really wonderful how my thoughts jump from one thing to another! A funeral passed through the street. A young and beautiful woman lay on a bier decked with garlands of flowers, and attended by torches which quite overpowered my light. In crowds all along the street stood the people from the houses, ready to join the procession. But when the torches had passed and I could look round, I saw one person alone, leaning against my post and weeping. Never shall I forget the sorrowful eyes that looked up at me."

These and similar reflections occupied the old street lamp, on this the last time that his light would shine. The sentry, when he is relieved from his post, knows at least who will succeed him, and may whisper a few words to him. But the lamp did not know his successor, or he could have given him a few hints respecting rain or mist, and could have informed him how far the moon's rays would rest on the pavement, and from which side the wind generally blew, and so on.

On the bridge over the canal stood three persons who wished to recommend themselves to the lamp, for they thought he could give the office to whomsoever he chose. The first was a herring's head, which could emit light in the darkness. He remarked that it would be a great saving of oil if they placed him on the lamppost. Number two was a piece of rotten wood, which also shone in the dark. He considered himself descended from an old stem, once the pride of the forest. The third was a glowworm; how he found his way there the lamp could not imagine, yet there he was, and could really give light as well as the others. But the rotten wood and the herring's head declared most solemnly that the glowworm gave light only at certain times, and must not be allowed to compete with themselves. The old lamp assured them that not one of them could give sufficient light to fill the position of a street lamp, but they would believe nothing he said. And when they discovered that he had not the power of naming his successor, they said they were very glad to hear it, for the lamp was too old and worn-out to make a proper choice.

At this moment the wind came rushing round the corner of the street, and through the air holes of the old lamp.

"What is this I hear?" said he. "Are you going away tomorrow? Is this evening the last time we shall meet? Then I must present you with a farewell gift. I will blow into your brain, so that in future you shall not only be able to remember all that you have seen or heard in the past, but your light within shall be so bright that you shall be able to understand all that is said or done in your presence."

"Oh, that is really a very, very great gift," said the old lamp. "I thank you most heartily. I only hope I shall not be melted down."

"That is not likely to happen yet," said the wind. "And I will also blow a memory into you, so that should you receive other similar presents your old age will pass very pleasantly."

"That is if I am not melted down," said the lamp. "But should I in that case still retain my memory?"

"Do be reasonable, old lamp," said the wind, puffing away.

At this moment the moon burst forth from the clouds. "What will you give the old lamp?" asked the wind.

"I can give nothing," she replied. "I am on the wane, and no lamps have ever given me light, though I have frequently shone upon them." With these words the moon hid herself again behind the clouds that she might be saved from further requests. Just then a drop fell on the lamp from the roof of the house, but the drop explained that he was a gift from those gray clouds, and perhaps the best of all gifts. "I shall penetrate you so thoroughly," he said, "that you will have the power of becoming rusty, and, if you wish it, to crumble into dust in one night."

But this seemed to the lamp a very shabby present, and the wind thought so, too. "Does no one give any more? Will no one give any more?" shouted the breath of the wind, as loud as it could. Then a bright falling star came down, leaving a broad, luminous streak behind it.

"What was that?" cried the herring's head. "Did not a star fall? I really believe it went into the lamp. Certainly, when such highborn personages try for the office, we may as well say 'good night,' and go home." And so they did, while the old lamp threw a strong light all around him.

"This is a glorious gift," said he. "The bright stars have always been a joy to me and have always shone more brilliantly than I ever could shine, though I have tried with my whole might. And now they have noticed me, a poor old lamp, and have sent me a gift that will enable me to see everything that I remember as clearly as if it still stood before me, and to be seen by all those who love me. And herein lies the truest pleasure, for joy which we cannot share with others is only half enjoyed."

"That sentiment does you honor," said the wind. "But for this purpose wax lights will be necessary. If these are not lighted in you, your peculiar faculties will not benefit others in the least. The stars have not thought of this. They suppose that you and every other light must be a wax taper. But I must go down now." So he laid himself to rest.

"Wax tapers, indeed!" said the lamp. "I have never yet held them nor is it likely I ever shall. If I could only be sure of not being melted down!"

The next day—well, perhaps we had better pass over the next day. Evening came and the lamp was resting in a grandfather's chair and guess where—why, at the old watchman's house! He had begged, as a favor, that the mayor and corporation would allow him to keep the street lamp in consideration of his long and faithful service, as he had himself hung it up and lit it on the day he commenced his duties, four and twenty years ago. He looked upon it almost as his own child: he had no children, so the lamp was given to him. There it lay in the great armchair near to the warm stove. It seemed almost as if it had grown larger, for it appeared quite to fill the chair.

The old people sat at their supper, casting friendly glances at the old lamp, whom they would willingly have admitted to a place at the table. It is quite true that they dwelt in a cellar two yards deep in the earth, and that they had to cross a stone passage to get to their room; but within it was warm and comfortable, and strips had been nailed round the door. The bed and the little window had curtains and everything looked clean and neat. On the window seat stood two curious flowerpots which a sailor named Christian had brought over from the East or West Indies. They were of clay in the form of two elephants, with open backs. They were hollow and filled with earth, and through the open space flowers bloomed. In one grew some very fine chives or leeks; this was the kitchen garden. The other elephant, which contained a beautiful geranium, they called their flower garden. On the wall hung a large colored print, representing all the kings and emperors at the Congress of Vienna. A clock, with heavy weights, also hung on the wall, and went "tick, tick," steadily enough; yet it was always rather too fast, which the old people said was better than being too slow.

They were now eating their supper, while the old street lamp, as we have heard, lay in the grandfather's armchair near the stove. It seemed to the lamp as if the whole world had turned round. But after a while the old watchman looked at the lamp and spoke of what they had both gone through together, in rain and in fog; during the short bright nights of summer, or in the long winter nights; through the drifting snowstorms, when he longed to be at home in the cellar. Then the lamp felt it was all right again. He saw everything that had happened quite clearly, as if it were passing before him. Surely the wind had given him an excellent gift. The old people were very active and industrious; they were never idle for even a single hour. On Sunday afternoons they would bring out some books, generally a book of travels of which they were very fond. The old man would read aloud about Africa with its great forests and the wild elephants, while his wife would listen attentively, stealing a glance now and then at the clay elephants which served as flowerpots.

"I can almost imagine I am seeing it all," she said. And then how the lamp wished for a wax taper to be lighted in him, for then the old woman would have seen the smallest detail as clearly as he did himself. He saw the lofty trees with their thickly entwined branches, the naked negroes on horseback, and whole herds of elephants treading down bamboo thickets with their broad, heavy feet.

"What is the use of all my capabilities," sighed the old lamp, "when I cannot obtain any wax lights? They have only oil and tallow here, and these will not do."

One day a great heap of wax candle ends found their way into the cellar. The larger pieces were burnt, and the old woman kept the smaller ones for waxing her thread. So there were now candles enough, but it never occurred to anyone to put a little piece in the lamp.

"Here I am now with my rare powers," thought the lamp. "I have faculties within me, but I cannot share them. They do not know that I could cover these white walls with beautiful tapestry, or change them into noble forests, or indeed to anything else they might wish for."

The lamp, however, was always kept clean and shining in a corner where it attracted all eyes. Strangers thought of it as junk, but the old people did not care for that; they loved the lamp.

One day—it was the watchman's birthday—the old woman approached the lamp, smiling to herself, and said, "I will have an illumination today in honor of my old man."

The lamp rattled in his metal frame, for he thought, "Now at last I shall have a light within me." But after all no wax light was placed in the lamp, but oil as usual. The lamp burned through the whole evening, and began to perceive too clearly that the gift of the stars would remain a hidden treasure all his life.

Then he had a dream, for to one with his faculties dreaming was no difficulty. It appeared to him that the old people were dead and that he had been taken to the iron foundry to be melted down. It caused him quite as much anxiety as on the day when he had been called upon to appear before the mayor and the council at the town hall. But though he had been endowed with the power of falling into decay from rust when he pleased, he did not make use of it. He was therefore put into the melting furnace and changed into as elegant an iron candlestick as you could wish to see, one intended to hold a wax taper. The candlestick was in the form of an angel holding a nosegay, in the center of which the wax taper was to be placed. It was to stand on a green writing table in a very pleasant room. Many books were scattered about, and splendid paintings hung on the walls.

The owner of the room was a poet, and a man of intellect. Everything he thought or wrote was pictured around him. Nature showed herself to him sometimes in the dark forests, at others in cheerful meadows where the storks were strutting about, or on the deck of a ship sailing across the foaming sea with the clear blue sky above, or at night the glittering stars.

"What powers I possess!" said the lamp, awaking from his dream. "I could almost wish to be melted down. But no, that must not be while the old people live. They love me for myself alone. They keep me bright and supply me with oil. I am as well off as the picture of the Congress, in which they take so much pleasure." And from that time he felt at rest in himself, and not more so than such an honorable old lamp really deserved to be.

The Tinder Box

A SOLDIER came marching along the highroad. One, two! One, two! He had his knapsack on his back and his sword at his side, for he had been to the wars and now he was on his way home. He met an old witch on the road. She was so ugly that her lower lip hung right down onto her chin.

She said, "Good evening, soldier! What a nice sword you've got, and such a big knapsack. You are a real soldier! You shall have as much money as ever you like."

"Thank you kindly, you old witch," said the soldier.

"Do you see that big tree?" said the witch, pointing to a tree close by. "It is hollow inside. Climb up to the top and you will see a hole into which you can let yourself down, right down under the tree. I will tie a rope round your waist so that I can haul you up again when you call."

"What am I to do down under the tree?" asked the soldier.

"Fetch money," said the witch. "You must know that when you get down to the bottom of the tree you will find yourself in a wide passage. It's quite light there, for there are over a hundred blazing lamps. You will see three doors which you can open, for the keys are there. If you go into the first room you will see a big box in the middle of the floor. A dog is sitting on the top of it and he has eyes as big as saucers, but you needn't mind that. I will give you my blue-checked apron, which you can spread out on the floor. Go quickly forward, take up the dog, and put him on my apron.

"*Do you see that big tree?*"

Then open the box and take out as much money as you like. It is all copper, but if you like silver better, go into the next room. There you will find a dog with eyes as big as millstones. But never mind that. Put him on my apron and take the money. If you prefer gold you can have it too, and as much as you can carry, if you go into the third room. But the dog sitting on that box has eyes each as big as the Round Tower. He *is* a dog, indeed, as you may imagine. Bu don't let it trouble you. You only have to put him on my apron. Then he won't hurt you, and you can take as much gold out of the box as you like!"

"That's not so bad," said the soldier. "But what am I to give you, old witch? You'll want something, I'll be bound."

"No," said the witch. "Not a single penny do I want. I only want you to bring me an old tinder box that my grandmother forgot the last time she was down there."

"Well, tie the rope round my waist," said the soldier.

"Here it is," said the witch. "And here is my blue-checked apron."

Then the soldier climbed up the tree, let himself slide down the hollow trunk, and found himself, as the witch had said, in the wide passage where the many hundred lamps were burning.

Now he opened the first door. Ugh! There sat the dog with eyes as big as saucers staring at him.

"You are a nice fellow!" said the soldier, as he put him onto the witch's apron and took out as many pennies as he could cram into his pockets. Then he shut the box, put the dog on the top of it again, and went into the next room. Hallo! There sat the dog with eyes as big as millstones.

"You shouldn't stare at me so hard. You might get a pain in your eyes!" Then he put the dog on the apron, but when he saw all the silver in the box he threw away all the coppers and stuffed his pockets and his knapsack with silver. Then he went into the third room. Oh, how horrible! That dog really had two eyes as big as the Round Tower, and they rolled around and around like wheels.

"Good evening," said the soldier, saluting, for he had never seen such a dog in his life. But after looking at him for a bit he thought, "That will do." And then he lifted him down onto the apron and opened the chest. Heavens! What a lot of gold! He could buy the whole of Copenhagen with it, and all the sugar pigs from the cake-woman, all the tin soldiers, whips, and rocking horses in the world. That was money indeed! Now the soldier threw away all the silver he had filled his pockets and his knapsack with and put gold in its place. Yes, he crammed all his pockets, his knapsack, his cap, and his boots so full that he could hardly walk. Now, he really had got a lot of money. He put the dog back onto the box, shut the door, and shouted up through the tree, "Haul me up, you old witch!"

"Have you got the tinder box?"

"Oh, to be sure!" said the soldier. "I had quite forgotten it." And he went back to fetch it. The witch hauled him up, and there he was standing on the highroad again with his pockets, boots, knapsack, and cap full of gold.

"What do you want the tinder box for?" asked the soldier.

"That's no business of yours," said the witch. "You've got the money. Give me the tinder box!"

"Rubbish!" said the soldier. "Tell me directly what you want with it or I will draw my sword and cut off your head."

"I won't!" said the witch.

Then the soldier cut off her head. There she lay! But he tied all the money up in her apron, slung it on his back like a pack, put the tinder box in his pocket, and marched off to the town.

It was a beautiful town. He went straight to the finest hotel and ordered the grandest rooms and all the food he liked best, because he was a rich man now that he had so much money.

Certainly the servant who had to clean his boots thought they were funny old things for such a rich gentleman, but he had not had time yet to buy any new ones. The next day he bought new boots and fine clothes. The soldier now became a fine gentleman, and the people told him all about the grand things in the town, and about their king, and what a lovely princess his daughter was.

"Where is she to be seen?" asked the soldier.

"You can't see her at all," they all said. "She lives in a great copper castle surrounded with walls and towers. Nobody but the King dares to go in and out, for it has been prophesied that she will marry a common soldier, and the King doesn't like that!"

"I should like to see her well enough," thought the soldier. But there was no way of getting leave for that.

He now led a very merry life. He went to theaters, drove about in the King's Park, and gave away a lot of money to poor people, which was very nice of him. He remembered how disagreeable it used to be not to have a penny in his pocket. Now he was rich, wore fine clothes, and had a great many friends who all said what a nice fellow he was—a thorough gentleman—and he liked to be told that.

But as he went on spending money every day and his store was never renewed, he at last found himself with only two pence left. Then he was obliged to move out of his fine rooms. He had to take a tiny little attic up under the roof, clean his own boots, and mend them himself with a darning needle. None of his friends went to see him because there were far too many stairs.

One dark evening when he had not even enough money to buy a candle with, he suddenly remembered that there was a little bit in the old tinder box he had brought out of the hollow tree, when the witch helped him down. He got out the tinder box with the candle end in it and struck fire. But as the sparks flew out from the flint, the door burst open and the dog with eyes as big as saucers, which he had seen down under the tree, stood before him and said, "What does my lord command?"

"By heaven!" said the soldier, "this is a nice kind of tinder box, if I can get whatever I want like this. Get me some money," he said to the dog, and away it went.

It was back in a twinkling with a bag full of pennies in its mouth.

Now the soldier saw what a treasure he had in the tinder box. If he struck once, the dog which sat on the box of copper came. If he struck twice, the dog on the silver box came. And if he struck three times, the one from the box of gold.

He now moved down to the grand rooms and got his fine clothes again, and then all his friends knew him once more and liked him as much as ever.

Then he suddenly began to think, "After all, it's a curious thing that no man can get a sight of the Princess. Everyone says she is so beautiful! But what is the good of that when she always has to be shut up in that big copper palace with all the towers. Can I not somehow manage to see her? Where is my tinder box?" Then he struck the flint and, whisk! came the dog with eyes as big as saucers.

"It certainly is the middle of the night," said the soldier, "but I am very anxious to see the Princess, if only for a single moment."

The dog was out of the door in an instant, and before the soldier had time to think about it, he was back again with the Princess. There she was, fast asleep on the dog's back, and she was so lovely that anybody could see that she must be a real princess. The soldier could not help it, but he was obliged to kiss her, for he was a true soldier.

Then the dog ran back again with the Princess, but in the

morning, when the King and Queen were having breakfast, the Princess said that she had such a wonderful dream about a dog and a soldier. She had ridden on the dog's back and the soldier had kissed her.

"That's a pretty tale," said the Queen.

After this an old lady-in-waiting had to sit by her bed at night to see if this was really a dream, or what it could be.

The soldier longed so intensely to see the Princess again that at night the dog came to fetch her. He took her up and ran off with her as fast as he could, but the old lady-in-waiting put on her galoshes and ran just as fast behind them. When she saw that they disappeared into a large house, she thought, "Now I know where it is," and made a big cross with chalk on the gate. Then she went home and lay down, and presently the dog came back with the Princess. When he saw that there was a cross on the gate, he took a bit of chalk, too, and made crosses on all the gates in the town. Now this was very clever of him, for the lady-in-waiting could not possibly find the gate when there were crosses on all the gates.

Early next morning the King, the Queen, the lady-in-waiting, and all the court officials went to see where the Princess had been.

"There it is," said the King, when he saw the first door with the cross on it.

"No, my dear husband, it is there," said the Queen, who saw another door with a cross on it.

"But there is one! And there is another!" they all cried out.

They soon saw that it was hopeless to try to find it.

Now the Queen was a very clever woman. She knew more than how to drive in a chariot. She took her big gold scissors and cut up a large piece of silk into small pieces, and made a pretty little bag which she filled with fine grains of buckwheat. She then tied it onto the back of the Princess.

And when that was done she cut a little hole in the bag, so that the grains could drop out all the way wherever the Princess went.

At night the dog came again, took the Princess on his back, and ran off with her to the soldier, who was so fond of her that he longed to be a prince, so that he might have her for his wife.

The dog never noticed how the grain dropped out all along the road from the palace to the soldier's window, where he ran up the wall with the Princess.

In the morning the King and the Queen easily saw where their daughter had been, and they seized the soldier and threw him into the dungeons.

There he lay. Oh, how dark and tiresome it was! And then one day they said to him, "Tomorrow you are to be hanged." It was not amusing to be told that, especially as he had left his tinder box behind him at the hotel.

In the morning he could see through the bars in the little window that the people were hurrying out of the town to see him hanged. He heard the drums and saw the soldiers marching along. All the world was going. Among them was a shoemaker's boy in his leather apron and slippers. He was in such a hurry that he lost one of his slippers, and it fell close under the soldier's window where he was peeping out through the bars.

"I say, you boy! Don't be in such a hurry," said the soldier to him. "Nothing will happen till I get there. But if you will run to the house where I used to live and fetch me my tinder box, you shall have a penny. You must put your best foot foremost."

The boy was only too glad to have the penny and tore off to get the tinder box. He gave it to the soldier and—yes, now we shall hear.

Outside the town a high scaffold had been raised, and the soldiers were drawn up round about it as well as crowds of the townspeople. The King and the Queen sat upon a beautiful throne exactly opposite the judge and all the councilors.

The soldier mounted the ladder, but when they were about to put the rope round his neck, he said that before undergoing his punishment a criminal was always allowed the gratification of a harmless wish, and he wanted very much to smoke a pipe as it would be his last in this world.

The King would not deny him this, so the soldier took out his tinder box and struck fire, once, twice, three times. And there were all the dogs—the one with eyes like saucers, the one with eyes like millstones, and the one whose eyes were as big as the Round Tower.

"Help me! Save me from being hanged," cried the soldier.

And then the dogs rushed at the soldiers and the councilors. They took one by the legs and another by the nose and threw them up many fathoms into the air, and when they fell down they were broken all to pieces.

"I won't!" cried the King, but the biggest dog took both him and the Queen and threw them after all the others. Then the soldiers became alarmed, and the people shouted, "Oh, good soldier, you shall be our King and marry the beautiful Princess!"

Then they conducted the soldier to the King's chariot, and all three dogs danced along in front of him and shouted "Hurrah!" The boys all put their fingers in their mouths and whistled, and the soldiers presented arms. The Princess came out of the copper palace and became Queen, which pleased her very much. The wedding took place in a week, and the dogs all had seats at the table, where they sat staring with all their eyes.

Grimms' Fairy Tales

Not to know these magical tales, filled with adventure, romance, and human trials, is to have missed one of the most priceless reading experiences of all time.

To be able to enter the famous world of fantasy, where dwell princes and princesses, giants and dwarfs, dragons and fairies, gnomes and talking animals, is to enlighten and enhance the imagination of young and old. For among this familiar and timeless collection of the Brothers Grimm, you will find all the favorites of folklore and fairyland, and all the enchanting people and places treasured and loved by millions throughout the world.

Classic stories like *The Twelve Dancing Princesses, The Elves and the Shoemaker, Hansel and Gretel, Rumpelstiltskin*, to be read and listened to, will delight and entertain all children and their parents as well.

Grimms' Fairy Tales

BY THE BROTHERS GRIMM

ILLUSTRATED BY ADELE WERBER

COMPANION LIBRARY

PUBLISHERS *Grosset & Dunlap* NEW YORK

CONTENTS

CONTENTS

Grimms' Fairy Tales

The Twelve Dancing Princesses

ONCE upon a time there was a king who had twelve daughters, each more beautiful than the other. They slept together in a hall where their beds stood close to one another. At night when they had gone to bed, the King locked the door and bolted it. But when he unlocked it in the morning, he noticed that their shoes had been danced to pieces, and nobody could explain how it happened.

So the King sent out a proclamation saying that anyone who could discover where the princesses did their night's dancing might choose one of them to be his wife and should reign after his death. But whoever presented himself, and failed to make the discovery after three days and nights, was to forfeit his life.

A prince soon appeared and offered to take the risk. He was well received, and at night was taken into a room adjoining the hall where the princesses slept. His bed was made up there, and he was to watch and see where they went to dance. And so that they could not do anything or leave without being seen, the door of the room was left open. But the eyes of the prince grew heavy and he fell asleep. When he woke up in the morning all twelve prin-

cesses had been dancing, for the soles of their shoes were full of holes. The second and third evenings passed with the same results. The prince was then granted no mercy, and his head was cut off. Many others came after him and offered to take the risk, but they all forfeited their lives.

Now it happened that a poor soldier, who had been wounded and could no longer serve, found himself on the road to the town where the King lived. There he fell in with an old woman who asked him where he intended to go.

"I really don't know," he said. And he added in fun, "I should like to discover where the King's daughters dance their shoes into holes, and after that I should like to become king."

"That is not so difficult," said the old woman. "You must not drink the wine which will be brought to you in the evening, but must pretend to be fast asleep." Whereupon she gave him a short cloak, saying, "When you wear this you will be invisible, and then you can slip out after the twelve princesses."

When the soldier heard this good advice he considered it seriously, plucked up the courage to appear before the King, and offered himself as suitor. He was as well received as the others and was dressed in royal garments.

In the evening, when bedtime came, he was conducted to the anteroom. As he was about to go to bed the eldest princess appeared, bringing him a cup of wine. But he had fastened a sponge under his chin and let the wine run down into it, so that he did not drink one drop. Then he lay down, and when he had been quiet a little while he began to snore as though in the deepest sleep.

The twelve princesses heard him and laughed. The eldest said, "He too must forfeit his life."

Then they got up, opened cupboards, chests, and cases,

[2]

and brought out their beautiful dresses. They decked themselves before the glass, skipping about and reveling in the prospect of the dance.

Only the youngest sister said, "I don't know what it is. You may rejoice, but I feel so strange. A misfortune is certainly hanging over us."

"You are a little goose," answered the eldest. "You are always frightened. Have you forgotten how many princes have come here in vain? Why, I need not have given the soldier a sleeping draught at all! The blockhead would never have awakened."

When they were all ready they looked at the soldier, but his eyes were shut and he did not stir. So they thought they would soon be quite safe. Then the eldest went up to one of the beds and knocked on it. It sank into the earth and they descended through the opening one after another, the eldest first.

The soldier, who had noticed everything, did not hesitate long, but threw on his cloak and went down behind the youngest. Halfway down he trod on her dress.

She was frightened and said, "What was that? Who is holding on to my dress?"

"Don't be so foolish. You must have caught it on a nail," said the eldest.

Then they went right down, and when they got quite underground they stood in a marvelously beautiful avenue of trees. All the leaves were silver, and glittered and shone.

The soldier thought, "I must take some token with me." And as he broke off a twig, a sharp crack came from the tree.

The youngest cried out, "All is not well! Did you hear that sound?"

"Those are triumphal salutes because we have eluded our 'prince'!" said the eldest.

[3]

Next they came to an avenue where all the leaves were of gold, and at last into a third where they were of shining diamonds. From both these the soldier broke off a twig, and there was a crack each time which made the youngest princess start with terror. But the eldest maintained that the sounds were only triumphal salutes. They went on faster and came to a great lake. Close to the bank lay twelve little boats and in every boat sat a handsome prince. They had expected the twelve princesses and each took one with him, but the soldier seated himself by the youngest.

Then said her prince, "I don't know why, but the boat is much heavier today. I am obliged to row with all my strength to get it along."

"I wonder why it is," said the youngest, "unless perhaps it is the hot weather. It is strangely hot."

On the opposite side of the lake stood a splendid brightly lighted castle from which came the sound of the joyous music of trumpets and drums. They rowed across, and every prince danced with his love. And the soldier danced too, unseen. If one of the princesses held a cup of wine he drank out of it, so that it was empty when she lifted it to her lips. This frightened the youngest one, but the eldest always silenced her.

They danced till three next morning, when their shoes were danced into holes and they were obliged to stop. The princes took them back across the lake, and this time the soldier took his seat beside the eldest. On the bank they said farewell to their princes and promised to come again the next night.

When they got to the steps the soldier ran on ahead, lay down in bed, and when the twelve came lagging by, slowly and wearily, he began to snore again very loud, so that they said, "We are quite safe so far as he is concerned." Then they took off their beautiful dresses, put them away, placed

[4]

the worn-out shoes under their beds, and lay down.

The next morning the soldier determined to say nothing, but to see the wonderful doings again. So he went with them the second and third nights. Everything was just the same as the first time, and they danced each time till their shoes were in holes. The third time the soldier took away a wine cup as a token.

When the appointed hour came for his answer, he took the three twigs and the cup with him and went before the King. The twelve princesses stood behind the door listening to hear what he would say.

When the King put the question, "Where did my daughters dance their shoes to pieces in the night?" he answered, "With twelve princes in an underground castle." Then he produced the tokens.

The King sent for his daughters and asked them whether the soldier had spoken the truth. As they saw that they were betrayed and would gain nothing by lies, they were obliged to admit all.

Thereupon the King asked the soldier which one he would choose as his wife. He answered, "I am no longer young. Give me the eldest."

So the wedding was celebrated that very day, and the kingdom was promised to him on the King's death. But for every night which the princes had spent in dancing with the princesses, a day was added to their time of enchantment.

The Golden Bird

A LONG time ago there was a king who had a lovely pleasure garden around his palace, and in it stood a tree which bore golden apples. When the apples were nearly ripe they were counted, but the very next morning one was missing. This was reported to the King, and he ordered a watch to be set every night under the tree.

The King had three sons, and he sent the eldest into the garden at nightfall, but by midnight he was overcome with sleep, and in the morning another apple was missing.

On the following night the second son had to keep watch, but he fared no better. When the clock struck twelve, he too was fast asleep, and in the morning another apple was gone.

The turn to watch now came to the third son. He was quite ready, but the King had not much confidence in him and thought that he would accomplish even less than his brothers. At last, however, he gave permission. So the youth lay down under the tree to watch, determined not to let sleep master him.

As the clock struck twelve, there was a rustling in the air,

and by the light of the moon he saw a bird whose shining feathers were of pure gold. The bird settled on the tree and was just plucking an apple when the young Prince shot an arrow at it. The bird flew away, but the arrow hit its plumage and one of the golden feathers fell to the ground. The Prince picked it up, and in the morning took it to the King and told him all that he had seen in the night.

The King assembled his council, and everybody declared that a feather like that was worth more than the whole kingdom.

"If the feather is worth so much," said the King, "one will not satisfy me. I must and will have the whole bird."

The eldest son, relying on his cleverness, set out in search of the bird, thinking that he would be sure to find it soon. When he had gone some distance he saw a fox sitting by the edge of a wood. He raised his gun and aimed at it.

The fox cried out, "Do not shoot me, and I will give you some good advice. You are going to look for the Golden Bird. At nightfall you will come to a village where you will find two inns opposite each other. One of them will be brightly lighted and there will be noise and revelry going on in it. Be sure you do not choose that one, but go into the other, even if you don't like the looks of it so well."

"How can a stupid animal like that give me good advice?" thought the King's son, and he pulled the trigger. But he missed the fox, who turned tail and made off into the wood.

Thereupon the Prince continued his journey and at nightfall reached the village with the two inns. Singing and dancing were going on in the one, and the other looked poverty-stricken and decayed. "I should be a fool," he said, "if I were to go to that miserable place when this good one is so near."

[7]

So he went into the noisy one and lived there in rioting and revelry, forgetting the bird, his father, and all his good counsels.

When some time had passed and the eldest son did not come back, the second started in quest of the Golden Bird. He met the fox, as the eldest son had done, and it gave him the same good advice, to which he paid just as little attention.

He came to the two inns and saw his brother standing at the window of the one from which came the sounds of revelry. He could not withstand his brother's calling, so he went in and gave himself up to a life of pleasure.

Again some time passed and the King's youngest son wanted to go out to try his luck, but his father would not let him go.

"It is useless," he said. "He will be even less able to find the Golden Bird than his brothers. And when any ill luck overtakes him, he will not be able to help himself. He has no backbone."

But at last, because the son gave him no peace, the King let him go. The fox again sat at the edge of the wood, begged for its life, and gave its good advice. The Prince was good-natured and said, "Be calm, little fox, I will do thee no harm."

"You won't repent it," answered the fox. "And so that you may get along faster, come and mount on my tail."

No sooner had he seated himself than the fox began to run; and away they flew over stock and stone, at such a pace that his hair whistled in the wind. When they reached the village, the Prince dismounted. And following the good advice of the fox, he went straight to the shabby inn without looking about him, and there he passed a peaceful night.

In the morning, when he went out into the fields, there

sat the fox, who said, "I will now tell you what you must do next. Walk straight on till you come to a castle in front of which a whole regiment of soldiers is encamped. Don't be afraid of them—they will all be asleep and snoring. Walk through the midst of them straight into the castle, and walk through all the rooms. At last you will reach an apartment where the Golden Bird will be hanging in a common wooden cage. A golden cage stands near it for show, but beware! Whatever you do, you must not take the bird out of the wooden cage to put it into the other, or it will be the worse for you."

After these words the fox again stretched out his tail, the Prince took his seat on it, and away they flew over stock and stone, till his hair whistled in the wind. When he arrived at the castle, he found everything just as the fox had said.

The Prince went to the room where the Golden Bird hung in the wooden cage. A golden cage was standing near by, and the three golden apples were scattered about the room. He thought it would be absurd to leave the beautiful bird in the common old cage, so he opened the door, caught it, and put it into the golden cage. But as he did it, the bird uttered a piercing shriek. The soldiers woke up, rushed in, and carried him away to prison. Next morning he was taken before a judge, and as he confessed all, he was sentenced to death. The King, however, said that he would spare his life on one condition, and this was that he should bring him the Golden Horse which runs faster than the wind. In addition, he should have the Golden Bird as a reward. So the Prince set off with many sighs. He was very sad, for where was he to find the Golden Horse? Then suddenly he saw his old friend the fox sitting on the road.

"Now you see!" said the fox. "All this has happened be-

cause you did not listen to me. All the same, keep up your spirits. I will protect you and tell you how to find the Golden Horse. You must keep straight along the road and you will come to a palace in the stable of which stands the Golden Horse. The grooms will be lying around the stable, but they will be fast asleep and snoring, and you can safely lead the horse through them. Only one thing you must beware of: put the old saddle of wood and leather upon it, and not the golden one hanging near, or you will rue it."

Then the fox stretched out his tail, the Prince took his seat, and away they flew over stock and stone, till his hair whistled in the wind.

Everything happened just as the fox had said. The Prince came to the stable where the Golden Horse stood. But when he was about to put the old saddle on its back, he thought, "Such a beautiful animal will be disgraced if I don't put the good saddle upon him, as he deserves." Hardly had the golden saddle touched the horse than he began neighing loudly. The grooms awoke, seized the Prince, and threw him into a dungeon.

The next morning he was taken before a judge and condemned to death, but the King promised to spare his life and give him the Golden Horse as well, if he could bring him the beautiful Princess out of the Golden Palace. With a heavy heart the Prince set out, but to his delight he soon met the faithful fox.

"I should leave you to your fate," the fox said, "but I will have pity on you and once more help you out of trouble. Your road leads straight to the Golden Palace. You will reach it in the evening. And at night, when everything is quiet, the beautiful Princess will go to the bathroom to take a bath. As she goes along, spring forward and give her a kiss, and she will follow you. Lead her away with you.

Only on no account allow her to bid her parents good-by, or it will go badly with you."

Again the fox stretched out his tail, the Prince seated himself upon it, and off they flew over stock and stone, till his hair whistled in the wind.

When he got to the Golden Palace, it was just as the fox had said. He waited till midnight, and when the whole palace was wrapped in sleep and the maiden went to take a bath, he sprang forward and gave her a kiss. She said she was quite willing to go with him, but she implored him to let her say good-by to her parents. At first he refused, but as she cried and fell at his feet, at last he gave her leave. Hardly had the maiden stepped up to her father's bed when he and everyone else in the palace woke up. The Prince was seized and thrown into prison.

Next morning the King said to him, "Your life is forfeited, and it can be spared only if you clear away from in front of my window the mountain which shuts out the view. It must be done in eight days, and if you accomplish the task you shall have my daughter as a reward."

So the Prince began his labors, and he dug and shoveled without ceasing. On the seventh day, when he saw how little he had done, he became very sad and gave up all hope. In the evening, however, the fox appeared and said, "You do not deserve any help from me, but lie down and go to sleep. I will do the work." In the morning when he woke and looked out of the window, the mountain had disappeared.

Overjoyed, the Prince hurried to the King and told him that his condition was fulfilled, and whether he liked it or not he must keep his word and give him his daughter.

So the Prince and the King's daughter went away together, and before long the faithful fox joined them.

"You certainly have got the best thing of all," said he, "but the Golden Horse belongs to the maiden of the Golden Palace."

"How am I to get it?" asked the Prince.

"Oh, I will tell you that," answered the fox. "First take the beautiful maiden to the King who sent you to the Golden Palace. There will be great joy when you appear, and they will bring out the Golden Horse to you. Mount it at once and shake hands with everybody, but last of all with the beautiful maiden. And when you have taken her hand firmly, swing her up beside you and gallop away. No one will be able to catch you, for the horse goes faster than the wind."

All this was successfully done and the Prince carried off the beautiful maiden on the Golden Horse.

The fox was not far off and he said to the Prince, "Now I will help you to get the Golden Bird, too. When you approach the castle where the Golden Bird lives, let the maiden dismount and I will take care of her. Then ride with the Golden Horse into the courtyard of the castle. There will be great rejoicing when they see you, and they will bring out the Golden Bird to you. As soon as you have the cage in your hand, gallop back to us and take up the maiden again."

When these plans had succeeded, and the Prince was ready to ride on with all his treasures, the fox said to him, "Now you must reward me for my help."

"What do you want?" asked the Prince.

"When you reach the wood, shoot me dead and cut off my head and my paws."

"That would indeed be gratitude!" said the Prince. "I can't possibly promise to do such a thing."

The fox said, "If you won't do it I must leave you, but before I go I will give you one more piece of advice. Be-

ware of two things: buy no gallows birds, and don't sit on the edge of a well." After saying this he ran off into the wood.

The Prince thought, "That is a strange animal. What whims he has! Who on earth would want to buy gallows birds? And the desire to sit on the edge of a well has never yet seized me."

He rode on with the beautiful maiden, and the road led him through the village where his two brothers had stayed behind. There was a great hubbub in the village, and when he asked what it was about he was told that two persons were going to be hanged. When he got nearer he saw that they were his brothers, who had wasted their possessions and done all sorts of evil deeds. He asked if they could not be set free.

"Yes, if you'll ransom them," answered the people. "But why will you throw your money away in buying off such wicked people?"

He did not stop to reflect, however, but paid the ransom for them. And when they were set free they all journeyed on together.

They came to the wood where they had first met the fox. It was deliciously cool there, though the sun was broiling outside. The two brothers said, "Let us sit down here by the well to rest a little and eat and drink." The Prince agreed, and during the conversation he forgot what he was about, and, never dreaming of any foul play, seated himself on the edge of the well. But his two brothers threw him backwards into it and went home to their father, taking with them the maiden, the horse, and the bird.

"Here we bring you not only the Golden Bird, but the Golden Horse and the maiden from the Golden Palace, as our booty."

Thereupon there was great rejoicing. But the horse would

not eat, the bird would not sing, and the maiden sat and wept all day. The youngest brother had not perished, however. Happily, the well was dry, and he fell upon soft moss without being harmed. Yet he could not get out.

Even in this great strait the faithful fox did not forsake him, but came leaping down and scolded him for not taking his advice. "I can't leave you to your fate, though. I must help you to get back to the light of day." He told him to take tight hold of his tail, and then he dragged him up. "You are not out of every danger even now," said the fox. "Your brothers were not sure of your death, so they have set watches all over the wood to kill you if they see you."

A poor old man was sitting by the roadside and the Prince exchanged clothes with him, and by this means he succeeded in reaching the King's court.

Nobody recognized him; but the bird began to sing, the horse began to eat, and the beautiful maiden left off crying.

In astonishment the King asked, "What does all this mean?"

The maiden answered, "I do not know, but I was very sad and now I am gay. It seems to me that my true bridegroom must have come."

She told the King all that had happened, although the two brothers had threatened her with death if she betrayed anything. The King ordered every person in the palace to be brought before him. Among them came the Prince disguised as an old man in all his rags, but the maiden knew him at once and fell on his neck. The wicked brothers were seized and put to death, but the Prince was married to the beautiful maiden and proclaimed heir to the King.

But what became of the poor fox? Long afterwards, when the Prince went out into the fields one day, he met the fox, who said, "You have everything that you can desire, but there is no end to my misery. It still lies in your

power to release me." And again he implored the Prince to shoot him dead and to cut off his head and his paws.

At last the Prince consented to do as he was asked. And no sooner was it done than the fox was changed into a man. He was no other than the brother of the beautiful Princess, at last set free from the evil spell which so long had lain upon him.

There was nothing now wanting to their happiness for the rest of their lives.

The Three Spinning Fairies

THERE was once upon a time a girl who was lazy and hated work, and nothing her mother could say would induce her to spin. At last the mother grew angry and, losing all patience with her, gave her a beating. At this the girl began to cry so loudly that the Queen, who was driving past at the time, heard her cries and stopped.

She went into the house and asked the mother why she was beating her daughter like that. "Her screams," she said, "can be heard outside in the street."

The mother was ashamed to confess the truth about her daughter's laziness, and so she answered, "I cannot get her to leave off spinning! She is forever at her wheel, and I am too poor to keep on buying her fresh flax."

"Is that all?" said the Queen. "There is nothing I like so much as the sound of spinning. I am never happier than when I can hear the humming of the wheels. Let me have your daughter and I will take her home with me to the castle. I have plenty of flax and she can go on spinning there to her heart's content."

The mother was heartily pleased at this proposal and so the Queen left, taking the girl with her. On their arrival at the castle, she took her upstairs and showed her three rooms filled from floor to ceiling with the most beautiful flax.

"Spin me all this," said the Queen, "and when it is finished, you shall have my eldest son for your husband. Your poverty is a matter of no consequence to me, for I consider that your unremitting industry is an all-sufficient dowry."

The girl dared not say anything but she inwardly trembled with fear, for she knew that she could never spin all that flax even if she were to sit at her spinning wheel from morning till night for three hundred years. As soon as she was alone she began to weep, and she sat like that for three days without doing a stroke of work.

When the Queen came again on the third day, she was surprised to find that the flax had not been touched. The girl excused herself by saying that she had felt so lonely and homesick that she had not been able to begin her spinning. The Queen was satisfied with this excuse, but as she was leaving she said, "Tomorrow, mind, I shall expect you to begin your work."

Alone once more, the girl was at her wit's end to know what to do, and in her distress of mind went and looked out of the window. There she saw three funny-looking women coming towards her. One had a big flat foot, another had a large underlip that hung over her chin, and the third had a very broad thumb. They stood still under the window and, looking up, they asked the girl what was the matter. She told them her trouble, and they offered to help her.

"If you will invite us to your wedding," they said, "and will not be ashamed of us, but will introduce us as your

cousins and let us sit at your table, we will soon spin all that flax for you."

"That I will gladly promise," said the girl, "if you will but come in and begin working for me at once."

So she let in the three women, and what queer little figures they looked! She cleared a space for them in the first room, and they all sat down and began spinning. The first drew out the thread and turned the wheel, and the second moistened the thread. The third twisted it, striking with her fingers on the table; and every time she did this a beautiful skein of the finest spun yarn fell on the ground.

Whenever the Queen came, the girl hid the three women and then showed her skein upon skein of spun yarn, till the Queen did not know how to find words enough to praise her.

As soon as the first room was empty, the spinners went on to the second, and finally they went on to the third, which like the others was very quickly cleared of the flax. Then the three women took leave of the girl, saying to her as they parted, "Do not forget the promise you made us, for it will bring you good fortune."

When the Queen was shown the empty rooms and the great piles of yarn, she began at once to make preparations for the wedding. The bridegroom was delighted to think he should have such a clever and industrious wife, and showered his praises upon her.

"I have three cousins," said the girl, "and they have shown me such great kindness in the past that I should not like to forget them, now that I am happy and prosperous. Will you give me permission to invite them to the wedding, and allow them to sit at our table?" The Queen and the bridegroom both willingly consented to this request.

The wedding feast was beginning when in walked the three women, attired in the most wonderful dresses. The

bride greeted them and said, "Welcome, dear cousins," but the bridegroom could not help exclaiming, "How came you to have such ugly friends?"

The he went up to the first and asked her what had given her such a broad foot.

"Turning the wheel," she answered.

Then he went to the second and asked what had caused her to have such a large lip.

"Moistening the thread," she answered.

Then he went to the third and asked what made her thumb so broad.

"Twisting the thread," she answered.

"Then," cried the Prince, horrified at these answers, "my beautiful wife shall never go near a spinning wheel again as long as she lives." And so henceforth she was rid of the hated task of spinning.

The Three Children of Fortune

ONCE upon a time a father sent for his three sons and gave to the eldest a cock, to the second a scythe, and to the third a cat.

"I am now old," said he. "My end is approaching, and I would fain provide for you before I die. Money I have none, and what I give you seems of but little worth. It rests with yourselves alone to turn my gifts to good account. Only seek out a land where what you have is still unknown, and your fortune is made."

After the death of the father, the eldest set out with his cock. But wherever he went, in every town he saw from afar off a cock sitting upon the church steeple and turning round with the wind. In the villages he always heard plenty of them crowing, and his bird was therefore nothing new. So there did not seem much chance of his making his fortune.

At length it happened that he came to an island where the people who lived there had never heard of a cock, and knew not even how to reckon the time. They knew, indeed,

if it were morning or evening, but at night, if they lay awake, they had no means of knowing how time went.

"Behold," said he to them, "what a noble animal this is! How like a knight he is! He carries a bright red crest upon his head and spurs upon his heels. He crows three times every night at stated hours, and at the third time the sun is about to rise. But this is not all. Sometimes he screams in broad daylight, and then you must take warning, for the weather is surely about to change."

This pleased the natives mightily. They kept awake one whole night and heard to their great joy how gloriously the cock called the hour at two, four, and six o'clock. Then they asked him whether the bird was for sale, and how much he would sell it for.

"About as much gold as an ass can carry," said he.

"A very fair price for such an animal," cried they with one voice, and they agreed to give him what he asked.

When he returned home with his wealth, his brothers wondered greatly, and the second said, "I will now set forth likewise and see if I can turn my scythe to as good an account."

There did not seem, however, much likelihood of this, for go where he would, he was met by peasants who had as good scythes on their shoulders as he had. But at last, as good luck would have it, he came to an island where the people had never heard of a scythe. There, as soon as the corn was ripe they went into the fields and pulled it up, but this was very hard work and a great deal of it was lost. The man then set to work with his scythe, and he mowed down their whole crop so quickly that the people stood staring openmouthed with wonder. They were willing to give him what he asked for such a marvelous thing, but he only took a horse laden with as much gold as it could carry.

Now the third brother had a great longing to go and see

what he could make of his cat. So he set out, and at first it happened to him as it had to the others. So long as he kept upon the mainland he met with no success. There were plenty of cats everywhere—indeed far too many—so that most of the young ones were drowned in the water as soon as they came into the world.

At last he passed over to an island, where, as it chanced most luckily for him, nobody had ever seen a cat. And they were overrun with mice to such a degree that the little wretches danced upon the tables and chairs, whether the master of the house was at home or not. The people complained loudly of this grievance. The King knew not how to rid himself of them in his palace. In every corner mice were squeaking, and they gnawed everything that their teeth could lay hold of.

Here was a fine field for puss! She soon began her chase, and had cleared two rooms in the twinkling of an eye. The people then besought their king to buy the wonderful animal at any price, for the good of the public. The King willingly gave what was asked—a mule laden with gold and jewels. And thus the third brother returned home with a richer prize than each of the others.

Meantime the cat feasted away upon the mice in the royal palace and devoured so many that they were no longer in any great numbers. At length, quite spent and tired with her work, she became extremely thirsty. So she stood still, drew up her head, and cried, "Miau, Miau!"

The King gathered together all his subjects when they heard this strange cry, and many ran shrieking in a great fright out of the palace. But the King held a council to decide what was best to be done, and it was at length agreed to send a herald to the cat, to warn her to leave the castle forthwith, or else force would be used to remove her.

"For," said the counselors, "we would far more willingly

put up with the mice—since we are used to that evil—than get rid of them at the risk of our lives."

A page accordingly went and asked the cat whether she was willing to quit the castle. But puss, whose thirst became every moment more and more pressing, answered nothing but "Miau! Miau!"

The page interpreted this to mean "No! No!" and therefore carried this answer to the King.

"Well," said the counselors, "then we must try what force will do."

So the guns were planted and the palace was fired upon from all sides. When the fire reached the room where the cat was, she sprang out of the window and ran away, but the besiegers did not see her and went on firing until the whole palace was burnt to the ground.

King Thrushbeard

THERE was once a king who had a daughter. She was more beautiful than words can tell, but at the same time so proud and haughty that no man who came to woo her was good enough for her. She turned away one after another, and even mocked them.

One day her father ordered a great feast to be given and invited to it all the marriageable young men from far and near. They were all placed in a row, according to their rank and position. First came kings, then princes, then dukes, earls, and barons. The Princess was led through the ranks, but she had some fault to find with all of them.

One was too stout. "That barrel!" she said. The next was too tall. "Long and lean is no good!" The third was too short. "Short and stout, can't turn about!" The fourth was too white. "Pale as death!" The fifth was too red. "Turkey cock!" The sixth was not straight. "Oven-dried!"

So there was something against each of them. But she made specially merry over one good king who stood quite at the head of the row and whose chin was a little hooked.

"Why," she cried, "he has a chin like the beak of a thrush." After that he was always called "King Thrushbeard."

When the old King saw that his daughter only made fun of them, and that she despised all the suitors who were assembled, he was very angry. He swore that the first beggar who came to the door should be her husband. A few days afterwards, a wandering musician began to sing at the window, hoping to receive charity.

When the King heard him he said, "Let him be brought in."

The musician came in, dressed in dirty rags, and sang to the King and his daughter. And when he had finished, he begged alms of them.

The King said, "Your song has pleased me so much that I will give you my daughter for wife."

The Princess was horror-stricken, but the King said, "I have sworn an oath to give you to the first beggar who came, and I will keep my word."

No entreaties were of any avail. A parson was brought and she had to marry the musician there and then.

When the ceremony was completed the King said, "Now that you are a begger woman, you can't stay in my castle any longer. You must go away with your husband." The beggar took her by the hand and led her away, and she was obliged to go with him on foot.

When they came to a big wood she asked:

> *"Ah, who is the lord of this forest so fine?"*
> *"It belongs to King Thrushbeard. It might*
> * have been thine,*
> * If his queen you had been."*
> *"Ah, sad must I sing!*
> * I would I'd accepted the love of the King."*

[25]

After that they reached a great meadow and she asked again:

> *"Ah, who is the lord of these meadows so fine?"*
> *"They belong to King Thrushbeard, and*
> *would have been thine,*
> *If his queen you had been."*
> *"Ah, sad must I sing!*
> *I would I'd accepted the hand of the King."*

Then they passed through a large town and again she asked:

> *"Ah, who is the lord of this city so fine?"*
> *"It belongs to King Thrushbeard, and it*
> *might have been thine,*
> *If his queen you had been."*
> *"Ah, sad must I sing!*
> *I would I'd accepted the heart of the King."*

"It doesn't please me at all," said the musician, "that you are always wishing for another husband. Am I not good enough for you?"

At last they came to a miserable little hovel and she said:

> *"Ah heavens! what's this house, so mean and small?*
> *This wretched little hut's no house at all."*

The musician answered, "This is my house and yours, where we are to live together." The door was so low that she had to stoop to get in.

"Where are the servants?" asked the Princess.

"Servants indeed!" answered the beggar. "Whatever you want done, you must do for yourself. Light the fire and put the kettle on to make my supper. I am very tired."

But the Princess knew nothing about lighting fires or cooking, and to get it done at all the begger had to do it

himself. When they had finished their humble fare they went to bed, but in the morning the man made her get up very early to do the housework. They lived like this for a few days, till they had eaten up all their store of food.

Then the man said, "Wife, this won't do any longer. You can't live here without working. You shall make baskets." So he went out and cut some willow twigs and brought them home. She began to weave them, but the hard twigs bruised her tender hands.

"I see that won't do," said the beggar. "You had better spin. Perhaps you can manage that." So she sat down and tried to spin, but the harsh yarn soon cut her delicate fingers and made them bleed.

"Now you see," said the man, "what a good-for-nothing you are. I have made a bad bargain in you. But I will try to start a trade in earthenware. You must sit in the market and offer your goods for sale."

"Alas!" she thought. "If any of the people from my father's kingdom come and see me sitting in the market place offering goods for sale, they will scoff at me." But it was no good. She had to obey unless she meant to die of hunger.

All went well the first time. The people willingly bought her wares because she was so handsome, and they paid what she asked them—nay, some even gave her the money and left her the pots as well.

They lived on the gains as long as they lasted and then the man laid in a new stock of wares. She took her seat in a corner of the market, set out her crockery about her, and began to cry her wares. Suddenly a drunken Hussar came galloping up and rode right in among the pots, breaking them into thousands of bits. She began to cry, and was so frightened that she did not know what to do.

"Oh, what will become of me?" she cried. "What will my

He rode right in among the pots

husband say to me?" She ran home and told him her misfortune.

"Who would ever think of sitting at the corner of the market with crockery?" he said. "Stop that crying. I see you are no manner of use for any decent kind of work. I have been to our King's palace and asked if they do not want a kitchen wench, and they have promised to try you. You will get your victuals free, at any rate."

So the Princess became a kitchen wench and had to wait upon the cook and do all the dirty work. She tied a pot into each of her pockets and in them took home her share of the scraps and leavings, and upon these they lived.

It so happened that the marriage of the eldest Princess just then took place, and the poor girl went upstairs and stood behind the curtains to peep at all the splendor. When the rooms were lighted up and she saw the guests streaming in, one more beautiful than the other, and the scene grew more and more brilliant, she thought with a heavy heart of her sad fate. She cursed the pride and haughtiness which was the cause of her humiliation, and of her being brought to such depths.

Every now and then the servants would throw her bits from the savory dishes they were carrying away from the feast, and these she put into her pots to take home with her.

All at once the King's son came in. He was dressed in silk and velvet and he had a golden chain round his neck. When he saw the beautiful girl standing at the door, he seized her by the hand and wanted to dance with her. But she shrank and refused, because she saw that it was King Thrushbeard, who had been one of the suitors for her hand, and whom she had most scornfully driven away.

Her resistance was no use and he dragged her into the hall. The string by which her pockets were suspended

broke. Down fell the pots, and the soup and savory morsels were spilt all over the floor.

When the guests saw it they burst into shouts of mocking laughter. She was so ashamed that she would gladly have sunk into the earth. She rushed to the door and tried to escape, but on the stairs a man stopped her and brought her back. When she looked at him she saw that it was no other than King Thrushbeard again.

He spoke kindly to her and said, "Do not be afraid. I and the beggar man who lived in the poor little hovel with you are one and the same. For love of you I disguised myself. And I was also the Hussar who rode among your pots. All this I did to bend your proud spirit and to punish you for the haughtiness with which you mocked me."

She wept bitterly and said, "I was very wicked and I am not worthy to be your wife."

But he said, "Be happy! Those evil days are over. Now we will celebrate our true wedding."

The waiting-women came and put rich clothing upon her, and her father with all his court came and wished her joy on her marriage with King Thrushbeard.

Then in truth her happiness began. I wish we had been there to see it, you and I.

Jorinda and Joringel

THERE was once an old castle in the middle of a vast thick wood. In it there lived an old woman quite alone, and she was a witch. By day she made herself into a cat or a screech owl, but regularly at night she became a human being again. In this way she was able to decoy wild beasts and birds, which she would kill and boil or roast. If any man came within a hundred paces of the castle, he was forced to stand still; he could not move from the place till she gave the word of release. But if an innocent maiden came within the circle, she changed her into a bird and shut her up in a cage, which she carried into a room in the castle. She must have had seven thousand cages of this kind, containing pretty birds.

Now there was once a maiden called Jorinda who was more beautiful than all other maidens. She had promised to marry a very handsome youth named Joringel, and it was in the days of their courtship, when they took the greatest joy in being alone together, that one day they wandered out into the forest. "Take care," said Joringel. "Do not let us go too near the castle."

It was a lovely evening. The sunshine glanced between the tree trunks of the dark greenwood, while the turtledoves sang plaintively in the old beech trees. Yet Jorinda sat down

in the sunshine and could not help weeping and bewailing, while Joringel, too, soon became just as mournful. They both felt as miserable as if they had been going to die. Gazing around them, they found they had lost their way and did not know how they should find the path home. Half the sun still appeared above the mountain; half had sunk below.

Joringel peered into the bushes and saw the old walls of the castle quite close to them. He was terror-stricken and became pale as death. Jorinda was singing:

> *"My birdie with its ring so red*
> *Sings sorrow, sorrow, sorrow;*
> *My love will mourn when I am dead,*
> *Tomorrow, morrow, mor—jug, jug."*

Joringel looked toward her, but she had changed into a nightingale who sang "Jug, jug." A screech owl with glowing eyes flew three times around her, and cried three times "Shu hu-hu." Joringel could not stir. He stood like a stone without being able to speak or cry, or to move hand or foot.

The sun had now set. The owl flew into a bush, out of which appeared almost at the same moment a crooked old woman, skinny and yellow. She had big red eyes and a crooked nose whose tip reached her chin. She mumbled something, caught the nightingale, and carried it away in her hand. Joringel could not say a word nor move from the spot, and the nightingale was gone.

At last the old woman came back, and said in a droning voice, "Greeting to thee, Zachiel! When the moon shines on the cage, unloose the captive, Zachiel."

Then Joringel was free. He fell on his knees before the witch and implored her to give back his Jorinda, but she

said he should never have her again, and went away. He pleaded, he wept, he lamented, but all in vain. "Alas! What is to become of me?" said Joringel.

At last he went away, and arrived at a strange village where he spent a long time as a shepherd. He often wandered around about the castle, but did not go too near it. At last he dreamt one night that he found a blood-red flower in the middle of which was a beautiful large pearl. He plucked the flower and took it to the castle. Whatever he touched with it was made free of enchantment. He dreamt also that by this means he had found his Jorinda again.

In the morning when he awoke, he began to search over hill and dale in the hope of finding a flower like this. He searched till the ninth day, when he found the flower early in the morning. In the middle was a big dewdrop, as big as the finest pearl. This flower he carried day and night till he reached the castle. He was not held fast as before when he came within the hundred paces of the castle, but walked straight up to the door.

Joringel was filled with joy. He touched the door with the flower, and it flew open. He went in through the court and listened for the sound of birds. He went on and found the hall, where the witch was feeding the birds in the seven thousand cages. When she saw Joringel she was angry, very angry. She scolded him and spat poison and gall at him. He paid no attention to her but turned away and searched among the bird cages. Yes, there were many hundred nightingales, but how was he to find his Jorinda?

While he was looking about in this way he noticed that the old woman was secretly removing a cage with a bird inside, and was making for the door. He sprang swiftly towards her, touched the cage and the witch with the flower,

and then she no longer had power to exercise her spells. Jorinda stood there, as beautiful as before, and threw her arms around Joringel's neck.

After that he changed all the other birds back into maidens again and went home with Jorinda, and they lived long and happily together.

The Wren and the Bear

ONCE upon a time a bear and a wolf were taking a walk in a wood. It was summer, and the bear heard a bird singing most beautifully. He said, "Brother Wolf, what kind of bird is that singing so beautifully?"

"That is the King of the birds, and we must bow down to it." But really it was a wren.

"If that is so," said the bear, "I should like to see his royal palace. Come, you must take me to it."

"That's not so easy," said the wolf. "You must wait till the Queen comes."

Soon afterwards the Queen made her appearance, bringing food in her beak, and the King came with her to feed their little ones. The bear would have liked to go in at once, but the wolf held him by the sleeve and said, "No, you must wait till the King and Queen fly away again."

So they marked the opening of the nest and trudged on. But the bear had no rest till he could see the royal palace, and before long he went back. The King and the Queen had gone out again. He peeped in and saw five or six young lying in the nest.

"Is that the royal palace?" cried the bear. "What a miserable place! And do you mean to say that you are royal children? You must be changelings."

When the young wrens heard this, they were furious.

They shrieked, "No, indeed we're not. Our parents are honest people. We must have this out with you."

The bear and the wolf were very much frightened. They turned around and ran home to their dens.

But the young wrens continued to shriek and scream aloud. And when their parents came back with more food, they said, "We won't touch so much as the leg of a fly, even if we starve, till you tell us whether we are really your children. The bear has been here calling us names."

Then said the old King, "Only be quiet, and this shall be seen to."

Thereupon he and his wife flew off to the bear in his den and called in to him, "Old Bruin, why have you been calling our children names? It will turn out badly for you, and it will lead to a bloody war between us."

So war was declared, and all the four-footed animals were called together—the ox, the ass, the cow, the stag, the deer, and every other creature on the earth.

But the wren called together every creature which flew in the air. He called not only the birds both large and small, but also the gnats, the hornets, the bees, and the flies.

When the time came for the war to begin, the wrens sent out scouts to discover where the commanding generals of the enemy were to be found. The gnats were the most cunning of all. They swarmed into the wood where the enemy were assembled, and at last they hid themselves under a leaf of the tree where the orders were being given.

The bear called the fox up to him and said, "You are the slyest of all the animals, Reynard. You shall be our general and lead us."

"Very good," said the fox, "but what shall we have for a signal?" But nobody could think of anything. Then said the fox, "I have a fine, long, bushy tail which looks almost like a red feather brush. When I hold my tail erect, things

are going well and you must march forward at once. But if it droops, you must all run away as hard as ever you can."

When the gnats heard this they flew straight home and told the wrens every detail.

When the day broke, all the four-footed animals came rushing to the spot where the battle was to take place. They came with such a tramping that the earth shook. The wren and his army also came swarming through the air. They fluttered and buzzed enough to terrify one.

And then they made for one another.

The wren sent the hornet down with orders to seat herself on the tail of the fox and sting him with all her might.

When the fox felt the first sting, he quivered and raised one leg in the air. But he bore it bravely and kept his tail erect. At the second sting he was forced to let it droop for a moment. But the third time he could bear it no longer: he screamed, and down went his tail between his legs. When the animals saw this they thought all was lost, and off they ran helter-skelter as fast as they could go, each to his own den.

So the birds won the battle.

When it was over, the King and the Queen flew home to their children and cried, "Children, be happy! Eat and drink to your hearts' content. We have won the battle."

But the young wrens said, "We won't eat till the bear comes here to make an apology, and says that we are really and truly your lawful children."

The wren flew to the bear's den and cried, "Old Bruin, you will have to come and apologize to my children for calling them names, or else you will have all your ribs broken."

So in great terror the bear crept to the nest and apologized, and at last the young wrens were satisfied. They ate and drank and made merry till far into the night.

[37]

The Twelve Brothers

ONCE upon a time there lived a king and a queen very peacefully together. They had twelve children, all boys.

Now the King said to the Queen one day, "If our thirteenth child should be a girl the twelve boys shall die so that the kingdom may fall to her alone."

Then he caused twelve coffins to be made, and they were filled with shavings and a little pillow laid in each, and they were brought and put into a locked-up room. And the King gave the key to the Queen and told her to say nothing about it to anyone. But the mother sat the whole day sorrowing, so that her youngest son, who never left her and to whom she had given the Biblical name Benjamin, said to her, "Dear mother, why are you so sad?"

"Dearest child," answered she, "I dare not tell you."

But he let her have no peace until she went and unlocked the room and showed him the twelve coffins with the shavings and the little pillows.

Then she said, "My dear Benjamin, your father has caused these coffins to be made for you and your eleven brothers, and if I bring a little girl into the world you are all to be put to death together and buried therein."

She wept as she spoke, and her little son comforted her

and said, "Weep not, dear mother. We will save ourselves and go far away."

Then she answered, "Yes, go with your eleven brothers out into the world, and let one of you always sit on the top of the highest tree that can be found and keep watch upon the tower of this castle. If a little son is born I will put out a white flag, and then you may safely venture back again. But if it is a little daughter I will put out a red flag, and then flee away as fast as you can, and the dear God watch over you. Every night will I arise and pray for you—in winter that you may have a fire to warm yourselves by, and in summer that you may not languish in the heat."

After that, when she had given her sons her blessing, they went away out into the wood. One after another kept watch, sitting on the highest oak tree and looking towards the tower. When eleven days had passed and Benjamin's turn came, he saw a flag put out. It was not white, but blood red, to warn them that they were to die.

When the brothers learned this they were angry and said, "Shall we suffer death because of a girl? We swear to be revenged. Wherever we find a girl we will shed her blood."

Then they went deeper into the wood, and in the middle where it was darkest they found a little enchanted house standing empty. Then they said, "Here will we dwell. And you, Benjamin, the youngest and weakest, shall stay at home and keep house. We others will go and find food."

Then they went into the wood and caught hares, wild does, birds and pigeons, and whatever else is good to eat, and brought them to Benjamin for him to prepare and cook to satisfy their hunger. So they lived together in the little house for ten years and the time did not seem long.

By this time the Queen's little daughter was growing up. She had a kind heart and a beautiful face, and a golden star on her forehead.

[39]

Once when there was a great wash she saw among the clothes twelve shirts, and she asked her mother, "Whose are these twelve shirts? They are too small to be my father's."

Then the mother answered with a sore heart, "Dear child, they belong to your twelve brothers."

The little girl said, "Where are my twelve brothers? I have never heard of them."

And her mother answered, "God only knows where they are wandering about in the world." Then she led the little girl to the secret room, and unlocked it and showed her the twelve coffins with the shavings and the little pillows.

"These coffins," said she, "were intended for your twelve brothers, but they went far away when you were born." And she related how everything had come to pass.

Then said the little girl, "Dear mother, do not weep. I will go and seek my brothers." So she took the twelve shirts and went far and wide in the great forest. The day sped on, and in the evening she came to the enchanted house.

She went in and found a youth, who asked, "Whence do you come, and what do you want?" And he marveled at her beauty, her royal garments, and the star on her forehead.

Then she answered, "I am a king's daughter and I seek my twelve brothers. I will go everywhere under the blue sky until I find them." And she showed him the twelve shirts which belonged to them.

Then Benjamin saw that it must be his sister and said, "I am Benjamin, your youngest brother."

And she began weeping for joy, and Benjamin also, and they kissed and cheered each other with great love.

After a while he said, "Dear sister, there is still a hindrance. We have sworn that any maiden whom we meet must die, as it was because of a maiden that we had to leave our kingdom."

Then she said, "I will willingly die, if by doing so I may benefit my twelve brothers."

"No," answered he, "you shall not die. Sit down under this tub until the eleven brothers get home and we come to an agreement about it." She did so, and as night came on they returned from hunting, and supper was ready.

And as they were sitting at table and eating, they asked, "What news?"

And Benjamin said, "Don't you know any?"

"No," answered they.

So he said, "You have been in the wood and I have stayed at home, and yet I know more than you."

"Tell us!" cried they.

He answered, "Promise me that the first maiden we see shall not be put to death."

"Yes, we promise," cried they all. "She shall have mercy."

Then he said, "Our sister is here." He lifted up the tub and the King's daughter came forth in her royal garments with her golden star on her forehead, and she seemed so beautiful, delicate, and sweet that they all rejoiced. And they fell on her neck and kissed her and loved her with all their hearts.

After this she remained in the house with Benjamin and helped him with the work. The others went forth into the woods to catch wild animals, does, birds, and pigeons for food for them all, and their sister and Benjamin took care that all was made ready for them. She fetched the wood for cooking, and the vegetables, and watched the pots on the fire, so that supper was always ready when the others came in. She also kept great order in the house, and the beds were always beautifully white and clean, and the brothers were contented and lived in unity.

One day the two got ready a fine feast, and when they were all assembled they sat down and ate and drank, and

were full of joy. Now there was a little garden belonging
to the enchanted house, in which grew twelve lilies. The
maiden, thinking to please her brothers, went out to gather
the twelve flowers, meaning to give one to each as they sat
at meat. But as she broke off the flowers, in the same moment the brothers were changed into twelve ravens and
flew over the wood far away, and the house with the
garden also disappeared. So the poor maiden stood alone
in the wildwood.

And as she was looking around her she saw an old
woman standing by her who said, "My child, what hast
thou done? Why couldst thou not leave the twelve flowers
standing? They were thy twelve brothers, who are now
changed to ravens forever."

The maiden said, weeping, "Is there no means of setting
them free?"

"No," said the old woman. "There is in the whole world
no way but one, and that is difficult. Thou canst not release
them but by being dumb for seven years. Thou must neither
speak nor laugh, and wert thou to speak one single word,
and it wanted but one hour of the seven years, all would
be in vain. Thy brothers would perish because of that one
word."

Then the maiden said in her heart, "I am quite sure that
I can set my brothers free." And she went and sought a
tall tree, climbed up, and sat there spinning, and never
spoke or laughed.

Now it happened that a king who was hunting in the
wood had with him a large greyhound, who ran to the tree
where the maiden was, sprang up at it, and barked loudly.
Up came the King and saw the beautiful Princess with the
golden star on her forehead, and he was so charmed with
her beauty that he prayed her to become his wife. She
gave no answer, only a little nod of her head. Then he him-

self climbed the tree and brought her down, set her on his horse, and took her home. The wedding was held with great splendor, but the bride neither spoke nor laughed.

After they had lived pleasantly together for a few years, the King's mother, who was a wicked woman, began to slander the young Queen, and said to the King, "She is only a low beggar maid that you have taken to yourself. Who knows what mean tricks she is playing? Even if she is really dumb and cannot speak she might at least laugh. Not to laugh is the sign of a bad conscience."

At first the King would believe nothing of it, but the old woman talked so long and suggested so many bad things that he at last let himself be persuaded and condemned the Queen to death.

Now a great fire was kindled in the courtyard, and she was to be burned in it. And the King stood above at the window and watched it all with weeping eyes, for he had held her very dear. And when she was already bound fast to the stake and the fire was licking her garments with red tongues, the last moment of the seven years came to an end.

Then a rushing sound was heard in the air and twelve ravens came flying and sank downwards. And as they touched the earth they became her twelve brothers that she had lost. They rushed through the fire and quenched the flames and set their sister free, kissing and consoling her.

And now that her mouth was opened and she might venture to speak, she told the King the reason of her dumbness and why she had never laughed. The King rejoiced when he heard of her innocence, and they all lived together in happiness until their death.

But the wicked mother-in-law was very unhappy, and died miserably.

The Mouse, the Bird,
and the Sausage

ONCE upon a time a mouse and a bird and a sausage lived
and kept house together in perfect peace among themselves, and in great prosperity. It was the bird's business
to fly to the forest every day and bring back wood. The
mouse had to draw the water, make the fire, and set the
table. And the sausage had to do the cooking. Nobody is
content in this world: much will have more. One day the
bird met another bird on the way, and told him of his excellent condition in life. But the other bird called him a
poor simpleton to do so much work while the two others
led easy lives at home.

When the mouse had made up her fire and drawn water,
she went to rest in her little room until it was time to lay
the cloth. The sausage stayed by the saucepans, looked to
it that the victuals were well cooked, and just before dinnertime he stirred the broth or the stew three or four times
well around himself, so as to enrich and season and flavor
it. Then the bird used to come home and lay down his load,
and they sat down at table; and after a good meal they
would go to bed and sleep their fill till the next morning.
It really was a most satisfactory life.

But the bird came to the resolution next day never again

to fetch wood. He had, he said, been their slave long enough. Now they must change about and make a new arrangement. So in spite of all the mouse and the sausage could say, the bird was determined to have his own way. So they drew lots to settle it, and as the lot fell, the sausage was to fetch wood, the mouse was to cook, and the bird was to draw water and make the fire.

Now see what happened. The sausage went away after wood, the bird made up the fire, and the mouse put on the pot, and they waited until the sausage should come home, bringing the wood for the next day. But the sausage was absent so long that they thought something must have happened to him, and the bird went part of the way to see if he could see anything of him. Not far off he met a dog on the road, who, looking upon the sausage as lawful prey, had picked him up and made an end of him. The bird then lodged a complaint against the dog, but it was all no good, as the dog swore that he had found forged letters on the sausage, so that he deserved to lose his life.

The bird then very sadly took up the wood and carried it home himself, and related to the mouse all he had seen and heard. They were both very troubled, but determined to look on the bright side of things and still to remain together. And so the bird laid the cloth, and the mouse prepared the food and finally got into the pot, as the sausage used to do, to stir and flavor the broth, but then she had to part with fur and skin and finally with life!

And when the bird came to dish up the dinner, there was no cook to be seen. And he turned over the heap of wood, and looked and looked, but the cook never appeared again. By accident the wood caught fire, and the bird hastened to fetch water to put it out, but he let fall the bucket in the well and himself after it, and as he could not get out again he was drowned.

The Wolf and the
Seven Kids

THERE was once an old nanny goat who had seven kids, and she was just as fond of them as a mother is of her children. One day she was going into the woods to fetch some food for them, so she called them all up to her and said, "My dear children, I am going out into the woods. Beware of the wolf! If once he gets into the house, he will eat you up—skin, and hair, and all. The rascal often disguises himself, but you will know him by his rough voice and his black feet."

The kids said, "Oh, we will be very careful, dear mother. You may be quite happy about us."

Bleating tenderly, the old goat went off to her work. Before long, someone knocked at the door and cried, "Open the door, dear children! Your mother has come back and brought something for each of you."

But the kids knew quite well by the voice that it was the wolf.

"We won't open the door," they cried. "You are not our mother. She has a soft, gentle voice, but yours is rough, and we are quite sure that you are the wolf."

So he went away to a shop and bought a lump of chalk, which he ate, and it made his voice quite soft.

He went back, knocked at the door again, and cried, "Open the door, dear children. Your mother has come back and brought something for each of you."

But the wolf had put one of his paws on the window sill, where the kids saw it, and they cried, "We won't open the door. Our mother has not got a black foot as you have. You are the wolf."

Then the wolf ran to a baker and said, "I have bruised my foot. Please put some dough on it." And when the baker put some dough on his foot, he ran to the miller and said, "Strew some flour on my foot."

The miller thought, "The old wolf is going to take somebody in," and refused.

But the wolf said, "If you don't do it, I will eat you up." So the miller was frightened, and whitened his paws. People are like that, you know.

Now the wretch went for the third time to the door, and knocked and said, "Open the door, children. Your dear mother has come home and has brought something for each of you out of the wood."

The kids cried, "Show us your feet first, so that we may be sure you are our mother." He put his paws on the window sill, and when they saw that they were white they believed all he said and opened the door.

Alas, it was the wolf who walked in. They were terrified and tried to hide themselves. One ran under the table, the second jumped into bed, the third into the oven. The fourth ran into the kitchen, the fifth got into the cupboard, the sixth into the washtub, and the seventh hid in the tall clockcase. But the wolf found them all but one and made short work of them. He swallowed one after the other, except the youngest one in the clockcase, whom he did not

find. When he had satisfied his appetite, he took himself off and lay down in a meadow outside, where he soon fell asleep.

Not long afterwards the old nanny goat came back from the woods. Oh, what a terrible sight met her eyes! The house door was wide open. Tables, chairs, and benches were overturned. The washing bowl was smashed to atoms, the covers and pillows torn from the bed. She searched all over the house for her children, but nowhere were they to be found. She called them by name, one by one, but no one answered.

At last when she came to the youngest, a tiny voice cried, "I am here, dear mother, hidden in the clockcase."

She brought him out and he told her that the wolf had come and eaten all the others. You may imagine how she wept over her children.

At last in her grief she went out, and the youngest kid ran by her side. When they went into the meadow, there lay the wolf under a tree, making the branches shake with his snores. They examined him from every side, and they could plainly see movements within his distended body.

"Ah, heavens!" thought the goat. "Is it possible that my

poor children, whom he ate for his supper, should be still alive?"

She sent the kid running to the house to fetch scissors, needles, and thread. Then she cut a hole in the monster's side, and hardly had she begun when a kid popped out its head. And as soon as the hole was big enough, all six jumped out, one after the other—all alive and without having suffered the least injury, for in his greed the monster had swallowed them whole. You may imagine the mother's joy! She hugged them and skipped about like a tailor on his wedding day.

At last she said, "Go and fetch some big stones, children, and we will fill up the brute's body while he is asleep."

Then the seven kids brought a lot of stones as fast as they could carry them, and stuffed the wolf with them till he could hold no more. The old mother quickly sewed him up, without his having noticed anything or even moved.

At last when the wolf had had his sleep out he got up, and as the stones made him feel very thirsty he wanted to go to a spring to drink. But as soon as he moved, the stones began to roll about and rattle inside him. Then he cried:

> *"What's the rumbling and tumbling*
> *That sets my stomach grumbling?*
> *I thought 'twas six kids, flesh and bones,*
> *Now I find it's nought but rolling stones."*

When he reached the spring and stooped over the water to drink, the heavy stones dragged him down, and he was drowned miserably. When the seven kids saw what had happened, they came running up and cried aloud, "The wolf is dead! The wolf is dead!" And they and their mother capered and danced around the spring in their joy.

Thumbling the Dwarf and Thumbling the Giant

AN honest husbandman once upon a time had a son born to him who was no bigger than my thumb, and who for many years did not grow one hairbreadth taller.

One day as the father was going to plow in his field, the little fellow said, "Father, let me go too."

"No," said his father, "stay where you are. You can do no good out of doors, and if you go perhaps I may lose you."

Then little Thumbling began to cry, and his father, to quiet him, at last said he might go. So he put him in his pocket, and when he was in the field pulled him out and set him upon the top of a newly made furrow, that he might be able to look about him. While he was sitting there, a great giant came striding over the hill.

"Do you see that steeple man?" said the father. "If you don't take care he will run away with you."

Now he only said this to frighten the little boy and keep him from straying away. But the giant had long legs, and with two or three strides he really came close to the furrow and picked up Master Thumbling to look at him as he would at a beetle or a cockchafer. Then he let him run

about his broad hand, and taking a liking to the little chap went off with him. The father stood by all the time, but could not say a word for fright. He thought his child was really lost, and that he should never see him again. But the giant took care of him at his house in the woods, and laid him in his bosom, and fed him with the same food that he lived upon himself. So Thumbling, instead of being a little dwarf, became like the giant—tall, and stout, and strong.

At the end of two years, when the old giant took him into the woods to try him and said, "Pull up that birch tree for yourself to walk with," the lad was so strong that he tore it up by the root. The giant thought he would make him a still stronger man than this, so after taking care of him two years more he took him into the wood to try his strength again. This time he took hold of one of the thickest oaks and pulled it up as if it were mere sport to him. Then the old giant said, "Well done, my man, you will do now." So he carried him back to the field where he first found him.

His father happened just then to be plowing his field again, as he was when he lost his son. The young giant went up to him and said, "Look here, father, see who I am! Don't you know your own son?"

But the husbandman was frightened and cried out, "No, no. You are not my son. Begone about your business."

"Indeed, I am your son. Let me plow a little. I can plow as well as you."

"No, go your way," said the father. But as he was afraid of the tall man he at last let go the plow and sat down on the ground beside it. Then the youth laid hold of the plow-share, and though he only pushed with one hand he drove it deep into the earth.

The plowman cried out, "If you must plow, pray do not push so hard. You are doing more harm than good."

But his son took off the horses and said, "Father, go home and tell my mother to get ready a good dinner. I'll go round the field meanwhile." So he went on driving the plow without any horses till he had done two mornings' work by himself. Then he harrowed it. And when all was over, he took up plow, harrow, horses, and all, and carried them home like a bundle of straw.

When he reached the house he sat himself down on the bench saying, "Now, mother, is dinner ready?"

"Yes," said she, for she dared not deny him anything. So she brought two large dishes full, enough to have lasted herself and her husband eight days. However, he soon ate it all up and said that was but a taste.

"I see very well, father, that I shall not get enough to eat at your house; so if you give me an iron walking stick so strong that I cannot break it against my knees, I will go away again."

The husbandman very gladly put his two horses to the cart and drove them to the forge, and brought back a bar of iron as long and as thick as his two horses could draw. But the lad laid it against his knee, and snap it went like a beanstalk.

"I see, father," said he, "you can get no stick that will do for me, so I'll go and try my luck by myself."

Then away he went and turned blacksmith, and traveled till he came to a village where lived a miserly smith who earned a great deal of money, but kept all he got to himself and gave nothing away to anybody. The first thing he did was to step into the smithy and ask if the smith did not want to hire a journeyman.

"Aye," said the cunning fellow, as he looked at him and thought what a stout chap he was and how lustily he would work and earn his bread. "What wages do you ask?"

"I want no pay," said he. "But every fortnight when the

other workmen are paid, you shall let me give you two strokes over the shoulders, just to amuse myself." The old smith thought to himself he could bear this very well and reckoned on saving a great deal of money, so the bargain was soon struck.

The next morning the new workman was about to begin to work but at the first stroke that he hit, when his master brought him the iron red-hot, he shivered it to pieces and the anvil sank so deep into the earth that he could not get it out again. This made the old fellow very angry.

"Holla!" cried he. "I can't have you for a workman. You are too clumsy. We must put an end to our bargain."

"Very well," said the other, "but you must pay for what I have done. So let me give you only one little stroke and then the bargain is all over." So saying, he gave him a thump that tossed him over a load of hay that stood near. Then he took the thickest bar of iron in the forge for a walking stick and went on his way.

When he had journeyed some way, he came to a farm-house and asked the farmer if he wanted a foreman.

The farmer said, "Yes," and the same wages were agreed on as before with the blacksmith.

The next morning the workmen were all to go into the wood, but the giant was found to be fast asleep in his bed when the rest were all up and ready to start.

"Come get up," said one of them to him. "It is high time to be stirring. You must go with us."

"Go your way," muttered he sulkily. "I shall do my work and get home long before you." So he lay in bed two hours longer and at last got up and cooked and ate his breakfast, and then at his leisure harnessed his horses to go to the wood.

Just before the wood was a hollow way through which all must pass, so he drove the cart on first and built up behind

him such a mound of faggots and briars that no horse could pass. This done, he drove on. And as he was going into the wood he met the others coming out on their road home.

"Drive away," said he. "I shall be home before you still." However, after going only a very little way into the wood he tore up one of the largest timber trees, put it into his cart, and turned about homewards. When he came to the pile of faggots he found all the others standing there, not being able to pass by. "So," said he, "you see if you had stayed with me, you would have been home just as soon and might have slept an hour or two longer."

Then he took his tree on one shoulder and his cart on the other, and pushed through as easily as though he were laden with feathers. And when he reached the yard he showed the tree to the farmer, and asked if it was not a fine walking stick.

"Wife," said the farmer," this man is worth something. If he does sleep longer, still he works better than the rest."

Time rolled on, and he had worked for the farmer his whole year. So when his fellow laborers were paid, he said he also had a right to take his wages. But great dread came upon the farmer at the thought of the blows he was to have, so he begged him to give up the old bargain and take his whole farm and stock instead.

"Not I," said he. "I will be no farmer. I am foreman, and so I mean to stay and to be paid as we agreed."

Finding that he could do nothing with him, the farmer begged one fortnight's respite, and called together all his friends to ask their advice in the matter. They bethought themselves for a long time and at last agreed that the shortest way was to kill this troublesome foreman. The next thing was to settle how it was to be done, and it was agreed that

he should be ordered to carry into the yard some great mill-stones and put them on the edge of the well. Then he should be sent down to clean it out, and when he was at the bottom the millstones should be pushed down upon his head.

Everything went right, and when the foreman was safe in the well the stones were rolled in. As they struck the bottom, the water splashed to the very top. Of course they thought his head must be crushed to pieces, but he only cried out, "Drive away the chickens from the well! They are scratching about in the sand above, and they throw it into my eyes so that I cannot see."

When his job was done, up he sprang from the well, saying, "Look here! See what a fine neckcloth I have!" And he pointed to one of the millstones that had fallen over his head and hung about his neck.

The farmer was again overcome with fear and begged another fortnight to think of it. So his freinds were called together again and at last gave this advice: that the foreman should be sent and made to grind corn by night at the haunted mill, whence no man had ever yet come out alive in the morning. That very evening he was told to carry eight bushels of corn to the mill and grind them in the night. Away he went to the loft, put two bushels into his right pocket, two into his left, and four into a long sack slung over his shoulders, and then set off to the mill. The miller told him he might grind there in the daytime but not by night, for the mill was bewitched and whoever went in at night had been found dead in the morning.

"Never mind, miller, I shall come out safe," said he. "Only make haste and get out of the way, and look out for me in the morning."

So he went into the mill and put the corn into the hopper, and about twelve o'clock sat down on the bench in the

miller's room. After a little time the door all at once opened of itself and in came a large table. On the table stood wine and meat and many good things besides. All seemed placed there by themselves—at any rate, there was no one to be seen. The chairs next moved themselves around it but still neither guests nor servants came, till all at once he saw fingers handling the knives and forks and putting food on the plates, but still nothing else was to be seen. Now our friend felt somewhat hungry as he looked at the dishes, so he sat himself down at the table and ate whatever he liked best.

"A little wine would be well after this cheer," said he. "But the good folks of this house seem to take but little of it." Just as he spoke, however, a flagon of the best moved on, and our guest filled a bumper, smacked his lips, and drank "Health and long life to all the company, and success to our next merry meeting!"

When they had had enough and the plates and dishes, bottle, and glasses, were all empty, of a sudden something unseen blew out the lights. "Never mind!" thought he. "One wants no candle to go to sleep by." But now that it was pitch dark he felt a huge blow fall upon his head. "Foul play!" cried he. "If I get such another box on the ear I shall just give it back again." And this he really did when the next blow came. Thus the game went on all night and he never let fear get the better of him, but kept dealing his blows, till at daybreak all was still.

"Well, miller," said he in the morning, "I have had some little slaps on the face but I've given as good, I warrant you. And meantime I have eaten just as much as I liked." The miller was glad to find the charm was broken and would have given him a great deal of money. "I want no money. I have quite enough," said he as he took his meal on his back and went home to his master to claim his wages.

But the farmer was in great trouble, knowing there was now no help for him. He paced the room up and down, while the drops of sweat ran down his forehead. Then he opened the window for a little fresh air, and before he was aware his foreman gave him the first blow, and such a blow that off he flew over the hills and far away. The next blow sent his wife after him, and for aught I know they may not have reached the ground yet. But without waiting to find out, the young giant took up his iron walking stick and walked off.

Sweetheart Roland

ONCE upon a time there was a woman who was a real witch, and she had two daughters. One was ugly and wicked, but she loved her because she was her own daughter. The other was good and lovely, but she hated her for she was only her foster child.

Now this foster child had a beautiful apron which the other daughter envied, and she said to her mother that she must and would have it.

"Just wait quietly, my child," said her mother. "You shall have it. Tonight when she is asleep I will go and chop off your sister's head. Only take care to lie on the farther side of the bed, against the wall, and push her well to this side."

Now all this would certainly have come to pass if the poor girl had not been standing in a corner and heard what they said. She was not even allowed to go near the door all day, and when bedtime came the witch's daughter got into bed first so as to lie at the farther side. But when she was asleep the other gently changed places with her and put herself next the wall.

In the middle of the night the witch crept up holding an ax in her right hand, while with her left she felt to find if

anyone was there. Then she seized the ax with both hands, struck—and struck off her own child's head.

When she had gone away, the maiden got up and went to the house of her sweetheart, Roland, and knocked at his door. When he came out, she said to him, "Listen, dear Roland, we must quickly fly. My foster mother tried to kill me, but she hit her own child instead. When day comes and she sees what she has done, we shall be lost."

"But," said Roland, "you must first get her magic wand, or we shall not be able to escape if she comes after us.'"

The maiden fetched the magic wand, and then she took her foster sister's head and dropped three drops of blood from it—one by the bed, one in the kitchen, and one on the stairs. After that, she hurried away with her sweetheart, Roland.

When the old witch got up in the morning she called her daughter in order to give her the apron, but she did not come. Then she called, "Where are you?"

"Here on the stairs," answered one drop of blood.

The witch went to the stairs but saw nothing. So she called again, "Where are you?"

"Here in the kitchen warming myself," answered the second drop of blood.

The witch went into the kitchen but found nothing. Then she called again, "Where are you?"

"Here in bed, sleeping," answered the third drop of blood.

So she went into the bedroom, and there she found her own child, whose head she had chopped off herself.

The witch flew into a violent passion and sprang out of the window. As she could see for many miles around, she soon discovered the maiden hurrying away with Roland.

"That won't do you any good!" she cried. "However far you may go, you won't escape me."

She put on her seven-league boots, and before long she overtook them. When the maiden saw her coming, with the magic wand she changed her sweetheart into a lake, and changed herself into a duck swimming in it. The witch stood on the shore and threw bread crumbs into the water, and did everything she could think of to entice the duck ashore. But it was all to no purpose, and she was obliged to go back at night without having accomplished her object.

When she had gone away, the maiden and Roland resumed their own shapes, and they walked the whole night till break of day.

Then the maiden changed herself into a beautiful rose in the middle of a briar hedge, and Roland into a fiddler. Before long the witch came striding along and said to the fiddler, "Good fiddler, may I pick this beautiful rose?"

"By all means," he said, "and I will play to you."

As she crept into the hedge in great haste to pick the flower (for she knew well who the flower was), Roland began to play. And she had to dance, whether she liked or not, for it was a magic dance. The faster he played, the higher she had to jump, and the thorns tore her clothes to ribbons and scratched her till she bled. He would not stop a moment, so she had to dance till she fell down dead.

When the maiden was freed from the spell, Roland said, "Now I will go to my father and order the wedding."

"Then I will stay here in the meantime," said the maiden. "And so that no one shall recognize me while I am waiting, I will change myself into a common red stone."

So Roland went away and the maiden stayed in the field as a stone, waiting his return.

But when Roland reached home he fell into the snares of another woman, who made him forget all about his

love. The poor maiden waited a long, long time, but when he did not come back, she became very sad and changed herself into a flower. "Somebody at least will tread upon me," she thought.

Now it so happened that a shepherd was watching his sheep in the field, and he saw the flower and picked it because he thought it was so pretty. He took it home and put it carefully away in a chest. From that time forward a wonderful change took place in the shepherd's hut. When he got up in the morning, all the work was done. The tables and benches were dusted, the fire was lighted, and the water was carried in. At dinnertime, when he came home, the table was laid and a well-cooked meal stood ready.

He could not imagine how it all came about, for he never saw a creature in his house, and nobody could be hidden in the tiny hut. He was much pleased at being so well served, but at last he got rather frightened and went to a wisewoman to ask her advice.

The wisewoman said, "There is magic behind it. You must look carefully about the room early in the morning, and whatever you see, throw a white cloth over it and the spell will be broken."

The shepherd did what she told him, and next morning just as the day broke he saw his chest open and the flower come out. So he sprang up quickly and threw a white cloth over it. Immediately the spell was broken and a lovely maiden stood before him, who confessed that she had been the flower and that it was she who had done all the work of his hut. She also told him her story, and he was so pleased with her that he asked her to marry him.

But she answered, "No, I want my sweetheart, Roland. Though he has forsaken me I will always be true to him."

She promised not to go away, however, but to go on with the housekeeping for the present.

Now the time came for Roland's marriage to be celebrated. According to old custom, a proclamation was made that every maiden in the land should present herself to sing at the marriage in honor of the bridal pair.

When the faithful maiden heard this she grew very sad, so sad that she thought her heart would break. She had no wish to go to the wedding but the others came and fetched her. But each time as her turn came to sing, she slipped behind the others till she was the only one left and she could not help herself.

As soon as she began to sing and her voice reached Roland's ears, he sprang up and cried, "That is the true bride and I will have no other."

Everything that he had forgotten came back, and his heart was filled with joy. So the faithful maiden was married to her sweetheart, Roland. All her grief and pain were over, and only happiness lay before her.

The Goose Girl

THERE was once an old queen whose husband had been dead for many years, and she had a very beautiful daughter. When she grew up she was betrothed to a prince in a distant country. When the time came for the maiden to be sent into this distant country to be married, the old Queen packed up quantities of clothes and jewels, gold and silver, cups and ornaments, and in fact everything suitable to a royal outfit, for she loved her daughter very dearly.

She also sent a waiting-woman to travel with her and to put her hand into that of the bridegroom. They each had a horse. The Princess' horse was called Falada, and it could speak.

When the hour of departure came, the old Queen went to her bedroom and with a sharp little knife cut her finger and made it bleed. Then she held a piece of white cambric under it and let three drops of blood fall on it. This cambric she gave to her daughter and said, "Dear child, take good care of this. It will stand you in good stead on the journey."

They then bade each other a sorrowful farewell. The Princess hid the piece of cambric in her bosom, mounted her horse, and set out to her bridegroom's country.

When they had ridden for a time, the Princess became

very thirsty and said to the waiting-woman, "Get down and fetch me some water in my cup from the stream. I must have something to drink."

"If you are thirsty," said the waiting-woman, "dismount yourself, lie down by the water, and drink. I don't choose to be your servant."

So in her great thirst the Princess dismounted and stooped down to the stream and drank, since she could not have her golden cup. The poor Princess said, "Alas!" And the drops of blood answered, "If your mother knew this it would break her heart."

The royal bride was humble, so she said nothing but mounted her horse again. Then they rode several miles farther, but the day was warm, the sun was scorching, and the Princess was soon very thirsty again.

When they reached a river she called out again to her waiting-woman, "Get down and give me some water in my golden cup." She had forgotten all about the rude words which had been said to her.

But the waiting-woman answered more haughtily than ever, "If you want to drink, get the water for yourself. I won't be your servant."

Being very thirsty, the Princess dismounted and knelt by the flowing water. She cried, "Ah me!" And the drops of blood answered, "If your mother knew this it would break her heart."

While she stooped over the water to drink, the piece of cambric with the drops of blood on it fell out of her bosom and floated away on the stream, but she never noticed this in her great fear. The waiting-woman, however, had seen it and rejoiced at getting more power over the bride, who by losing the drops of blood had become weak and powerless.

Now when she was about to mount her horse Falada

again, the waiting-woman said, "By rights, Falada belongs to me. This jade will do for you!"

The poor little Princess was obliged to give way. Then the waiting-woman in a harsh voice ordered her to take off her royal robes, and to put on her own mean garments. Finally she forced her to swear before heaven that she would not tell a creature at the court what had taken place. Had she not taken the oath she would have been killed on the spot. But Falada saw all this and marked it.

The waiting-woman then mounted Falada and put the real bride on her poor jade, and they continued their journey.

There was great rejoicing when they arrived at the castle. The Prince hurried towards them and lifted the waiting-woman from her horse, thinking she was his bride. She was led upstairs, but the real Princess had to stay below.

The old King looked out of the window and saw the delicate, pretty little creature standing in the courtyard. So he went to the bridal apartment and asked the bride about her companion, who was left standing in the courtyard, and wished to know who she was.

"I picked her up on the way and brought her with me for company. Give the girl something to do to keep her from idling."

But the old King had no work for her and could not think of anything. At last he said, "I have a little lad who looks after the geese. She may help him."

The boy was called Little Conrad, and the real bride was sent with him to look after the geese.

Soon afterwards the false bride said to the Prince, "Dear husband, I pray you do me a favor."

He answered, "That will I gladly do."

"Well then, let the knacker be called to cut off the head of the horse I rode. It angered me on the way."

Really she was afraid that the horse would speak and tell of her treatment of the Princess. So it was settled, and the faithful Falada had to die.

When this came to the ear of the real Princess, she promised the knacker a piece of gold if he would do her a slight service. There was a great dark gateway to the town, through which she had to pass every morning and evening. Would he nail up Falada's head in this gateway so that she might see him as she passed?

The knacker promised to do as she wished, and when the horse's head was cut off he hung it up in the dark gateway. In the early morning, when she and Conrad went through the gateway, she said in passing:

> *"Alas! dear Falada, there thou hangest."*

And the head answered:

> *"Alas! Queen's daughter, there thou gangest.*
> *If thy mother knew thy fate,*
> *Her heart would break with grief so great."*

Then they passed on out of the town and right into the fields with the geese. When they reached the meadow, the Princess sat down on the grass and let down her hair. It shone like pure gold, and when Little Conrad saw it he was so delighted that he wanted to pluck some out. But she said:

> *"Blow, blow, little breeze,*
> *And Conrad's hat seize.*
> *Let him join in the chase*
> *While away it is whirled,*
> *Till my tresses are curled*
> *And I rest in my place."*

Then a strong wind sprang up which blew away Conrad's hat right over the fields, and he had to run after it.

When he came back, she had finished combing her hair and it was all put up again, so he could not get a single hair. This made him very sulky and he would not say another word to her. And they tended the geese till evening, when they went home.

Next morning when they passed under the gateway, the Princess said:

> "Alas! dear Falada, there thou hangest."

Falada answered:

> "Alas! Queen's daughter, there thou gangest,
> If thy mother knew thy fate,
> Her heart would break with grief so great."

Again when they reached the meadows, the Princess undid her hair and began combing it. Conrad ran to pluck some out, but she said quickly:

> "Blow, blow, little breeze,
> And Conrad's hat seize.
> Let him join in the chase
> While away it is whirled,
> Till my tresses are curled
> And I rest in my place."

The wind again sprang up and blew Conrad's hat far away over the fields, and he had to run after it. When he came back, the hair was all put up again and he could not pull out a single hair. And they tended the geese till the evening.

When they got home Conrad went to the old King and said, "I won't tend the geese with that maiden again."

"Why not?" asked the King.

"Oh, she vexes me every day."

The old King ordered him to tell what she did to vex him.

Conrad said, "In the morning when we pass under the dark gateway with the geese, she talks to a horse's head which is hung up on the wall. She says:

'Alas! Falada, there thou hangest.'

And the head answers:

'Alas! Queen's daughter, there thou gangest.
If thy mother knew thy fate,
Her heart would break with grief so great.' "

Then Conrad went on to tell the King all that had happened in the meadow, and how he had to run after his hat in the wind.

The old King ordered Conrad to go out next day as usual. Then he placed himself behind the dark gateway and heard the Princess speaking to Falada's head. He also followed her into the field and hid himself behind a bush. And with his own eyes he saw the Goose Girl and the lad come driving the geese into the field. Then after a time he saw the girl let down her hair, which glittered in the sun. Directly after this, she said:

"Blow, blow, little breeze,
And Conrad's hat seize.
Let him join in the chase
While away it is whirled,
Till my tresses are curled
And I rest in my place."

Then came a puff of wind which carried off Conrad's hat, and he had to run after it. While he was away, the maiden combed and did up her hair, and all this the old

King observed. Thereupon he went away unnoticed, and in the evening when the Goose Girl came home, he called her aside and asked why she did all these things.

"I may not tell you that, nor may I tell any human creature, for I have sworn it under the open sky. If I had not done so, I should have lost my life."

He pressed her sorely and gave her no peace, but he could get nothing out of her. Then he said, "If you won't tell me, then tell your sorrows to the iron stove there." And he went away.

She crept up to the stove and, beginning to weep and lament, unburdened her heart to it and said, "Here I am, forsaken by all the world, and yet I am a princess. A false waiting-woman brought me to such a pass that I had to take off my royal robes. Then she took my place with my bridegroom, while I have to do mean service as a goose girl. If my mother knew it, it would break her heart."

The old King stood outside by the pipes of the stove and heard all that she said. Then he came back and told her to go away from the stove. He caused royal robes to be put upon her, and her beauty was a marvel. The old King called his son and told him that he had a false bride—she was only a waiting-woman, but the true bride was here, the so-called Goose Girl.

The young Prince was charmed with her youth and beauty. A great banquet was prepared to which all the courtiers and good friends were bidden. The bridegroom sat at the head of the table with the Princess on one side and the waiting-woman at the other, but she was dazzled and did not recognize the Princess in her brilliant apparel.

When they had eaten and drunk and were all very merry, the old King put a riddle to the waiting-woman. "What does a person deserve who deceives his master?"

Then he told the whole story and ended by asking, "What doom does he deserve?"

The false bride answered, "No better than this: he must be put stark naked into a barrel stuck with nails, and be dragged along by two white horses from street to street till he is dead."

"That is your own doom," said the King, "and the judgment shall be carried out!"

When the sentence was fulfilled, the young Prince married his true bride, and they ruled their kingdom together in peace and happiness.

The Cat and Mouse
in Partnership

A CAT, having made acquaintance with a mouse, professed such great love and friendship for her that the mouse at last agreed that they should live and keep house together.

"We must make provision for the winter," said the cat, "or we shall suffer hunger. And you, little mouse, must not stir out, or you will be caught in a trap."

So they took counsel together and bought a little pot of fat. Then they could not tell where to put it for safety, but after long consideration the cat said there could not be a better place than the church, for nobody would steal there. And they decided to put it under the altar and not touch it until they were really in want. So the little pot was placed in safety. But before long the cat was seized with a great wish to taste it.

"Listen to me, little mouse," said he. "I have been asked by my cousin to stand godfather to a little son she has brought into the world. He is white with brown spots, and they want to have the christening today. So let me go to it, and you stay at home and keep house."

"Oh yes, certainly," answered the mouse. "Pray go, by all means. And when you are feasting on all the good things, think of me. I should so like a drop of the sweet red wine."

But there was not a word of truth in all this. The cat had no cousin and had not been asked to stand godfather. He went to the church, straight up to the little pot, and licked the fat off the top. Then he took a walk over the roofs of the town, saw his acquaintances, stretched himself in the sun, and licked his whiskers as often as he thought of the little pot of fat. And then when it was evening he went home.

"Here you are at last," said the mouse. "I expect you have had a merry time."

"Oh, pretty well," answered the cat.

"And what name did you give the child?" asked the mouse.

"Top-off," answered the cat dryly.

"Top-off!" cried the mouse. "That is a singular and wonderful name. Is it common in your family?"

"What does it matter?" said the cat. "It's not any worse than Crumb-picker, like your godchild."

A little time after this the cat was again seized with a longing for the pot of fat.

"Again I must ask you," said he to the mouse, "to do me a favor and keep house alone for a day. I have been asked a second time to stand godfather, and as the little one has a white ring round its neck, I cannot well refuse."

So the kind little mouse consented, and the cat crept along by the town wall until he reached the church, where he went straight to the little pot of fat and ate half of it.

"Nothing tastes so well as what one keeps to oneself," said he, feeling quite content with his day's work. When he reached home, the mouse asked what name had been given to the child.

"Half-gone," answered the cat.

"Half-gone!" cried the mouse. "I never heard such a name in my life. I'll bet it's not to be found in the calendar."

Soon after that the cat's mouth began to water again for the fat.

"Good things always come in threes," said he to the mouse. "Again I have been asked to stand godfather. The little one is quite black with white feet, and not any white hair on its body. Such a thing does not happen every day, so you will let me go, won't you?"

"Top-off, Half-gone," murmured the mouse. "They are such curious names, I cannot but wonder at them."

"That's because you are always sitting at home," said the cat, "in your little gray frock and hairy tail, never seeing the world, and fancying all sorts of things."

So the little mouse cleaned up the house and set it all in order. Meanwhile the greedy cat went and made an end of the little pot of fat.

"Now all is finished one's mind will be easy," said he, and came home in the evening quite sleek and comfortable. The mouse asked what name had been given to the third child.

"It won't please you any better than the others," answered the cat. "It is called All-gone."

"All-gone!" cried the mouse. "What an unheard-of name! I never met with anything like it. All-gone! Whatever can it mean?" And shaking her head, she curled herself round and went to sleep. After that the cat was not again asked to stand godfather.

When the winter had come and there was nothing more to be had out of doors, the mouse began to think of their store.

"Come, cat," said she, "we will fetch our pot of fat. How good it will taste, to be sure!"

"Of course it will," said the cat. "Just as good as if you stuck your tongue out of the window."

So they set out, and when they reached the place they found the pot, but it was standing empty.

"Oh, now I know what it all meant," cried the mouse. "Now I see what sort of partner you have been! Instead of standing godfather you have eaten it all up. First Top-off! Then Half-gone! Then—"

"Hold your tongue!" screamed the cat. "Another word, and I eat you too!"

And the poor little mouse, having "All-gone" on her tongue, out it came, and the cat leaped upon her and made an end of her. And that is the way of the world.

The White Snake

A LONG time ago there lived a king whose wisdom was celebrated far and wide. Nothing was unknown to him, and the news of the most secret transactions seemed to reach him through the air.

Now he had one very odd habit. Every day at dinner, when the courtiers had withdrawn and he was quite alone, a trusted servant had to bring in another dish. It was always covered. Even the servant did not know what it contained, nor anyone else, for the King never uncovered it till he was alone. This had gone on for a long time, when one day the servant who carried the dish was overcome by his curiosity and took the dish to his own room.

When he had carefully locked the door, he took the cover off the dish and saw a white snake lying in it. At the sight of it, he could not resist tasting it, so he cut off a piece and put it into his mouth. Hardly had he tasted it, however, when he heard a wonderful whispering of delicate voices.

He went to the window and listened, and he noticed that the whispers came from the sparrows outside. They were chattering away and telling each other all kinds of things

that they had heard in the woods and fields. Eating the snake had given him the power of understanding the language of birds and animals.

Now it happened on this day that the Queen lost her most precious ring, and suspicion fell upon this trusted servant who went about everywhere. The King sent for him, and threatened that if it was not found by the next day, he would be sent to prison. In vain he protested his innocence; but he was not believed.

In his grief and anxiety he went down into the courtyard and wondered how he should get out of his difficulty. A number of ducks were lying peaceably together by a stream, stroking down their feathers with their bills while they chattered gaily. The servant stood still to listen to them. They were telling each other of their morning's walks and experiences.

Then one of them said somewhat fretfully, "I have something lying heavy on my stomach. In my haste I swallowed the Queen's ring this morning."

The servant quickly seized it by the neck, carried it off into the kitchen, and said to the cook, "Here's a fine fat duck. You had better kill it at once."

"Yes, indeed," said the cook, weighing it in her hand. "It has spared no pains in stuffing itself. It should have been roasted long ago." So she killed it and cut it open, and there, sure enough, was the Queen's ring.

The servant now had no difficulty in proving his innocence. The King, to make up for his injustice, gave the servant leave to ask any favor he liked, and promised him the highest post about the court which he might desire. The servant, however, declined everything but a horse and some money to travel with, as he wanted to wander about for a while to see the world.

His request being granted, he set off on his travels, and

one day came to a pond where he saw three fishes caught among the reeds, gasping for breath. Although it is said that fishes are dumb, he understood their complaint at perishing thus miserably. As he had a compassionate heart, he got off his horse and put the three captives back into the water. They wriggled in their joy, stretched up their heads above the water, and cried, "We will remember that you saved us and will reward you for it."

He rode on again, and after a time he seemed to hear a voice in the sand at his feet. He listened, and heard an ant king complain, "I wish these human beings and their animals would keep out of our way. A clumsy horse has just put his hoof down upon a number of my people in the most heartless way."

He turned his horse into a side path, and the ant king cried, "We will remember and reward you."

The road now ran through a forest, and he saw a pair of ravens standing by their nest throwing out their young.

"Away with you, you gallows birds," they were saying. "We can't feed you any longer. You are old enough to look after yourselves."

The poor little nestlings lay on the ground, fluttering and flapping their wings and crying: "We poor helpless children must feed ourselves, and we can't even fly! We shall die of hunger. There is nothing else for it."

The good youth dismounted, killed his horse with his sword, and left the carcass as food for the young ravens. They hopped up to it and cried, "We will remember and reward you."

Now he had to depend upon his own legs, and after going a long way he came to a large town. There was much noise and bustle in the streets, where a man on horseback was making a proclamation.

"The King's daughter seeks a husband, but anyone who

wishes to sue for her hand must accomplish a hard task. And if he does not bring it to a successful issue, he will forfeit his life." Many had already attempted the task, but they had risked their lives in vain.

When the youth saw the Princess, he was so dazzled by her beauty that he forgot all danger, at once sought an audience of the King, and announced himself as a suitor.

He was immediately led out to the seashore, and a golden ring was thrown into the water before his eyes. Then the King ordered him to fetch it out from the depths of the sea, adding, "If you come to land without it, you will be thrown back every time till you perish in the waves."

Everyone pitied the handsome youth, but they had to go and leave him standing solitary on the seashore.

He was pondering over what he should do when all at once he saw three fishes swimming towards him. They were no others than the very ones whose lives he had saved. The middle one carried a mussel shell in its mouth, which it laid on the sand at the feet of the youth. When he picked it up and opened it, there lay the ring.

Full of joy, he took it to the King, expecting that he would give him the promised reward. The proud Princess, however, when she heard that he was not her equal, despised him and demanded that he should perform yet another task. So she went into the garden herself, and strewed ten sacks of millet seeds among the grass.

"He must pick up every one of the seeds before the sun rises tomorrow morning," said she. "Not a grain must be missing."

The youth sat miserably in the garden, wondering how it could possibly be done. But as he could not think of a plan, he remained sadly waiting for the dawn which would bring death to him.

But when the first sunbeams fell on the garden, he saw the ten sacks full to the top, and not a grain was missing. The ant king had come in the night with thousands and thousands of his ants, and the grateful creatures had picked up the millet and filled the sacks.

The Princess came into the garden herself, and saw with amazement that the youth had completed the task.

But still she could not control her proud heart, and she said, "Even if he has accomplished these two tasks, he shall not become my husband till he brings me an apple from the tree of life."

The youth had no idea where to find the tree of life. He started off, however, meaning to walk as far as his legs would carry him, but he had no hope of finding it.

When he had traveled through three kingdoms, he was one night passing through a great forest, and he lay down under a tree to sleep. He heard a rustling among the branches, and a golden apple fell into his hand.

At the same time three ravens flew down and perched on his knee, and said, "We are the young ravens you saved from death. When we grew big and heard that you were looking for the golden apple, we flew across the sea to the end of the world, where the tree of life stands, and brought you the apple."

The youth, delighted, started on his homeward journey and took the golden apple to the beautiful Princess, who had now no further excuse to offer.

They divided the apple of life and ate it together, and then her heart was filled with love for him, and they lived happily to a great age.

The Frog Prince

IN the old times, when it was still of some use to wish for the thing one wanted, there lived a king whose daughters were all handsome, but the youngest was so beautiful that the sun himself, who has seen so much, wondered at her beauty each time he shone over her. Near the royal castle there was a great dark wood, and in the wood under an old linden tree was a well. When the day was hot, the King's daughter used to go forth into the wood and sit by the brink of the cool well. And if the time seemed long, she would take out a golden ball and throw it up and catch it again, and this was her favorite pastime.

Now it happened one day that the golden ball, instead of falling back into the maiden's little hand which had sent it aloft, dropped to the ground near the edge of the well and rolled in. The King's daughter followed it with her eyes as it sank, but the well was deep—so deep that the bottom could not be seen. Then she began to weep, and she wept and wept as if she could never be comforted.

And in the midst of her weeping she heard a voice saying to her, "What ails you, King's daughter? Your tears would melt a heart of stone."

And when she looked to see where the voice came from, there was nothing but a frog stretching his thick ugly head out of the water.

"Oh, is it you, old waddler?" said she. "I weep because my golden ball has fallen into the well."

"Never mind. Do not weep," answered the frog. "I can help you. But what will you give me if I fetch up your ball again?"

"Whatever you like, dear frog," said she. "Any of my clothes, my pearls and jewels, or even the golden crown that I wear."

"Your clothes, your pearls and jewels, and your golden

crown are not for me," answered the frog. "But if you would love me, and have me for your companion and play-fellow, and let me sit by you at table and eat from your plate and drink from your cup, and sleep in your little bed—if you would promise all this, then would I dive below the water and fetch you your golden ball again."

"Oh yes," she answered, "I will promise it all, whatever you want, if you will only get me my ball again."

But the frog, as soon as he heard her promise, drew his head under the water and sank down out of sight. But after a while he came to the surface again with the ball in his mouth, and he threw it on the grass.

The King's daughter was overjoyed to see her pretty plaything again, and she caught it up and ran off with it.

"Stop, stop!" cried the frog. "Take me up too. I cannot run as fast as you!" But it was of no use, for croak, croak after her as he might, she would not listen to him. Instead, she hastened home and soon forgot all about the poor frog.

The next day, when the King's daughter was sitting at table with the King and all the court, and was eating from her golden plate, there came something pitter-patter up the marble stairs, and then there came a knocking at the door and a voice crying, "King's youngest daughter, let me in!"

And she got up and ran to see who it could be, but when she opened the door, there was the frog sitting outside. Then she shut the door hastily and went back to her seat, feeling very uneasy.

The King noticed how quickly her heart was beating and said, "My child, what are you afraid of? Is there a giant standing at the door ready to carry you away?"

"Oh no," answered she. "No giant, but a horrid frog."

"And what does the frog want?" asked the King.

"Oh, dear father," answered she, "when I was sitting by the well yesterday playing with my golden ball, it fell into the water. And while I was crying for the loss of it, the frog came and got it again for me on condition I would let him be my companion. I never thought that he could leave the water and come after me, but there he is now outside the door, and he wants to come in to me."

And then they all heard him knocking the second time and crying:

THE FROG PRINCE

"King's youngest daughter,
Open to me!
By the well water
What promised you me?
King's youngest daughter,
Now open to me!"

"That which you have promised must you perform," said the King sternly. "So go now and let him in."

So she went and opened the door and the frog hopped in, following at her heels till she reached her chair.

Then he stopped and cried, "Lift me up to sit by you." But she delayed doing so until the King ordered her.

When once the frog was on the chair, he wanted to get on the table, and there he sat and said, "Now push your golden plate a little nearer so that we may eat together."

And so she did, but everybody could see how unwilling she was. And the frog feasted heartily, but every morsel seemed to stick in her throat.

"I have had enough now," said the frog at last. "And as I am tired, you must carry me to your room and make ready your bed, and we will lie down and go to sleep."

Then the King's daughter began to weep, and was afraid of the cold frog, whom nothing would satisfy but he must sleep in her pretty clean bed.

Now the King grew angry with her and said, "What you have promised in your time of necessity, you must now perform."

So she picked up the frog with her finger and thumb, carried him upstairs, and put him in a corner. And when she had lain down to sleep, he came creeping up, saying, "I am tired and want sleep as much as you. Take me up or I will tell your father."

Then she felt beside herself with rage and, picking him

up, she threw him with all her strength against the wall, crying, "Now will you be quiet, you horrid frog?"

But as he fell he ceased to be a frog, and became all at once a prince with beautiful kind eyes. And it came to pass that with her father's consent they became bride and bridegroom. And he told her how a wicked witch had bound him by her spells, and how no one but she alone could have released him, and that they two would go together to his father's kingdom at once.

And there came to the door a carriage drawn by eight white horses, with white plumes on their heads and with golden harness, and behind the carriage, faithful Henry, the servant of the young Prince, was standing. Now, faithful Henry had suffered such care and pain when his master was turned into a frog that he had been obliged to wear three iron bands over his heart, to keep it from breaking with trouble and anxiety. When the carriage started to take the Prince to his kingdom, and faithful Henry had helped them both in, he got up behind and was full of joy at his master's deliverance.

When they had gone a part of the way, the Prince heard a sound at the back of the carriage as if something had broken, and he cried, "Henry, the wheel must be breaking!"

But Henry answered:

> *"The wheel does not break,*
> *'Tis the band round my heart*
> *That, to lessen its ache,*
> *When I grieved for your sake,*
> *I bound round my heart."*

Again and yet once again there was the same sound, and the Prince thought it must be the wheel breaking, but it was the breaking of the other bands from faithful Henry's heart, because it was now so relieved and happy.

The Pink

THERE was once a queen who had not been blessed with children. She prayed every morning as she walked in her garden that a son or daughter might be given to her. Then one day an angel came and said to her, "Be content. You shall have a son, and he shall be endowed with the power of wishing, so that whatsoever he wishes for shall be granted to him." She hurried to the King and told him the joyful news. When the time came, a son was born to them and they were filled with delight.

Every morning the Queen used to take her little son into the gardens where the wild animals were kept, to bathe him in a clear sparkling fountain. It happened one day, when the child was a little older, that as she sat with him on her lap she fell asleep.

The old cook, who knew that the child had the power of wishing, came by and stole it. He also killed a chicken and dropped some of its blood on the Queen's garments. Then he took the child away to a secret place where he placed it out to be nursed. Then he ran back to the King and accused the Queen of having allowed her child to be carried off by a wild animal.

When the King saw the blood on the Queen's garments, he believed the story and was overwhelmed with anger. He caused a high tower to be built, into which neither the sun nor the moon could penetrate. Then he ordered his wife to be shut up in it and the door walled up. She was to stay there for seven years without eating or drinking, so as gradually to pine away. But two angels from heaven, in the shape of white doves, came to her, bringing food twice a day till the seven years were ended.

Meanwhile the cook thought, "If the child really has the power of wishing, and I stay here, I might easily fall into disgrace." So he left the palace and went to the boy, who was then old enough to talk, and said to him, "Wish for a beautiful castle, with a garden and everything belonging to it." Hardly had the words passed the boy's lips than all that he had asked for was there.

After a time the cook said, "It is not good for you to be so much alone. Wish for a beautiful maiden to be your companion."

The Prince uttered the wish and immediately a maiden stood before them, more beautiful than any painter could paint. So they grew very fond of each other and played together, while the old cook went out hunting like any grand gentleman. But the idea came to him one day that the Prince might wish to go to his father sometime, and he would thereby be placed in a very awkward position. So he took the maiden aside, and said to her, "Tonight when the boy is asleep, go and drive this knife into his heart. Then bring me his heart and his tongue. If you fail to do it you will lose your own life."

Then he went away, but when the next day came the maiden had not yet obeyed his command. She said, "Why should I shed his innocent blood, when he has never done harm to any creature in his life?"

The cook again said, "If you do not obey me you will lose your own life."

When he had gone away, she ordered a young hind to be brought and killed. Then she cut out its heart and its tongue and put them on a dish. When she saw the old man coming she said to the boy, "Get into bed and cover yourself completely."

The old scoundrel came in and said, "Where are the tongue and the heart of the boy?"

The maiden gave him the dish, but the Prince threw off the coverings and said, "You old sinner, why did you want to kill me? Now hear your sentence. You shall be turned into a black poodle with a gold chain round your neck, and you shall be made to eat live coals so that flames of fire will come out of your mouth."

As he said the words, the old man was changed into a black poodle with a gold chain round his neck, and the scullions brought live coals which he had to eat till the flames poured out of his mouth.

The prince stayed on at the castle for a time, thinking of his mother, and wondering if she were still alive. At last he said to the maiden, "I am going into my own country. If you like you can go with me. I will take you."

She answered, "Alas, it is so far off, and what should I do in a strange country where I know no one?"

As she did not wish to go and yet they could not bear to be parted, he changed her into a beautiful pink which he took with him. Then he set out on his journey and the poodle was made to run alongside till the Prince reached his own country. Arrived there, he went straight to the tower where his mother was imprisoned, and as the tower was so high, he wished for a ladder to reach the top. Then he climbed up, looked in, and cried, "Dearest mother, lady Queen, are you still alive?"

She, thinking it was the angels who brought her food, said, "I have just eaten. I do not want anything more."

Then he said, "I am your own dear son whom the wild animals were supposed to have devoured. But I am still alive and I shall soon come and rescue you."

Then he got down and went to his father. He had himself announced as a strange huntsman, anxious to take service with the King. The King said, "Yes, if he is skilled in game preserving, and can procure plenty of venison, I will engage him. But there has never before been any game in the whole district."

The huntsman promised to procure as much game as the King could possibly require for the royal table.

Then he called the whole hunt together and ordered them all to come into the forest with him. He caused a great circle to be enclosed, with only one outlet. Then he took his place in the middle and began to wish as hard as he could. Immediately, over two hundred head of game came running into the enclosure. These the huntsmen had to shoot, and then they were piled onto sixty country wagons and driven home to the King. So for once he was able to load his board with game, after having had none for many years.

The King was much pleased and commanded his whole court to a banquet on the following day. When they were all assembled, he said to the huntsman, "You shall sit by me, as you are so clever."

He answered, "My lord and King, may it please Your Majesty, I am only a poor huntsman!"

The King, however, insisted and said, "I command you to sit by me."

As he sat there, his thoughts wandered to his dear mother, and he wished one of the courtiers would speak of

her. Hardly had he wished it than the Lord High Marshal said, "Your Majesty, we are all rejoicing here. How fares it with Her Majesty the Queen? Is she still alive in the tower or has she perished?"

But the King answered, "She allowed my beloved son to be devoured by wild animals, and I do not wish to hear anything about her."

Then the huntsman stood up and said, "Gracious father, she is still alive, and I am her son. I was not devoured by wild animals. I was taken away by the scoundrel of a cook. He stole me while my mother was asleep, and sprinkled her garments with the blood of a chicken." Then he brought up the black poodle with the golden chain and said, "This is the villain."

He ordered some live coals to be brought, which he made the dog eat in the sight of all the people till the flames poured out of his mouth. Then he asked the King if he would like to see the cook in his true shape, and wished him back, and there he stood in his long white apron with his big knife at his side.

The King was furious when he saw him and ordered him to be thrown into the deepest dungeon. Then the huntsman said further, "My father, would you like to see the maiden who so tenderly saved my life when she was ordered to kill me, although by so doing she might have lost her own life?"

The King answered, "Yes, I will gladly see her."

Then his son said, "Gracious father, I will show her to you first in the guise of a beautiful flower."

He put his hand into his pocket and brought out the pink. It was a finer one than the King had ever seen before. Then his son said, "Now I will show her to you in her true form."

The moment his wish was uttered, she stood before them in all her beauty, which was greater than any artist could paint.

The King sent ladies- and gentlemen-in-waiting to the tower to bring the Queen back to his royal table. But when they reached the tower they found that she would no longer eat or drink. She said, "The merciful God, who has preserved my life so long, will soon release me now."

Three days afterwards she died. At her burial the two white doves which had brought her food during her captivity followed and hovered over her grave.

The old King caused the wicked cook to be torn into four quarters, but his own heart was filled with grief and remorse, and he died soon after.

His son married the beautiful maiden he had brought home with him as a flower, and for all I know they may be living still.

The Queen Bee

Two king's sons once started to seek adventures, and they fell into a wild, reckless way of living and gave up all thoughts of going home again. Their third and youngest brother, who was called Witling, had remained behind, and now he started off to seek them. When at last he found them, they jeered at his simplicity in thinking that he could make his way in the world, when they who were so much cleverer were unsuccessful.

But they all three went on together until they came to an anthill. This the two elder brothers wished to stir up, to see the little ants hurrying about in their fright and carrying off their eggs.

But Witling said, "Leave the little creatures alone. I will not suffer them to be disturbed."

And they went on farther until they came to a lake where a number of ducks were swimming about. The two elder brothers wanted to catch a couple and cook them, but Witling again would not allow it.

He said, "Leave the creatures alone. I will not suffer them to be killed."

And then they came to a bees' nest in a tree, and there was so much honey in it that it overflowed and ran down the trunk. The two elder brothers then wanted to make a fire beneath the tree, that the bees might be stifled by the smoke and then they could get at the honey.

But Witling prevented them, saying, "Leave the little creatures alone. I will not suffer them to be stifled."

At last the three brothers came to a castle where there were many horses standing in the stables, all of stone. The brothers went through all the rooms until they came to a door at the end, secured with three locks, and in the middle of the door was a small opening through which they could look into the room. There they saw a little gray-haired man sitting at a table.

They called out to him once, twice, and he did not hear, but at the third time he got up, undid the locks, and came out. Without speaking a word he led them to a table loaded with all sorts of good things, and when they had eaten and drunk he showed to each his bedchamber.

The next morning the little gray man came to the eldest brother and, beckoning him, brought him to a table of stone on which were written three things, directing by what means the castle could be delivered from its enchantment. The first thing was that in the wood under the moss lay the pearls belonging to the Princess—a thousand in number. And they were to be sought for and collected; and if he who should undertake the task had not finished it by sunset, if but one pearl were missing, he must be turned to stone.

So the eldest brother went out and searched all day, but at the end of it he had found only one hundred. And just as it was said, so it came to pass, and he was turned into stone.

The second brother undertook the adventure next day,

but it fared no better with him than with the first: he found two hundred pearls and was turned into stone.

And so at last it was Witling's turn, and he began to search in the moss. But it was a very tedious business to find the pearls and he grew so out of heart that he sat down on a stone and began to weep. As he was sitting thus, up came the ant king with five thousand ants whose lives had been saved through Witling's pity, and it was not very long before the little insects had collected all the pearls and put them in a heap.

Now the second thing ordered by the table of stone was to get the key of the Princess' sleeping chamber out of the lake. And when Witling came to the lake, the ducks whose lives he had saved came swimming, and they dived down and brought up the key from the bottom.

The third thing that had to be done was the most difficult, and that was to choose out the youngest and loveliest of the three princesses as they lay sleeping. All bore a perfect resemblance each to the other, and differed only in this: that before they went to sleep each one had eaten a different sweetmeat—the eldest a piece of sugar, the second a little syrup, and the third a spoonful of honey. Now the queen bee of those bees that Witling had protected from the fire came at this moment and, trying the lips of all three, settled on those of the one who had eaten honey, and so it was that the King's son knew which to choose. Then the spell was broken. Everyone awoke from stony sleep and took his right form again.

And Witling married the youngest and loveliest princess and became king after her father's death. But his two brothers had to put up with the two other sisters.

Briar Rose
(Sleeping Beauty)

A LONG time ago there lived a king and a queen, who said every day, "If only we had a child!" But for a long time they had none.

It happened once as the Queen was bathing that a frog crept out of the water onto the land and said to her, "Your wish shall be fulfilled. Before a year has passed you shall bring a daughter into the world."

The frog's words came true. The Queen had a little girl who was so beautiful that the King could not contain himself for joy, and he prepared a great feast. He invited his relatives, friends and acquaintances, and also the fairies, in order that they might be favorably and kindly disposed towards the child. There were thirteen of them in the kingdom, but as the King had only twelve golden plates for them to eat from, one of the fairies had to stay at home.

The feast was held with all splendor, and when it came to an end the fairies all presented the child with a magic gift. One gave her virtue, another beauty, a third riches, and so on, with everything in the world that she could wish for.

When eleven of the fairies had said their say, the thir-

teenth suddenly appeared. She wanted to revenge herself for not having been invited.

Without greeting anyone or even glancing at the company, she called out in a loud voice, "The Princess shall prick herself with a distaff in her fifteenth year and shall fall down dead." And without another word she turned and left the hall.

Everyone was terror-stricken, but the twelfth fairy, whose wish was still unspoken, stepped forward. She could not cancel the curse but could only soften it, so she said, "It shall not be death, but a deep sleep lasting a hundred years, into which your daughter shall fall."

The King was so anxious to guard his dear child from the misfortune that he sent out a command that all the distaffs in the whole kingdom should be burned.

As time went on, all the promises of the fairies came true. The Princess grew up so beautiful, modest, kind, and clever that everyone who saw her could not but love her. Now it happened that on the very day when she was fifteen years old, the King and Queen were away from home and the Princess was left quite alone in the castle. She wandered about over the whole place, looking at rooms and halls as she pleased, and at last she came to an old tower. She ascended a narrow winding staircase and reached a little door. A rusty key was sticking in the lock, and when she turned it the door flew open. In a little room sat an old woman with a spindle, spinning her flax busily.

"Good day, Granny," said the Princess. "What are you doing?"

"I am spinning," said the old woman, and nodded her head.

"What is the thing that whirls around so merrily?" asked the Princess. And she took the spindle and tried to spin too.

But she had scarcely touched it before the curse was fulfilled, and she pricked her finger with the spindle. The instant she felt the prick she fell upon the bed which was standing near, and lay still in a deep sleep which spread over the whole castle.

The King and Queen, who had just come home and had stepped into the hall, went to sleep, and all their courtiers with them. The horses went to sleep in the stable, the dogs in the yard, the doves on the roof, the flies on the wall. Yes, even the fire flickering on the hearth grew still and went to sleep, and the roast meat stopped crackling. The cook, who was pulling the scullion's hair because he had made some mistake, let him go and went to sleep. The wind dropped, and on the trees in front of the castle not a leaf stirred.

But round the castle a hedge of briar roses began to grow up. Every year it grew higher, till at last it surrounded the whole castle so that nothing could be seen of it, not even the flags on the roof.

But there was a legend in the land about the lovely sleeping Briar Rose, as the King's daughter was called. And from time to time princes came and tried to force a way through the hedge into the castle. They found it impossible; for the thorns, as though they had hands, held them fast, and the princes remained caught in them without being able to free themselves. And so they died a miserable death.

After many, many years a prince came again to the country and heard an old man tell of the castle which stood behind the briar hedge, in which a most beautiful maiden called Briar Rose had been asleep for the last hundred years, and with her the King, the Queen, and all their courtiers. He knew also from his grandfather that many

princes had already come and sought to pierce through the briar hedge, and had remained caught in it and died a sad death.

Then the young Prince said, "I am not afraid. I am determined to go and look upon the lovely Briar Rose."

The good old man did all in his power to dissuade him, but the Prince would not listen to his words.

Now, however, the hundred years were just ended, and the day had come when Briar Rose was to wake up again. When the Prince approached the briar hedge it was in blossom, and was covered with beautiful large flowers which made way for him of their own accord and let him pass unharmed, and then closed up again into a hedge behind him.

In the courtyard he saw the horses and brindled hounds lying asleep. On the roof sat the doves with their heads under their wings. And when he went into the house, the flies were asleep on the walls. And near the throne lay the King and Queen.

In the kitchen was the cook, with his hand raised as though about to strike the scullion, and the maid sat with the black fowl in her lap which she had been about to pluck.

He went on farther, and all was so still that he could hear his own breathing. At last he reached the tower and opened the door into the little room where Briar Rose was asleep. There she lay, looking so beautiful that he could not take his eyes off her. He bent down and gave her a kiss.

As he touched her, Briar Rose opened her eyes and looked lovingly at him. Then they went down together, and the King woke up, and the Queen, and all the courtiers, and looked at each other with astonished eyes. The horses in the stable stood up and shook themselves, the

hounds leaped about and wagged their tails, the doves on the roof lifted their heads from under their wings, looked around, and flew into the fields.

The flies on the walls began to crawl again; the fire in the kitchen roused itself and blazed up and cooked the food. The meat began to crackle, and the cook boxed the scullion's ears so soundly that he screamed aloud, while the maid finished plucking the fowl.

Then the wedding of the Prince and Briar Rose was celebrated with all splendor, and they lived happily till they died.

The Six Swans

ONCE upon a time a king was hunting in a great wood, and he pursued a wild animal so eagerly that none of his people could follow him. When evening came he stood still; then looking round him he found that he had lost his way, and seeking a path, he found none. Then all at once he saw an old woman with a nodding head coming up to him, and she was a witch.

"My good woman," said he, "can you show me the way out of the wood?"

"Oh yes, my Lord King," answered she. "Certainly I can, but I must make a condition. And if you do not fulfill it, you will never get out of the wood again, but will die there of hunger."

"What is the condition?" asked the King.

"I have a daughter," said the old woman, "who is as fair as any in the world. If you will take her for your bride and make her your Queen, I will show you the way out of the wood."

The King consented because of the difficulty he was in, and the old woman led him into her little house, where her daughter was sitting by the fire.

She received the King just as if she had been expecting

him. And though he saw that she was very beautiful, she did not please him, and he could not look at her without an inward shudder. Nevertheless, he took the maiden before him on his horse, and the old woman showed him the way, and soon he was in his royal castle again, where the wedding was held.

The King had been married before and his first wife had left seven children, six boys and one girl, whom he loved better than all the world. And as he was afraid the stepmother might not behave well to them, and perhaps would do them some mischief, he took them to a lonely castle standing in the middle of a wood.

There they remained hidden, for the road to it was so hard to find that the King himself could not have found it had it not been for a ball of yarn with wonderful properties, which a wisewoman had given him. When he threw this down before him, it unrolled itself and showed him the way.

But the King went so often to see his dear children that the Queen was displeased at his absence. She became curious and wanted to know why he went out alone into the wood so often. She bribed the King's servants with much money, and they showed her the secret and told her of the ball of yarn, which alone could point out the way. Then she gave herself no rest until she had found out where the King kept the ball, and then she made some little white silk shirts and sewed a charm in each, since she had learned witchcraft from her mother. And once when the King had ridden to the hunt, she took the little shirts and went into the wood, and the ball of yarn showed her the way. The children, who saw someone in the distance, thought it was their dear father coming to see them and came jumping for joy to meet him. Then the wicked Queen threw over each of them one of the little shirts, and

as soon as the shirts touched their bodies, they were changed into swans and flew away through the wood.

So the Queen went home much pleased to think she had got rid of her stepchildren, but since the maiden had not run out with her brothers the Queen knew nothing about her. The next day the King went to see his children, but he found nobody but his daughter.

"Where are your brothers?" asked the King.

"Ah, dear father," answered she, "they have gone away and have left me behind." And then she told him how from her window she had seen her brothers in the guise of swans fly away through the wood. And she showed him the feathers which they had let fall in the courtyard, and which she had picked up. The King was grieved, but he never dreamt that it was the Queen who had done this wicked deed. And as he feared lest the maiden also should be stolen away from him, he wished to take her away with him. But she was afraid of the stepmother and begged the King to let her remain one more night in the castle in the wood.

Then she said to herself, "I must stay here no longer, but go and seek my brothers." And when night came, she ran away straight into the wood.

She went on all that night and the next day, until she could go no longer for weariness. At last she saw a rude hut, and she went in and found a room with six little beds in it. She did not dare to lie down in one, but she crept under one and lay on the hard boards and wished for night. When it was near sunset she heard a rustling sound and saw six swans come flying in at the window. They alighted on the ground and blew at one another until they had blown all their feathers off, and then they stripped off their swan skins as if they had been shirts. When the maiden looked at them and knew them for her brothers,

she was very glad and crept out from under the bed. The brothers were not less glad when their sister appeared, but their joy did not last long.

"You must not stay here," they said to her. "This is a robbers' haunt, and if they were to come and find you here they would kill you."

"And cannot you defend me?" asked the little sister.

"No," answered they, "for we can only get rid of our swan skins and keep our human shape every evening for a quarter of an hour. After that we must be changed again into swans."

Their sister wept at hearing this and said, "Can nothing be done to set you free?"

"Oh no," answered they, "the work would be too hard for you. For six whole years you would be obliged never to speak or laugh, and during that time you would have to make six little shirts out of aster flowers. If you were to let fall a single word before the work was finished, all would be of no avail."

And just as the brothers had finished telling her this, the quarter of an hour came to an end and they changed into swans and flew out the window.

But the maiden made up her mind to set her brothers free, even though it should cost her her life. She left the hut and went into the middle of the wood, where she climbed a tree and there passed the night. The next morning she set to work and gathered asters and began sewing them together. As for speaking, there was no one to speak to. And as for laughing, she had no mind to laugh. So she sat there and looked at nothing but her work.

When she had been going on like this for a long time, it happened that the King of that country went hunting in the wood, and some of his huntsmen came up to the tree in which the maiden sat.

They called out to her, "Who are you?" But she gave no answer.

"Come down," they cried. "We will do you no harm." But she only shook her head.

When they tormented her further with questions she threw down to them her gold necklace, hoping they would be content with that, but they would not leave off. So she threw down to them her sash, and when that did no good she threw down her garters, and one after another everything she had on and could possibly spare, until she had nothing left but her smock. But it all did no good; the huntsmen would not be put off any longer. And they climbed the tree, carried the maiden off, and brought her to the King.

The King asked, "Who are you? What were you doing in the tree?" But she answered nothing.

He spoke to her in all the languages he knew, but she remained dumb. But since she was very beautiful, the King felt a great love rise up in his heart towards her, and casting his mantle round her, he put her before him on his horse and brought her to his castle. Then he caused rich clothing to be put upon her, and her beauty shone as bright as the morning, but no word would she utter.

He seated her by his side at table, and her modesty and gentle mien so pleased him that he said, "This maiden I choose for a wife, and no other in all the world." And accordingly after a few days they were married.

But the King had a wicked mother, who was displeased with the marriage, and spoke ill of the young Queen.

"Who knows where this maid can have come from," said she, "who is not able to speak a word? She is not worthy of a king!"

After a year had passed and the Queen brought her first child into the world, the old woman carried it away, and

marked the Queen's mouth with blood as she lay sleeping. Then she went to the King and declared that his wife was an eater of human flesh. The King would not believe such a thing and ordered that no one should do her any harm. And the Queen went on quietly sewing the shirts and caring for nothing else. The next time that a fine boy was born, the wicked woman used the same deceit, but the King would give no credence to her words.

He said, "She is too tender and good to do any such thing, and if she were only not dumb, and could defend herself, then her innocence would be as clear as day."

When for the third time the old woman stole away the newborn child and accused the Queen, who was unable to say a word in her own defense, the King could do nothing but give her up to justice, and she was sentenced to suffer death by fire.

The day on which her sentence was to be carried out was the very last day of the six years during which she was neither to speak nor laugh, in order to free her dear brothers from the evil spell. The six shirts were ready, all except one which lacked the left sleeve. And when she was led to the pile of wood, she carried the six shirts on her arm. When she mounted the pile and the fire was about to be kindled, all at once she cried out aloud, for there were six swans flying through the air towards her. She saw that her deliverance was near, and her heart beat for joy.

The swans came close up to her with rushing wings and stooped round her, so that she could throw the shirts over them. And when that had been done the swan skins fell off them, and her brothers stood before her in their own bodies quite safe and sound. But as one shirt wanted the left sleeve, so the youngest brother had a swan's wing instead of a left arm. They embraced and kissed each other,

and the Queen went up to the King, who looked on with astonishment, and began to speak to him.

"Dearest husband," she said, "now I may dare to speak and tell you that I am innocent, and have been falsely accused." And she related to him the treachery of the old woman who had taken away the three children and hidden them. And she was reconciled to the King with great joy, and the wicked mother was bound to the stake on the pile of wood and burnt to ashes.

And the King and Queen lived many years with their six brothers in peace and joy.

The Fisherman and His Wife

THERE was once a fisherman who lived with his wife in a miserable little hovel close to the sea. He went to fish every day, and he fished and fished, and at last one day as he was sitting looking deep down into the shining water, he felt something on his line. When he hauled it up there was a big flounder on the end of the line.

The flounder said to him, "Listen, fisherman, I beg you not to kill me. I am no common flounder. I am an enchanted prince! What good will it do you to kill me? I shan't be good to eat. Put me back into the water and leave me to swim about."

"Ho! ho!" said the fisherman. "You need not make so many words about it. I am quite ready to put back a flounder that can talk." And so saying, he put back the flounder into the shining water and it sank down to the bottom, leaving a streak of blood behind it. Then the fisherman got up and went back to his wife in the hovel.

"Husband," she said, "have you caught nothing today?"

"No," said the man. "All I caught was one flounder. And he said he was an enchanted prince, so I let him go again."

"Did you not wish for anything then?" asked the good-wife.

"No," said the man. "What was there to wish for?"

"Alas," said his wife, "isn't it bad enough always to live in this wretched hovel? You might at least have wished for a nice clean cottage. Go back and call him! Tell him I want a pretty cottage. He will surely give us that."

"Alas," said the man, "what am I to go back there for?"

"Well," said the woman, "it was you who caught him and let him go again. He will certainly do that for you. Be off now.'"

The man was still not very willing to go, but he did not want to vex his wife and at last he went back to the sea.

He found the sea no longer bright and shining, but dull and green. He stood by it and said:

> "Flounder, flounder in the sea,
> Prithee, hearken unto me:
> My wife, Ilsebil, must have her own will,
> And sends me to beg a boon of thee."

The flounder came swimming up and said, "Well, what do you want?'"

"Alas," said the man, "I had to call you, for my wife said I ought to have wished for something as I caught you. She doesn't want to live in our miserable hovel any longer. She wants a pretty cottage."

"Go home again then," said the flounder. "She has her wish fully."

The man went home and found his wife no longer in the old hut, but a pretty little cottage stood in its place and his wife was sitting on a bench by the door.

She took him by the hand and said, "Come and look in here. Isn't this much better?"

They went inside and found a pretty sitting room, a bedroom with a bed in it, a kitchen, and a larder furnished with everything of the best in tin and brass and every possible requisite. Outside there was a little yard with chickens and ducks and a little garden full of vegetables and fruit.

"Look!" said the woman. "Is not this nice?"

"Yes," said the man, "and so let it remain. We can live here very happily."

"We will see about that," said the woman. With that they ate something and went to bed.

Everything went well for a week or more, and then the wife said, "Listen, husband, this cottage is too cramped

and the garden is too small. The flounder could have given us a bigger house. I want to live in a big stone castle. Go to the flounder and tell him to give us a castle."

"Alas, wife," said the man, "the cottage is good enough for us. What should we do with a castle?"

"Never mind," said his wife. "You just go to the flounder and he will manage it."

"No, wife," said the man. "The flounder gave us the cottage. I don't want to go back. As likely as not he'll be angry."

"Go, all the same," said the woman. "He can do it easily enough and willingly into the bargain. Just go!"

The man's heart was heavy and he was very unwilling to go. He said to himself, "It's not right." But at last he went.

He found the sea was no longer green: it was still calm, but dark violet and gray. He stood by it and said:

> "Flounder, flounder in the sea,
> Prithee, hearken unto me:
> My wife, Ilsebil, must have her own will,
> And sends me to beg a boon of thee."

"Now what do you want?" said the flounder.

"Alas," said the man, half scared, "my wife wants a big stone castle."

"Go home again," said the flounder. "She is standing at the door of it."

Then the man went away thinking he would find no house, but when he got back he found a great stone palace, and his wife was standing at the top of the steps waiting to go in.

She took him by the hand and said, "Come in with me." With that they went in and found a great hall paved with marble slabs, and numbers of servants in attendance

who opened the great doors for them. The walls were hung with beautiful tapestries and the rooms were furnished with golden chairs and tables, while rich carpets covered the floors and crystal chandeliers hung from the ceilings. The tables groaned under every kind of delicate food and the most costly wines. Outside the house there was a great courtyard, with stables for horses and cows, and many fine carriages. Beyond this there was a great garden filled with the loveliest flowers and fine fruit trees. There was also a park half a mile long, and in it were stags, hinds and hares, and everything that one could wish for.

"Now," said the woman, "is not this worth having?"

"Oh yes," said the man, "and so let it remain. We will live in this beautiful palace and be content."

"We will think about that," said his wife, "and sleep upon it."

With that they went to bed.

Next morning the wife woke up first. Day was just dawning, and from her bed she could see the beautiful country around her. Her husband was still asleep, but she pushed him with her elbow and said, "Husband, get up and peep out of the window. See here, now, could we not be King over all this land? Go to the flounder. We will be King."

"Alas, wife," said the man, "why should we be King? I don't want to be King."

"Ah," said his wife, "if you will not be King, I will. Go to the flounder. I will be King."

"Alas, wife," said the man, "why do you want to be King? I don't want to ask the flounder."

"Why not?" said the woman. "Go you must. I will be King."

So the man went, but he was quite sad because his wife would be King.

[*113*]

"It is not right," he said. "It is not right."

When he reached the sea, he found it dark, gray, and rough, and evil smelling. He stood there and said:

> *"Flounder, flounder in the sea,*
> *Prithee, hearken unto me:*
> *My wife, Ilsebil, must have her own will,*
> *And sends me to beg a boon of thee."*

"Now what does she want?" said the flounder.

"Alas," said the man, "she wants to be King now."

"Go back. She is King already," said the flounder.

So the man went back, and when he reached the palace he found that it had grown much larger and a great tower had been added with handsome decorations. There was a sentry at the door and numbers of soldiers were playing drums and trumpets. As soon as he got inside the house he found everything was marble and gold, and the hangings were of velvet with great golden tassels.

The doors of the saloon were thrown wide open, and he saw the whole court assembled. His wife was sitting on a lofty throne of gold and diamonds. She wore a golden crown and carried in one hand a scepter of pure gold. On each side of her stood her ladies in a long row, each one a head shorter than the next.

He stood before her and said, "Alas, wife, are you now King?"

"Yes," she said. "Now I am King."

He stood looking at her for some time, and then he said, "Ah, wife, it is a fine thing for you to be King. Now we will not wish to be anything more."

"No, husband," she answered, quite uneasily, "I find that time hangs very heavy on my hands. I can't bear it any longer. Go back to the flounder. King I am, but I must also be Emperor."

"Alas, wife," said the man, "why do you now want to be Emperor?"

"Husband," she answered, "go to the flounder. Emperor I will be."

"Alas, wife," said the man, "Emperor he can't make you, and I won't ask him. There is only one Emperor in the country, and Emperor the flounder cannot make you. That he can't."

"What?" said the woman. "I am King, and you are but my husband. To him you must go and that right quickly. If he can make a king, he can also make an emperor. Emperor I will be, so go quickly."

He had to go, but he was quite frightened. And as he went he thought, "This won't end well. Emperor is too shameless. The flounder will make an end of the whole thing."

With that he came to the sea, but now he found it quite black and heaving up from below in great waves. It tossed to and fro and a sharp wind blew over it, and the man trembled. So he stood there and said:

> "Flounder, flounder in the sea,
> Prithee, hearken unto me:
> My wife, Ilsebil, must have her own will,
> And sends me to beg a boon of thee."

"What does she want now?" said the flounder.

"Alas, flounder," he said, "my wife wants to be Emperor."

"Go back," said the flounder. "She is Emperor."

So the man went back, and when he got to the door he found that the whole palace was made of polished marble, with alabaster figures and golden decorations. Soldiers marched up and down before the doors, blowing their trumpets and beating their drums. Inside the palace,

counts, barons, and dukes walked about as attendants, and they opened to him the doors, which were of pure gold.

He went in and saw his wife sitting on a huge throne made of solid gold. It was at least two miles high. She had on her head a great golden crown set with diamonds three yards high. In one hand she held the scepter, and in the other the orb of empire. On each side of her stood the gentlemen-at-arms in two rows, each one a little smaller than the other, from giants two miles high down to the tiniest dwarf no bigger than my little finger. She was surrounded by princes and dukes.

Her husband stood still and said, "Wife, are you now Emperor?"

"Yes," said she. "Now I am Emperor."

Then he looked at her for some time and said, "Alas, wife, how much better off are you for being Emperor?"

"Husband," she said, "what are you standing there for? Now I am Emperor, I mean to be Pope! Go back to the flounder."

"Alas, wife," said the man, "what won't you want next? Pope you cannot be. There is only one Pope in Christendom. That's more than the flounder can do."

"Husband," she said, "Pope I will be, so go at once! I must be Pope this very day."

"No, wife," he said, "I dare not tell him. It's no good. It's too monstrous altogether. The flounder cannot make you Pope."

"Husband," said the woman, "don't talk nonsense. If he can make an emperor, he can make a pope. Go immediately. I am Emperor, and you are but my husband, and you must obey."

So he was frightened and went, but he was quite dazed. He shivered and shook and his knees trembled.

A great wind arose over the land, the clouds flew across the sky, and it grew as dark as night. The leaves fell from the trees, and the water foamed and dashed upon the shore. In the distance the ships were being tossed to and fro on the waves, and he heard them firing signals of distress. There was still a little patch of blue in the sky among the dark clouds, but towards the south they were red and heavy, as in a bad storm. In despair, he stood and said:

> *"Flounder, flounder in the sea,*
> *Prithee, hearken unto me:*
> *My wife, Ilsebil, must have her own will,*
> *And sends me to beg a boon of thee."*

"Now what does she want?" said the flounder.

"Alas," said the man, "she wants to be Pope!"

"Go back. Pope she is," said the flounder.

So back he went, and he found a great church surrounded with palaces. He pressed through the crowd, and inside he found thousands and thousands of lights. And his wife, entirely clad in gold, was sitting on a still higher throne with three golden crowns upon her head, and she was surrounded with priestly state.

On each side of her were two rows of candles, from the biggest as thick as a tower down to the tiniest little taper. Kings and emperors were on their knees before her, kissing her shoe.

"Wife," said the man, looking at her, "are you now Pope?"

"Yes," said she. "Now I am Pope."

So there he stood gazing at her, and it was like looking at a shining sun.

"Alas, wife," he said, "are you better off for being Pope?"

At first she sat as stiff as a post, without stirring. Then he said, "Now, wife, be content with being Pope. Higher you cannot go."

"I will think about that," said the woman, and with that they both went to bed. Still she was not content and could not sleep for her inordinate desires. The man slept well and soundly, for he had walked about a great deal in the day. But his wife could think of nothing but what further grandeur she could demand. When the dawn reddened the sky she raised herself up in bed and looked out the window, and when she saw the sun rise she said:

"Ha! Can I not cause the sun and the moon to rise? Husband!" she cried, digging her elbow into his side. "Wake up and go to the flounder. I will be Lord of the Universe."

Her husband, who was still more than half asleep, was so shocked that he fell out of bed. He thought he must have heard wrong. He rubbed his eyes and said, "Alas, wife, what did you say?"

"Husband," she said, "if I cannot be Lord of the Universe, and cause the sun and moon to set and rise, I shall not be able to bear it. I shall never have another happy moment."

She looked at him so wildly that it caused a shudder to run through him.

"Alas, wife," he said, falling on his knees before her, "the flounder can't do that. Emperor and Pope he can make, but this is indeed beyond him. I pray you, control yourself and remain Pope."

Then she flew into a terrible rage. Her hair stood on end. She kicked him and screamed, "I won't bear it any longer. Now go!"

Then he pulled on his trousers and tore away like a madman. Such a storm was raging that he could hardly keep his feet. Houses and trees quivered and swayed, and

mountains trembled, and the rocks rolled into the sea. The sky was pitchy black.

It thundered and lightened, and the sea ran in black waves mountains high, crested with white foam. He shrieked out, but could hardly make himself heard:

> *"Flounder, flounder in the sea,*
> *Prithee, hearken unto me:*
> *My wife, Ilsebil, must have her own will,*
> *And sends me to beg a boon of thee."*

"Now what does she want?" asked the flounder.

"Alas," he said, "she wants to be Lord of the Universe."

"Now she must go back to her old hovel," said the flounder, "and there she is!" So there they are to this very day.

Rumpelstiltskin

THERE was once a miller who was very poor, but he had a beautiful daughter. Now it once happened that he had occasion to speak with the King, and in order to give himself an air of importance he said, "I have a daughter who can spin gold out of straw."

The King said to the miller, "That is an art in which I am much interested. If your daughter is as skillful as you say she is, bring her to my castle tomorrow, and I will put her to the test."

Accordingly, when the girl was brought to the castle, the King conducted her to a chamber which was quite full of straw, gave her a spinning wheel and a reel, and said, "Now set to work. And if between tonight and tomorrow at dawn you have not spun this straw into gold, you must die." Thereupon he carefully locked the chamber door, and she remained alone.

There sat the unfortunate miller's daughter, and for the life of her did not know what to do. She had not the least idea how to spin straw into gold, and she became more

and more distressed until at last she began to weep. Then all at once the door sprang open, and in stepped a little man who said, "Good evening, Mistress Miller. Why are you weeping so?"

"Alas," answered the maiden, "I've got to spin gold out of straw, and don't know how to do it."

Then the little man said, "What will you give me if I spin it for you?"

"My necklace," said the maid.

The little man took the necklace, sat down before the spinning wheel, and whir—whir—whir, in a trice the reel was full.

Then he fixed another reel, and whir—whir—whir, thrice round, and that too was full. And so it went on until morning, when all the straw was spun and all the reels were full of gold.

Immediately at sunrise the King came, and when he saw the gold he was astonished and much pleased, but his mind became only the more avaricious. So he had the miller's daughter taken to another chamber full of straw, larger than the former one, and he ordered her to spin it also in one night, if she valued her life.

The maiden was at her wit's end and began to weep. Then again the door sprang open, and the little man appeared and said, "What will you give me if I spin the straw into gold for you?"

"The ring off my finger," answered the maiden.

The little man took the ring, began to whir again at the wheel, and by morning had spun all the straw into gold.

The King was delighted at sight of the masses of gold, but was not even yet satisfied. So he had the miller's daughter taken to a still larger chamber full of straw, and said, "This must you spin tonight into gold, but if you succeed you shall become my Queen." "Even if she is only a mill-

er's daughter," thought he, "I shan't find a richer woman in the whole world."

When the girl was alone the little man came again and said for the third time, "What will you give me if I spin the straw for you this time?"

"I have nothing more that I can give," answered the girl.

"Well, promise me your first child if you become Queen."

"Who knows what may happen?" thought the miller's daughter, but she did not see any other way of getting out of the difficulty. So she promised the little man what he demanded, and in return he spun the straw into gold once more.

When the King came in the morning and found everything as he had wished, he celebrated his marriage with her, and the miller's daughter became Queen.

About a year afterwards a beautiful child was born, but the Queen had forgotten all about the little man. However, he suddenly entered her chamber and said, "Now, give me what you promised."

The Queen was terrified, and offered the little man all the wealth of the kingdom if he would let her keep the child. But the little man said, "No, I would rather have some living thing than all the treasures of the world."

Then the Queen began to moan and weep to such an extent that the little man felt sorry for her. "I will give you three days," said he, "and if within that time you discover my name you shall keep the child."

Then during the night the Queen called to mind all the names that she had ever heard, and sent a messenger all over the country to inquire far and wide what other names there were.

When the little man appeared the next day, she began with Caspar, Melchior, Balthazar, and mentioned all the

names which she knew, one after the other. But at every one the little man said, "No. No. That's not my name."

The second day she had inquiries made all round the neighborhood for the names of people living there, and suggested to the little man all the most unusual and strange names. "Perhaps your name is Cowribs, or Spindleshanks, or Spiderlegs?"

But he answered every time, "No. That's not my name."

On the third day the messenger came back and said, "I haven't been able to find any new names, but as I came round the corner of a wood on a lofty mountain, where the fox says good night to the hare, I saw a little house, and in front of the house a fire was burning. And around the fire a most ridiculous little man was leaping. He was hopping on one leg and singing:

'Today I bake; tomorrow I brew my beer;
The next day I will bring the Queen's child here.
Ah! lucky 'tis that not a soul doth know
That Rumpelstiltskin is my name. Ho! Ho!' "

You can imagine how delighted the Queen was when she heard the name! And soon afterwards when the little man came in and asked, "Now, Your Majesty, what is my name?" at first she asked, "Is your name Tom?"

"No."

"Is it Dick?"

"No."

"Is it, by chance, Rumpelstiltskin?"

"The devil told you that! The devil told you that!" shrieked the little man. And in his rage he stamped his right foot into the ground so deep that he sank up to his waist.

Then in his rage he seized his left leg with both hands and tore himself asunder in the middle.

Rapunzel

THERE was once a man and his wife who had long wished in vain for a child, and at last they had reason to hope that heaven would grant their wish. There was a little window at the back of their house, which overlooked a beautiful garden full of lovely flowers and shrubs. It was, however, surrounded by a high wall, and nobody dared to enter it, because it belonged to a powerful witch who was feared by everybody.

One day the woman, standing at this window and looking into the garden, saw a bed planted with beautiful rampion. It looked so fresh and green that she longed to eat some of it. This longing increased every day; and as she knew it could never be satisfied, she began to look pale and miserable and to pine away. Then her husband was alarmed and said, "What ails you, my dear wife?"

"Alas!" she answered. "If I cannot get any of the rampion to eat from the garden behind our house, I shall die."

Her husband, who loved her, thought. "Before you let your wife die you must fetch her some of that rampion, cost what it may." So in the twilight he climbed over the wall into the witch's garden, hastily picked a handful of

rampion, and took it back to his wife. She immediately prepared it and ate it very eagerly. It was so very, very nice that the next day her longing for it increased threefold. She could have no peace unless her husband fetched her some more. So in the twilight he set out again, but when he got over the wall he was terrified to see the witch before him.

"How dare you come into my garden like a thief and steal my rampion?" she said, with angry looks. "It shall be the worse for you!"

"Alas!" he answered. "Be merciful to me. I am only here from necessity. My wife sees your rampion from the window, and she has such a longing for it that she would die if she could not get some of it."

The anger of the witch abated and she said to him, "If it is as you say, I will allow you to take away with you as much rampion as you like, but on one condition. You must give me the child which your wife is about to bring into the world. I will care for it like a mother, and all will be well with it."

In his fear the man consented to everything. And when the baby was born, the witch appeared, gave it the name of Rapunzel (rampion), and took it away with her.

Rapunzel was the most beautiful child under the sun. When she was twelve years old, the witch shut her up in a tower which stood in a wood. It had neither staircase nor doors, but only a little window quite high up in the wall.

When the witch wanted to enter the tower, she stood at the foot of it and cried, "Rapunzel, Rapunzel, let down your hair!"

Rapunzel had splendid long hair, as fine as spun gold. As soon as she heard the voice of the witch, she unfastened her plaits and twisted her hair round a hook by the window. It fell twenty ells downwards, and the witch climbed up by it.

It happened a couple of years later that the King's son rode through the forest and came close to the tower. From thence he heard a song so lovely that he stopped to listen. It was Rapunzel who in her loneliness made her sweet voice resound to pass away the time. The King's son wanted to join her, and he sought for the door of the tower but there was none to find.

He rode home, but the song had touched his heart so deeply that he went into the forest every day to listen to it. Once when he was hidden behind a tree he saw a witch come to the tower and call out, "Rapunzel, Rapunzel, let down your hair!"

Then Rapunzel lowered her plaits of hair and the witch climbed up to her. "If that is the ladder by which one ascends," he thought, "I will try my luck myself." And the next day, when it began to grow dark, he went to the tower and cried, "Rapunzel, Rapunzel, let down your hair!"

The hair fell down and the King's son climbed up it.

At first Rapunzel was terrified, for she had never set eyes on a man before. But the King's son talked to her kindly, and told her that his heart had been so deeply touched by her song that he had no peace and was obliged to see her. Then Rapunzel lost her fear. And when he asked if she would have him for her husband, and she saw that he was young and handsome, she thought, "He will love me better than old Mother Gothel." So she said, "Yes," and laid her hand in his. She said, "I will gladly go with you, but I do not know how I am to get down from this tower. When you come, will you bring a skein of silk with you every time? I will twist it into a ladder, and when it is long enough I will descend by it, and you can take me away with you on your horse."

She arranged with him that he should come and see her every evening, for the old witch came in the daytime.

The witch discovered nothing till suddenly Rapunzel said to her, "Tell me, Mother Gothel, how can it be that you are so much heavier to draw up than the young prince who will be here before long?"

"Oh, you wicked child, what do you say? I thought I had separated you from all the world, and yet you have deceived me." In her rage she seized Rapunzel's beautiful hair, twisted it twice round her left hand, snatched up a pair of shears, and cut off the plaits, which fell to the ground. She was so merciless that she took poor Rapunzel away into a wilderness, where she forced her to live in the greatest grief and misery.

In the evening of the day on which she had banished Rapunzel, the witch fastened the plaits which she had cut off to the hook by the window. And when the Prince came and called:

"Rapunzel, Rapunzel, let down your hair!"
—she lowered the hair. The Prince climbed up, but there he found, not his beloved Rapunzel, but the witch, who looked at him with angry and wicked eyes.

"Ah!" she cried mockingly. "You have come to fetch your ladylove, but the pretty bird is no longer in her nest. And she can sing no more, for the cat has seized her and it will scratch your own eyes out too. Rapunzel is lost to you. You will never see her again."

The Prince was beside himself with grief, and in his despair he sprang out of the window. He was not killed, but his eyes were scratched out by the thorns among which he fell. He wandered about blind in the wood and had nothing but roots and berries to eat. He did nothing but weep and lament over the loss of his beloved wife Rapunzel. In this way he wandered about for some years, till at last he reached the wilderness where Rapunzel had been living very sadly in great poverty.

He heard a voice which seemed very familiar to him and he went towards it. Rapunzel knew him at once and fell weeping upon his neck. Two of her tears fell upon his eyes, and they immediately grew quite clear and he could see as well as ever.

He took her to his kingdom, where he was received with joy, and they lived long and happily together.

The Salad

THERE was once a merry young huntsman who went into the forest to hunt. He was gay and lighthearted, and whistled a tune upon a leaf as he went along.

Suddenly an ugly old crone spoke to him and said, "Good morning, dear huntsman. You are merry and happy enough, while I am hungry and thirsty. Pray give me an alms."

The huntsman pitied the poor old woman, put his hand in his pocket, and made her a present according to his means.

Then he wanted to go on, but the old woman held him back and said, "Hark ye, dear huntsman, I will make you a present because of your good heart. Go on your way and you will come to a tree on which nine birds are sitting. They will have a cloak in their claws, over which they are fighting. Take aim with your gun and shoot into the middle of them. They will drop the cloak and one of the birds will fall down dead. Take the cloak with you. It is a wishing cloak. When you throw it round your shoulders you only have to wish yourself at a place to be there at once.

Take the heart out of the dead bird and swallow it whole. Then you will find a gold coin under your pillow every single morning when you wake."

The huntsman thanked the wisewoman and thought, "She promises fine things. If only they turn out as well!"

When he had gone about a hundred paces he heard above him, in the branches of a tree, such a chattering and screaming that he looked up. There he saw a flock of birds tearing a garment with their beaks and claws. They were snatching and tearing at it as if each one wanted to have it for himself.

"Well," said the huntsman, "this is extraordinary. It is exactly what the old woman said."

He put his gun to his shoulder, took aim, and fired right into the middle of them, making the feathers fly about. The birds took flight with a great noise, all except one, which fell down dead, and the cloak dropped at his feet.

He did as the old woman had told him: he cut the heart out of the bird and swallowed it whole. Then he took the cloak home with him. When he woke in the morning, he remembered the old woman's promise, and looked under his pillow to see if all was true. There, sure enough, lay the golden coin shining before him. The next morning he found another, and found the same every morning when he got up.

He collected quite a heap of gold and at last he thought, "What is the good of all my gold if I stay at home here? I will go and look about me in the world." So he took leave of his parents, shouldered his gun, and started off into the world.

It so happened that one day he came to a thick forest, and when he got through it he saw a fine castle lying in the plain beyond. He saw an old woman standing in one of the windows looking out, with a beautiful golden-haired maiden beside her.

But the old woman was a witch and she said to the maiden, "Here comes someone out of the forest. He has a wonderful treasure inside him. We must try to get it from him, my darling. It will suit us better than him. He has a bird's heart about him, and so he finds a gold coin every morning under his pillow."

She told the girl how he had got it and at last said, "If you don't get it from him it will be the worse for you."

When the huntsman got nearer, he saw the maiden and said, "I have been wandering about for a long time. I will go into this castle and take a rest. I have plenty of money."

But the real reason was that he had caught sight of the pretty picture at the window. He went in and he was kindly received and hospitably treated. Before long, he was so enamored of the witch maiden that he thought of nothing else and cared for nothing but pleasing her.

The old woman said to the maiden, "Now we must get the bird's heart. He will never miss it."

They concocted a potion, and when it was ready they put it into a goblet. And the maiden took it to him and said, "Now, my beloved, you must drink to me."

He took the cup and drank the potion, and when he was overpowered by it the bird's heart came out of his mouth. The maiden took it away secretly and swallowed it herself, for the old woman wanted to have it.

From this time on the huntsman found no more gold under his pillow, but the coin was always under the maiden's instead, and the old woman used to fetch it away every morning. But he was so much in love that he thought of nothing but enjoying himself in the maiden's company.

Then the old woman said, "We have got the bird's heart, but we must have his wishing cloak too."

The maiden said, "Let us leave him that. We have taken away his wealth."

The old woman was very angry and said, "A cloak like that is a very wonderful thing and not often to be got. Have it I must and will." So the maiden obeyed the witch's orders, placed herself at the window, and looked sadly out at the distant range of hills.

The huntsman said, "Why are you so sad?"

"Alas, my love," was her answer, "over there are the garnet mountains, where the precious stones are found. I long for them so much that I grow sad whenever I think of them. But who could ever get them? The birds which fly, perhaps. No mortal could ever reach them."

"If that is all your trouble," said the huntsman, "I can soon lift that load from your heart."

Then he drew her under his cloak and in a moment they were both sitting on the mountain. The precious stones were glittering around them. Their hearts rejoiced at the sight of them and they soon gathered together some of the finest and largest.

Now the witch had so managed that the huntsman began to feel his eyes grow very heavy. Then he said to the maiden, "We will sit down to rest. I am so tired I can hardly stand."

So they sat down and he laid his head on her lap and was soon fast asleep. As soon as he was asleep, the maiden slipped the cloak from his shoulders and put it on her own, loaded herself with the precious garnets, and wished herself at home. When the huntsman had had his sleep out, he woke up and saw that his beloved had betrayed him and left him alone on the wild mountain.

"Oh, what treachery there is in the world!" he exclaimed, as he sat down in grief. He did not know what to do.

Now the mountain belonged to some wild and savage giants who lived on it, and before long he saw three of

them striding along. He quickly lay down again and pretended to be fast asleep.

The first one, as he came along, stumbled against him and said, "What kind of earthworm is this?"

The second said, "Tread on him and kill him."

But the third said, "It isn't worth the trouble. Let him alone! He can't live here, and when he climbs higher up the mountain the clouds will roll down and carry him off."

Then they passed on, and as soon as they were gone the huntsman, who had heard all they said, got up and climbed to the top of the mountain. After he had sat there for a time, a cloud floated over him and carried him away. At first he was swept through the air, but then he was gently lowered and deposited within a large walled garden, upon a soft bed of lettuce and other herbs.

He looked around him and said, "If only I had something to eat! I am so hungry, and it will be difficult to get away from here. I see neither apples nor pears nor any other fruit—nothing but salad and herbs."

At last, however, he thought, "At the worst, I can eat some of this salad. It does not taste very good, but it will at least be refreshing."

He picked out a fine head of lettuce and began eating it. But he had hardly swallowed a little piece when he began to feel very odd and quite changed. He felt four legs growing, a big head, and two long ears, and he saw to his horror that he was changed into an ass.

As he still felt as hungry as ever and the juicy salad was now very much to his taste, he went on eating greedily. At last he reached another kind of salad, which he had hardly tasted when he felt a new change taking place, and found himself back in his human shape. After this he lay down and slept off his fatigue.

When he woke next morning he broke off a head of the bad salad and a head of the good and thought, "These will help me to regain my own and also to punish the traitors."

He put the salad into his wallet, climbed over the wall, and went off to find the castle of his beloved.

After wandering about for a few days, he was fortunate enough to find it. Then he stained his face and disguised himself so that his own mother would not have known him, and went to the castle to ask for shelter.

"I am so tired," he said. "I cannot go any farther."

The witch said, "Who are you, countryman, and what do you want?

He answered, "I am a messenger from the King. He sent me to find the rarest salad which grows under the sun. I have been lucky enough to find it and I carry it with me. But the sun is so burning that I am afraid the tender plant will be withered, and I don't know if I shall be able to take it any farther."

When the old witch heard about the rare salad, she felt a great desire to have some and said, "Good countryman, let me try the wonderful salad."

"By all means," he answered. "I have two heads with me and you shall have one." So saying, he opened his sack and handed her the bad one.

The witch had no suspicions, and her mouth so watered for the new dish that she went to the kitchen herself to prepare it. When it was ready, she could not wait till it was put upon the table, but put a few leaves into her mouth at once. Hardly had she swallowed them when she lost her human shape, and she ran out into the courtyard as an old she-ass.

Then the maid came into the kitchen, saw the salad standing ready, and was about to put it on the table. But on the way the fancy to taste it seized her, according to her

usual habit, and she ate a few leaves. The power of the salad at once became apparent, because she also turned into an ass and ran out into the yard to join the old witch, while the dish of salad fell to the ground.

In the meantime the messenger was sitting with the beautiful maiden, and as no one appeared with the salad, she also was seized with a desire to taste it. She said, "I don't know what has become of the salad."

But the huntsman thought, "The plant must have done its work," and said, "I will go into the kitchen and see."

As soon as he got downstairs he saw the two asses running about and the salad lying on the ground.

"This is all right," he said. "Two of them are done for." Then he picked up the leaves, put them on a dish, and took them to the maiden.

"I am bringing the precious food to you myself," said he, "so that you will not have to wait any longer."

She ate some, and like the others was immediately changed into an ass, and ran out to them in the yard.

When the huntsman had washed his face so that the transformed creatures might know him, he went into the courtyard and said, "Now you shall be paid for your treachery."

He tied them all together with a rope and drove them along till he came to a mill. He tapped at the window, and the miller put his head out and asked what he wanted.

"I have three bad animals here," he said, "that I want to get rid of. If you will take them and feed them and treat them as I wish, I will pay you what you like to ask."

"Why not?" said the miller. "How do you want them treated?"

The huntsman said he wanted the old she-ass (the witch) to be well beaten three times a day and fed once. The younger one, which was the maid, beaten once and

fed three times. The youngest of all, who was the beautiful maiden, was to be fed three times and not beaten at all. He could not find it in his heart to have her beaten.

Then he went back to the castle and found everything he wanted in it.

A few days later the miller came and told him that the old ass which was to be beaten three times and fed once was dead. "The other two," he said, "which are to be fed three times, are not dead, but they are pining away and won't last long."

The huntsman's heart was stirred with pity and he told the miller to bring them back to him. When they came he gave them some of the other salad to eat, so that they took their human shapes again.

The beautiful maiden fell on her knees before him and said, "Oh, my beloved, forgive me all the wrong I have done you. My mother forced me to do it. It was against my own will, for I love you dearly. Your wishing cloak is hanging in the cupboard, and you shall have the bird's heart back too."

But he said, "Keep it. It will be all the same, as I will take you to be my own true wife."

Their marriage was soon after celebrated and they lived happily together till they died.

The Bremen Town Musicians

A CERTAIN man had an ass which for many years carried sacks to the mill without tiring. At last, however, its strength was worn out and it was no longer of any use for work. Accordingly, its master began to ponder as to how best to cut down its keep. But the ass, seeing there was mischief in the air, ran away and started on the road to Bremen. There he thought he could become a town musician.

When he had been traveling a short time, he fell in with a hound, who was lying panting on the road as though he had run himself off his legs.

"Well, what are you panting so for, Growler?" said the ass.

"Ah," said the hound, "just because I am old, and every day I get weaker. And also, because I can no longer keep up with the pack, my master wanted to kill me, so I took my departure. But now how am I to earn my bread?"

"Do you know what?" said the ass. "I am going to Bremen and shall there become a town musician. Come with me and take your part in the music. I shall play the lute, and you shall beat the kettledrum."

The hound agreed and they went on.

A short time afterwards they came upon a cat sitting in the road, with a face as long as a wet week.

"Well, why are you so cross, Whiskers?" asked the ass.

"Who can be cheerful when he is out at elbows?" said the cat. "I am getting on in years and my teeth are blunted, and I prefer to sit by the stove and purr instead of hunting round after mice. Just because of this my mistress wanted to drown me. I made myself scarce, but now I don't know where to turn."

"Come with us to Bremen," said the ass. "You are a great hand at serenading, so you can become a town musician."

The cat consented and joined them.

Next the fugitives passed by a yard where a barnyard fowl was sitting on the door, crowing with all its might.

"You crow so loud you pierce one through and through," said the ass. "What is the matter?"

"Why, didn't I prophesy fine weather for Lady Day, when Our Lady washes the Christ Child's little garment and wants to dry it? But notwithstanding this, because Sunday visitors are coming tomorrow, the mistress has no pity, and she has ordered the cook to make me into soup. So I shall have my neck wrung tonight. Now I am crowing with all my might while I can."

"Come along, Red-comb," said the ass. "You had much better come with us. We are going to Bremen and you will find a much better fate there. You have a good voice, and when we make music together there will be quality in it."

The cock allowed himself to be persuaded and they all four went off together. They could not, however, reach the town in one day, and by evening they arrived at a wood, where they determined to spend the night. The ass and the hound lay down under a big tree. The cat and the cock

settled themselves in the branches, the cock flying right up to the top, which was the safest place for him. Before going to sleep he looked round once more in every direction. Suddenly it seemed that he saw a light burning in the distance. He called out to his comrades that there must be a house not far off, for he saw a light.

"Very well," said the ass. "Let us set out and make our way to it, for the entertainment here is very bad."

The hound thought some bones or meat would suit him too, so they set out in the direction of the light. They soon saw it shining more clearly and getting bigger and bigger, till they reached a brightly lighted robbers' den. The ass, being the tallest, approached the window and looked in.

"What do you see, old Jackass?" asked the cock.

"What do I see?" answered the ass. "Why, a table spread with delicious food and drink, and robbers seated at it enjoying themselves."

"That would just suit us," said the cock.

"Yes, if we were only there," answered the ass.

Then the animals took counsel as to how to set about driving the robbers out. At last they hit upon a plan.

The ass was to take up his position with his forefeet on the window sill, the hound was to jump on his back, the cat to climb up onto the hound, and last of all the cock was to fly up and perch on the cat's head. When they were thus arranged, at a given signal they all began to perform their music. The ass brayed, the hound barked, the cat mewed, and the cock crowed. Then they dashed through the window, shivering the panes. The robbers jumped up at the terrible noise. They thought nothing less than the devil was coming in upon them and fled into the wood in the greatest alarm. Then the four animals sat down to table and helped themselves according to taste, and they ate as though they had been starving for weeks. When they had finished,

The ass brayed, the hound barked, the cat mewed, and the cock crowed

they extinguished the light and looked for sleeping places, each one to suit his taste.

The ass lay down on a pile of straw, the hound behind the door, the cat on the hearth near the warm ashes, and the cock flew up to the rafters. As they were tired from the long journey, they soon went to sleep.

When midnight was past, and the robbers saw from a distance that the light was no longer burning and that all seemed quiet, the chief said, "We ought not to have been scared by a false alarm." And he ordered one of the robbers to go and examine the house.

Finding all quiet, the messenger went into the kitchen to kindle a light. And taking the cat's glowing, fiery eyes for live coals, he held a match close to them so as to light it. But the cat would stand no nonsense—it flew at his face, spat, and scratched. He was terribly frightened and ran away.

He tried to get out the back door, but the hound, who was lying there, jumped up and bit his leg. As he ran across the pile of straw in front of the house, the ass gave him a good sound kick with his hind legs; while the cock, who had awakened at the uproar quite fresh and gay, cried out from his perch, "Cock-a-doodle-doo."

Thereupon the robber ran back as fast as he could to his chief and said, "There is a gruesome witch in the house who breathed on me and scratched me with her long fingers. Behind the door there stands a man with a knife, who stabbed me, while in the yard lies a black monster who hit me with a club. And upon the roof the judge is seated, and he called out, 'Bring the rogue here!' So I hurried away as fast as I could."

Thenceforward the robbers did not venture again to the house, which, however, pleased the four Bremen musicians so much that they never wished to leave it again.

The Raven

THERE was once a queen who had a little daughter still in arms. One day the child was naughty and would not be quiet, whatever her mother might say.

Then she grew impatient, and as the ravens were flying round the castle, she opened the window and said, "I wish you were a raven, that you might fly away, and then I should have peace."

She had hardly said the words when the child was changed into a raven and flew out the window. She flew straight into a dark wood, and her parents did not know what had become of her. One day a man was passing through this wood and heard the raven calling.

When he was near enough, the raven said, "I am a princess by birth, and I am bewitched, but you can deliver me from the spell."

"What must I do?" asked the man.

"Go farther into the wood," she said, "and you will come to a house with an old woman in it. She will offer you food and drink, but you must not take any. If you eat or drink what she offers you, you will fall into a deep sleep, and then you will never be able to deliver me. There is a great heap of tanbark in the garden behind the house. You must stand on it and wait for me. I will come for three days in a coach drawn by four horses which on the

first day will be white. On the second day the horses will be chestnut, and on the last day black. If you are not awake, I shall not be delivered."

The man promised to do everything that she asked, but the raven said, "Alas, I know that you will not deliver me! You will take what the woman offers you, and I shall never be freed from the spell."

He promised once more not to touch either the food or the drink, but when he reached the house the old woman said to him, "Poor man, how tired you are! Come and refresh yourself. Eat and drink."

"No," said the man, "I will neither eat nor drink."

But she persisted and said, "Well, if you won't eat, take a sip out of the glass. One sip is nothing." Then he yielded and took a little sip.

About two o'clock he went down into the garden and stood on the tan heap to wait for the raven. All at once he became so tired that he could not keep on his feet, and he lay down for a moment, not meaning to go to sleep. But he had hardly stretched himself out before his eyelids closed, and he fell fast asleep. He slept so soundly that nothing in the world could have awakened him.

At two o'clock the raven came, drawn by her four white horses. But now she was already very sad, for she said, "I know he is asleep." She alighted from the carriage, went to him, shook him, and called him, but he did not wake.

Next day at dinnertime the old woman came again and brought him food and drink, but again he refused to touch it. But she left him no peace, till at last she induced him to take a sip from the glass.

Towards two o'clock he again went into the garden and stood on the tan heap, meaning to wait for the raven. But he suddenly became so tired that he sank down and fell into a deep sleep.

When the raven drove up with her chestnut horses, she was very mournful and said, "I know he is asleep." She went to him but he was fast asleep, and she could not wake him.

Next day the old woman said, "What is the meaning of this? If you don't eat or drink you will die."

He said, "I must not, and I will not, either eat or drink." She put the dish of food and the glass of wine before him, and when the scent of the wine reached him he could withstand it no longer and swallowed a good draught.

When the time came he went into the garden and stood on the tan heap and waited for the raven. But he was more tired than ever, and lay down and slept like a log.

At two o'clock the raven came, drawn by four black horses. The coach and everything about it was black. She herself was in the deepest mourning and said, "Alas! I know he is asleep." She shook him and called him, but she could not wake him.

Finding her efforts in vain, she placed a loaf beside him, a piece of meat, and a bottle of wine. Then she took a golden ring on which her name was engraved, and put it on his finger. Last, she laid a letter by him, saying that the bread, the meat, and the wine were inexhaustible. She also said, "I see that you cannot deliver me here, but if you still wish to do so, come to the Golden Castle of Stromberg. I know that it is still in your power."

Then she seated herself in her coach again and drove to the Golden Castle of Stromberg.

When the man woke and found that he had been asleep, his heart grew heavy and he said, "She certainly must have passed, and I have not delivered her."

Then his eyes fell on the things lying by him and he read the letter which told him all that had occurred. So he

got up and went away to find the Golden Castle of Stromberg, but he had no idea where to find it.

When he had wandered about for a long time he came to a dark wood whence he could not find his way out. After walking about in it for a fortnight, he lay down one night under a bush to sleep, for he was very tired. But he heard such lamentations and howling that he could not go to sleep. Then he saw a light glimmering in the distance and went towards it. When he reached it, he found that it came from a house which looked very tiny because a huge giant was standing at the door.

He thought, "If I go in and the giant sees me, I shan't escape with my life." But at last he ventured to go forward.

When the giant saw him, he said, "It's a good thing you have appeared, for I have had nothing to eat for an age. I will just swallow you for my supper."

"I had much rather that you did not," said the man. "I do not really like to be eaten. But if you only want something to eat, I have plenty here to satisfy you."

"If you are speaking the truth," said the giant, "you may be quite easy. I was only going to eat you because I had nothing else."

Then they went in and sat down at the table, and the man produced the bread, the meat, and the wine, which were all inexhaustible. "This just suits me fine," said the giant, and he ate as much as ever he could.

The man said to him, "Can you tell me where to find the Golden Castle of Stromberg?"

The giant said, "I will look at my map. Every town, village, and house is marked upon it."

He fetched the map, but the castle was not to be found.

"It doesn't matter," he said. "I have bigger maps upstairs in my chest. We will look for it there."

At last on a very old map they found the Golden Castle of Stromberg, but it was many thousands of miles away.

"How am I ever to get there?" asked the man.

The giant said, "I have a couple of hours to spare, and I can carry you rather near it. But then I must come back home to look after my wife and child."

Then the giant transported him to within a hundred leagues of the castle and said, "You will be able to find your way easily from here alone." Then he went back, and the man went on till at last he came to the Golden Castle.

It stood on a mountain of glass, and the bewitched maiden drove round and round it every day in her coach. He was delighted to see her again and wanted to go to her at once, but when he tried to climb the mountain, he found it was so slippery that he slid back at every step.

When he found he could not reach her, he grew very sad and said to himself, "I will stay down here below and wait for her."

So he built himself a little hut and lived in it for a whole year, and every day he could see the Princess above, driving round and round the castle, but he could never get to her.

Then one day he saw three robbers fighting, and called out to them, "God be with you!"

They stopped at the sound of his voice, but seeing nothing they began to fight again.

Then he cried again, "God be with you!"

They stopped and looked about, but seeing no one, went on fighting.

Then he cried for the third time, "God be with you!"

Again they stopped and looked about, but as there was no one visible they fell to fighting more savagely than ever.

He said to himself, "I must go and see what it is all about."

He went up and asked them why they were fighting. One of them said he had found a stick which made any door fly open which it touched. The second said he had found a cloak which made him invisible when he wore it. The third said he had caught a horse which could go anywhere, even up the mountain of glass. They could not decide whether these things should be common property or whether they should divide them.

Then said the man, "I will give you something in exchange for them if you like. I have no money, but I have something more valuable. First, however, I must test your things to see if you are speaking the truth."

They let him get onto the horse, put on the cloak, and take the stick in his hand. When he had got them all, he was nowhere to be seen.

Then he gave them each a sound drubbing and said, "Now you have your deserts, you rascals!"

Then he rode up the glass mountain, and when he reached the castle he found the gate was shut. He touched it with his stick and it flew open.

He entered and went straight up the stairs into the gallery, where the maiden sat with a golden cup of wine before her. She, however, could not see him because he had the cloak on. Then he took the ring she had given him and dropped it into the cup, where it fell with a clink.

She cried, "That is my ring! The man who is to deliver me must be here."

They searched for him all over the castle but could not find him, for he had gone outside, taken off the cloak, and mounted his horse. When the people came to the gate and saw him, they raised cries of joy.

Then he dismounted and took the Princess in his arms. She kissed him and said, "Now you have delivered me, and tomorrow we will celebrate our marriage."

Cinderella

THE wife of a rich man fell ill, and when she felt that she was nearing her end she called her only daughter to her bedside and said, "Dear child, continue devout and good. Then God will always help you, and I will look down upon you from heaven and watch over you."

Thereupon she closed her eyes and breathed her last.

The maiden went to her mother's grave every day and wept, and she continued to be devout and good. When the winter came, the snow spread a white covering on the grave. And when the sun of spring had unveiled it again, the husband took another wife. The new wife brought home with her two daughters who were fair and beautiful to look upon, but base and black at heart.

Then began a sad time for the unfortunate stepchild.

"Is this stupid goose to sit with us in the parlor?" they said.

"Whoever wants to eat bread must earn it. Go and sit with the kitchenmaid."

They took away her pretty clothes and made her put on an old gray frock, and gave her wooden clogs.

"Just look at the proud princess! How well she's dressed," they laughed, as they led her to the kitchen.

There the girl was obliged to do hard work from morn-

ing till night, to get up at daybreak, carry water, light the fire, cook, and wash. Not content with that, the sisters inflicted on her every vexation they could think of. They made fun of her, and tossed the peas and lentils among the ashes, so that she had to sit down and pick them out again. In the evening, when she was worn out with work, she had no bed to go to but had to lie on the hearth among the cinders. And because, on account of that, she always looked dusty and dirty, they called her Cinderella.

It happened one day that the father had a mind to go to the fair. So he asked both his stepdaughters what he should bring home for them.

"Fine clothes," said one.

"Pearls and jewels," said the other.

"But you, Cinderella," said he, "what will you have?"

"Father, break off for me the first twig which brushes against your hat on your way home."

Well, for his two stepdaughters he brought beautiful clothes, pearls, and jewels. And on his way home, as he was riding through a green copse, a hazel twig grazed against him and knocked his hat off. Then he broke off the branch and took it with him.

When he got home he gave his stepdaughters what they had asked for, and to Cinderella he gave the twig from the hazel tree.

Cinderella thanked him, and went to her mother's grave and planted the twig upon it. She wept so much that her tears fell and watered it, and it took root and became a fine tree.

Cinderella went to the grave three times every day. She wept and prayed there, and every time she went a little white bird came and perched upon the tree. And when she uttered a wish, the little bird threw down to her what she had wished for.

Now it happened that the King proclaimed a festival which was to last three days, and to which all the beautiful maidens in the country were invited, in order that his son might choose a bride.

When the two stepdaughters heard that they were also to be present, they were in high spirits.

They called Cinderella and said, "Brush our hair and clean our shoes and fasten our buckles, for we are going to the feast at the King's palace."

Cinderella obeyed but wept, for she also would gladly have gone to the ball with them, and she begged her stepmother to give her leave to go.

"You, Cinderella?" she said. "Why, you are covered with dust and dirt. You go to the festival? You have no clothes or shoes, and yet you want to go to the ball."

As she went on asking, however, her stepmother said, "Well, I have thrown a dishful of lentils into the cinders. If you have picked them all out in two hours you shall go with us."

The girl went through the back door into the garden and cried, "Ye gentle doves, ye turtledoves, and all ye little birds under heaven, come and help me—

> *The good into a dish to throw,*
> *The bad into your crops can go."*

Then two white doves came in by the kitchen window and were followed by the turtledoves, and finally all the little birds under heaven flocked in chirping and settled down among the ashes. And the doves gave a nod with their little heads, peck, peck, peck. And then the rest began also, peck, peck, peck, and collected all the good lentils into the dish. Scarcely had an hour passed by before they had finished and had all flown out again.

Then the girl brought the dish to her stepmother, and

was delighted to think that now she would be able to go to the feast with them. But she said, "No, Cinderella, you have no clothes and cannot dance. You will only be laughed at."

But when she began to cry, the stepmother said, "If you can pick out two whole dishes of lentils from the ashes in an hour, you shall go with us." And she thought, "She will never be able to do that."

When her stepmother had thrown the dishes of lentils among the ashes, the girl went out through the back door and cried, "Ye gentle doves, ye turtledoves, and all ye little birds under heaven, come and help me—

> *The good into a dish to throw,*
> *The bad into your crops can go."*

Then two white doves came in by the kitchen window, and were followed by the turtledoves and all the other little birds under heaven. And in less than an hour the whole had been picked up, and they had all flown away.

Then the girl carried the dish to her stepmother and was delighted to think that she would now be able to go to the ball.

But she said, "It's not a bit of good. You can't go with us, for you've got no clothes and you can't dance. We should be quite ashamed of you."

Thereupon she turned her back upon her and hurried off with her two proud daughters.

As soon as everyone had left the house, Cinderella went out to her mother's grave under the hazel tree, and cried:

> *"Shiver and shake, dear little tree,*
> *Gold and silver shower on me."*

Then the bird threw down to her a gold and silver robe and a pair of slippers embroidered with silk and silver.

[*151*]

With all speed she put on the robe and went to the feast. But her stepsisters and their mother did not recognize her. They supposed that she was some foreign princess, so beautiful did she appear in her golden dress. They never gave a thought to Cinderella, but imagined that she was sitting at home in the dirt, picking the lentils out of the cinders.

The Prince came up to the stranger, took her by the hand, and danced with her. In fact he would not dance with anyone else and never let go of her hand. If anyone came up to ask her to dance, he said, "This is my partner."

She danced until nightfall and then wanted to go home, but the Prince said, "I will go with you and escort you."

He wanted to see to whom the beautiful maiden belonged. But she slipped out of his way and sprang into the pigeon house.

Then the Prince waited till her father came, and told him that the unknown maiden had vanished into the pigeon house.

The old man thought, "Could it be Cinderella?" And he had an ax brought to him so that he might break down the pigeon house, but there was no one inside.

When they went home, there lay Cinderella in her dirty clothes among the cinders, and a dismal oil lamp was burning in the chimney corner, for Cinderella had quietly jumped down out of the pigeon house and run back to the hazel tree. There she had taken off her beautiful clothes and laid them on the grave, and the bird had taken them away again. Then she had settled herself among the ashes on the hearth in her old gray frock.

On the second day, when the festival was renewed and her parents and stepsisters had started forth again, Cinderella went to the hazel tree and said:

CINDERELLA

"Shiver and shake, dear little tree,
Gold and silver shower on me."

Then the bird threw down a still more gorgeous robe than on the previous day. And when she appeared at the festival in this robe, everyone was astounded by her beauty. The King's son had waited till she came and at once took her hand, and she danced with no one but him. When others came forward and invited her to dance, he said, "This is my partner."

At nightfall she wished to leave; but the Prince went after her, hoping to see into what house she went, but she sprang out into the garden behind the house. There stood a fine big tree on which the most delicious pears hung. She climbed up among the branches as nimbly as a squirrel, and the Prince could not make out what had become of her.

But he waited till her father came and then said to him, "The unknown maiden has slipped away from me, and I think that she has jumped into the pear tree."

The father thought, "Can it be Cinderella?" And he had the ax brought to cut down the tree, but there was no one in it. When they went home and looked into the kitchen, there lay Cinderella among the cinders as usual, for she had jumped down on the other side of the tree, taken back the beautiful clothes to the bird on the hazel tree, and put on her old gray frock.

On the third day, when her parents and sisters had started, Cinderella went again to her mother's grave and said:

"Shiver and shake, dear little tree,
Gold and silver shower on me."

Then the bird threw down a dress which was so magnificent that no one had ever seen the like before, and the

[*153*]

slippers were entirely of gold. When she appeared at the festival in this attire, they were all speechless with astonishment. The Prince danced only with her, and if anyone else asked her to dance he said, "This is my partner."

When night fell and she wanted to leave, the Prince was more desirous than ever to accompany her, but she darted away from him so quickly that he could not keep up with her. But the Prince had used a stratagem, and had caused the steps to be covered with cobbler's wax. The consequence was that, as the maiden sprang down them, her left slipper remained sticking there. The Prince took it up. It was small and dainty and made entirely of gold. The next morning he went with it to Cinderella's father and said to him, "No other shall become my wife but she whose foot this golden slipper fits."

The two sisters were delighted at that, for they both had beautiful feet. The eldest went into the room intending to try on the slipper, and her mother stood beside her. But her great toe prevented her getting it on. Her foot was too long.

Then her mother handed her a knife and said, "Cut off the toe. When you are Queen you won't have to walk any more."

The girl cut off her toe, forced her foot into the slipper, stifled her pain, and went out to the Prince. Then he took her up on his horse as his bride and rode away with her.

However, they had to pass the grave on the way, and there sat the two doves on the hazel tree and cried:

> "Prithee, look back, prithee, look back,
> There's blood on the track.
> The shoe is too small;
> At home the true bride is waiting thy call."

Then he looked at her foot and saw how the blood was

streaming from it. So he turned his horse round and carried the false bride back to her home, and said that she was not the right one.

Then the second sister must try the shoe. She went into the room and succeeded in getting her toes into the shoe, but her heel was too big.

Then her mother handed her a knife and said, "Cut a bit off your heel. When you are Queen you won't have to walk any more."

The maiden cut a bit off her heel, forced her foot into the shoe, stifled her pain, and went out to the Prince. Then he took her up on his horse as his bride and rode off with her.

As they passed the grave, the two doves were sitting on the hazel tree, crying:

> "Prithee, look back, prithee, look back,
> There's blood on the track.
> The shoe is too small;
> At home the true bride is waiting thy call."

He looked down at her foot and saw that it was streaming with blood and that there were dark red spots on her stockings. Then he turned his horse and brought the false bride back to her home. "This is not the right one either," he said. "Have you no other daughter?"

"No," said the man. "There is only a daughter of my late wife's, a puny, stunted drudge, but she cannot possibly be the bride."

The Prince said that she must be sent for.

But the mother answered, "Oh no. She is much too dirty. She mustn't be seen on any account."

He was absolutely determined, however, to have his way, and they were obliged to summon Cinderella.

When she had washed her hands and face, she went up

and curtsied to the Prince, who handed her the golden slipper. Then she sat down on a bench, pulled off her wooden clog, and put on the slipper, which fitted to a nicety.

And when she stood up and the Prince looked into her face, he recognized the beautiful maiden that he had danced with and cried, "This is the true bride!"

The stepmother and the two sisters were dismayed and turned white with rage. But he took Cinderella on his horse and rode off with her.

As they rode past the hazel tree the two white doves cried:

> *"Prithee, look back, prithee, look back,*
> *No blood's on the track.*
> *The shoe's not too small;*
> *You carry the true bride home to your hall."*

And when they had said this they both came flying down and settled on Cinderella's shoulders, one on the right and one on the left, and they remained perched there.

When the wedding was going to take place, the two false sisters came and wanted to curry favor with her and take part in her good fortune. As the bridal party was going to the church, the elder was on the right side, the younger on the left, and the doves picked out one of the eyes of each of them.

Afterwards when they were coming out of the church, the elder was on the left, the younger on the right, and the doves picked out the other eye of each of them. And so for their wickedness and falseness they were punished with blindness for the rest of their days.

Snow-White and the Seven Dwarfs

ONCE upon a time in the middle of winter, when the snow-flakes were falling like feathers from the sky, a queen sat at her window working, and her embroidery frame was of ebony. And as she worked, gazing at times out on the snow, she pricked her finger, and there fell from it three drops of blood on the snow. And when she saw how bright and red it looked, she said to herself, "Oh, that I had a child as white as snow, as red as blood, and as black as the wood of the embroidery frame!"

Not very long afterwards she had a daughter, with skin as white as snow, lips as red as blood, and hair as black as ebony, and she was named Snow-White. And when she was born the Queen died.

After a year had gone by, the King took another wife, a beautiful woman, but proud and overbearing, and she could not bear to be surpassed in beauty by anyone. She had a magic looking glass, and she used to stand before it and look in it and say:

> *"Looking glass upon the wall,*
> *Who is fairest of us all?"*

And the looking glass would answer:

"You are fairest of them all."

And she was contented, for she knew that the looking glass spoke the truth.

Now Snow-White was growing prettier and prettier, and when she was seven years old she was as beautiful as day, far more so than the Queen herself. So one day when the Queen went to her mirror and said:

"Looking glass upon the wall,
Who is fairest of us all?"

It answered:

"Queen, you are full fair, 'tis true,
But Snow-White fairer is than you."

This gave the Queen a great shock, and she became yellow and green with envy, and from that hour her heart turned against Snow-White and she hated her. And envy and pride like ill weeds grew higher in her heart every day until she had no peace day or night.

At last she sent for a huntsman and said, "Take the child out into the woods, so that I may set eyes on her no more. You must put her to death and bring me her heart for a token."

The huntsman consented and led her away. But when he drew his cutlass to pierce Snow-White's innocent heart, she began to weep and to say, "Oh, dear huntsman, do not take my life. I will go away into the woods and never come home again."

And as she was so lovely the huntsman had pity on her and said, "Away with you then, poor child."

He thought the wild animals would be sure to devour her, and it was as if a stone had been rolled away from his heart when he was spared putting her to death.

Just at that moment a young wild boar came running by, so he caught and killed it. And taking out its heart, he brought it to the Queen for a token. And it was salted and cooked and the wicked woman ate it up, thinking that there was an end of Snow-White.

Now when the poor child found herself quite alone in the wild woods, she felt full of terror, even of the very leaves on the trees, and she did not know what to do for fright. Then she began to run over the sharp stones and

through the thornbushes, and the wild beasts ran about her but they did her no harm. She ran as long as her feet would carry her.

And when the evening drew near she came to a little house and she went inside to rest. Everything there was very small, but as pretty and clean as possible. There stood a little table, ready laid. It was covered with a white cloth, and seven little plates, and seven knives and forks, and drinking cups. By the wall stood seven little beds side by side, covered with clean white quilts.

Snow-White, being very hungry and thirsty, ate from each plate a little porridge and bread, and drank out of each little cup a drop of wine, so as not to finish up any one portion. After that she felt so tired that she lay down in turn on each of the beds, but none of them seemed to suit her. One was too long, another too short; but at last the seventh was right, and so she lay down upon it, committed herself to heaven, and fell asleep.

When it was quite dark, the masters of the house came home. They were seven dwarfs whose work it was to dig underground among the mountains. When they had lighted their seven candles and it was quite light in the little house, they saw that someone must have been in, as everything was not in the same order in which they had left it.

The first said, "Who has been sitting in my little chair?"

The second said, "Who has been eating from my little plate?"

The third said, "Who has been taking from my little loaf?"

The fourth said, "Who has been tasting my porridge?"

The fifth said, "Who has been using my little fork?"

The sixth said, "Who has been cutting with my little knife?"

The seventh said, "Who has been drinking from my little cup?"

Then the first one, looking round, saw a hollow in his bed and cried, "Who has been lying on my bed?"

And the others came running and cried, "Someone has been on our beds too!"

But when the seventh looked at his bed, he saw little Snow-White lying there asleep. Then he told the others, who came running up, crying out in their astonishment and holding up their seven little candles to throw a light upon Snow-White.

"Goodness gracious!" they cried. "What beautiful child is this?" And they were so full of joy to see her that they did not wake her, but let her sleep on. And the seventh dwarf slept with his comrades, an hour at a time with each, until the night had passed.

When it was morning, and Snow-White awoke and saw the seven dwarfs, she was very frightened. But they seemed quite friendly and asked her what her name was, and she told them. Then they asked her how she came to be in their house. And she related to them how her stepmother had wished her to be put to death, and how the huntsman had spared her life, and how she had run the whole day long until at last she had found their little house.

Then the dwarfs said, "If you will keep our house for us, and cook, and wash, and make the beds, and sew and knit, and keep everything tidy and clean, you may stay with us, and you shall lack nothing."

"With all my heart," said Snow-White. And so she stayed and kept the house in good order. In the morning the dwarfs went to the mountain to dig for gold. In the evening they came home, and their supper had to be ready for them.

All the day long the maiden was left alone, and the good

little dwarfs warned her, saying, "Beware of your step-mother! She will soon know you are here. Let no one into the house."

Now the Queen, having eaten Snow-White's heart, as she supposed, felt quite sure that now she was the first and fairest, and so she came to her mirror and said:

> "Looking glass upon the wall,
> Who is fairest of us all?"

And the glass answered:

> "Queen, thou art of beauty rare,
> But Snow-White living in the glen
> With the seven little men
> Is a thousand times more fair."

Then she was very angry, for the glass always spoke the truth, and she knew that the huntsman must have deceived her and that Snow-White must still be living. And she thought and thought how she could manage to make an end of her, for as long as she was not the fairest in the land, envy left her no rest. At last she thought of a plan. She painted her face and dressed herself like an old ped-dler woman, so that no one would have known her. In this disguise she went across the seven mountains, until she came upon the house of the seven little dwarfs.

And she knocked at the door and cried, "Fine wares to sell! Fine wares to sell!"

Snow-White peeped out the window and cried, "Good day, good woman, what have you to sell?"

"Good wares, fine wares," answered she. "Laces of all colors." And she held up a piece that was woven of many-colored silk.

"I need not be afraid of letting in this good woman," thought Snow-White, and she unbarred the door and bought the pretty lace.

"What a figure you are, child!" said the old woman. "Come and let me lace your bodice properly for once."

Snow-White, suspecting nothing, stood up before her and let her lace her with the new lace. But the old woman laced so quickly and tightly that it took Snow-White's breath away, and she fell down as dead.

"Now you are no longer the fairest," said the old woman as she hastened away.

Not long after that, towards evening, the seven dwarfs came home, and they were terrified to see their dear Snow-White lying on the ground without life or motion. They raised her up, and when they saw how tightly she was laced, they cut the lace in two. Then she began to draw breath, and little by little she returned to life.

When the dwarfs heard what had happened they said, "The old peddler woman was no other than the wicked Queen. You must beware of letting anyone in when we are not here!"

And when the wicked woman got home she went to her glass and said:

"*Looking glass against the wall,*
Who is fairest of us all?"

And it answered as before:

"*Queen, thou art of beauty rare,*
But Snow-White living in the glen
With the seven little men
Is a thousand times more fair."

When she heard that, she was so struck with surprise that all the blood left her heart, for she knew that Snow-White must still be living.

"But now," said she, "I will think of something that will be her ruin." And by witchcraft she made a poisoned

comb. Then she dressed herself up to look like another and different sort of old woman.

So she went across the seven mountains and came to the house of the seven dwarfs, and knocked at the door and cried, "Good wares to sell! Good wares to sell!"

Snow-White looked out and said, "Go away, I must not let anybody in."

"But you are not forbidden to look," said the old woman, taking out the poisoned comb and holding it up. It pleased the poor child so much that she was tempted to open the door.

And when the bargain was made the old woman said, "Now for once your hair shall be properly combed."

Poor Snow-White, thinking no harm, let the old woman do as she would, but no sooner was the comb put in her hair than the poison began to work, and the poor girl fell down senseless.

"Now, you paragon of beauty," said the wicked woman, "this is the end of you!" And she went off.

By good luck it was now near evening and the seven little dwarfs came home. When they saw Snow-White lying on the ground as dead, they thought directly that it was the stepmother's doing. They looked about and found the poisoned comb, and no sooner had they drawn it out of her hair than Snow-White came to herself and related all that had passed. Then they warned her once more to be on her guard, and never again to let anyone in at the door.

And the Queen went home and stood before the looking glass and said:

> *"Looking glass against the wall,*
> *Who is fairest of us all?"*

And the looking glass answered as before:

"Queen, thou are of beauty rare,
But Snow-White living in the glen
With the seven little men
Is a thousand times more fair."

When she heard the looking glass speak thus she trembled and shook with anger.

"Snow-White shall die," cried she, "though it should cost me my own life!"

And then she went to a secret lonely chamber where no one was likely to come, and there she made a poisonous apple. It was beautiful to look upon, being white with red cheeks, so that anyone who should see it must long for it, but whoever ate even a little bit of it must die. When the apple was ready, she painted her face and clothed herself like a peasant woman, and went across the seven mountains to where the seven dwarfs lived.

And when she knocked at the door Snow-White put her head out the window and said, "I dare not let anybody in. The seven dwarfs told me not to."

"All right," answered the woman. "I can easily get rid of my apples elsewhere. There, I will give you one."

"No," answered Snow-White. "I dare not take anything."

"Are you afraid of poison?" said the woman. "Look here, I will cut the apple in two pieces. You shall have the red side. I will have the white one."

The apple was so cunningly made that all of the poison was in the rosy half of it. Snow-White longed for the beautiful apple. And as she saw the peasant woman eating a piece of it she could no longer refrain, but stretched out her hand and took the poisoned half. But no sooner had she taken a morsel of it into her mouth than she fell to the earth as dead.

And the Queen, casting on her a terrible glance, laughed aloud and cried, "As white as snow, as red as blood, as black as ebony! This time the dwarfs will not be able to bring you to life again."

And when she went home and asked the looking glass:

> *"Looking glass against the wall,*
> *Who is fairest of us all?"*

—at last it answered, "You are the fairest now of all."

Then her envious heart had peace, as much as an envious heart can have.

The dwarfs, when they came home in the evening, found Snow-White lying on the ground, and there came no breath out of her mouth, and she was dead. They lifted her up, sought if anything poisonous was to be found, cut her laces, combed her hair, washed her with water and wine, but all was of no avail. The poor child was dead, and remained dead. Then they laid her on a bier, and all seven of them sat around it, and wept and lamented three whole days. And then they would have buried her, except that she still looked as if she were living, with her beautiful blooming cheeks.

So they said, "We cannot hide her away in the black ground."

And they had made a coffin of clear glass that could be looked into from all sides. They laid her in it and wrote upon it in golden letters her name, and that she was a king's daughter. Then they sat the coffin out upon the mountain and one of them always remained by it to watch. And the birds came too and mourned for Snow-White; first an owl, then a raven, and last, a dove.

Now for a long while Snow-White lay in the coffin and never changed, but looked as if she were asleep, for she was still as white as snow, as red as blood, and her hair

[*166*]

was as black as ebony. It happened, however, that one day a king's son rode through the wood and up to the dwarfs' house, which was near it. He saw on the mountain the coffin, and beautiful Snow-White within it, and he read what was written in golden letters upon it.

Then he said to the dwarfs, "Let me have the coffin, and I will give you whatever you like to ask for it."

But the dwarfs told him that they could not part with it for all the gold in the world.

But he said, "I beseech you give it to me, for I cannot live without looking upon Snow-White. If you consent, I will bring you to great honor and care for you as if you were my brethren."

When he pleaded, the good little dwarfs had pity upon him and gave him the coffin, and the King's son called his servants and bid them carry it away on their shoulders. Now it happened that as they were going along they stumbled over a bush, and with the shaking the bit of poisoned apple flew out of her throat. It was not long before she opened her eyes, threw up the cover of the coffin, and sat up, alive and well.

"Oh dear, where am I?" cried she.

The King's son answered, full of joy, "You are near me." And relating all that had happened, he said, "I would rather have you than anything in the world. Come with me to my father's castle and you shall be my bride."

And Snow-White was kind and went with him, and their wedding was held with pomp and great splendor.

But Snow-White's wicked stepmother also was bidden to the feast. And when she had dressed herself in beautiful clothes she went to her looking glass and said:

> *"Looking glass upon the wall,*
> *Who is fairest of us all?"*

[*167*]

The looking glass answered:

"O Queen, although you are of beauty rare,
The young bride is a thousand times more fair."

Then she railed and cursed, and was beside herself with disappointment and anger. First she thought she would not go to the wedding, but then she felt she should have no peace until she went and saw the bride. And when she saw her she knew her for Snow-White, and could not stir from the place for anger and terror. For they had ready red-hot iron shoes, in which she had to dance until she fell down dead.

The Elves and the Shoemaker

THERE was once a shoemaker who through no fault of his own had become so poor that at last he had only leather enough left for one pair of shoes. At evening he cut out the shoes which he intended to begin upon the next morning, and since he had a good conscience, he lay down quietly, said his prayers, and fell asleep.

In the morning, when he had said his prayers and was preparing to sit down to work, he found the pair of shoes standing finished on his table. He was amazed and could not understand it in the least.

He took the shoes in his hand to examine them more closely. They were so neatly sewn that not a stitch was out of place, and were as good as the work of a master hand.

Soon afterwards a purchaser came in and, as he was much pleased with the shoes, he paid more than the ordinary price for them, so that the shoemaker was able to buy leather for two pairs of shoes with the money.

He cut them out in the evening, and the next day with fresh courage was about to go to work. But he had no need to, for when he got up the shoes were finished, and buyers were not lacking. These gave him so much money that he was able to buy leather for four pairs of shoes.

Early next morning he found the four pairs finished, and so it went on. What he cut out at evening was finished in the morning, so that he was soon again in comfortable circumstances and became a well-to-do man.

Now it happened one evening not long before Christmas, when he had cut out some shoes as usual, that he said to his wife, "How would it be if we were to sit up tonight to see who it is that lends us such a helping hand?"

The wife agreed and lighted a candle, and they hid themselves in the corner of the room behind the clothes which were hanging there.

At midnight came two little naked men who sat down at the shoemaker's table, took up the cutout work, and began with their tiny fingers to stitch, sew, and hammer so neatly and quickly that the shoemaker could not believe his eyes. They did not stop till everything was quite finished. Then they ran swiftly away.

The next day the wife said, "The little men have made us rich, and we ought to show our gratitude. They were running about with nothing on, and must freeze with cold. Now I will make them little shirts, coats, waistcoats, and hose, and will even knit them a pair of stockings. And you shall make them each a pair of shoes."

The husband agreed. And at evening, when they had everything ready, they laid out the presents on the table and hid themselves to see how the little men would behave.

At midnight they came skipping in and were about to set to work. But instead of the leather ready cut out, they found the charming little clothes.

At first they were surprised, then excessively delighted. With the greatest speed they put on and smoothed down the pretty clothes, singing:

> "Now we're boys so fine and neat,
> Why cobble more for others' feet?"

Then they hopped and danced about, and leapt over chairs and tables and out the door. Henceforward they came back no more, but the shoemaker fared well as long as he lived, and had good luck in all his undertakings.

The Water of Life

THERE was once a king who was so ill that it was thought impossible his life could be saved. He had three sons, and they were all in great distress on his account, and they went into the castle gardens and wept at the thought that he must die. An old man came up to them and asked the cause of their grief. They told him that their father was dying, and nothing could save him.

The old man said, "There is only one remedy which I know. It is the Water of Life. If he drinks of it he will recover, but it is very difficult to find."

The eldest son said, "I will soon find it." And he went to the sick man to ask permission to go in search of the Water of Life, as that was the only thing to cure him.

"No," said the King. "The danger is too great. I would rather die." But he persisted so long that at last the King gave his permission.

The Prince thought, "If I bring this water I shall be the favorite, and I shall inherit the kingdom." So he set off, and when he had ridden some distance he came upon a dwarf standing in the road, who cried, "Whither away so fast?"

"Stupid little fellow," said the Prince proudly, "what business is it of yours?" And he rode on.

The little man was very angry and made an evil vow.

Soon afterwards, the Prince came to a gorge in the mountains, and the farther he rode the narrower it became, till he could go no farther. His horse could neither go forward nor turn round for him to dismount. So there he sat, jammed in.

The sick King waited a long time for him, but he never came back. Then the second son said, "Father, let me go and find the Water of Life." He was thinking, "If my brother is dead I shall have the kingdom."

The King at first refused to let him go but at last he gave his consent. So the Prince started on the same road as his brother and met the same dwarf, who stopped him and asked where he was going in such a hurry.

"Little snippet, what does it matter to you?" he said, and rode away without looking back.

But the dwarf cast a spell over him, and he, too, got into a narrow gorge like his brother, where he could neither go backwards nor forwards. That is what happens to the haughty.

As the second son also stayed away, the youngest one offered to go and fetch the Water of Life, and at last the King was obliged to let him go.

When he met the dwarf, and the dwarf asked him where he was hurrying to, he stopped and said, "I am searching for the Water of Life, because my father is dying."

"Do you know where it is to be found?"

"No," said the Prince.

"As you have spoken pleasantly to me, and not been haughty like your false brothers, I will help you and tell you how to find the Water of Life. It flows from a fountain

in the courtyard of an enchanted castle. But you will never get in unless I give you an iron rod and two loaves of bread. With the rod strike three times on the iron gate of the castle and it will spring open. Inside you will find two lions with wide-open jaws, but if you throw a loaf to each they will be quiet. Then you must make haste to fetch the Water of Life before it strikes twelve, or the gates of the castle will close and you will be shut in."

The Prince thanked him, took the rod and the loaves, and set off. When he reached the castle all was just as the dwarf had said. At the third knock the gate flew open, and when he had pacified the lions with the loaves, he walked into the castle. In the great hall he found several enchanted princes, and he took the rings from their fingers. He also took a sword and a loaf which were lying by them.

On passing into the next room he found a beautiful maiden, who rejoiced at his coming. She embraced him and said that he had saved her, and should have the whole of her kingdom, and if he would come back in a year she would marry him. She also told him where to find the fountain with the enchanted water, but she said he must make haste to get out of the castle before the clock struck twelve.

Then he went on and came to a room where there was a beautiful bed freshly made, and as he was very tired he thought he would take a little rest. So he lay down and fell asleep. When he woke it was striking a quarter to twelve. He sprang up in a fright, and ran to the fountain and took some of the water in a cup which was lying near, and then hurried away. The clock struck just as he reached the iron gate, and it banged so quickly that it took off a bit of his heel.

He rejoiced at having got some of the Water of Life, and hastened on his homeward journey. He again passed the

dwarf, who said when he saw the sword and the loaf, "Those things will be of much service to you. You will be able to strike down whole armies with the sword, and the loaf will never come to an end."

The Prince did not want to go home without his brothers and he said, "Good dwarf, can you not tell me where my brothers are? They went in search of the Water of Life before I did, but they never came back."

"They are both stuck fast in a narrow mountain gorge. I cast a spell over them because of their pride."

Then the Prince begged so hard that they might be released that at last the dwarf yielded. But he warned him against them and said, "Beware of them! They have bad hearts."

He was delighted to see his brothers when they came back, and told them all that had happened to him: how he had found the Water of Life and brought a gobletful with him; how he had released a beautiful princess, who would wait a year for him and then marry him, and he would then become a great prince.

Then they rode away together and came to a land where famine and war were raging. The King thought he would be utterly ruined, so great was the destitution.

The Prince went to him and gave him the loaf, and with it he fed and satisfied his whole kingdom. The Prince also gave him his sword, and he smote the whole army of his enemies with it, and then he was able to live in peace and quiet. Then the Prince took back his sword and his loaf, and the three brothers rode on.

But later they had to pass through two more countries where war and famine were raging, and each time the Prince gave his sword and his loaf to the King and in this way he saved three kingdoms.

After that they took a ship and crossed the sea. During

the passage the two elder brothers said to each other, "Our youngest brother found the Water of Life, and we did not. So our father will give him the kingdom which we ought to have, and he will take away our fortune from us."

This thought made them very vindictive and they made up their minds to get rid of him. They waited till he was asleep, and then they emptied the Water of Life from his goblet and took it themselves, and filled up his cup with salt sea water.

As soon as they got home the youngest Prince took his goblet to the King so that he might drink of the water which was to make him well. But after drinking only a few drops of the sea water he became more ill than ever. As he was bewailing himself, his two elder sons came to him and accused the youngest of trying to poison him, and said that they had the real Water of Life, and gave him some. No sooner had he drunk it than he felt better, and he soon became as strong and well as he had been in his youth.

Then the two went to the youngest brother and mocked him, saying, "It was you who found the Water of Life. You had all the trouble, while we have the reward. You should have been wiser and kept your eyes open. We stole it from you while you were asleep on the ship. When the end of the year comes, one of us will go and bring away the beautiful Princess. But don't dare to betray us. Our father will certainly not believe you, and if you say a single word you will surely lose your life. Your one and only chance is to keep silence."

The old King was very angry with his youngest son, thinking that he had tried to take his life. So he had the court assembled to give judgment upon him, and it was decided that he must be secretly got out of the way.

One day when the Prince was going out hunting, think-

ing no evil, the King's huntsman was ordered to go with him. Seeing the huntsman look sad, the Prince said to him, "My good huntsman, what is the matter with you?"

The huntsman answered, "I can't bear to tell you, and yet I must."

The Prince said, "Say it out. Whatever it is I will forgive you."

"Alas!" said the huntsman. "I am to shoot you dead. It is the King's command."

The Prince was horror-stricken and said, "Dear huntsman, do not kill me. Give me my life. Let me have your dress, and you shall have my royal robes."

The huntsman said, "I will gladly do so. I could never have shot you." So they changed clothes and the huntsman went home, but the Prince wandered away into the forest.

After a time three wagonloads of gold and precious stones came to the King for his youngest son. They were sent by the kings who had been saved by the Prince's sword and his miraculous loaf, and who now wished to show their gratitude.

Then the old King thought, "What if my son really was innocent?" And he said to his people, "If only he were still alive! How sorry I am that I ordered him to be killed."

"He is still alive," said the huntsman. "I could not find it in my heart to carry out your commands." And he told the King what had taken place.

A load fell from the King's heart on hearing the good news, and he sent out a proclamation to all parts of his kingdom that his son was to come home, where he would be received with great favor.

In the meantime, the Princess had caused a road to be made of pure shining gold leading to her castle, and told her people that whoever came riding straight along it would be the true bridegroom, and they were to admit

him. But anyone who came either on one side of the road or the other would not be the right one, and he was not to be let in.

When the year had almost passed, the eldest Prince thought that he would hurry to the Princess, and by giving himself out as her deliverer would gain a wife and a kingdom as well. So he rode away, and when he saw the beautiful golden road he thought it would be a thousand pities to ride upon it, so he turned aside and rode to the right of it. But when he reached the gate the people told him that he was not the true bridegroom, and he had to go away.

Soon after the second Prince came, and when he saw the golden road he thought it would a thousand pities for his horse to tread upon it, so he turned and rode up on the left of it. But when he reached the gate he also was told that he was not the true bridegroom, and like his brother was turned away.

When the year had quite come to an end, the third Prince came out of the wood to ride to his beloved, and through her to forget all his past sorrows. So on he went, thinking only of her and wishing to be with her, and he never even saw the golden road. His horse cantered right along the middle of it, and when he reached the gate it was flung open and the Princess received him joyfully, and called him her deliverer and the lord of her kingdom. Their marriage was celebrated without delay and with much rejoicing. When it was over, she told him that his father had called him back and forgiven him. So he went to him and told him everything: how his brothers had deceived him, and how they had forced him to keep silence. The old King wanted to punish them, but they had taken a ship and sailed away over the sea, and never came back as long as they lived.

The Gallant Tailor

ONE summer morning a little tailor was sitting at his bench near the window, working cheerfully with all his might, when an old woman came down the street.

She was crying, "Good jelly to sell! Good jelly to sell!"

The cry sounded pleasant in the little tailor's ears, so he put his head out the window and called out, "Here, my good woman! Come here, if you want a customer."

So the poor woman climbed the steps with her heavy basket, and was obliged to unpack and display all her pots to the tailor. He looked at every one of them and, lifting all the lids, applied his nose to each.

At last he said, "The jelly seems pretty good. You may weigh me out four half ounces, or I don't mind having a quarter of a pound."

The woman, who had expected to find a good customer, gave him what he asked for but went off angry and grumbling.

"This jelly is the very thing for me!" cried the little tailor. "It will give me strength and cunning." And he took down the bread from the cupboard, cut a big slice off the loaf and spread the jelly on it, laid it near him, and went on stitching more gallantly than ever. All the while the scent of the sweet jelly was spreading throughout the

room, where there were quantities of flies. They were attracted by it and flew down to eat of it.

"Now then, who invited you here?" said the tailor, and drove the unbidden guests away. But the flies, not understanding his language, were not to be got rid of like that, and returned in larger numbers than before. Then the tailor, unable to stand it any longer, took from his chimney corner a ragged cloth.

"Now, I'll let you have it!" he said, and beat it among them unmercifully. When he ceased and counted the slain, he found seven lying dead before him.

"This is indeed somewhat," he said, wondering at his own bravery. "The whole town shall know about this."

So he hastened to cut out a belt, and he stitched it and put on it in large capitals: "Seven at one blow!"

"The town, did I say?" said the little tailor. "The whole world shall know it!" And his heart quivered with joy, like a lamb's tail.

The tailor fastened the belt round him and began to think of going out into the world, for his workshop seemed too small for his valor. So he looked about in all the house for something that would be useful to take with him, but he found nothing but an old cheese, which he put in his pocket. Outside the door he noticed that a bird had got caught in the bushes, so he took that and put it in his pocket with the cheese. Then he set out gallantly on his way, and as he was light and active he felt no fatigue.

The way led over a mountain, and when he reached the topmost peak he saw a terrible giant sitting there, and looking about him at his ease.

The tailor went bravely up to him, called out to him, and said, "Good day, comrade! There you sit looking over the wide world. I am on the way thither to seek my fortune. Have you a fancy to go with me?"

The giant looked at the tailor contemptuously and said, "You vagabond! You miserable little creature!"

"That may be," answered the little tailor, and undoing his coat he showed the giant his belt. "You can read there whether I am a man or not."

The giant read, "Seven at one blow!" And thinking it meant men that the tailor had killed, he at once felt more respect for the little fellow. But as he wanted to test him, he took a stone and squeezed it so hard that water came out of it.

"Now you can do that," said the giant, "that is, if you have the strength for it."

"That's not much!" said the little tailor. "I call that play." And he put his hand in his pocket and took out the cheese and squeezed it till the whey ran out of it.

"Well," said he, "what do you think of that?"

The giant did not know what to say to it, for he could not have believed it of the little man. Then the giant took up a stone and threw it so high that it was nearly out of sight.

"Now, little fellow, suppose you do that!"

"Well thrown!" said the tailor. "But the stone fell back to earth again. I will throw you one that will never come back." So he felt in his pocket, took out the bird, and threw it into the air. And the bird, when it found itself at liberty, took wing, flew off, and returned no more.

"What do you think of that, comrade?" asked the tailor.

"There is no doubt that you can throw," said the giant. "Now we will see if you can carry."

He led the little tailor to a mighty oak tree which had been felled and was lying on the ground, and said, "Now, if you are strong enough, help me to carry this tree out of the wood."

"Willingly," answered the little man. "You take the

trunk on your shoulders and I will take the branches with all their foliage. That is by far the biggest end."

So the giant took the trunk on his shoulders, and the tailor seated himself on a branch. And the giant, who could not see what he was doing, had the whole tree to carry, and the little man on it as well. And the little man was very cheerful and merry and whistled the tune, *"There were three tailors riding by,"* as if carrying the tree was mere child's play.

The giant, when he had struggled on under his heavy load a part of the way, was tired out and cried, "Look here, I must let go the tree!"

The tailor jumped off quickly. Then, taking hold of the tree with both arms as if he were carrying it, he said to the giant, "You see you can't carry the tree, though you are such a big fellow!"

They went on together a little farther and presently they came to a cherry tree. And the giant took hold of the topmost branches, where the ripest fruit hung, and pulling them downward gave them to the tailor to hold, bidding him eat. But the little tailor was much too weak to hold the tree, and as the giant let go, the tree sprang back and the tailor was thrown up into the air.

And when he dropped down again without any damage, the giant said to him, "How is this? Haven't you strength enough to hold such a weak sprig as that?"

"It is not strength that is lacking," answered the little tailor. "How should it to one who has slain seven at one blow? I just jumped over the tree because the hunters are shooting down there in the bushes. Why don't you jump it too, if you can?"

The giant made the attempt and, not being able to vault the tree, he remained hanging in the branches, so that once more the little tailor got the better of him.

Then said the giant, "As you are such a gallant fellow, suppose you come with me to our den and stay the night."

The tailor was quite willing and followed him. When they reached the den, there sat some other giants by the fire and all gladly welcomed him.

The little tailor looked round and thought, "There is more elbow room here than in my workshop."

The giant showed him a bed and told him he had better lie down on it and go to sleep. The bed, however, was too big for the tailor, so he did not stay in it but crept into a corner to sleep. As soon as it was midnight the giant got up, took a great staff of iron and beat the bed through with one stroke, and supposed he had made an end of that grasshopper of a tailor. Very early in the morning the giants went into the wood and forgot all about the little tailor, and when they saw him coming after them alive and merry, they were terribly frightened. And thinking he was going to kill them, they ran away in all haste.

So the little tailor marched on, always following his nose. And after he had gone a great way he entered the courtyard belonging to a king's palace, and there he felt so overpowered with fatigue that he lay down and fell asleep. In the meanwhile came various people, who looked at him very curiously and read on his belt, "Seven at one blow!"

"Oh," said they, "why should this great lord come here in time of peace? What a mighty champion he must be!"

Then they went and told the King about him. They thought that if war should break out what a worthy and useful man he would be, and he ought not to be allowed to depart at any price. The King then summoned his council and sent one of his courtiers to the little tailor to beg him, as soon as he should wake up, to consent to serve in the King's army. So the messenger stood and waited at the sleeper's side until he began to stretch his limbs and to

open his eyes, and then he carried his answer back: "I am ready to enter the King's service."

So he was received into it very honorably, and a separate dwelling was set apart for him.

But the rest of the soldiers were very much set against the little tailor, and wished him a thousand miles away.

"What shall be done about it?" they said among themselves. "If we pick a quarrel and fight with him, then seven of us will fall at each blow. That will be of no good to us."

So they came to a resolution, and went all together to the King to ask for their discharge.

"We never intended," said they, "to serve with a man who kills seven at a blow."

The King felt sorry to lose all his faithful servants because of one man. He wished that he had never seen him, and would willingly get rid of him if he might. But he did not dare to dismiss the little tailor for fear he should kill all the King's people and place himself upon the throne. He thought a long while about it, and at last made up his mind what to do.

He sent for the little tailor and told him that as he was so great a warrior he had a proposal to make to him. He told him that in a wood in his dominions dwelt two giants who did great damage by robbery, murder, and fire, and that no man dared go near them for fear of his life. But that if the tailor should overcome and slay both these giants the King would give him his only daughter in marriage and half his kingdom as dowry, and that a hundred horsemen should go with him to give him assistance.

"That would be a fine thing for a man like me," thought the little tailor. "A beautiful princess and half a kingdom are not to be had every day."

So he said to the King, "Oh yes, I can soon overcome the giants, and yet I have no need of the hundred horse-

men. He who can kill seven at one blow has no need to be afraid of two."

So the little tailor set out and the hundred horsemen followed him.

When he came to the border of the wood he said to his escort, "Stay here while I go to attack the giants."

Then he sprang into the wood and looked about him right and left. After a while he caught sight of the two giants. They were lying down under a tree asleep, and snoring so that all the branches shook. The little tailor, all alert, filled both his pockets with stones and climbed up into the tree, and made his way to an overhanging bough so that he could seat himself just above the sleepers. And from there he let one stone after another fall on the chest of one of the giants.

For a long time the giant was quite unaware of this, but at last he waked up and pushed his comrade and said, "What are you hitting me for?"

"Are you dreaming?" said the other. "I am not touching you." And they composed themselves again to sleep, and the tailor let fall a stone on the other giant.

"What can that be?" cried he. "What are you casting at me?"

"I am casting nothing at you," answered the first, grumbling.

They disputed about it for a while, but as they were tired they gave it up at last, and their eyes closed once more. Then the little tailor began his game anew. He picked out a heavier stone and threw it down with force upon the first giant's chest.

"This is too much!" cried he, and sprang up like a madman and struck his companion such a blow that the tree shook above them. The other paid him back with ready coin, and they fought with such fury that they tore

up trees by their roots to use for weapons against each other, so that at last both of them lay dead upon the ground. And now the little tailor got down. "What a lucky thing," he said, "that the tree I was sitting in did not get torn up, too! Or else I should have had to jump like a squirrel from one tree to another."

Then he drew his sword and gave each of the giants a few hacks in the breast, and went back to the horsemen and said, "The deed is done. I have made an end of both of them, though it went hard with me. In the struggle they rooted up trees to defend themselves, but it was of no use."

"Then are you not wounded?" asked the horsemen.

"Nothing of the sort!" answered the tailor. "They have not injured a hair."

The horsemen still would not believe it and rode into the wood to see, and there they found the giants wallowing in their blood, and all about them lying the uprooted trees. The little tailor then claimed the promised boon, but the King repented of his offer and again sought how to rid himself of the hero.

"Before you can possess my daughter and the half of my kingdom," said he to the tailor, "you must perform another heroic act. In the wood lives a unicorn who does great damage. You must capture him."

"A unicorn does not strike more terror into me than two giants. Seven at one blow! That is my way," was the tailor's answer.

So taking a rope and an ax with him, he went out into the wood and told those who were ordered to attend him to wait outside. He had not far to seek. The unicorn soon came out and sprang at him, as if he would make an end of him without delay.

"Softly, softly!" said the tailor. "Most haste, worst speed." And he remained standing until the animal came

quite near; then he slipped quickly behind a tree. The unicorn ran with all his might against the tree and stuck his horn so deep into the trunk that he could not get it out again, and so was captured.

"Now I have you," said the tailor, coming out from behind the tree. And putting the rope around the unicorn's neck, he took the ax and cut free the horn, and when all his party was assembled he led forth the animal and brought it to the King.

The King did not yet wish to give him the promised reward and set him a third task to do. Before the wedding could take place the tailor was to secure a wild boar which had done a great deal of damage in the wood.

The huntsmen were to accompany him and help him.

"All right," said the tailor. "This is child's play."

But he did not take the huntsmen into the wood, and they were all the better pleased, for the wild boar had many a time before received them in such a way that they had no fancy to disturb him.

When the boar caught sight of the tailor he ran at him with foaming mouth and gleaming tusks to bear him to the ground, but the nimble hero rushed into a chapel which chanced to be near and jumped quickly out a window on the other side. The boar ran after him, and when he got inside the tailor shut the door after him, and there he was imprisoned, for the creature was too big and unwieldy to jump out the window too.

Then the tailor called the huntsmen that they might see the prisoner with their own eyes. And then he betook himself to the King, who now, whether he liked it or not, was obliged to fulfill his promise and give him his daughter and the half of his kingdom. But if he had known that the great warrior was only a little tailor he would have taken it still more to heart.

So the wedding was celebrated with great splendor and little joy, and the tailor was made into a king. One night the young Queen heard her husband talking in his sleep and saying, "Boy, make me that waistcoat and patch me those breeches, or I will wrap my yardstick about your shoulders!"

And as she perceived of what low birth her husband was, she went to her father the next morning and told him all, and begged him to set her free from a man who was nothing better than a tailor.

The King bade her be comforted, saying, "Tonight leave your bedroom door open. My guards shall stand outside, and when he is asleep they shall come in and bind him and carry him off to a ship that will take him to the other side of the world."

So the wife felt consoled, but the King's water bearer, who had been listening all the while, went to the little tailor and disclosed to him the whole plan.

"I shall put a stop to all this," said he.

At night he lay down as usual in bed, and when his wife thought that he was asleep she got up, opened the door, and lay down again. The little tailor, who only made believe to be asleep, began to murmur plainly.

"Boy, make me that waistcoat and patch me those breeches, or I will wrap my yardstick about your shoulders! I have slain seven at one blow, killed two giants, caught a unicorn, and taken a wild boar. And shall I be afraid of those who are standing outside of my room door?"

And when they heard the tailor say this, a great fear seized the guards. They fled away as if they had been wild hares and none of them would venture to attack him.

And so the little tailor all his lifetime remained a king.

The Golden Goose

THERE was once a man who had three sons, the youngest of whom was called Simpleton. He was scorned and despised by the others and kept in the background.

The eldest son was going into the forest to cut wood, and before he started his mother gave him a nice sweet cake and a bottle of wine to take with him so that he might not suffer from hunger or thirst.

In the wood he met a little old gray man, who bade him good day and said, "Give me a bit of the cake in your pocket, and let me have a drop of your wine. I am so hungry and thirsty."

But the clever son said, "If I give you my cake and wine, I shan't have enough for myself. Be off with you!"

He left the little man standing there and went on his way. But he had not been long at work, cutting down a tree, before he made a false stroke. He dug the ax into his own arm and he was obliged to go home to have it bound up. Now this was no accident. It was brought about by the little gray man.

The second son now had to go into the forest to cut wood, and like the eldest, his mother gave him a sweet cake and a bottle of wine. In the same way the little gray man met him and asked for a piece of his cake and a drop

of his wine. But the second son made the same sensible answer, "If I give you any, I shall have the less for myself. Be off and out of my way!" And he went on.

His punishment, however, was not long delayed. After a few blows at the tree, he hit his own leg and had to be carried home.

Then Simpleton said, "Let me go to cut the wood, father."

But his father said, "Your brothers have only come to harm by it. You had better leave it alone. You know nothing about it." But Simpleton begged so hard to be allowed to go that at last his father said, "Well, off you go then. You will be wiser when you have hurt yourself."

His mother gave him a cake which was mixed only with water and baked in the ashes, and a bottle of sour beer. When he reached the forest, like the others he met the little gray man.

"Give me a bit of the cake in your pocket and a drop of your wine. I am so hungry and thirsty," said the little man.

Simpleton answered, "I only have a cake baked in the ashes, and some sour beer. But if you like such fare, we will sit down and eat it together."

So they sat down. But when Simpleton pulled out his cake it was a nice sweet cake, and his sour beer was turned into good wine. So they ate and drank, and the little man said, "As you have such a good heart and are willing to share your goods, I will give you good luck. There stands an old tree. Cut it down and you will find something at the roots."

So saying, he disappeared.

Simpleton cut down the tree, and when it fell, lo and behold! a goose was sitting among the roots, and its feathers were of pure gold. He picked it up and took it with him to an inn where he meant to stay the night. The land-

lord had three daughters, who saw the goose and were very curious as to what kind of bird it could be, and wanted to get one of its golden feathers.

The eldest thought, "There will soon be some opportunity for me to pull out one of the feathers." And when Simpleton went outside, she took hold of its wing to pluck out a feather, but her hand stuck fast and she could not get away.

Soon afterwards the second sister came up, meaning also to pluck out one of the golden feathers. But she had hardly touched her sister when she found herself held fast.

Finally the third one came with the same intention, but the others screamed out, "Keep away! For goodness' sake, keep away!"

But she, not knowing why she was to keep away, thought, "Why should I not be there if they are there?"

So she ran up. But as soon as she touched her sisters she had to stay hanging on to them, and they all had to pass the night like this.

In the morning, Simpleton took up the goose under his arm without noticing the three girls hanging on behind. They had to keep running behind, dodging his legs.

In the middle of the fields they met the parson, who when he saw the procession cried out, "For shame, you bold girls! Why do you run after the lad like that? Do you call that proper behavior?"

Then he took hold of the hand of the youngest girl to pull her away. But no sooner had he touched her than he felt himself held fast, and he too had to run behind.

Soon afterwards the sexton came up and, seeing his master the parson treading on the heels of the three girls, cried out in amazement, "Hallo, your reverence! Where are you going so fast? Don't forget that we have a christening!"

So saying, he plucked the parson by the sleeve and soon found that he could not get away.

As this party of five, one behind the other, tramped on, two peasants came along the road, carrying their hoes. The parson called them and asked them to set the sexton and himself free, but as soon as ever they touched the sexton they were held fast. So now there were seven people running behind Simpleton and his goose.

By and by they reached a town where a king ruled whose only daughter was so solemn that nothing and nobody could make her laugh. So the King had proclaimed that whoever could make her laugh should marry her.

When Simpleton heard this he took his goose, with all his following, before her, and when she saw these seven people running one behind another, she burst into fits of laughter and seemed as if she could never stop. Thereupon Simpleton asked her in marriage. But the King did not like him for a son-in-law and made all sorts of conditions. First, he said Simpleton must bring him a man who could drink up a cellarful of wine.

Then Simpleton at once thought of the little gray man who might be able to help him, and he went out to the forest to look for him. On the very spot where the tree that he had cut down had stood, he saw a man sitting with a very sad face.

Simpleton asked him what was the matter and he answered, "I am so thirsty, and I can't quench my thirst. I hate cold water, and I have already emptied a cask of wine. But what is a drop like that on a burning stone?"

"Well, there I can help you," said Simpleton. "Come with me and you shall soon have enough to drink."

He led him to the King's cellar, and the man started upon the great casks. And he drank and drank till his sides ached, and by the end of the day the cellar was empty.

Then again Simpleton demanded his bride. But the King was annoyed that a wretched fellow called "Simpleton" should have his daughter and he made new conditions. He was now to find a man who could eat up a mountain of bread.

Simpleton did not reflect long, but went straight to the forest. And there in the selfsame place sat a man tightening a strap round his body and making a miserable face.

He said, "I have eaten up a whole ovenful of rolls. But what is the good of that when anyone is as hungry as I am? I am never satisfied. I have to tighten my belt every day if I am not to die of hunger."

Simpleton was delighted and said, "Get up and come with me. You shall have enough to eat."

And he took him to the court, where the King had caused all the flour in the kingdom to be brought together and a huge mountain of bread to be baked. The man from the forest sat down before it and began to eat, and at the end of the day the whole mountain had disappeared.

Now for the third time Simpleton asked for his bride. But again the King tried to find an excuse, and demanded a ship which could sail on land as well as at sea.

"As soon as you sail up in it, you shall have my daughter," he said.

Simpleton went straight to the forest, and there sat the little gray man to whom he had given his cake. The little man said, "I have eaten and drunk for you, and now I will give you the ship, too. I do it all because you were merciful to me."

Then he gave him the ship which could sail on land as well as at sea, and when the King saw it he could no longer withhold his daughter. The marriage was celebrated, and at the King's death Simpleton inherited the kingdom, and lived long and happily with his wife.

The Blue Light

THERE was once a soldier who had served his king well and faithfully for many years, but on account of his many wounds he could serve no longer. The King said, "You can go home now. I have no further need for you, and I can only pay those who serve me."

The soldier did not know what to do for a living, and he went sadly away. He walked all day till he reached a wood, and there in the distance he saw a light. On approaching it, he found a house inhabited by a witch.

"Pray give me shelter for the night and something to eat and drink," he said, "or I shall perish."

"Oh ho!" she said. "Who gives anything to a runaway soldier, I should like to know? But I will be merciful and take you in if you will do something for me."

"What is it?" asked the soldier.

"I want you to dig up my garden tomorrow."

The soldier agreed to this and the next day he worked as hard as he could, but he could not finish before evening.

"I see," said the witch, "that you can do no more this evening. I will keep you one night more, and tomorrow you shall split up some logs for firewood."

The soldier took the whole day over this task, and in the evening the witch proposed that he should again stay another night.

"You shall only have a very light task tomorrow," she said. "There is an old dry well behind my house. My light, which burns blue and never goes out, has fallen into it and I want you to bring it back."

Next day the witch led him to the well, and let him down in a basket. He found the light and made a sign to be pulled up, but when he was near the top, the witch put out her hand and wanted to take it from him.

But seeing her evil designs he said, "No. I will not give you the light till I have both feet safe on dry land again."

The witch flew into a passion, let him fall back into the well again, and went away. The poor soldier fell on the damp ground without being harmed, and the blue light burnt as brightly as ever. But what was the good of that? He saw that he could not escape death.

He sat for some time feeling very sad. Then, happening to put his hand into his pocket, he found his pipe still half full. "This will be my last pleasure," he thought, as he lighted it at the blue light and began to smoke.

When the cloud of smoke he made cleared off a little, a tiny black man appeared before him and asked, "What orders, master?"

"What do you mean?" the soldier asked in amazement.

"I must do anything that you command," said the little man.

"Oh, if that is so," said the soldier, "get me out of this well first."

The little man took him by the hand and led him through an underground passage, but the soldier did not forget to take the blue light with him. On the way he showed the soldier all the treasures the witch had amassed

there, and the soldier took as much gold as he could carry.

When they reached the top he said to the little man, "Now go and bind the witch and take her before the judge."

Before long the witch came by, riding at a furious pace on a tomcat and screaming at the top of her voice.

The little man soon after appeared and said, "Everything is done as you commanded and the witch hangs on the gallows. What further orders have you, master?"

"Nothing at this moment," answered the soldier. "You can go home. Only be at hand when I call."

"You only have to light your pipe at the blue light and I will be there," said the little man, and then he vanished.

The soldier went back to the town that he had left and ordered some new clothes. Then he went to the best inn and told the landlord to give him the best rooms.

When he had taken possession, he summoned the little black man and said, "I served my king faithfully, but he sent me away to die of hunger. Now I will have my revenge."

"What do you wish me to do?" asked the little man.

"Late at night when the Princess is sleeping in her bed, bring her asleep to me and I will make her do menial service for me."

"It is an easy enough thing for me to do," said the little man. "But it will be a bad business for you if it happens."

As the clock struck twelve the door sprang open and the little man bore the maiden in.

"Ah ha! There you are!" cried the soldier. "Set about your work at once. Fetch the broom and sweep the floor."

When she had finished he sat down and ordered her to take off his boots. Then he threw them at her and made

her pick them up and clean them. She did everything he ordered without resistance, silently and with half-shut eyes.

At the first cockcrow, the little man carried her away to the royal palace and put her back in bed. In the morning when the Princess got up, she went to her father and told him that she had had an extraordinary dream.

"I was carried through the streets at lightning speed and taken to the room of a soldier, whom I had to serve as a maid and do all kinds of menial work. I had to sweep the room and clean his boots. Of course it was only a dream, and yet I am as tired this morning as if I had done it all."

"The dream could not have been true," said the King, "but I will give you a piece of advice. Fill your pocket with peas, and cut a little hole in it. Then if you are carried away again, they will drop out and leave a trail on the road."

When the King said this, the little man was standing by, invisible, and heard it all.

That night, when he again carried off the Princess, the peas certainly fell out of her pocket, but they were useless to trace her by, for the cunning little man had scattered peas all over the streets. Again the Princess had to perform her menial duties till cockcrow.

The next morning the King sent out people who were to find the trail. But they were unable to do so, because in every street the poor children were picking up peas and saying, "It must have rained peas in the night."

"We must devise a better plan," said the King. "Keep your shoes on when you go to bed, and before you come away from the place where you are taken, hide one of them. I shall be sure to find it."

The little man heard this plan also, and when the soldier told him to bring the Princess again, he advised him to put it off. He said he knew no further means against their

craftiness, and if the shoe was found it would be very dangerous for his master.

"Do what I tell you," answered the soldier. And for the third time the Princess was brought and made to work like a servant. But before leaving, she hid one of her shoes under the bed.

Next morning the King ordered the whole town to be searched for his daughter's shoe, and it was soon found in the soldier's room. He himself, at the request of the little man, had gone outside the gates, but before long he was seized and thrown into prison. In his flight he had forgotten his greatest treasures, the blue light and his gold. He had but one ducat in his pocket. As he stood loaded with chains at his window in the prison, he saw one of his comrades going by.

He tapped on the pane and said, "Be so good as to fetch me the little bundle I left behind at the inn and I will give you a ducat."

His comrade hurried off and brought him the bundle. As soon as the soldier was alone, he lighted his pipe and summoned the little man.

"Don't be afraid," he said to his master. "Go where they take you and let what will happen. Only take the blue light with you."

Next day a trial was held and, although the soldier had done nothing wicked, the judge sentenced him to death. When he was led out to execution he asked a last favor of the King.

"What is your wish?" asked the King.

"That I may smoke a last pipe."

"You may smoke three," answered the King. "But don't imagine that I will therefore grant you your life."

Then the soldier drew out his pipe and lighted it at the blue light.

As soon as a few rings of smoke arose, the little man appeared with a little cudgel in his hand and said, "What is my master's command?"

"Strike the false judge and his minions to the ground. And do not spare the King either for all his cruelty to me."

Then the little man flew about like lightning—zigzag, hither and thither! And whomever he touched with his cudgel fell to the ground and dared not move. The King was now seized with alarm. And begging on his knees that his life might be spared, he rendered up his kingdom and gave his daughter to the soldier to be his wife.

The Straw, the Coal, and the Bean

ONCE there was a poor old woman who lived in a village. She had collected a bundle of beans and was going to cook them. So she prepared a fire on her hearth, and to make it burn up quickly she lighted it with a handful of straw. When she threw the beans into the pot, one escaped her unnoticed and slipped onto the floor, where it lay by a straw. Soon afterwards a glowing coal jumped out of the fire and joined the others.

Then the straw began and said, "Little friends, how did you come here?"

The coal answered, "I have happily escaped the fire, and if I had not done so by force of will, my death would certainly have been a most cruel one. I should have been burnt to a cinder."

The bean said, "I also have escaped so far with a whole skin. But if the old woman had put me into the pot, I should have been pitilessly boiled down to broth like my comrades."

"Would a better fate have befallen me, then?" asked the straw. "The old woman packed all my brothers into the fire and smoke. Sixty of them were all done for at once. Fortunately I slipped through her fingers."

"What are we to do now, though?" asked the coal.

"My opinion is," said the bean, "that, as we have escaped death, we must all keep together like good comrades. And so that we may run no further risks, we had better quit the country."

This proposal pleased both the others, and they set out together. Before long they came to a little stream where there was neither path nor bridge, and they did not know how to get over.

The straw at last had an idea and said, "I will throw myself over and then you can walk across upon me like a bridge."

So the straw stretched himself across from one side to the other, and the coal, which was of a fiery nature, tripped gaily over the newly built bridge. But when it got to the middle and heard the water rushing below, it was frightened and remained speechless, not daring to go any farther. The straw, beginning to burn, broke in two and fell into the stream. The coal, falling with it, fizzled out in the water. The bean, who had cautiously remained on the bank, could not help laughing over the whole business, and having begun could not stop, but laughed till she split her sides. Now all would have been up with her had not, fortunately, a wandering tailor been taking a rest by the stream. As he had a sympathethic heart, he brought out a needle and thread and stitched her up again, but as he used black thread all beans have a black seam to this day.

Fundevogel

THERE was once a forester who went into the woods to hunt, and he heard a cry like that of a little child. He followed the sound and at last came to a big tree where a tiny child was sitting high up on one of the top branches. The mother had gone to sleep under the tree, and a bird of prey, seeing the child on her lap, had flown down and carried it off in its beak to the top of the tree.

The forester climbed the tree and brought down the child, thinking to himself, "I will take it home, and bring it up with my own little Lina."

So he took it home, and the two children were brought up together. The foundling was called Fundevogel, because it had been found by a bird. Fundevogel and Lina were so fond of each other that they could not bear to be out of each other's sight.

Now the forester had an old cook, who one evening took two pails and began carrying water. She did not go once but many times, backwards and forwards to the well.

Lina saw this and said, "Dear me, Sanna, why are you carrying so much water?"

"If you will not tell anyone, I will tell you why."

Lina said no, she would not tell anyone.

So then the cook said, "Tomorrow morning early, when the forester goes out hunting, I am going to boil the water. And when it bubbles in the kettle, I am going to throw Fundevogel into it and boil him."

Next morning the forester got up very early and went out hunting, leaving the children still in bed.

Then said Lina to Fundevogel, "Never forsake me, and I will never forsake you."

And Fundevogel answered, "I will never forsake you."

Then Lina said, "I must tell you now. Old Sanna brought in so many pails of water last night that I asked her what she was doing. She said if I would not tell anybody she would tell me what it was for. So I promised not to tell anybody, and she said that in the morning, when our father had gone out hunting, she would fill the kettle, and when it was boiling she would throw you into it and boil you. Now we must get up quickly, dress ourselves, and run away."

So the children got up, dressed quickly, and left the house.

When the water boiled, the cook went to their bedroom to fetch Fundevogel to throw him into it. But when she entered the room and went to the bed, both the children were gone. She was terribly frightened and said to herself, "Whatever am I to say to the forester when he comes home and finds the children gone? We must hurry after them and get them back." So the cook dispatched three menservants to catch up with the children and bring them back.

The children were sitting near a wood, and when they saw the three men a great way off, Lina said to Fundevogel, "Do not forsake me, and I will never forsake you."

And Fundevogel answered, "I will never forsake you as long as I live."

Then Lina said, "You must turn into a rosebush, and I will be a rosebud upon it."

When the three men reached the wood, they found nothing but a rosebush with one rosebud on it. No children were to be seen. They said to each other, "There is nothing to be done here."

So they went home and told the cook that they had seen nothing whatever but a rosebush with one rosebud on it.

The old cook scolded them and said, "You boobies, you ought to have hacked the rosebush to pieces, broken off the bud, and brought it home to me. Off with you at once and do it." So they had to start off again on their search.

But the children saw them a long way off and Lina said to Fundevogel, "Do not forsake me, and I will never forsake you."

Fundevogel said, "I will never forsake you as long as I live."

Then said Lina, "You must become a church, and I will be the chandelier in it."

Now when the three men came up they found nothing but a church with a chandelier in it. And they said to each other, "What are we to do here? We had better go home again."

When they reached the house, the cook asked if they had not found anything. They said, "Nothing but a church with a chandelier in it."

"You fools!" screamed the cook. "Why did you not destroy the church and bring me the chandelier?" Then the old cook put her best foot foremost and started herself with the three men in pursuit of the children.

But the children saw the three men in the distance, and the old cook waddling behind them. Then said Lina, "Fundevogel, do not forsake me, and I will never forsake you."

And he said, "I will never forsake you as long as I live."

Lina said, "You must become a pond, and I will be the duck swimming upon it."

When the cook reached the pond, she lay down beside it to drink it up, but the duck swam quickly forward, seized her head with his bill, and dragged her under water. So the old witch was drowned.

Then the children went home together as happy as possible, and if they are not dead yet, then they are still alive.

Karl Katz

In the midst of the Hartz forests there is a high mountain of which the neighbors tell all sorts of stories: how the goblins and fairies dance on it by night, and how the old Emperor Redbeard holds his court there and sits on his marble throne, with his long beard sweeping on the ground.

A great many years ago there lived in a village at the foot of this mountain one Karl Katz. Now Karl was a goatherd, and every morning he drove his flock to feed upon the green spots that are here and there found on the mountainside. In the evening he sometimes thought it too late to drive his charges home, so then he would shut them up in a spot in the woods, where the old ruined walls of some castle that had long ago been deserted were left standing. They were high enough to form a fold, in which he could count his goats and let them rest for the night.

One evening he found that the prettiest goat of his flock had vanished soon after they were driven into this fold. He searched everywhere for it in vain but, to his surprise and delight, when he counted his flock in the morning what should he see but his lost goat! Again and again the same thing happened.

At last he thought he would watch still more narrowly. And having looked carefully over the old walls, he found a narrow doorway through which it seemed that his favorite made her way. Karl followed and found a path leading downwards through a cleft in the rocks. On he went, scrambling as well as he could, down the side of the rock and at last came to the mouth of a cave, where he lost sight of his goat. Just then he saw that his faithful dog was not with him. He whistled but no dog was there. He was therefore forced to go into the cave and try to find his goat by himself.

He groped his way for a while and at last came to a place where a little light found its way in. And there he wondered not a little to find his goat employing itself, very much at its ease in the cavern, in eating corn which kept dropping from some place over its head. He went up and looked about him to see where all this corn, that rattled about his ears like a hailstorm, could come from, but all overhead was dark and he could find no clew to this strange business.

At last, as he stood listening, he thought he heard the neighing and stamping of horses. He listened again; it was plainly so. And after a while he was sure that horses were feeding above him and that the corn fell from their mangers. What could these horses be, which were thus kept in the clefts of rocks where none but the goat's foot ever trod? There must be people of some sort or other living here, and who could they be? Was it safe to trust himself in such company? Karl pondered awhile but his wonder only grew greater and greater, when of a sudden he heard his own name, "Karl Katz!" echo through the cavern. He turned round, but could see nothing. "Karl Katz!" again sounded sharply in his ears. And soon out came a little dwarfish page with a high-peaked hat and a scarlet cloak, from a dark corner at one end of the cave.

The dwarf nodded and beckoned him to follow. Karl thought he should first like to know a little about who it was that thus sought his company. He asked, but the dwarf shook his head, answering not a word, and again beckoned him to follow. He did so, and winding his way through ruins he soon heard rolling overhead what sounded like peals of thunder echoing among the rocks. The noise grew louder and louder as he went on, and at last he came to a courtyard surrounded by old ivy-grown walls. The spot seemed to be the bosom of a little valley. Above rose on every hand high masses of rock. Wide-branching trees threw their arms overhead so that nothing but a glimmering twilight made its way through. And here on the cool smooth-shaven turf, Karl saw twelve strange old figures amusing themselves very sedately with a game of ninepins.

Their dress did not seem altogether strange to Karl, for in the church of the town whither he went every week to market there was an old monument, with figures of queer old knights upon it, dressed in the very same fashion. Not a word fell from any of their lips. They moved about soberly and gravely, each taking his turn at the game; but the oldest of them ordered Karl Katz, by dumb signs, to busy himself in setting up the pins as they knocked them down. At first his knees trembled, and he hardly dared snatch a stolen sidelong glance at the long beards and old-fashioned dresses of the worthy knights. But he soon saw that as each knight played out his game he went to his seat and there took a hearty draught at a flagon, which the dwarf kept filled and which sent up the smell of the richest old wine.

Little by little Karl got bolder, and at last he plucked up his heart so far as to beg the dwarf, by signs, to let him too take his turn at the flagon. The dwarf gave it to him with a grave bow, and Karl thought he had never tasted anything

half so good. This gave him new strength for his work, and as often as he flagged at all he turned to the same kind friend for help in his need.

Which was tired first, he or the knights, Karl never could tell, or whether the wine got the better of his head. What he knew was that sleep at last overpowered him, and that when he awoke he found himself stretched out upon the old spot within the walls where he had folded his flock, and saw that the bright sun was high up in the heavens. The same green turf was spread beneath, and the same tottering ivy-clad walls surrounded him. He rubbed his eyes and called his dog, but neither dog nor goat was to be seen. And when he looked about him again, the grass seemed to be longer under his feet than it was yesterday. And trees hung over his head, which he had either never seen before or had quite forgotten. Shaking his head and hardly knowing whether he was in his right mind, he got up and stretched himself. Somehow or other his joints felt stiffer than they were. "It serves me right," said he. "This comes of sleeping out of one's own bed." Little by little he recollected his evening's sport and licked his lips as he thought of the charming wine he had taken so much of. "But who," thought he, "can those people be that come to this odd place to play ninepins?"

His first step was to look for the doorway through which he had followed his goat, but to his astonishment not the least trace of an opening of any sort was to be seen. There stood the wall, without chink or crack big enough for a rat to pass through. Again he paused and scratched his head. His hat was full of holes. "Why, it was new last Shrovetide!" said he. By chance his eyes fell next on his shoes, which were almost new when he last left home. But now they looked so old that they were likely to fall to pieces before he could get home. All his clothes seemed in

the same sad plight. The more he looked, the more he pondered, and the more he was at a loss to know what could have happened to him.

At length he turned round and left the old walls to look for his flock. Slow and out of heart he wound his way among the mountain steeps, through paths where his flocks were wont to wander. Still not a goat was to be seen. Again he whistled and called his dog, but no dog came. Below him in the plain lay the village where his home was, so at length he took the downward path and set out with a heavy heart and a faltering step in search of his flock.

"Surely," said he, "I shall soon meet some neighbor who can tell me where my goats are." But the people who met him as he drew near to the village were all unknown to him. They were not even dressed as his neighbors were, and they seemed as if they hardly spoke the same tongue. When he eagerly asked each, as he came up, after his goats, they only stared at him and stroked their chins. At last he did the same too—and what was his wonder to find that his beard was grown at least a foot long!

"The world," said he to himself, "is surely turned upside down. If not, I must be bewitched." Yet he knew the mountain, as he turned round again and looked back on its woody heights. And he knew the houses and cottages also, with their little gardens, as he entered the village. All were where he had always known them to be. And he heard some children, too (as a traveler that passed by was asking his way), call the village by the very same name he had always known it to bear.

Again he shook his head and went straight through the village to his own cottage. Alas, it looked sadly out of repair. The windows were broken, the door off its hinges, and in the courtyard lay an unknown child in a ragged dress, playing with a rough, toothless old dog, whom he

thought he ought to know, but who snarled and barked in his face when he called to him. He went in at the open doorway, but he found all so dreary and empty that he staggered out again like a drunken man, and called his wife and children loudly by their names. But no one heard —at least no one answered him.

A crowd of women and children soon flocked around the strange-looking man with the long gray beard, and all broke upon him at once with the questions, "Who are you?" "Who is it that you want?" It seemed to him so odd to ask other people, at his own door, after his wife and children that, in order to get rid of the gaping crowd, he named the first man that came into his head.

"Hans the blacksmith," said he. Most held their tongues and stared, but at last an old woman said, "He went these seven years ago to a place that you will not reach today."

"Fritz the tailor, then."

"Heaven rest his soul!" said an old beldam upon crutches. "He has lain these ten years in a house that he'll never leave."

Karl Katz looked at the old woman again and shuddered, as he knew her to be one of the old gossips, but saw she had a strangely altered face. All wish to ask further questions was gone, but at last a young woman made her way through the gaping throng. She had a baby in one arm and a little girl of about three years old clinging to her other hand. All three looked the very image of his own wife.

"What is your name?" he asked wildly.

"Liese," said she.

"And your father's?"

"Karl Katz, heaven bless him!" said she. "But, poor man, he is lost and gone. It is now full twenty years since we sought for him day and night on the mountain. His dog

and his flock came back, but he never was heard of any more. I was then seven years old."

Poor Karl could restrain himself no longer. "I am Karl Katz and no other," said he, as he took the child from his daughter's arms and kissed it over and over again.

All stood gaping, hardly knowing what to say or think, when old Stropken the schoolmaster hobbled by and took a long and close look at him. "Karl Katz! Karl Katz!" said he slowly. "Why, it *is* Karl Katz sure enough. There is my own mark upon him. There is the scar over his right eye that I gave him myself one day with my oak stick."

Then several others also cried out, "Yes, it is! It is Karl Katz. Welcome, neighbor, welcome home!"

"But where," said or thought all, "can an honest steady fellow like you have been these twenty years?"

And now the whole village had flocked around. The children laughed, the dogs barked, and all were glad to see neighbor Karl home alive and well. As to where he had been for the twenty years, that was a part of the story at which Karl shrugged up his shoulders. For he never could very well explain it, and he seemed to think the less that was said about it the better. But it was plain enough that what dwelt most in his memory was the noble wine that had tickled his mouth while the knights played their game of ninepins.

The Table, the Ass, and the Stick

THERE was once an old tailor who had three sons and one goat. And as the goat nourished them all with her milk, she was obliged to have good food, and so she was led every day down to the willows by the waterside. And this business the sons did in turn. One day the eldest took the goat to the churchyard, where the best sprouts are, that she might eat her fill and gambol about.

In the evening, when it was time to go home, he said, "Well, goat, have you had enough?"

The goat answered:

> *"I am so full,*
> *I cannot pull*
> *Another blade of grass—ba! baa!"*

"Then come home," said the youth, and he fastened a string to her, led her to her stall, and fastened her up.

"Now," said the tailor, "has the goat had her proper food?"

"Oh," answered the son, "she is so full, she no more can pull."

But the father, wishing to see for himself, went out to the stall, stroked his dear goat, and said, "My dear goat, are you full?"

And the goat answered:

> *"How can I be full?*
> *There was nothing to pull*
> *Though I looked all about me—ba! baa!"*

"What is this that I hear?" cried the tailor. And he ran and called out to the youth, "Oh, you liar, to say that the goat was full, and she was hungry all the time!" And in his wrath he took up his yardstick and drove his son out of the house with many blows.

The next day came the turn of the second son, and he found a fine place in the garden hedge where there were good green sprouts, and the goat ate them all up...

In the evening, when he came to lead her home, he said, "Well, goat, have you had enough?"

And the goat answered:

> *"I am so full,*
> *I cannot pull*
> *Another blade of grass—ba! baa!"*

"Then come home," said the youth, and led her home and tied her up.

"Now," said the old tailor, "has the goat had her proper food?"

"Oh," answered the son, "she is so full, she no more can pull."

The tailor, not feeling satisfied, went out to the stall and said, "My dear goat, are you really full?"

And the goat answered:

> *"How can I be full?*
> *There was nothing to pull,*
> *Though I looked all about me—ba! baa!"*

"The good-for-nothing rascal," cried the tailor, "to let the dear creature go hungry!" And running back, he chased the youth with his yardstick out of the house.

Then came the turn of the third son, who, meaning to make all sure, found some shrubs with the finest sprouts possible and left the goat to eat them.

In the evening, when he came to lead her home, he said, "Well, goat, are you full?" And the goat answered:

> *"I am so full,*
> *I cannot pull*
> *Another blade of grass—ba! baa!"*

"Then come home," said the youth. And he took her to her stall and fastened her up.

"Now," said the old tailor, "has the goat had her proper food?"

"Oh," answered the son, "she is so full, she no more can pull."

But the tailor, not trusting his word, went to the goat and said, "My dear goat, are you really full?"

The malicious animal answered:

> *"How can I be full?*
> *There was nothing to pull,*
> *Though I looked all about me—ba! baa!"*

"Oh, the wretches!" cried the tailor. "The one as good for nothing and careless as the other. I will no longer have such fools about me." And rushing back, in his wrath he laid about him with his yardstick and belabored his son's back so unmercifully that he ran away out of the house.

So the old tailor was left alone with the goat. The next day he went out to the stall and let out the goat, saying, "Come, my dear creature, I will take you myself to the willows."

So he led her by the string and brought her to the green hedges and pastures where there was plenty of food to her taste, and said to her, "Now for once you can eat to your heart's content."

He left her there till the evening. Then he returned and said, "Well, goat, are you full?"

She answered:

> *"I am so full,*
> *I cannot pull*
> *Another blade of grass—ba! baa!"*

"Then come home," said the tailor. And leading her to her stall, he fastened her up.

Before he left her he turned once more, saying, "Now then, for once you are full."

But the goat actually cried:

> *"How can I be full?*
> *There was nothing to pull,*
> *Though I looked all about me—ba! baa!"*

When the tailor heard that, he marveled, and saw at once that his three sons had been sent away without reason.

"Wait a minute," cried he, "you ungrateful creature! It is not enough merely to drive you away—I will teach you to show your face again among honorable tailors."

So in haste he went and fetched his razor, and seizing the goat he shaved her head as smooth as the palm of his hand. And as the yardstick was too honorable a weapon, he took the whip and fetched her such a crack that with many a jump and spring she ran away.

The tailor felt very sad as he sat alone in his house, and he would willingly have had his sons back again, but no one knew where they had gone, so he could not send for them.

The eldest son, when he was driven from home, apprenticed himself to a joiner and applied himself diligently to his trade. And when the time came for him to travel, his master gave him a little table, nothing much to look at and

made of common wood, but it had one great quality. When anyone set it down and said, "Table, be covered!" all at once the good little table had a clean cloth on it, and a plate and knife and fork, and dishes with roast and boiled meat, and a large glass of red wine sparkling so as to cheer the heart. The young apprentice thought he was set up for life and went merrily out into the world, and he never cared whether an inn were good or bad or whether he could get anything to eat there or not. When he was hungry, it did not matter where he was, whether in the fields, in the woods, or in a meadow, he set down his table and said, "Be covered!" And there he was provided with everything that heart could wish. At last it occurred to him that he would go back to his father, whose wrath might by this time have subsided, and perhaps because of the wonderful table he might receive him again gladly. It happened that one evening during his journey home he came to an inn that was quite full of guests, who bade him welcome and asked him to sit down with them and eat, as otherwise he would have found some difficulty in getting anything.

"No," answered the young joiner, "I could not think of depriving you. You had much better be my guests."

Then they laughed and thought he must be joking. But he brought his little wooden table and put it in the middle of the room, and said, "Table, be covered!" Immediately it was set with food much better than the landlord had been able to provide.

"Fall to, good friends!" said the joiner. And the guests, when they saw how it was, needed no second asking, but taking up knife and fork fell to valiantly. And what seemed most wonderful was that when a dish was empty, immediately a full one stood in its place.

All the while the landlord stood in a corner and watched all that went on. He did not know at all what to say about

it but thought, "Such cooking as that would make my inn prosper."

The joiner and his companions kept it up very merrily until late at night. At last they went to sleep, and the young joiner, going to bed, left his wishing table standing against the wall. The landlord, however, could not sleep for thinking of the table. And he remembered that there was in his lumber room an old table very like it, so he fetched it, took away the joiner's table, and left the other in its place. The next morning the joiner paid his reckoning, took up the table, not dreaming that he was carrying off the wrong one, and went on his way. About noon he reached home, and his father received him with great joy.

"Now, my dear son, what have you learned?" said he.

"I have learned to be a joiner, father," he answered.

"That is a good trade," returned the father. "But what have you brought back with you from your travels?"

"The best thing I've got, father, is this little table," said he.

The tailor looked at it on all sides and said, "You have certainly produced no masterpiece. It is a shabby old table."

"But it is a very wonderful one," answered the son. "When I set it down and tell it to be covered, at once the finest meats are standing on it, and wine so good that it cheers the heart. Let us invite all the friends and neighbors that they may feast and enjoy themselves, for the table will provide enough for all."

When the company was all assembled, he put his table in the middle of the room and said, "Table, be covered!"

But the table never stirred, and remained just as empty as any other table that does not understand talking. When the poor joiner saw that the table remained unfurnished, he felt ashamed to stand there like a fool. The company

[217]

laughed at him freely, and were obliged to return unfilled and uncheered to their houses. The father gathered his pieces together and returned to his tailoring, and the son went to work under another master. The second son had bound himself apprentice to a miller. And when his time was up, his master said to him, "As you have behaved yourself so well, I will give you an ass of a remarkable kind. He will draw no cart and carry no sack."

"What is the good of him then?" asked the young apprentice.

"He spits out gold," answered the miller. "If you put a cloth before him and say, 'Bricklebrit,' out come gold pieces."

"That is a capital thing!" said the apprentice, and thanking his master he went out into the world.

Whenever he wanted gold he had only to say, "Bricklebrit," to his ass, and there was a shower of gold pieces. And so he had no cares as he traveled about. Wherever he went he lived on the best, and the dearer the better, as his purse was always full. And when he had been looking about the world a long time, he thought he would go and seek out his father, who would perhaps forget his anger and receive him kindly because of his gold-ass. And it happened that he came to lodge in the same inn where his brother's table had been exchanged.

He was leading his ass, and the landlord was about to take the ass from him to tie it up, but the young apprentice said, "Don't trouble yourself, old fellow. I will take him into the stable myself and tie him up."

The landlord thought this was very strange, and he never supposed that a man who was accustomed to look after his ass himself could have much to spend. But when the stranger, feeling in his pocket, took out two gold pieces and told him to get him something good for supper, the land-

lord stared, and ran and fetched the best that could be got.

After supper the guest called for the reckoning, and the landlord, wanting to get all the profit he could, said that it would amount to two gold pieces more. The apprentice felt in his pocket, but his gold had come to an end.

"Wait a moment, landlord," said he. "I will go and fetch some money." And he went out of the room, carrying the tablecloth with him.

The landlord could not tell what to make of it, and, curious to know his proceedings, slipped after him. And as the guest shut the stable door, he peeped in through a knothole. Then he saw how the stranger spread the cloth before the ass, saying, "Bricklebrit," and directly the ass spat out gold, which rained upon the ground.

"Dear me!" said the landlord. "That is an easy way of getting ducats. A purse of money like that is no bad thing."

After that the guest paid his reckoning and went to bed. But the landlord slipped down to the stable in the middle of the night, led the gold-ass away, and tied up another ass in his place. Early the next morning the apprentice set forth with his ass, never doubting that it was the right one. By noon he came to his father's house, who rejoiced to see him again and received him gladly.

"What trade have you taken up, my son?" he asked.

"I am a miller, dear father," answered he.

"What have you brought home from your travels?" continued the father.

"Nothing but an ass," answered the son.

"We have plenty of asses here," said the father. "You had much better have brought me a nice goat!"

"Yes," answered the son, "but this is no common ass. When I say, 'Bricklebrit,' the good creature spits out a whole clothful of gold pieces. Let me call all the neighbors together. I will make rich people of them all."

"That will be fine!" said the tailor. "Then I need labor no more at my needle.'" And he rushed out himself and called the neighbors together. As soon as they were all assembled, the miller called out to them to make room, and brought in the ass and spread his cloth before him.

"Now, pay attention!" said he, and he cried, "Bricklebrit!" But no gold pieces came, and that showed that the animal was no more scientific than any other ass.

So the poor miller made a long face when he saw that he had been taken in, and begged pardon of the neighbors, who all went home as poor as they had come. And there was nothing for it but that the old man must take to his needle again and that the young one should take service with a miller.

The third brother had bound himself apprentice to a turner. And as turning is a very ingenious handicraft, it took him a long time to learn it. His brothers told him in a letter how badly things had gone with them, and how on the last night of their travels the landlord deprived them of their treasures. When the young turner had learned his trade and was ready to travel, his master, to reward him for his good conduct, gave him a sack and told him that there was a stick inside it.

"I can hang up the sack, and it may be very useful to me," said the young man. "But what is the good of the stick?"

"I will tell you," answered the master. "If anyone does you any harm, and you say, 'Stick, out of the sack!' the stick will jump out upon them and will belabor them so soundly that they shall not be able to move. And it will not stop until you say, 'Stick, into the sack!' "

The apprentice thanked him and took up the sack and started on his travels, and when anyone attacked him he would say, "Stick, out of the sack!" And directly out

jumped the stick and dealt a shower of blows on the coat or jerkin, and the back beneath, which quickly ended the affair. One evening the young turner reached the inn where his two brothers had been taken in. He laid his knapsack on the table and began to describe all the wonderful things he had seen in the world.

"Yes," said he, "you may talk of your self-spreading table, your gold-supplying ass, and so forth. Very good, things, I do not deny, but they are nothing in comparison with the treasure that I have acquired and carry with me in that sack!"

Then the landlord opened his ears.

"What in the world can it be?" thought he. "Very likely the sack is full of precious stones. And I have a perfect right to it, for all good things come in threes."

When bedtime came, the guest stretched himself on a bench and put his sack under his head for a pillow. And the landlord, when he thought the young man was sound asleep, came, stooped down, pulled gently at the sack so as to remove it cautiously, and put another in its place. The turner had only been waiting for this to happen. And just as the landlord was giving a last courageous pull, he cried, "Stick, out of the sack!" Out flew the stick directly and laid to heartily on the landlord's back. And in vain he begged for mercy! The louder he cried, the harder the stick beat time on his back, until he fell exhausted to the ground.

Then the turner said, "If you do not give me the table and the ass directly, this game shall begin all over again."

"Oh dear!" cried the landlord, quite overcome. "I will gladly give it all back again if you will only make this terrible goblin go back into the sack."

Then said the young man, "I will be generous instead of just. But beware!" Then he cried, "Stick, into the sack!"

The next morning the turner set out with the table and

the ass on his way home to his father. The tailor was very glad indeed to see him again and asked him what he had learned abroad.

"My dear father," answered he, "I am become a turner."

"A very ingenious handicraft," said the father. "And what have you brought with you from your travels?"

"A very valuable thing, dear father," answered the son. "A stick in a sack!"

"What?" cried the father. "A stick! The thing is not worth so much when you can cut one from any tree."

"But it is not a common stick, dear father," said the young man. "When I say, 'Stick, out of the sack!' out jumps the stick upon anyone who means harm to me, and makes him dance, and does not leave off till he is beaten to the earth and asks pardon. Just look here! With this stick I have recovered the table and the ass which the thieving landlord took from my two brothers. Now let them both be sent for, and bid all the neighbors too, and they shall eat and drink to their hearts' content, and I will fill their pockets with gold."

The old tailor could not quite believe in such a thing, but he called his sons and all the neighbors together.

Then the turner brought in the ass, opened a cloth before him, and said to his brother, "Now, my dear brother, speak to him."

And the miller said, "Bricklebrit!" And immediately the cloth was covered with gold pieces, until they had all got more than they could carry away. (I tell you this because it is a pity you were not there.)

Then the turner set down the table and said, "Now, my dear brother, speak to it."

And the joiner said, "Table, be covered!" And directly it was covered and set forth plentifully with the richest dishes. Then they held such a feast as had never taken place in

the tailor's house before, and the whole company remained through the night, merry and content.

After that the tailor locked up in a cupboard his needle and thread, his yardstick and goose, and lived ever after with his three sons in great joy and splendor.

But what became of the goat, the unlucky cause of the tailor's sons being driven out? I will tell you. She felt so ashamed of her bald head that she ran into a fox's hole and hid herself. When the fox came home he saw two great eyes staring at him out of the darkness, and was very frightened and ran away.

A bear met him, and seeing that he looked very disturbed asked him, "What is the matter, brother fox, that you should look like that?"

"Oh dear," answered the fox, "a horrible beast is sitting in my hole, and he stared at me with fiery eyes."

"We will soon drive him out," said the bear, and went to the hole and looked in. But when he caught sight of the fiery eyes he likewise felt great terror seize him, and not wishing to have anything to do with so grisly a beast, he made off.

He was soon met by a bee, who remarked that he had not a very courageous air and said to him, "Bear, you have a very depressed countenance. What has become of your high spirit?"

"You may well ask," answered the bear. "In the fox's hole there sits a beast with fiery eyes, and we cannot drive him out."

The bee answered, "I know you despise me, bear. I am a poor feeble little creature, but I think I can help you."

So she flew into the fox's hole and, settling on the goat's smooth-shaven head, stung her so severely that she jumped up crying, "Ba-baa!" and ran out like mad into the world. And to this hour no one knows where she ran.

Red Riding Hood

ONCE upon a time there was a sweet little maiden who was loved by all who knew her, but she was especially dear to her grandmother, who did not know how to make enough of the child. Once she gave her a little red velvet cloak. It was so becoming and she liked it so much that she would never wear anything else, and so she got the name of Red Riding Hood.

One day her mother said to her, "Come here, Red Riding Hood! Take this cake and bottle of wine to grandmother. She is weak and ill, and they will do her good. Go quickly, before it gets hot. And don't loiter by the way, or run, or you will fall down and break the bottle, and there will be no wine for grandmother. When you get there, don't forget to say 'Good morning' prettily, without staring about you."

"I will do just as you tell me," Red Riding Hood promised her mother.

Her grandmother lived away in the wood, a good half hour from the village. When she got to the wood she met a wolf, but Red Riding Hood did not know what a wicked animal he was, so she was not a bit afraid of him.

"Good morning, Red Riding Hood," he said.

"Good morning, Red Riding Hood," said the wolf

"Good morning, wolf," she answered.

"Whither away so early, Red Riding Hood?"

"To grandmother's."

"What have you got in your basket?"

"Cake and wine. We baked yesterday, so I'm taking a cake to grandmother. She wants something to make her well."

"Where does your grandmother live, Red Riding Hood?"

"A good quarter of an hour farther into the wood. Her house stands under three big oak trees, near a hedge of nut trees which you must know," said Red Riding Hood.

The wolf thought, "This tender little creature will be a plump morsel! She will be nicer than the old woman. I must be cunning and snap them both up."

He walked along with Red Riding Hood for a while. Then he said, "Look at the pretty flowers, Red Riding Hood. Why don't you look about you? I don't believe you even hear the birds sing. You are just as solemn as if you were going to school. Everything else is so gay out here in the woods."

Red Riding Hood raised her eyes, and when she saw the sunlight dancing through the trees, and all the bright flowers, she thought, "I'm sure grandmother would be pleased if I took her a bunch of fresh flowers. It is still quite early. I shall have plenty of time to pick them."

So she left the path and wandered off among the trees to pick the flowers. Each time she picked one, she always saw another prettier one farther on. So she went deeper and deeper into the forest.

In the meantime the wolf went straight off to the grandmother's cottage and knocked at the door.

"Who is there?"

"Red Riding Hood, bringing you a cake and some wine. Open the door!"

"Lift the latch," called out the old woman. "I am too weak to get up."

The wolf lifted the latch and the door sprang open. He went straight in and up to the bed without saying a word, and ate up the poor old woman. Then he put on her nightdress and nightcap, got into bed and drew the curtains.

Red Riding Hood ran about picking flowers till she could carry no more, and then she remembered her grandmother again. She was astonished when she got to the house to find the door open, and when she entered the room everything seemed so strange.

She felt quite frightened but she did not know why. "Generally I like coming to see grandmother so much," she thought. "Good morning, grandmother," she cried. But she received no answer.

Then she went up to the bed and drew the curtain back. There lay her grandmother, but she had drawn her cap down over her face and she looked very odd.

"Oh grandmother, what big ears you have," she said.

"The better to hear you with, my dear."

"Grandmother, what big eyes you have."

"The better to see you with, my dear."

"What big hands you have, grandmother."

"The better to catch hold of you with, my dear."

"But grandmother, what big teeth you have."

"The better to eat you up with, my dear."

Hardly had the wolf said this than he made a spring out of bed and swallowed poor little Red Riding Hood. When the wolf had satisfied himself he went back to bed, and he was soon snoring loudly.

A huntsman went past the house and thought, "How loudly the old lady is snoring. I must see if there is anything the matter with her."

So he went into the house and up to the bed, where he found the wolf fast asleep. "Do I find you here, you old sinner!" he said. "Long enough have I sought you!"

He raised his gun to shoot, when it just occurred to him that perhaps the wolf had eaten up the old lady, and that she might still be saved. So he took a knife and began cutting open the sleeping wolf. At the first cut he saw the little red cloak, and after a few more slashes, the little girl sprang out and cried, "Oh, how frightened I was! It was so dark inside the wolf." Next the old grandmother came out, alive but hardly able to breathe.

Red Riding Hood brought some big stones with which they filled the wolf, so that when he woke up and tried to spring away, the stones dragged him back and he fell down dead.

They were all quite happy now. The huntsman skinned the wolf and took the skin home. The grandmother ate the cake and drank the wine which Red Riding Hood had brought, and she soon felt quite strong. Red Riding Hood thought to herself, "I will never again wander off into the forest as long as I live, when my mother forbids it."

Snow-White and Rose-Red

THERE was once a poor widow who lived alone in her hut with her two children, who were called Snow-White and Rose-Red because they were like the flowers which bloomed on two rosebushes which grew before the cottage. These two children were as good, happy, industrious, and amiable as any in the world; only Snow-White was more quiet and gentle than Rose-Red.

Rose-Red would run and jump about the meadows, seeking flowers and catching butterflies, while Snow-White sat at home helping her mother to keep house, or reading to her if there were nothing else to do.

The two children loved each other so dearly that they always walked hand in hand when they went out together, and when Snow-White said, "We will never separate from each other," Rose-Red replied, "Not so long as we live!" And their mother said, "What each girl has, she must share with the other."

Often they ran deep into the forest and gathered wild berries, but no beast ever harmed them. For the hare

would eat cabbage leaves out of their hands, the fawn grazed by their side, the goats frisked about them in play, and the birds sat perched on the boughs singing as if nobody were near.

No accident ever befell them, and if they stayed late in the forest and night came upon them, they used to lie down on the moss and sleep till morning. And because their mother knew they would do so, she felt no concern about them.

Once when they had passed the night in the forest and the dawn of morning awoke them, they saw a beautiful child dressed in shining white dress sitting near their couch. The child rose up and looked at them kindly, but without saying anything went into the forest. And when the children looked round they saw that they had slept close to the edge of a pit, into which they would have certainly fallen had they walked a couple of steps farther in the dark. Their mother told them the figure they had seen was doubtless the good angel who watches over children.

Snow-White and Rose-Red kept their mother's cottage so clean that it was a pleasure to look in it. Every morning in the summertime Rose-Red would put the house in order, and then lay a wreath of flowers at her mother's bed before she woke up, in which she always placed a bud from each rose tree. Every winter in the morning Snow-White would light the fire and put the kettle on to boil, and although the kettle was made of copper it shone like gold because it was polished so well.

In the evening when the flakes of snow were falling, the mother would say, "Go, Snow-White, and bolt the door." And then they would sit down at the hearth, and the mother would put on her spectacles and read out of a great book, while the two girls sat spinning. By their side

lay a little lamb, and on a perch behind them a white dove sat with its head under a wing.

One evening when they were sitting comfortably together, there came a knock at the door, as if someone wished to come in.

"Make haste, Rose-Red," cried her mother. "Make haste and open the door. Perhaps there is some traveler outside who needs shelter."

So Rose-Red went and drew the bolt and opened the door, thinking it was some poor man outside. But instead a great bear poked his black head in. Rose-Red cried out and ran back, the little lamb bleated, the dove fluttered on her perch, and Snow-White hid herself behind her mother's bed.

The bear, however, began to speak and said, "Do not be afraid. I will do you no harm. I am half frozen and only wish to come in and warm myself."

"Poor bear!" cried the mother. "Come in and lie down by the fire, but take care you do not burn your coat." Then she continued, "Come here, Rose-Red and Snow-White. The bear will not harm you. He means well."

So they both came back, and at last the lamb and the dove came near and were no longer afraid of him.

"Come here, children," said the bear, as he entered. "Come and knock the snow off my coat."

So they brought the broom and swept him clean. Then he stretched himself before the fire and growled cheerfully and comfortably, and in a little while the children became friendly enough to play tricks with their unwieldy guest. They tugged at his long shaggy hair, put their feet against his back and rolled him about, and even ventured to hit him with a hazel stick, laughing when he grumbled. The bear bore all their play in good temper, and only when they hit too hard he cried out:

"Leave me my life, you children,
Snow-White and Rose-Red,
Or you'll never wed."

When bedtime came and the others had gone to bed, the mother said to the bear, "You may sleep here by the hearth if you like, and then you will be safe from the cold and the bad weather."

As soon as day came the two children let the bear out again, and he trotted away over the snow, and every evening afterwards he came back at a certain hour. He would lie down on the hearth and allow the children to play with him as much as they liked. And at last they became so used to him that the door was left unbolted till their black friend had arrived.

But as soon as spring returned and everything out of doors was green again, the bear said to Snow-White one morning, "Now I must leave, and I cannot return during the whole summer."

"Where are you going, then, dear bear?" asked Snow-White.

"I must go into the forest and guard my treasures from the evil dwarfs. In winter, when the ground is hard, they are obliged to keep in their holes and cannot break through. But now, since the sun has thawed the earth and warmed it, the dwarfs break through and steal all they can find. And what has once passed into their hands and is hidden by them in their caves is not easily brought to light."

Snow-White, however, was very sad at the departure of the bear, and opened the door so slowly that when he hurried through it he left behind on the latch a piece of his hairy coat. And through the hole which was made in his

coat Snow-White thought she saw the glittering of gold, but she was not certain about it. The bear, however, ran hastily away and was soon hidden behind the trees.

Soon afterwards the mother sent the children into the wood to gather sticks. While doing so they came to a tree lying across the path, and near its trunk something was bobbing up and down in the grass, and they could not imagine what it was. When they came nearer they saw a dwarf, with an old wrinkled face and a snow-white beard a yard long. The end of this beard was caught in a split of the tree, and the little man kept jumping about like a dog tied by a chain, for he did not know how to free himself.

He glared at the maidens with his fiery red eyes and cried, "Why do you stand there? Are you going to pass by without offering me any help?"

"What have you done, little man?" asked Rose-Red.

"You foolish goose!" cried the dwarf. "I was going to split the tree, in order to get a little wood for my kitchen. The little food which we get is soon burnt up with great logs. We don't swallow down so much as you greedy people devour! I had just driven the wedge in properly and everything was going well, but the wretched wedge was too smooth and flew out! And the tree closed up so suddenly that I could not draw out my beautiful white beard. So here it sticks, and I cannot get away. Don't laugh there, you silly milk-faced creatures! Ugh! How horrid you are!"

The children tried as hard as they could to pull the dwarf's beard out, but it was caught too tightly. "I will run and get some help," cried Rose-Red at length.

"Oh you crackbrained sheep's head!" snarled the dwarf. "What are you going to call other people for? You are two too many for me now. Can't you think of anything better?"

"Don't be impatient," replied Snow-White. "I have thought of something." And pulling her scissors out of her pocket, she cut off the end of the beard.

As soon as the dwarf found himself at liberty, he snatched up his sack, which lay filled with gold between the roots of the tree, and throwing it over his shoulder he marched off, grumbling to himself, "Stupid people! To cut off a piece of my beautiful beard! Bad luck to you!" Away he went, without once even looking at the children.

Some time afterwards Snow-White and Rose-Red went to catch some fish, and as they came near the pond they saw something like a great grasshopper hopping about on the bank, as if it were going to jump into the water. They ran up and recognized the dwarf.

"What are you doing?" asked Rose-Red. "You will fall into the water."

"I am not quite such a simpleton as that," replied the dwarf. "But don't you see this fish trying to pull me in?"

The little man had been sitting there fishing and unfortunately the wind had entangled his beard with the fishing line. And so when a great fish bit the bait, the weak little fellow was not able to draw it out, and the fish had the upper hand. The drawf held onto the reeds and rushes which grew near, but to no purpose, for the fish pulled him where it liked and he would soon have been drawn into the pond. Luckily just then the two maidens arrived and tried to release the beard of the dwarf from the fishing line, but they were too closely entangled. So the maiden pulled out her scissors again and cut off another piece of beard.

When the dwarf saw this done he cried out in a great rage, "You donkey! Do you want to disfigure my face? Was it not enough to cut off the end of my beard? Now you have to take away the best part of my fine beard! I dare not

*They held him fast till the bird gave up the struggle
and flew off*

show myself again now to my own people. I wish you had run the soles off your boots before you had come here!"

So saying, he took up a bag of pearls which lay among the rushes, and without speaking another word slipped off and disappeared behind a stone.

Not many days after this adventure, it chanced that the mother sent the two maidens to the next town to buy thread, needles and pins, laces and ribbons. Their road led across a field where great pieces of rock lay strewn about. Just over their heads they saw a great bird flying round and round. Every now and then it dropped lower and lower, till at last it flew down behind a rock.

Then they heard a piercing shriek, and running up they saw with fright that the eagle had caught their old acquaintance the dwarf and was trying to carry him off. The gentle children at once laid tight hold of the little man and held him fast till the bird gave up the struggle and flew off.

As soon, then, as the dwarf had recovered from his fright, he cried out in his shrill voice, "Could you not have held me more gently? You pulled at my fine brown coat so hard that it is torn and full of holes. What meddling rubbish you are!"

With these words he shouldered a bag filled with precious stones and slipped away to his cave among the rocks.

The maidens were by now used to his ingratitude, and so they walked on to the town and completed their errand. On the way home they crossed the same field and again came suddenly upon the dwarf, who had emptied his bag of precious stones in a clean place, thinking that nobody was near. The sun shone on the bright stones, which glittered with so many colors that the two maidens stood still to admire them.

"What are you standing there gaping for?" asked the dwarf, and his face grew as red as copper with rage. He

continued to abuse the poor maidens till a loud growling noise was heard, and a great black bear came lumbering out of the forest. The dwarf jumped up, terrified; but he could not reach his cave before the bear overtook him.

Then, terror-stricken, he cried out, "Spare me, my dear Lord Bear! I will give you all my treasures. See these beautiful precious stones which lie here. Only give me my life. What have you to fear from a little weak fellow like me? You would not even feel me with your big teeth. Here, take the two wicked girls! They will make nice morsels for you! They're as fat as young quails! For heaven's sake, eat them!"

The bear, however, did not take the trouble to speak, but gave the wicked dwarf a single blow with his paw, and he did not move again.

The maidens were then going to run away, but the bear called after them, "Snow-White and Rose-Red, fear not! Wait and I will go with you."

They recognized his voice and stopped, and when the bear came up to them his rough coat suddenly fell off, and there stood a tall man, dressed entirely in gold.

"I am a king's son," he said, "and was condemned by the wicked dwarf, who stole all my treasures, to wander about in this forest in the form of a bear till his death freed me. Now he has got his well-deserved punishment."

Then they went home, and Snow-White was married to the Prince, and Rose-Red to his brother, with whom they shared the immense treasure which the dwarf had collected. The old mother also lived happily many years with her two children. And the rose trees which had stood before the cottage were now planted before the palace, and every year they bore beautiful red and white roses.

Hansel and Gretel

CLOSE to a large forest there lived a woodcutter with his wife and his two children. The boy was called Hansel and the girl Gretel. They were always very poor and had very little to live on. And at one time when there was famine in the land, he could no longer procure daily bread.

One night when he lay in bed worrying over his troubles, he sighed and said to his wife, "What is to become of us? And how are we to feed our poor children?"

"I'll tell you what, husband," answered the woman. "Tomorrow morning we will take the children out quite early into the thickest part of the forest. We will light a fire and give each of them a piece of bread. Then we will go to our work and leave them alone. They won't be able to find their way back, and so we shall be rid of them."

"Nay, wife," said the man, "we won't do that. I could never find it in my heart to leave my children alone in the forest. The wild animals would soon tear them to pieces."

"What a fool you are!" she said. "Then we must all four die of hunger. You may as well plane the boards for our coffins at once."

She gave him no peace till he consented. "But I grieve over the poor children all the same," said the man. The

two children could not go to sleep for hunger either, and they heard what their stepmother said to their father.

Gretel wept bitterly and said, "All is over with us now."

"Be quiet, Gretel," said Hansel. "Don't cry! I will find some way out of it."

When the old people had gone to sleep, he got up, put on his little coat, opened the door, and slipped out. The moon was shining brightly and the white pebbles round the house shone like newly minted coins. Hansel stooped down and put as many into his pockets as they would hold.

Then he went back to Gretel and said, "Take comfort, little sister, and go to sleep. God won't forsake us." And then he went to bed again.

At daybreak, before the sun had risen, the woman came and said, "Get up, you lazybones! We are going into the forest to fetch wood."

Then she gave them each a piece of bread and said, "Here is something for your dinner, but don't eat it before then, for you'll get no more."

Gretel put the bread under her apron, for Hansel had the stones in his pockets. Then they all started for the forest. When they had gone a little way, Hansel stopped and looked back at the cottage, and he did the same thing again and again.

His father said, "Hansel, what are you stopping to look back at? Take care and put your best foot foremost."

"Oh, father," said Hansel, "I am looking at my white cat. It is sitting on the roof, wanting to say good-by to me."

"Little fool, that's no cat! It's the morning sun shining on the chimney," said the mother.

But Hansel had not been looking at the cat. He had been dropping a pebble on the ground each time he stopped.

When they reached the middle of the forest, their father said, "Now, children, pick up some wood. I want to make a fire to warm you."

Hansel and Gretel gathered the twigs together and soon made a huge pile. Then the pile was lighted, and when it blazed up the woman said, "Now lie down by the fire and rest yourselves while we go and cut wood. When we have finished we will come back to fetch you."

Hansel and Gretel sat by the fire, and when dinnertime came they each ate their little bit of bread, and they thought their father was quite near because they could hear the sound of an ax. It was no ax, however, but a branch which the man had tied to a dead tree, and which blew backwards and forwards against it. They sat there so long a time that they got tired. Then their eyes began to close and they were soon fast asleep.

When they woke it was dark night. Gretel began to cry, "How shall we ever get out of the wood?"

But Hansel comforted her and said, "Wait a little while till the moon rises, and then we will soon find our way."

When the full moon rose, Hansel took his little sister's hand and they walked on, guided by the shiny pebbles. They walked the whole night, and at daybreak they found themselves back at their father's cottage.

They knocked at the door, and when the woman opened it and saw Hansel and Gretel she said, "You bad children, why did you sleep so long in the wood? We thought you did not mean to come back any more."

But their father was delighted, for it had gone to his heart to leave them behind alone.

Not long afterwards they were again in great destitution, and the children heard the woman at night in bed say to their father, "We have eaten up everything again but half a loaf, and then we will be at the end of everything.

The children must go away! We will take them farther into the forest so that they won't be able to find their way back. There is nothing else to be done."

The man took it much to heart and said, "We had better share our last crust with the children."

But the woman would not listen to a word he said. She only scolded and reproached him. Anyone who once says A must also say B, and as the father had given in the first time he had to do so the second. The children were again wide awake and heard what was said.

When the old people went to sleep Hansel again got up, meaning to go out and get some more pebbles, but the woman had locked the door and he couldn't get out. But he consoled his little sister and said, "Don't cry, Gretel. Go to sleep. God will help us."

In the early morning the woman made the children get up and gave them each a piece of bread, but it was smaller than the last. On the way to the forest Hansel crumbled it up in his pocket, and stopped every now and then to throw a crumb onto the ground.

"Hansel, what are you stopping to look about you for?" asked his father. "I am looking at my dove which is sitting on the roof and wants to say good-by to me," answered Hansel.

"Little fool," said the woman, "that is no dove! It is the morning sun shining on the chimney."

Nevertheless, Hansel strewed the crumbs from time to time on the ground. The woman led the children far into the forest, where they had never been in their lives before. Again they made a big fire, and the woman said, "Stay where you are, children. We are going farther on to cut wood, and in the evening when we have finished we will come back and fetch you."

At dinnertime Gretel shared her bread with Hansel, for

he had crumbled his upon the road. Then they went to sleep and the evening passed, but no one came to fetch the poor children.

It was quite dark when they woke up, and Hansel cheered his little sister. He said, "Wait a bit, Gretel, till the moon rises, and then we can see the bread crumbs which I scattered to show us the way home."

When the moon rose they started, but they found no bread crumbs, for all the thousands of birds in the forest had picked them up and eaten them.

Hansel said to Gretel, "We shall soon find the way." But they could not find it. They walked the whole night and all the next day from morning till night, but they could not get out of the wood.

They were very hungry, for they had nothing to eat but a few berries which they found. They were so tired that their legs would not carry them any farther, and they lay down under a tree and went to sleep.

When they woke in the morning, it was the third day

since they had left their father's cottage. They started to walk again, but they only got deeper and deeper into the wood, and if no help came they must perish.

At midday they saw a beautiful snow-white bird sitting on a tree. It sang so beautifully that they stood still to listen to it. When it stopped, it fluttered its wings and flew around them. They followed it till they came to a little cottage, on the roof of which it settled down.

When they got quite near, they saw that the little house was made of gingerbread and roofed with cake. The windows were transparent sugar.

"Here is something for us," said Hansel. "We will have a good meal. I will have a piece of the roof, Gretel, and you can have a bit of the window. It will be nice and sweet."

Hansel reached up and broke off a piece of the roof to see what it tasted like. Gretel went to the window and nibbled at that. A gentle voice called out from within:

> *"Nibbling, nibbling like a mouse,*
> *Who's nibbling at my little house?"*

The children answered:

> *"The wind, the wind doth blow*
> *From heaven to earth below."*

And they went on eating without disturbing themselves. Hansel, who found the roof very good, broke off a large piece for himself, and Gretel pushed a whole round pane out of the window and sat down on the ground to enjoy it.

All at once the door opened and an old, old woman, supporting herself on a crutch, came hobbling out. Hansel and Gretel were so frightened that they dropped what they held in their hands. But the old woman only shook her head and said, "Ah, dear children, who brought you here? Come in and stay with me. You will come to no harm."

She took them by the hand and led them into the little house. A nice dinner was set before them: pancakes and sugar, milk, apples, and nuts. After this she showed them two little white beds into which they crept, and they felt as if they were in heaven.

Although the old woman appeared to be so friendly, she was really a wicked old witch who was on the watch for children. She had built the gingerbread house on purpose to lure them to her. Whenever she could get a child into

her clutches she cooked it and ate it, and considered it a grand feast. Witches have red eyes and can't see very far, but they have keen noses like animals and can scent the approach of human beings.

When Hansel and Gretel came near her, she laughed wickedly to herself and said scornfully, "Now that I have them, they shan't escape me."

She got up early in the morning before the children were awake, and when she saw them sleeping, with their beautiful rosy cheeks, she murmured to herself, "They will be dainty morsels."

She seized Hansel with her bony hand and carried him off to a little stable, where she locked him up behind a barred door. He might shriek as loud as he liked, she took no notice of him.

Then she went to Gretel and shook her till she woke, and cried, "Get up, little lazybones! Fetch some water and cook something nice for your brother. He is in the stable and has to be fattened. When he is nice and fat, I will eat him."

Gretel began to cry bitterly, but it was no use; she had to obey the witch's orders. The best food was now cooked for poor Hansel, but Gretel got nothing but the shells of crayfish.

The old woman hobbled to the stable every morning and cried, "Hansel, put your finger out for me to feel how fat you are."

Hansel put out a knucklebone, and the old woman, whose eyes were too dim to see, thought it was his finger. And she was much astonished that he did not get fat.

When four weeks had passed and Hansel still kept thin, she became very impatient and would wait no longer.

"Now then, Gretel," she cried, fetch the water. Fat or thin, tomorrow I will kill Hansel and eat him."

Oh, how his poor little sister grieved! As she carried the water, the tears streamed down her cheeks.

"Dear God, help us!" she cried. "If only the wild animals in the forest had eaten us, we should at least have died together."

"You may spare your lamentations! They will do you no good," said the old woman.

Early in the morning Gretel had to go out to fill the kettle with water, and then she had to kindle a fire and hang the kettle over it.

"We will bake first," said the old witch. "I have heated the oven and kneaded the dough."

She pushed poor Gretel towards the oven and said, "Creep in and see if it is properly heated, and then we will put the bread in."

She meant, when Gretel had gone in, to shut the door and roast her, but Gretel saw her intention and said, "I don't know how to get in. How am I to manage it?"

"Stupid goose!" cried the witch. "The opening is big enough. You can see that I could get into it myself."

She hobbled up and stuck her head into the oven. But Gretel gave her a push which sent the witch right in, and then she banged the door and bolted it.

"Oh! oh!" the witch began to howl horribly. But Gretel ran away and left the wicked witch to perish miserably.

Gretel ran as fast as she could to the stable. She opened the door and cried, "Hansel, we are saved! The old witch is dead."

Hansel sprang out, like a bird out of a cage when the door is set open. How delighted they were. They fell upon each other's necks and kissed each other and danced about for joy. As they had nothing more to fear, they went into the witch's house, and in every corner they found chests full of pearls and precious stones.

"These are better than pebbles," said Hansel as he filled his pockets.

Gretel said, "I must take something home with me too." And she filled her apron.

"But now we must go," said Hansel, "so that we may get out of this enchanted wood."

Before they had gone very far, they came to a great piece of water. "We can't get across it," said Hansel. "I see no steppingstones and no bridge."

"And there are no boats either," answered Gretel, "but there is a duck swimming. It will help us over if we ask it."

So she cried:

> *"Little duck that cries quack, quack,*
> *Here Gretel and here Hansel stand.*
> *Quickly take us on your back,*
> *No path nor bridge is there at hand!"*

The duck came swimming towards them, and Hansel got on its back and told his sister to sit on his knee.

"No," answered Gretel, "it will be too heavy for the duck. It must take us over one after the other."

The good creature did this, and when they had got safely over and walked for a while the wood seemed to grow more and more familiar to them, and at last they saw their father's cottage in the distance. They began to run, and rushed inside, where they threw their arms around their father's neck. The man had not had a single happy moment since he deserted his children in the wood, and in the meantime his wife had died.

Gretel shook her apron and scattered the pearls and precious stones all over the floor, and Hansel added handful after handful out of his pockets.

So all their troubles came to an end, and they lived together as happily as possible.